NONE

BUT

THE LIVING

~

KENNETH P. SMITH

PHENIX BOOKS

MIDDLETON HOUSE PUBLISHING, Ltd, Co.

Greenville

Phenix Books®, an imprint and registered trademark of Middleton House Publishing, Ltd. Co. Printed in the United States.

Library of Congress Cataloging-in-Publication Data has been applied for.

ISBN 978-0-9981071-0-3

Dedicated to my father, E.E. Smith, who on a bright summer morning in 1931, at the age of eighteen, left a 25¢ an hour job at the Alice Manufacturing Company— a cotton mill—and vowed not to return; he never did.

PART ONE

CHAPTER 1

In the fading evening light Ezra Burke sat alone on the front porch smoking his pipe gazing out at Jones Mountain to the west. Clouds, dark and roiling, had begun to form over its narrow high ridge. Just beyond the porch the corn, green and high, spread westward toward the mountain, up to the edge of its thick, forest skirt. Except for the large vegetable garden on the east side of the house he again had sowed all the land, twenty acres, in corn. Tanner, who owned the land and the house, had advised him to do this. Good money in corn, Tanner had said, winking at him, and despite his instincts he had planted it all in corn.

**

On that cold blustery afternoon in late January, with a dusting of snow frosting the crowns of the surrounding peaks, he had hitched the mule to the wagon and driven the three miles to Lanford's store for staples—flour, corn meal, and kerosene for the lamps. He had a quarter in his pocket, enough for some pieces of hard-rock candy or licorice sticks and the blue ribbon his wife needed to finish sewing the baby's dressing gown. He smiled slightly as he thought how convinced she was that it was going to be a boy. They were struggling, for sure, but he knew he could get by through spring planting if old Lanford would continue to extend him the credit he needed.

When he finally pulled up in front of the store—both he and the mule stiff from the cold—there were several other wagons parked in the dirt lot next to the building. The mules, with steam coming from their nostrils in huge clouds, huddled together as best they could for warmth. He noticed the black Ford sedan, shiny and abstract, parked near the front door well away from the animals. It was one of the few automobiles in or around Waverley. It belonged to Pick Tanner. There was talk that it had a heater inside, but Tanner would never say for sure.

As much as he wished not to encounter Tanner, he pushed open the unpainted door and stepped into the welcoming warmth and familiar aroma of Lanford's Store. It was a large low-ceiling room filled with the necessary staples of rural mountain life. The shelves were stocked with canned goods. A wooden barrel of pickles and one of crackers sat squat near the door. Cloth sacks of flour were stacked against one wall, imprinted with flowery designs, that would likely be cut up and sewn into dresses when emptied. There were walls with hardware hanging from pegs, bolts of cloth, a few clothes, overalls mostly, and other things, all new and all practical.

Slightly to his left toward the rear of the store was the huge iron pot-belly stove, the heat from its hot, bulging midriff warming the room. The smell of beans heavily seasoned with pork, simmering slowly in a large covered cast-iron pot on the top of the stove, permeated the room. Four men sat in straight wooden chairs, semi-circled, in the open space near the stove. They spoke occasionally to each other in low, bored monotones but mostly stared blankly at the stove, chewing tobacco and spitting into empty coffee cans on the floor. Tanner, sitting in the far chair, had pulled a small pouch of tobacco out of his coat pocket and was skillfully rolling a cigarette between boney, claw-like fingers. He wore a soiled felt hat pulled low on his forehead. A thin scar ran from the left corner of his mouth to the edge of his chin, giving his mouth a permanent sinister smile. His eyes, though intelligent enough, were watery pools of colorless light.

None of the men at the stove had heard the door open or had noticed Ezra when he entered the store. Lanford was absentmindedly arranging various items behind the long counter that ran along the far left wall. He wore a dingy butcher's apron which did not obscure the rotund outline of his belly beneath it. His face was fleshy and pink with deep-set, kind eyes. He held an unlit half-smoked cigar tightly in a corner of his drooping mouth. He had turned to see the man come through the door and quickly resumed straightening the chewing tobacco and sundries on the shelves.

Lighting the cigarette, Tanner glanced up he and saw Ezra across the room.

"Well, if it ain't Ezra Burke done come into Waverley, and on such a god-awful day at that. How you been, Ezra?"

Ezra lightly touched the gleaming edge of the ax that he was examining, then placed it back on one of the wall pegs. He needed a new ax but he would have to settle for just a new handle, and not even that until spring, if then. He looked at Tanner and the other men and strode over to the stove.

"I'm all right. You?"

"Snug as a bug in a rug. Come on over here and warm yourself. Got to be half froze riding all the way over here in a mule wagon. How's the family?" Tanner's voice was thin and high pitched, without sympathy or sincerity.

"We're all fine." Ezra nodded to the other men and walked past them to the counter, ignoring Tanner. Lanford continued to unconvincingly busy himself with his shelves.

"Afternoon, Mr. Lanford."

"Hey, Ezra. Didn't see you come in. Ain't seen you in a while. How you been?"

"All right, I reckon. Just trying to get through the winter."

"Yeah, she's been a bugger this year, for sure. What can I help you with?"

"Well, I'm going to need a few things. A sack of flour and some cornmeal. A small can of lard and five gallons of kerosene."

"I can fix you up on all that, for sure. Just pick out what you need."

Ezra straightened himself slightly and started to clear his throat, but his pride would not allow it.

"If you can, I'm going to have to ask you to put it on my bill. Until my corn comes in, that is."

With both his large hands spread on the counter, he looked squarely into Lanford's face. Lanford hesitated, and looking away, pulled the cigar stub from his mouth. His countenance seemed to soften a little.

"Well, sure, Ezra, I suppose we can do that. Sure thing." He then lowered his voice, leaning across the counter toward Ezra. "I can carry you until spring, June at the latest, but we got to settle up then. Okay?"

"All right, as soon as I can. I hate asking for credit as much as you hate giving it. More, I'd say."

"I reckon you do, but I got to make a living too. Go ahead and load up your wagon with what you came for, then we'll tally up. Need any help?"

"No, I can manage. I appreciate it, the credit I mean." Lanford nodded slightly, chomped down on the cigar, and turned back to straightening his shelves.

After going back outside to give the mule water, Ezra returned to the store and began gathering the things he needed and loading them into the wagon. Mentally, he kept count of the cost of each item. When he got home he would record it. The numbers would join those of all the other past credit purchases in a small black notebook that he kept. He knew to the penny how much he owed Lanford as well as what he owed Tanner.

After he had finished loading the supplies, he went over to the far corner of the store. There the items mostly for housekeeping were arranged neatly on a long, low table. Oddly, at the insistence of his wife,

Lanford stocked an unusually large variety of needles, thread, thimbles, pins, buttons, cloth, and ribbons. The carefully arranged ribbon section was bright as a rainbow, but with even more colors. They came wound on large cardboard spools. There was a yardstick tacked flat on the edge at the end of the table. You could measure off how much ribbon you wanted and then cut the length with the scissors hanging from a string nailed to a nearby post.

He found the roll of sky-blue ribbon. It was five-cents a yard, but he then realized that he had not thought about how much to buy. He measured off a yard and snipped it with the scissors. He hesitated, then measured off and cut two more strands the same length. The shiny satin material felt strangely stiff but smooth sliding between his calloused fingers. He had expected it to feel softer.

The conversation of the men sitting around the stove had grown livelier as the topic had turned to politics. Tanner, with a presumed self-importance, expounded on how with Hoover as president the good times were here to stay. Just needed to keep those damned Democrats out of office. The others stared at the stove and nodded.

Ezra walked back over to Lanford at the counter. He was glad that Tanner was too distracted to notice him.

"All right, Ezra, let's see. What all did you get?" He jotted down each item on a lined sheet of paper beside the cash register as Ezra recited his purchases. He then quickly licked the pointed lead of his pencil and totaled the items.

"Looks like five dollars and seventy-cents. That sound right to you?

"Yes," said Ezra.

Lanford then noticed the three strands of ribbon that he was holding gently, but awkwardly, in his hand.

"Oh, I didn't see the ribbon. That will be fifteen-cents more." Lanford started to add the ribbon to the list.

"No, I don't want credit for the ribbon. I'll pay for it now." He pulled the quarter from his pocket and placed it on the counter beside Lanford's list.

"Oh. Yeah, sure. That's good," said Lanford, surprised with the cash purchase. "That's real good."

"And I'd like a small bag of hard-rock candy, with some peppermint if you've got it."

Lanford scooped out the candy from the large, glass case beneath the cash register and placed it a small paper bag. He carefully rolled up the ribbon without creasing it and placed it gently into another small bag. He placed both bags on the counter and picked up the quarter and rang up the sale.

"There you go, Ezra. A nickel change." Ezra dropped the coin into his pocket.

He walked away from the counter toward the front of the store, purposely avoiding the men at the stove. But Tanner had been watching him and called out, louder than he needed to be heard.

"You ain't leaving just yet are you, Ezra? Come and sit a spell. Want a chaw of tobacco? You ain't too good to have a chew with us are you?" He had crushed out the cigarette on the floor and was cutting off a slice from the dark brown plug with a pocketknife.

"Reckon I need to get back to the farm. It will be getting dark pretty soon."

Tanner rose from his chair, spat toward the coffee can but missed it. The spurt of tobacco splattered on the wooden floor, joining similar stains around the can. He had moved closer to the stove, his back to it, facing Ezra. He rubbed the dark beard stubble on his chin, looking up from the brim of his dirty hat.

"Well, I heard you been doing some planting this winter," he chuckled quietly under his breath and glanced at the men seating around the stove.

"No, nothing to plant in cold weather. I did bring in some sweet potatoes and collards late, though. After the frost."

"Not that kind of planting, man. I was joking with you. Thing is, I heard that the missus was expecting a young 'un. That so?"

Ezra felt the warmth of blood rising to his face. Between his fingers, unconsciously, he rubbed hard the nickel in his pocket.

"Yes, I reckon she is."

"When's she dropping it?"

"'Middle of July, doc says."

"Well, that's a good thing, I guess. Always can use another hand on the farm, right?" Tanner smirked, enjoying himself. "But there ain't no point it keeping it a secret now, is there?"

"It's not a secret." He turned to leave the store but Tanner wasn't finished.

"I'll send Mrs. Tanner around to look in on her."

"There's no need. She's fine."

"Maybe so, but sometimes the women folk need to talk to each other about these kinds of things. Can't hurt."

Ezra hated his meddling and he hated him. Tanner walked over and approached him.

"By the way, speaking of planting, what are you planning to grow this spring?"

"Same as usual, I guess. Stuff we can sell. Pole beans, squash, some corn, tomatoes. Just like last year. Thinking about maybe putting a little tobacco in."

"Well, truth is Ezra, last year you didn't quite clear enough to catch up the rent."

"I know that."

"Listen to me now. I'm suggesting you plant all twenty acres in corn this year, except for your garden of course. They's good money in corn. My brother Bud says he'll buy all the corn he can get his hands on. I believe that's the way you need to go."

Like everyone else in this part of the county Ezra knew Bud Tanner. He was nasty and mean. He lived alone in a cabin up a hollow near the state line. He made a living off bootleg whiskey, people said, but no one seemed to know where his still was located. Ezra wanted nothing to do with Bud Tanner anymore than he wanted anything to do with his brother.

"I don't know, Mr. Tanner. Think I'll stick to growing those vegetables, along with some corn. We'll do better this year. I plan to take my stuff down to the market in Corinth every week or so this summer. Maybe set up a roadside stand, too."

Tanner looked down, shaking his head. He edged nearer to Ezra.

"You ain't listening, man. I can't go another year without getting my rent money. You plant the farm in corn and you'll do fine. That's all I'm saying. 'Course I can't tell you what to plant, exactly, but you think about it, you hear."

"All right." He turned toward the door.

"You think real hard about it, Ezra Burke. That's a right good piece of land you're on."

***

It was not a bad piece of land, as mountain farms go but that was not saying much. Most of the good land had long been taken, sold and resold. Most, if not all, of the old forest had been clear-cut and never reseeded. What was left were small meager farms with thin, rocky soil that was barely tillable. Sometimes just good enough for a farmer to eke out a living, and maybe in a good year he could pay the landlord the back-rent and some of the interest on the money he had borrowed for seed.

Though not much more than a sharecropper himself, Ezra tried to convince himself that he was more fortunate than many of his neighbors. A little less than two of his acres was decent bottomland that bordered on a river at the south end of his field. The remainder sloped up sharply from the river and was rocky and hard, mostly red clay, the topsoil having long since washed away. With only himself and the mule, to have the ground ready for spring planting, he had begun ploughing the field earlier than usual this year. It had been late winter when there was still heavy frost in the mornings and barely enough light to see the blade of the plough. He had worked from the upper section of the field downward toward the river. He did it this way mainly because the morning sunlight in late February hit the high ground first. Down lower, the bottomland was still bathed in darkness and sometime in fog until well after sunrise.

CHAPTER 2

The corn was doing well, green and already chest high. There had been plenty of rain, almost too much at times, but by June the stalks were lush and laden with blooms turning soon to young corn. With good sun he reckoned they would be gathering corn come mid-July .

He bent low to relight his pipe and then placed the small box of Diamond matches back into the bib pocket of his overalls. The heavy sweet fragrance of honeysuckle drifted up on a light breeze from the river. There was a low rumble, thunder, from the west. He glanced up and looked hard at the high black clouds gathering rapidly in the distance. A storm was moving over the mountain, eastward toward the farm, moving slowly, but as inexorably as the approaching darkness.

We don't need more rain, he thought to himself as he moved to the front corner of the porch just above the steps. Just a lot of sun between now and July.

Leaning lightly on the porch post, he looked down across the cornfield toward the river and thought about maybe going fishing in the morning, early. He did not fish much, not nearly as much as he would like. His neighbors, some Presbyterians and Baptists, but mostly Pentecostals, did not fish on Sundays. The Lord's Day, they said. Day of rest. What could be more restful than fishing, he thought. Besides, according to the Good Book, Jesus Christ himself was some kind of fisherman or other. Probably fished on Sunday a time or two.

He wondered if the snake-handlers fished on Sunday. There was a small cult of them, a church, just over in North Carolina, back side of Jones Mountain. They pretty much stayed to themselves he reckoned. He had never seen it, but it was said that in church on Sunday evenings, when the Spirit hit them just right, they would gather around a box of timber rattlers and copperheads, and jabber away in what they called *tongues*. Then when someone felt especially blessed, they might reach into the box and pick up one of the hissing, gnarling serpents and hold it up high for all the congregation and perhaps the Spirit to see. Timber rattlers were mean and aggressive, and he had seen and killed a lot of them in these hills. He suspected that not a few of the holy-rollers had been bitten and maybe died. No, he had never been to a snake handling church but it would probably be something to see. After thinking about it, he reckoned that they probably didn't fish on Sundays either.

The river and the cornfield and the mountain soon faded in the darkness but there were flashes of lightning in the distant clouds, and the rumbling grew closer. He tapped his pipe on the porch post. The loosened ashes dispersed like red fireflies in the freshening westerly breeze, their glow dying quickly as they fell on the damp leaves covering the ground below the porch.

From the single front window of the house a pale ray of yellow light leapt out and spread across the weathered planks of the porch. Judith lit one of the lamps in the front room and came to the door, her thin silhouette framed by the dimly lit interior.

"The children are asleep," she said softly.

"Tired out, I reckon. They're doing mighty good with the chores, seeing they as young as they are."

"You coming in soon?"

"Yes, just listening to the thunder," he said, his back to her as he continued to stare into the darkness.

"I heard it, too. Is it coming up a cloud?"

"I reckon so. We sure don't need any more rain right now. It's been a mighty wet spring. The river's still up some."

"The corn will be all right, won't it? Rain won't hurt my garden."

"Corn just needs a lot of sun, now that it's up as high as it is. It's looking real good."

"You feel better now about planting it all in corn again this year?"

He bit the corner of his lower lip and sighed deeply.

"I reckon so. Anyway, it's done. No point in dwelling on it."

"Why don't you come and sit with me. It's getting late."

"All right." He turned and followed her into the house.

The front room, or the sitting room as she liked to call it, was small and sparsely furnished. A wood stove stood near the back wall, opposite the front door. There was a single window on the left that looked out over the cornfield. Beneath the window was a wooden table holding the kerosene lamp on a piece of white linen bordered by exquisite lace work. It had been made by his mother. Judith kept it washed and starched, as it gave her a strange sense of cultivation and civility in the otherwise austere interior of the house.

There were two chairs in the room on either side of the table, one was a rocker. This is where she read to the children most evenings after supper, either from the Bible or from the one book of poems that she possessed, and where she and her husband sat after the children were put to bed. Sometimes he would read the Corinth paper if he had been to

Lanford's store and someone had left an old copy which Lanford was throwing away. Sometimes they talked. And sometimes they just sat quietly, her knitting or patching clothes and him just sitting with his pipe. He was not a moody or melancholy man by nature, but he had a seriousness about him which sometimes made him seem so. Mostly he worried about the welfare of his family, the farm, and the future. The future especially seemed vague and formless to him sometimes. He could not quite envision it, and this bothered him a great deal, but he kept these thoughts mostly to himself.

Across the room near the door to the kitchen was a low, homemade book case which contained the few books that her father had left her. Ezra had built it from scraps of lumber that he had gotten at Tanner's sawmill when he had worked there a few weeks last winter. He even painted it a bright yellow, which had surprised and delighted his wife. Few things around the farm were painted and even fewer were bright and colorful. On the right wall next to the door to the front bedroom was a crucifix, a small wooden cross with the Christ, twisted and dying in pewter, hanging upon it.

She sat in the rocker and retrieved a small cloth bag from the floor beside the chair. In the bag were her sewing things. From it she took a threaded needle and and began mending the heel of one of Ezra's woolen socks. He sat across from her and scraped the bowl of his pipe with a pocketknife.

"Mrs. Tanner came by today when you were chopping weeds down by the river."

"What did she want?"

"Nothing, really. We talked a bit about the garden and she wanted to see the children. She said old Miss McBee died last week. Said she died alone, by herself in that old house. Seems sad to me. I mean to be that old and live alone all those years and then just die."

"It's sad enough, I reckon," he said, without looking up from his pipe cleaning. "That's about all you can say about it. Is that all Mrs. Tanner had to say?"

"Mostly. She's seems like a nice woman, Ezra."

"So it was just a neighborly visit? Nothing wrong with that I don't reckon." Finished with the pipe, he slipped it back into his pocket and looked at his wife. "I wish you had more company. I suppose Mrs. Tanner is all right."

Judith dropped her sewing to her lap. "She wants to help us if she can."

"What do mean? We need *her* help now?" he asked sharply.

"She said that she had more than she could do around the house with all those grandchildren, and she with a big garden herself. They got relatives stopping by all the time. She wanted to know if I might be interested in taking in some washing and ironing."

He leaned toward his wife.

"More charity from the Tanner's. Is going to her husband two or three times a year with my hat in my hand not enough for those folks? Enough for you?" They both fell silent.

"What did you tell her?" he finally asked.

"Well, I told her that I really appreciated her thinking of me. In offering me work, I mean. And that I thought two dollars a week was awfully generous, but I didn't have the time, what with all my own chores, at least the time to do her a good job."

"That's good. You didn't let her back you into it."

A slight smile crossed her mouth.

"Ezra, I don't generally let anyone back me into something I don't want to do or isn't right. Truth is, we could use the money right now and I'm not too good to work for wages. But I knew you wouldn't like it, so I told her no."

He did not reply. She resumed her darning.

A flash of lightning briefly lit up the room, followed closely by a sharp clap of thunder.

"Storm's moving in fast. I reckon Grace put the cow in the shed like I told her?" he asked.

"Yes, she did. Just before you came in for supper."

"I reckon I'd better go out and check on things just the same."

Just then there was a single clicking sound, foreign and distinct, as something hit the tin roof of the house. Then another, and another. Soon the sounds were continuous.

"The rain," Judith said, without looking up from her work.

"No, I don't reckon it is."

He went out on the porch, where clicking sounds were even louder on the porch roof. With another flash of lightning, he saw the small white pellets of ice starting to cover the yard. Not rain, but hail.

"It's hail," he said to her as he went back into the house. "I'm going out back to check on the animals."

Walking back into the kitchen, he took the lantern off the wall peg, lit it and went out the back door into the yard. The wind was now up and pellets of hail stung his face as he held the lantern low to follow the well-worn narrow path to the shed. He lowered his head in protection against the wind and ice. He had forgotten his hat.

The cow and mule stood vacuously in the shed, each tied loosely to a post, unconcerned about him or the weather outside. There were corn stalks in the small feed bin and a bucket of water on the floor near the animals.

Sweet Grace, he thought, you could always depend on her. Her mother all over again.

He closed and secured the shed door and made his way round back to the hog pen. The hail was now heavy and relentless, with frequent lightning, dry and sharp. The earth crunched beneath his feet. He found the hog lying in soft mud, awake and grunting softly, but safe under the piece of tin that covered part of the pen. He turned and walked back toward the house. Guided by the faint light of the kitchen window, he could hardly see through the white storm. The chickens would be all right roosting safely under the house which rested on large river rocks a foot or two feet off the ground.

In the kitchen he brushed away pieces of ice from his hair and shoulders. He snuffed out the lantern and returned it to its peg. He did not look at his wife as she entered the kitchen from the small lean-to room where the children slept.

"Is everything all right?" she asked.

"The animals are all right but all this hail's not good."

"Surely it will turn to rain soon."

"It better. The corn won't survive much of this."

"Strange weather. We just don't ever get hail much."

"Well, we got it now." The sound of the hail pounding the roof was almost deafening. "Grace and Andrew all right?"

"Yes. Sleeping like the babies they are. I'm going to bed, too."

"All right."

"You coming soon?"

"In a while. I need to see about this storm."

"I thought maybe…" she stopped in mid-sentence. "Don't stay up too late worrying. We'll be all right." She went into the bedroom.

He sat down in the rocker in the front room and listened as the hail continued to pound the house. It was as if it would go on forever.

Sometime during the night, after dozing off, he woke to a different, more muted sound. The hail had finally turned to rain. It was beating relentlessly against the window panes. They shook under the assault. The small house itself seemed to sway in a staccato rhythm from the wind that battered it from the west. The storm had moved in.

He stepped out onto the front porch and was met with sheets of rain, driven almost horizontally by the strong, constant wind. At the edge of the porch, his hand gripping the rough-hewn wood of the corner post, he peered into the howling darkness, oblivious to the wetness that had already soaked through his clothes to his skin. With a wet sleeve he wiped the rain from his even wetter face. He could see nothing. But he knew. It was all gone. They had lost the crop for sure. It would be light soon but it would only confirm what he already knew. Rain and reluctant bitter tears mixed briefly in his eyes.

Leaving wet tracks across the dry, wooden floor, he went into the kitchen to make coffee. He placed several pieces of dry, split oak in the stove and lit the kindling, which flared up into yellow flames almost instantly. He then sat down heavily at the table and waited, knowing that there was now nothing to be done.

CHAPTER 3

The day dawned gray and windless with a light drizzle falling
from low slate-hued clouds, remnants the storm had left behind in its
passing. She woke in the semi-darkness of the room and gently touched
the pillow beside her, but she somehow knew that she was alone in the
bed. She lay there in the dim. Beneath the thin cotton gown her breast
rose and fell almost imperceptibly with her breathing.

The only sound was the steady falling of heavy water drops from
the edge of the porch roof onto the ground. Dreading what lay ahead, she
slid effortlessly out of bed and slipped her feet into flat, leather shoes. In
the kitchen her husband was sitting slumped over the table, asleep, his
head resting on folded arms. The coffee pot was gurgling, steam pouring
from its spout. She moved it to the edge of the stove and added a length
of oak to the low, smoldering fire in the stove. Walking over to the table,
she touched his shoulder lightly and felt the warm dampness of the shirt.

"Ezra," she said softly, as her hand remained gently on him.

He stirred and looked up, not at her but across the room at
nothing. His eyes opened wide as he shook his head in quick, short jerks
to rouse himself from sleep. She poured coffee into a cup and placed it
on the table in front of him.

"I reckon I fell asleep waiting for the storm to pass. Has it quit
raining? I can't hear it now." He was still in that half-dream state that
feels unreal and confusing when you are suddenly woken from a deep
sleep, sleep born of fatigue and hopelessness.

"I don't know but you sat here all night in soaked clothes.
There's a clean shirt in the bureau. And socks. You need to get out of
those wet things. You ought not to have gone out in the storm."

"I didn't. Just stood on the porch listening to what it was doing
to us." He did not look at her. "I'm going out to the field. Need to go see
what shape the farm is in."

Ignoring the hot coffee and the discomfort of the damp clothing,
he went onto the porch and looked out across what only the day before
had been the cornfield. He was at the edge of the porch where he had
stood during the night when he had seen nothing but wet darkness. Now
it was all before him, real and undeniable.

What he saw through the drizzle, in the the gray but growing
light, was like the desolation of some ancient battle. The living
combatants, both the victors and the vanquished, having withdrawn from
the field, leaving behind their dead and dying. Hardly a stalk of corn was

left standing, and even those that were were broken or twisted, as if some great hand had reached down and assaulted them individually, one by one. The violent wind had yanked them from their shallow roots and scattered them randomly across the muddy acres.

Looking down to the south end of the field, he could see that the river had risen and poured over its banks, flooding the two acres of the bottomland. The best of the land. If any of the corn there had survived the hail and the wind, it was now under water.

God has forsaken these mountains. This farm, anyway, he thought bitterly. It cannot be raised back up. Not by me.

In the heavy dampness there seemed to be no air to breathe. It pressed down on him. He would suffocate and die here. He drew a ragged breath and sighed deeply. Stepping off the low porch onto the drenched earth, hot unrestrained tears mixed with the warm morning mist on his face. He walked out into the field. He wiped a sleeve across his eyes. He would not weep again.

He walked slowly out into the sloping field among what once had been rows of green corn, their hope and future. His shoes were caked and heavy with mud. There were no rows now, just the twisted broken stalks thickly strewn about on the ground like a loosely woven web. The rain and wind had washed away all of what was left of the topsoil, leaving deep, eroded trenches like open wounds on the earth's face. The flooded section of bottomland would be deep in useless, red silt washed down from the steep hillside.

He squatted and scooped up a handful of the soaked earth. Gritty and red, it ran through his fingers like thick blood. He recalled the bitter resignation he had felt, once he had relented to Tanner and agreed to plant the field in corn. This field, and maybe himself, was cursed.

Memory of the spring work flooded his thoughts like a suddenly-remembered dream. The hard and difficult labor of plowing had gone well. He had enjoyed the work, surrounded by the hills, dark and blue and misty, against a brightening sky in the early mornings. With spring had come the long mornings of bright sun warming the damp earth. The mellow fragrance of rhododendron and wild azaleas had floated down from the woods above, across the field, filling the air and his nostrils with its sweetness.

After completing their chores, the children had often joined the plowing. Andrew rode atop old Pete, holding onto to the hard leather collar. Grace, always industrious, walked behind him grappling with stones freshly turned up by the plow in the loose soil. She placed them in a burlap sack that she dragged along with her. She would use the stones for a border around the flower garden she dreamed of having and spoke about each day, her dark eyes sparkling with anticipation.

In late spring the rains had come almost every afternoon it seemed, and the plowing stopped for a day, sometimes two. But the forested mountains grew even more wild and lush with vegetation. The rows, plowed deep and straight, were finally ready for planting, and together all of them had worked dropping the seeds into the furrows. Once covered with earth, the corn sprouted quickly and seemed to grow taller overnight. Even with all the late rains things had gone well.

***

He felt a light touch from behind on his shoulder. Still hunched over the ground he turned to see Grace, small and serious. A faint, brief smile crossed his lips. She stood there barefoot in the mud, still in her long, cotton night shift with her small hand resting on his shoulder.

"The corn's gone, Papa," she said softly.

"Yes. Gone."

"Mama said the storm was real bad last night and that there was ice. Is that true? There was ice?" she asked innocently, with puzzled eyes.

"Hail. It was hail."

"Is hail ice?"

"Yes, small pieces of ice. Like small stones or marbles?"

"But, Papa, how can there be ice when it's summertime?"

"I don't rightly know exactly. It just happens sometimes."

"I wish I could have seen it. Me and Andrew were asleep. The storm didn't wake us up."

"That was good."

"But I wish I could see ice in summer."

Standing up, he wiped the dark wetness from his hand against his damp overalls. He reached down and picked up the child. It was almost like holding air, light as a bird he thought as he lifted her into his arms. She was small for six years old. Small, dark, and beautiful. Like her mother in so many ways. Already he could see the intelligence and energy. There was some kind of inner strength of his daughter emerging, which he again attributed to his wife. He gently brushed the damp dirt from her feet with his large, rough hand.

"Let's go back to the house. I think I might smell bacon frying. Mama's probably got breakfast about ready."

"Papa, can I ride on your shoulders?"

"All right."

Effortlessly he hoisted her up. On his shoulders, with her thin brown arms wrapped around his head, they walked silently through the muddy field back to the house. Although the gray clouds still hung low over the farm and the surrounding mountains, they were no longer a threat. They had done their work and would soon move on. The clouds hiding the eastern sky began to lighten more. A thin fog, like a translucent veil, hid the river and some of the flooded bottomland below. But finally the rain had stopped.

The storm that had destroyed the corn crop, and that would fundamentally change his life forever, had roared off to the southeast toward the city of Corinth, miles away.

CHAPTER 4

The lounge—the Club Room as it was officially designated and affectionately known at the newly renovated Corinth Country Club—was the pride of its two hundred thirty-five affluent members, all of which were white and male, as specified by the club's covenants. It was a large square room with walls of highly polished cherry paneling and no windows. The hardwood oak floor was equally polished where it was visible, but was mostly covered by a huge oriental rug woven in designs of muted reds, greens, and golds. Along one wall hung large portraits, prints actually, of famous golfers of the day and of an earlier era. The likes of Walter Hagen, Gene Sarazen, and the latest sensation, Bobby Jones. In still-life, the faces of these heroes of the links were brightly illuminated by small brass light fixtures beneath each frame. Their gazes, confident and smug, were fixed forever on the club members below, subtly, but most assuredly reminding them of who they were *and* who they were not.

On an adjacent wall were even larger portraits of the club's past presidents, all seven of them. Beyond these were photographs of each of the past club champions, all with brilliant white-toothed smiles holding the club trophy above their heads for all the world to see. That is, the world as defined and contained within the confines of the Corinth Country Club.

It was Sunday morning and the room was filled with impatient men, all ready for golf, dressed in the very appropriate attire of the day. They sat in the large, red leather chairs placed tastefully around the room, or on one of the several settees along three walls of the room. They chatted with a neighbor, or group of neighbors. The talk was mostly of golf or football. Some scanned a newspaper, bored and disinterested. Around four wooden game tables set in the middle of the room, men played gin rummy or pinochle. Cigar smoke mingled with the aroma of the overabundant leather in the room. The smell was not unpleasant and was completely masculine. The members were restless and annoyed at having to admit to themselves that there were still a few things in their privileged world which they could not control, the weather being one.

One of the doors on the right side of the club room opened onto a flagstone patio. Beyond the patio, caddies, all black and wearing identical green cotton smocks, huddled under a canvas awning that overlooked the tee box on the first fairway. It had been raining softly, but steadily, since early morning and the slate gray sky offered no promise of sun. Rain water dripped heavily off the drooping edges of the canopy, soaking the feet of the unfortunate men pressed to the perimeter of the group.

The caddies were restless, too. Some cursed the weather, and their inevitable loss of gratuities from the golfers. For many of them this was their primary source of income. Most just looked out at the rain in silence. They knew that no golf would be played here today. But everyone was waiting on the greenskeeper, Bobby Jack Cleveland, to give the word, that is, to make it official. However, at the moment, Bobby Jack was preoccupied in the equipment shed, his undivided attention focused on the newest of the club's kitchen help, a girl of nineteen.

Back inside the club room, a graying ageless black steward moved about the room, discretely attending to the needs of the men. Many of them had ordered coffee and were served efficiently by the white-jacketed servant who poured the hot liquid expertly into white china cups resting in white china saucers.

One of the men at a game table looked up from his cards and called across the room, causing many of the members to glance at each other, slightly shaking their heads in disapproval of his good-natured crassness.

"Hey, Jacob, when you get a chance step over here if you will please." The steward was expressionless as he strode over to the table.

"Yes, sir, Mr. Pinckney. What is it I can do for your?"

"Bring me a whiskey and soda on the rocks, please."

"Yes sir, Mr. Pinckney, right away."

"Damn, Scooter, it's hardly nine o'clock. A bit early, isn't it, even for you?" laughed the man sitting across the table from Pinckney, as he lay down one card and drew another from the deck.

"Ah, I'm not feeling all that good. You know how it is."

"Yeah, I'd say you were nursing a hangover. Hair of the dog, is it?"

"I'm not sure *nursing* is the right word. More like doctoring. I guess I'm not as young as I used to be. Sure not as young as Liz, that's for sure. I wanted to go home and she kept wanting to dance, so I just kept throwing down drinks. You know how I get sometimes, Cates."

"Yes, I do. I'm glad we left early. Anyway, Winky had a headache."

"Don't they always on Saturday night?"

"Be nice now, Scooter."

"Anyway, I had a good time."

"You always do."

J. Madison Pinckney, known as Scooter to his friends, of which there seemed to be many, was a rather short and slightly rotund man of about forty-five. His complexion was smooth with a pink, almost a reddish flush to it. His deep-set brown eyes always seemed to have a glint of mischievousness about them, but they complimented the openness of his smile, and of his face in general. Although he was always groomed and well-dressed there was a certain crumpled, unkempt aura about him. His closest friends said that he would never grow up and was the world's oldest frat-boy. Scooter loved these remarks and playfully vowed never to change, always looking for a good time, and was generally successful in finding it. In college he had pledged Kappa Alpha, naturally. Although some of the upper classmen may not have cared for his style, it didn't matter much. He'd been a legacy.

The Pinckney family had been prominent long before Corinth had become a city of any consequence. They owned or at least managed, among other things, the Corinth State Bank, of which Scooter Pinckney was president.

Of course the details and routine of bank administration did not come naturally nor did they appeal to Scooter's more facetious nature. He preferred the perks and schmoozing available to those of his station more than he did any actual work. He, therefore, was a member of all the right civic and charitable organizations, and was on the Mayor's Council for City Improvement. He and his third wife were among the most prominent and active members of the Cotton Exchange Club—his grandfather had been a founder. It was, to be sure, along with the Country Club, the exclusive domain of Corinth's social elite. One could rightly say that Scooter Pinckney was connected. But his real love was golf, mixed with a blend of partying friends and Irish whiskey, not necessarily in that order. Most everyone liked him.

***

The club professional, Jasper Hudson, stepped out onto the small covered veranda adjacent to his office and called across the lawn to the cadre of caddies.

"You can go on home, boys. Won't be any golf played here today. Likely not tomorrow either. Anybody seen that son of bitch Cleveland?"

The caddies ignored his question. Cleveland was white. They donned caps pulled from their back pockets and headed off in small groups. Resigned to their fate and now seemingly oblivious to the rain, most walked the four blocks to the bus stop to take the electric trolley back to their homes in Free Town, the section of Corinth where the black people lived. Some loitered on the street corner and pulled small, brown paper bags from their pockets, taking deep draughts from the bottles they contained. All would be soaked to the skin in five minutes.

Hudson opened a large, black umbrella and trotted across the end of the lawn, opposite to the awning where the caddies had taken shelter. With each step his saddle oxfords splashed water from the sodden grass, generously soaking his beige, cotton trousers up to the knees. His destination was the door of the club room, which he quickly reached and stepped inside.

"Damn if you don't look like a drowned rat, Jasper," Scooter called out. The room roared with laughter.

"I feel like one, too, Mr. Pinckney," said Hudson, grinning embarrassingly in a self-effacing way. "Sorry, gents. This rain's set in. The course is practically under water. Mr. Cleveland should have notified you an hour ago. I don't know why he didn't."

"Get on his ass, Jasper," Scooter continued, getting another round of guffaws from his friends.

"I will, Mr. Pinckney. Y'all can be sure of that. Gentlemen, there's plenty of umbrellas in the stand at the end of the walkway. Should be able to get to your cars without getting wet."

"Shoulda kept some of them darkies here to bring our cars 'round," Scooter slurred and laughed, halfway through his third whiskey and soda.

The other members began dispersing and seemed to ignore his latest attempt at humor. Scooter spoke across the table to his partner who had slid his chair back preparing to leave.

"Come on, sit down, Cates. Let's play a few more hands."

"I don't know, Scooter. Think I'll go on home and maybe attend services with Winky. She's always nagging me to go."

"Sounds like a hoot. Just a few hands. I'll buy you a drink. Tell you what let's do. Make it a nickel a point just to keep it interesting. Whatcha you say, old chum?"

"I don't know, Scooter," repeated Cates hesitantly, then pulled his chair back up to the table. "Hell, I'd probably fall asleep before the sermon started anyway. Deal the cards."

Scooter smiled, sipped his drink, and began dealing from the deck.

Other than Scooter and Cates Allgood, the room quickly cleared except for the man sitting in the near corner. He was deeply immersed in the thick, Sunday edition of the Corinth Gazette. His gold, wire-rimmed glasses were set purposely low astride a prominent but elegant aquiline nose. With thinning, gray hair and manicured nails he looked much more the bank president than did Scooter. He wore a starched, white shirt with an open collar beneath a forest green cardigan. The creases of his gray, woolen trousers were sharply honed as a knife blade. The paper rattled crisply as he flipped to the next page. Both men at the card table were suddenly aware of his presence.

"Good morning, Jameson," said Cates.

"Yeah, top of the morning to you Jameson," Scooter chimed in, absentmindedly. He was more interested in the fan of cards in his hand.

"Well, I don't know about good. Good and wet maybe. I sure was looking forward to a round of golf this morning, not this blasted rain," the man with the newspaper retorted in an especially distinct southern accent that many affluent Southerners seem to acquire sometime after their fortieth birthday. It was considered to be, by them at least, particularly patrician. Its primary purpose, unspoken of course, was to allow one to be identified as being in the desired social strata, as belonging to *the club*. He folded his paper neatly and placed in on the table beside his chair. He strode over to his two friends seated at the game table.

"Pull up a seat, Jameson. Cates just lost at gin rummy. Again. We can play pinochle. Just kill some time and chew the fat until the rain eases up," Scooter said.

"Eh, I'm not much of pinochle player. In fact, never learned the game," said Jameson, taking a seat at the table.

"Doesn't matter," retorted Scooter, as he shuffled the deck, "how about a little stud?"

"I'm afraid I couldn't afford to play poker with you two," laughed Jameson.

"And just who do you think you're kidding?" Allgood asked, drawing a cigarette from the silver case on the table and leaning forward in his chair to light it. After a few quick puffs he continued.

"Hell, you got more money than God, Phelps, so don't go poor-mouthing to us. We know you too well." All three men laughed.

"Yeah, everybody knows where all the cash in this country is. You insurance boys got it. I, of course, ain't got a problem with that. I just wish you'd put more of it in my bank," Scooter said, continuing the banter.

"Don't know where you got that idea," said Jameson, smiling smugly.

"Oh, come on, old boy," Scooter said, and then looked over at Allgood. "Now take my partner here. Cates, now just how many of those cotton mills you own? Ten, Twelve?" Nothing, nor anyone, was off-limits to Scooter.

"No, no, nothing like that. I own six outright. I mean the family does."

"And who's head of the family—the illustrious Allgood's?" Scooter was enjoying himself, emptying his glass with a final gulp.

"What are you getting at?" asked Allgood lightly. "I mean, please do tell before you order another whiskey."

"Watch it, Cates," said Scooter, feigning offense. "You're getting a little personal. Anyway, what I was saying, referring to Mr. Jameson C. Phelps here, is well, uh, what was I saying?"

"Getting ready to expound I'm sure," said Jameson.

"Oh, yes, of course. Just making a point about you insurance men. Now tell me, Cates. You own all those mills and God knows what else, but I bet you'd swap 'em even with Jameson here for the Freedom Life Insurance Company. Now, wouldn't you, Cates? Tell the truth."

"Truth is, I suspect," inserted Jameson, "you're drunk or about to be so."

"Now why would you say a thing like that about the fine upstanding Scooter Pinckney?" Allgood asked, warming to the friendly jibbing.

"Naw, I'll admit I may be a little tight but just trying to maintain, gents, just trying to maintain. Where the hell is Jacob anyway?"

"Probably hiding from you," said Allgood, bringing a guffaw from his pals.

"Yeah, he just might be, at that," agreed Scooter. Then looking over at Jameson across the table he continued, "I just want to know how it actually works, Jameson. You selling all these lint-heads—sorry Cates—that is, all these cotton mill workers life insurance. It seems that you're betting they won't die and they're betting they will. Is that about right?"

"There is a little more to it than that, I can assure you," responded Jameson sanctimoniously.

"I mean, I understand that they will eventually die and Freedom Life will have to pay up. So you're really always going to lose in the end, right?"

"That's not the point, but certainly we fulfill the obligations of the client's policy. That is, of course, if he has kept up with his premium payments."

Scooter nudged Allgood.

"Cates, you got insurance?"

"Yes, some."

"Point is, we don't need insurance. We got money. We're covered, so to speak. That's right, ain't it?" said Scooter, addressing both men.

"Everybody needs life insurance," said Jameson, with authority.

"No, they really don't. Not everybody. Anyway, how do just common working people, you know, folks living on the mill hill, afford to pay for life insurance?" asked Scooter, as if he was seriously contemplating the question.

"It isn't expensive. In fact, it's downright cheap. A real good bargain," said Jameson.

"But these people *are* all your customers?" asked Allgood to Jameson.

"Sure, not all but most of them, I suspect. Can we deal the cards?" asked Jameson somewhat self-consciously, wanting to change the subject.

"Okay, okay, don't get riled up, Mr. Phelps. Just tell me one thing and I'll shut my trap. How does it work, the mill workers buying it, I mean insuring their lives with you? Them betting they'll die, you betting they won't. Not anytime soon anyway."

"Damn it, Scooter. It's pretty simple. Our clients take out a policy and pay so much a week, usually."

"So that's the premium, the weekly payment?"

"Yes," said Phelps, slightly irritated at Scooter persistence.

"How much do they pay; I mean each week?"

"Usually twenty-five cents. Sometimes more."

"And what do they get for that?" asked a suddenly interested Allgood, as he tapped ashes from the cigarette into a gold plated ashtray.

"They get coverage, of course, as stated in their policy."

"How much coverage?" pressed Allgood.

"I don't know," replied Phelps hesitantly, "usually five hundred dollars at the time of their death. Enough to pay for a decent funeral, with plenty left over. Saves the family from having to worry about it. Enough, boys." He pushed away from the table and stood up. "Sounds like the rain has let up. I have to go."

"Damn, five-hundred dollars. That's it? Just five-hundred? Damn," said Scooter shaking his head, more to himself than anyone. "I need a drink.

CHAPTER 5

The large, vegetable garden was on the east side of the house away from the storm's approach and had been partially sheltered from the it. Also the upper edge of the plot was protected from the wind by the tree line on the sharply ascending hill which rose behind the house. Morning spears of warm, white sunlight shot down between the top of the trees, striking the earth at sharp angles. The wet leaves of the plants sparkled, the droplets of water rested on them like prisms struck by the dazzling rays of the sun.

Ezra's spirits brightened a bit as he walked down a row of red, ripe tomatoes closest to the house. A few of the vines were broken and the twine fixing them to the stakes had not been able to bear the dead weight. But mostly all of the vines, many already laden with ripening tomatoes, were intact. So it was for most of the garden. Some of the pole beans would have to be restrung and there were dead, wet leaves and weeds to be cleared, but the garden had, by and large, been spared.

After he had plowed the garden in late winter, Judith had been anxious to have it ready by early spring. She planted it, and all spring worked the garden while he laboriously plowed the acreage for the ill-fated corn. After breakfast and household chores each morning, she worked in the garden. It was, in many ways, her happiest time of the day. After dinner was prepared and eaten, with the sun high in the sky, he returned to his plowing. Grace helped her clear the table and wash the dishes. Then she was free again to spend a large portion of the afternoon in the garden, often working up until it was near time to fix supper. As the late spring and summer evenings grew longer, she and the children often went out to the garden to gather its bounty. They talked and laughed, not considering the gathering to be work at all.

***

By now it was mid-morning and with the aftermath of the storm all around them, the rhythm of the day—a farm day—had been disrupted and had gotten away from them. He had gone into the house and pulled the heavy damp clothing from his body. Judith had hung a clean neatly-patched pair of overalls, along with a faded and equally patched cotton shirt, on a wall peg just inside the bedroom door.

He dipped his large, cupped hands in the wash basin on the dresser and splashed the cool water on his face. There were things to be done, and right now he felt that work was what he needed most. He could think more clearly when he was working, doing something with his hands. Right now he just needed movement, activity. There was always hope in action, or at least that is the way it seemed to him. He walked out the back door into the yard, the chickens cackling as they scattered from his path.

"Got to get the cow milked, Grace. Want to help me?" he called out.

Judith came round to the corner of the house from the garden.

"She's already in the barn, waiting for you."

Barn, he thought with an almost ironical smile. The shed was not much more than a lean-to but she had always called it a barn. A real farm should have a real barn. She thought calling it a barn would make her husband feel better about the farm, their lives. It didn't.

***

"Go put your shoes on," Judith said to Grace, as she and her father entered the kitchen.

She was at the stove ladling grits from a small pot onto plates. He placed the plates on the table as she filled them. Also on the table was a plate of warm, buttered biscuits and fried bacon. A half-filled jar of honey had been placed in the center.

"Smells good. Looks good, too," he said.

"I gathered eggs but, well, we probably need to sell them all to Mr. Lanford for a while."

She paused and looked at him.

"Is the corn gone?"

"Yes. All of it." He sat down at the table, not looking across the room at her. She turned back to her cooking at the stove.

"Nothing left?"

"Nothing that is going to make a difference. We'll gather up the stalks in a few days when they dry out some. I'll chop them up to make feed for the livestock. That's about it."

"Well, that's something. We'll just have to figure out how to get by," she said after a brief silence, without looking up from her work at the stove. "We've done it before and we'll do it this time. God is watching over us."

"Judith, I just don't see it. Not this time. Everything turned on that corn crop. I'm already so deep in debt to Tanner I'll never get out."

"*We*, Ezra, *we*. We are a family here, you know."

"Yes, I reckon I know that. I didn't mean it any different. But I've made some bad turns. Seems like you and the children suffer on account of it. It's different this time." He looked down at his crossed hands resting on the table. "It's beat me, Judith, and I know it."

"No. You're just tired. I know you're discouraged. I am too but we've got to have hope. Without hope there's nothing."

"I don't know. I'm just not sure anymore. We can't go on like this. Sinking deeper and deeper. You deserve better, the children deserve better. It's too hard."

"We deserve what we've got and what we've got is good," she replied softly, but with conviction.

He looked over at his wife and knew that he had never loved her more than he did at this moment. If she did not feel as hopeless as he, then she must at least know that things were going to be very difficult, more difficult than they had been up to now. Yet she had this inexplicable strength deep in her soul, something that could not be touched or dissuaded by adversity or bad turns or hail storms. She had a peace within her, and her resiliency was somehow made even stronger by her small family, the land, and trust in a world the way it was. She was still young, they both were, but he knew how quickly this kind of life could take its toll, trying year after year to scrape a living out of a piece of disgruntled and worn earth. He had seen his father, an old man at fifty, lose courage by the day, and dead two years later leaving a widow, scared and without options, with five children. The family split up into pieces, to be allocated to reluctant relatives, as poor as them, dreading another mouth to feed and a body to clothe. This will not happen to me and my family, he vowed to himself.

Andrew, not yet five, stood in the doorway of the backroom, leaning sleepily against the door casing. His dark tousled hair and blue-gray eyes were those of his father. The hem of his rumpled nightshirt touched the floor.

"I'm hungry, Mama," he said, rubbing the sleep from his eyes with a plump fist in each.

"Go sit down at the table."

"Morning, Andrew. I don't believe you are awake yet, son. Not all the way, anyhow."

His countenance brightened when he saw the child who walked wearily across the room and climbed onto his lap. Judith came to the table with a plate of freshly-sliced tomatoes which she placed beside the biscuits.

"Andrew, let Papa eat. You have your own chair. Here, I'll help you fix your plate."

She opened a hot biscuit dripping with the melted butter on his plate and poured a spoon of the thick honey over it. Alongside the biscuit she placed a length of the cut bacon. The child climbed into his chair and folded his legs beneath him to negotiate the table's height. He began eating the honey-soaked biscuit and bacon, ignoring the thick slice of ripe tomato that was also on his plate.

"Grace, your breakfast will be cold. Come eat now."

"Coming, Mama." Grace ambled into the kitchen. She was wearing shoes. "These shoes hurt my feet. I don't like them and, anyway, why do I need shoes on in the summer time?"

"We don't come to the table barefoot, Grace. You know that."

"I know, but these shoes hurt. I couldn't find my moccasins," the child retorted.

Ezra looked down at his daughter's shoes as she walked across the room to the table, her face tightly screwed in a grimace. He could see the bulge in the shoes as the child's feet pressed against the restraint of the cracked leather. At the toes the soles were lose and flapped slightly when she walked.

"You need new shoes. We'll go over to Lanford's store as soon as we can, and buy you a pair," he said, wondering how they would be able to buy shoes or anything else anytime soon. They ate in silence.

"I'm going out to look at the garden. See if anything's left of it," he finally said, pushing his chair back from the table. His wife did not reply.

"I'm going with you, Papa," Grace said, wiping traces of milk from the corners of her mouth.

She bent over and started untying her shoes. Andrew quickly climbed down from his chair and raced toward the back door, excited over the prospect of escaping the confines of the house.

"No, you help your mother wash up in here. Then you got to turn to your chores. We're already late. We still got animals to look after, you know."

"Okay, Papa. Can I take off my shoes now?"

"All right."

***

He leaned against the post of the shed and watched Grace as she finished the milking. She grasped the milk-gorged teats expertly in her small but strong hands, directing a thin steady stream of the warm liquid into the nearly-full pail with each squeeze. He was proud of her quickness in learning and in her willingness to help with chores. An older child, or a boy, could have done no better.

"All right, I believe that's about it. You did good. I'll tote the bucket to the house."

"No, Papa, I can do it." She lifted the bucket with both hands and then shifted it to her right hand, steading it with her left. "It's near full, though. I'll go slow and not spill a drop. You'll see."

"See that you don't."

He pushed the shed door open for her and she walked slowly across the yard with her burden, occasionally setting it down on the ground to change hands on her journey to the back door. She was determined that the pail of milk arrive at the house with not one drop less that when it was removed from beneath the cow's udder.

Before she got to the steps leading up to the door and into the kitchen, her brother came around the corner of the house running, his face bright with excitement.

"Papa, there's a motor car in the front yard! A big black car! Come see! Quick, Papa!"

"Well, I reckon I've seen a car or two in my time and so far they have all been black." Ezra said, feigning disinterest as he closed and latched the shred door. He scraped manure off the soles of his shoes on a fence rail.

"Papa, you coming to look, ain't you?" The boy was almost beside himself.

"Yes, I'll be around there directly. Go tell your mama we got company."

"She's already seen it. She was on the front porch but then went back inside," Andrew replied, and then turned and ran, disappearing around the corner of the house to make sure that the source of his excitement had not vanished.

Grace had stopped midway to the back steps to observe Andrew's near-hysteria.

"Why does he get so worked up over things? Nothing but a motor car. Like he's never seen one before," she said, shaking her head.

"He's not seen many, now has he? He knows it's company come, that's all."

He absentmindedly wiped his hands across the bib of his faded overalls and walked to the front yard, his jaw set, and without lightness in his step. He had no curiosity about the newly arrived guest.

As he rounded the corner of the house with the devastated cornfield, a backdrop behind him, his saw that Tanner's automobile had indeed pulled into the yard. The car was black and shiny as always, except for the red mud caked on the tires and splattered along the edges of the fenders.

Judith had been sitting on the front porch stringing beans into a large pan on her lap when she saw the car approaching. She then quickly moved inside the house without looking up as the car pulled to a stop in the yard just beyond the porch. The driver of the car, a small wiry dark man, got out. He hesitated ever so slightly when he caught just a glance of her disappearing behind the screen door of the house. The car door slammed with a dull thud and he leaned on the hood with his arms folded on it, as Ezra rounded the far corner of the house.

"Howdy, Ezra." The man turned and extended a hand across the hood. There was a brief reluctant handshake.

"Mr. Tanner," he said, nodding almost imperceptibly. He withdrew his hand and lightly fingered the shiny chrome radiator cap on the front of the hood, and placed a foot on the gleaming bumper.

"Quite a cloud we had last night," Tanner said, and Ezra nodded again slightly. Tanner looked out at the cornfield.

"Damned sure messed up your corn crop. Never seen a field so tore up, not by rain anyhow."

"It was the hail, Mr. Tanner. We had hail here last night. Then rain and wind on top of it."

"Damned bad luck anyway you cut it. Bad luck for Bud too. He was counting on that corn."

Ezra involuntarily but noticeably tightened his grip on the radiator cap. Thoughts raced through his mind.

Bad luck for Bud, he thought. Bud, the bootlegger. What about me and my family, Tanner? Think about that? We go deeper in debt. Months of plowing with a worn out old mule. Seed bought with borrowed money—your money. I can't afford to buy my children shoes, I have to depend on my wife's garden to feed us and all you can say is bad luck for Bud. He did not respond to Tanner's comments.

Maybe he hated himself at the moment, but he hated Tanner more. In some perverse way he knew that Tanner was enjoying himself.

"Yes, bad luck all around, I guess." Tanner pulled a plug of Brown Mule from his pocket and sliced off a chunk of it with his pocketknife.

"Here, Ezra, have a chaw," he said, as he began to carve off another piece of the dark moist tobacco.

Ezra shook his head.

"No, I wouldn't care to."

"Nothing wrong with a friendly chaw is there? I seen you chew before, awhile back."

"No, nothing wrong with it. I quit chewing a ways back."

"Well, it don't differ." With a click, Tanner folded his knife and returned it to his trouser pocket along with the tobacco.

"Anyway, Ezra, things don't look good now do they?"

Tanner looked away from him out across the sodden field and down at the flooded bottomland. Ezra thrust his hands into the pockets of his overalls and did not reply. He had nothing to say.

"Just plain bad luck. Bad luck for you *and* for my brother. Hell, he'll be all right though. He's got a big patch up on the ridge. Course, he don't work it hisself."

Don't reckon he would, thought Ezra.

"But I guess that don't help you none, now does it?" Tanner continued.

"I reckon not."

"I spied your garden when I drove in. It looks pretty fair. Ought to have plenty of grub the balance of warm weather. You got a pretty good cow, too, don't you?"

"Pretty good, I reckon."

"And you got a hog coming along. It'll be ready to slaughter come first freeze wouldn't you say?"

He hated the fact that Tanner knew so much about his business that he could so readily give an account of the farm and his predicament. But what he really detested was what Tanner was actually doing. He was reminding him that the farm and almost everything that Ezra owned was due to loans from him. The hog, the cow, the seed, everything. This was Tanner's way of reminding him, as if he might somehow forget or not have the proper degree of gratitude. Inevitably, Tanner continued.

"But then we ain't talking about much cash coming in, are we?" Ezra sighed deeply but looked away from Tanner. "I guess that's the problem, wouldn't you say?"

"I reckon it is."

"Got any idees?"

"Look, Mr. Tanner, we both know I owe you money, a good bit of money. And I know I've not made a payment in awhile."

"It *has* been a spell," Tanner interrupted.

"All right, in a long time. I just don't have it. I was counting on this corn crop. But with it gone we're wiped out. Done, I reckon you'd say. To tell you the truth, I don't know what I'm going to do."

"Well, that's all fine. Bad luck, like I said. But you've had a run of bad luck it seems to me. Anyhow, where does all this put me? What about the money you owe me?"

"You know I'm good for it. I aim to pay you back like I said I would."

"Now, Ezra, just how you plan to do that?" Tanner chuckled, his pupilless eyes dark and sinister behind drooping eyelids. "I'd like to know that."

"Don't rightly know just yet, I've not had time to sort things out, but I'm good for the money. You know that."

"What I know is I ain't got a damn payment from you in more than six months. I *do* know that. You're just under, man, that's all there is to it. I believe even you can see that."

"I'll figure something out," he said, running a big calloused hand through his thick, dark hair.

"Yeah, you might. And then again you might not. Not much evidence to say you will. Ain't much here to hang my hat on, way I see it."

"Look, Mr. Tanner, what do you want me to tell you? Everything was riding on the corn. You know that. We're standing here looking at my losses. Farming's hard up here."

He immediately regretted saying it, the part about farming being hard. He was no whiner. He had grown up in these mountains. He had watched his own father try to scratch a living out of this rocky dirt and die trying in the effort. He detested himself at this moment—making excuses to Tanner.

"Hard or not, that's the way it is. Knew it the when you hitched that old mule to a plow."

Ezra nodded. He had it coming.

"Anyhow, it's done with."

"Yes, I reckon it might be."

"Ezra, you're a good man, I reckon. Might be a little uppity sometimes but you work hard trying to take care of your wife and them young 'uns of yours. And you're honest, 'least I reckon you are. You just ain't a very good farmer, that's all."

"Get to your point, Mr. Tanner."

"Well, point is you ain't never going to make this place pay. Least not near enough to feed yourselves and pay me what you owe. Hell, you can't even pay the ten dollars for rent each month. But I tell you what I'm going to do."

"And what might that be?" Ezra asked, becoming restless with this pointless conversation with his creditor. He turned and stepped away a few paces down the sloping field toward the river, his back to Tanner.

"I can use you over at the sawmill. You did a real fine job for me there awhile back. Helped you get through another rough time or two, as I recollect. Anyway, I need a good man on the loading end of the belt. I know it's a tough job, real hard work, but then you ain't never been afraid of hard work, have you?"

Not responding, Ezra sighed as he slightly shrugged his shoulders. Tanner continued.

"I can pay you three dollars a day. We knock off at noon on Saturdays so that's near sixteen dollars, maybe a little more. I'll need to take out five dollars a week for what you owe me but that'll still give you near fifty dollars a month. You won't get rich, but then again your family won't starve neither. And they'll be a roof over your head."

At five dollars a week toward his debt, he would be Tanner's peon for almost five years. That is, if Tanner did not increase the interest on the outstanding balance, as he was liable to do. He would basically be an indentured servant, almost worse than a sharecropper.

He cringed at the thought, the nasty dangerous work at the mill with unsavory men around him, drifters all, as co-workers. But most of all at the thought of being under Tanner's thumb for years to come. Yet he realized that he had no one to blame but himself for his predicament. This thought burned within him. He had rented the farm from him and with each failed season had gone to this foul man, hat in hand, for more loans. He had gotten in bed with the devil and now the devil was extracting his pound of flesh, his due.

He turned and looked at Tanner.

"What about the farm?"

"There won't be no farm, at least for your uses. I mean you can stay in the house. I reckon you could use the cow shed and pig pen if you wanted to, but I'll have to do something else with the land. Probably rent it out. Maynard Spearman's been looking for more land, he'd likely take it."

"What about the garden plot?" He hesitated. "It's just that we need the garden."

Tanner lightly rubbed the stubble on his chin and spat a line of tobacco on the ground between his shoes.

"Of course, I reckon you'd need the garden. But that's a chunk of property. I'd have to raise your rent a mite."

"I reckon I'll need to think about it," Ezra said, picking up a wet piece of a corn leaf off the ground, rubbing it between his fingers, and then absent-mindedly tearing it into small strips. He looked out across the field, down toward the river.

"Well, just don't think too long. Times is hard, Ezra. There's plenty of men who would take the job in a heartbeat and be glad to get it. And for less money than what I'm offering you. Three dollars a day is damned good pay, generous on my part. Yeah, you think about it and maybe talk it over with that pretty little wife of yours. She's smart. I believe she'll see this is a good deal."

Tanner turned and walked back toward the house. Ezra followed him.

"I reckon I ought to pay my respects to the missus. Wouldn't be neighborly to leave without speaking."

Stepping up onto the porch Tanner tapped on the screen door with his sharp, bony knuckles. Startled, she looked up from her chair across the room where she had continued to work with the beans. He was a hazy outline, like an apparition, as streaks of the afternoon sun behind him cast his shadow against the screen of the door. She looked back down into the pan in her lap.

Her heart raced for a few seconds. She suddenly felt strangely outside of herself, as if she was vanishing and could not be seen. Thoughts flooded over her. Then by force of will she fought to maintain herself, her control. She continued to look down into the pan and said nothing. He could plainly see her sitting there, knowing she sensed his presence.

"Good evening to you, Mrs. Burke," he spoke through the screen. "Shame about this mess with the storm. Sure looks bad. Just bad luck, that's what I told that husband of yourn. Just pure bad luck." She did not reply or look up at him.

"I see you're busy. Just wanted to pay my respects," said the shadow on the screen as he tipped his hat, half smiling—almost a smirk—the thin white scar pulling at the corner of his mouth. He then turned and stepped off the porch. Ezra was in the yard, just in front of the Ford watching him. Tanner came round and opened the driver's side door. He started to get in the car but hesitated and looked over at him.

"Mrs. Burke seems to be doing just fine in spite of things. Don't take much for 'em, does it?"

Ezra said nothing.

"Anyway, think about the job. I don't know what else you'd do. Don't see you have too much choice. I'll expect to hear from you in a day or so?"

"All right, Mr. Tanner. I'll let you know something."

Tanner got into his car and started the engine. He wheeled the car around in the yard and drove slowly away, trying not to splatter more mud on the shiny fenders of his nearly-new automobile.

CHAPTER 6

She had come to the doorway and watched the car drive away. He sat slumped-shouldered on the steps of the porch, his back to her. He stared out across the field down to the river.

"What was that about, Ezra? He knows there's no money. Is he turning us out?"

"No, not exactly. Not yet anyway. He offered me work. He wants me to come back to the sawmill."

"No," she said softly, but quicker and sharper than she had intended.

He sighed deeply, but did not reply. He pinched his bottom lips between his fingers, something he did when he was deep in thought. He just needed to think now.

Standing in the doorway, a cold shiver raced through her body as she thought of her husband working for Tanner—just having to be near him. She thought back to that autumn and winter when he had worked at the sawmill before, the last time. She could hardly bear the thought of it. And if he only knew. She had fought back the memory, but now it flooded over her like a heavy, black fog. It now seemed almost unreal, like a bad dream. A nightmare. But it was real. It had happened. It had happened to her. And she knew that this dark secret in her heart was something she could never share with him or anyone. It was her cross, her burden, and it lay open but hidden between them. If only she had stayed home that warm autumn day.

***

It had been Grace's birthday and she was thinking about the of eggs that had accumulated in the wire basket on the small table in the corner of the kitchen. She wanted it to be a special day for her daughter. There would be no presents of course, but maybe a cake, a cake with icing to celebrate. They would have a party at supper when her husband returned from the sawmill.

But the flour was almost gone and there probably would not be enough sugar for a cake, certainly not for icing. In her logical and independent mind, it did not make sense to do without when she had perfectly good eggs that could be easily bartered for the things she needed. Lanford's store was only three miles away, an hour's walk she had made many times before.

The day had begun like every other since he had gone to work for Tanner. He left for the sawmill very early each morning, rising before daybreak to hitch the mule to the wagon and to take care of the animals. She had woken with him. While he was outside preparing for the trip she lit a fire in the cold, iron stove and put on coffee. While the coffee was heating up she made a pan of biscuits which, when they were done, she pulled apart and sandwiched a generous slab of fried bacon between the halves. Wrapping them in a cotton cloth, she placed several of them, along with some apples, in a small, wrinkled, paper bag. He would bring the bag back neatly folded in the evening, when he returned from work. She then placed the bag of food and a jug of water in a burlap sack. Twisting and securing the opening end of the sack in a knot, she sat it on the floor beside the kitchen door. This would be his dinner.

He came in from the yard and ate one of the biscuits she had left in the pan, and sipped coffee. He did not sit down at the table to eat, but rather leaned against the wall beside the door, staring at the floor as he munched the warm bread. She knew that he was anxious to be on his way. Without finishing the coffee, he placed the cup in the sink and, with his fingers, lightly flicked crumbs from the bib of his faded overalls.

"Well, I best be on my way. The animals are fed. I didn't milk the cow. I was thinking Grace could do it. You might send her out by herself this morning. I've watched her do the milking so she'll be all right. Reckon it will make her feel like a real big girl to do it by herself without her Pa looking over her shoulder, being it's her birthday and all."

"All right."

"Andrew can help with the eggs. Just watch out for snakes when you gather from those nests under the porch." He was always warning her about the snakes though she had yet to come upon one while collecting eggs.

"I guess I know how to gather eggs by now," she said teasingly. He smiled at this as he looked at her.

"I reckon you do by now."

"We've got good hens, I think. We've been gathering a lot more eggs that we need. Mr. Lanford is always wanting more eggs to sell. I might go over to the store and do some trading. We need some things. We're almost out of flour and the sugar is almost gone." She wanted the birthday cake to be a surprise for them.

"That's fine, but I can do it Saturday evening when I get off work. I don't want you going over to Lanford's by yourself. Not while I'm gone."

"All right, Mr. Burke. Whatever you say," her teasing continued.

He stepped over to her and held her close. She pressed her face hard against his chest. She could feel the pulsing of his heart. Still in his embrace, she looked up at him and he kissed her. He then released her with a suddenness that almost startled her, and then turned to leave.

"Don't forget your dinner," she said. He reached down and picked up the bundle.

"See you late this evening. About dark as usual, I reckon."

They had looked at each other for a long moment before he turned and left. She walked to the back door and watched him cross the yard in the gray light of the early dawn. He mounted the wagon and took the worn leather straps of the reins in his huge hands. With a loud slap he cracked the reins across the rump of the mule. The wagon lurched forward and disappeared around the corner of the house and was gone. Sometimes she went through the house to the front porch and waved to him as he passed. But not this morning. She stood at the back door for a moment biting her lower lip, looking up at the hills that rose beyond the farm yard against the gray-pink sky. She then turned away from the door and called the children to breakfast.

***

"Grace, you and Andrew come here," she called from the half-opened screen door later in the morning. The children were out of sight, gathering late tomatoes in the garden. No answer came.

"Grace!"

"Yes, Mama. I'm coming," the child called back, still out of sight.

"Bring your brother."

Both children came around the corner of the house into the back yard swinging a half-filled basket of tomatoes between them. She took the basket and held the door open for them. She sat down, pulling a chair from the kitchen table and taking Andrew into her lap. Grace stood beside her mother and crossed her small brown hands on her knee.

"What's the matter, Mama? We've got a bunch more tomatoes to pick. Just look at that basket. Why, we can fill it up easy."

"I know you can. We'll finish getting them in later. Nothing's the matter. I just need talk to you, that's all."

"All right," replied Grace, her dark eyes luminous with curiosity, looked openly into her mother's face.

"I am going to take some eggs over to Lanford's store and buy some groceries so I can fix a good supper tomorrow night. And I might just have a surprise for everybody too."

"A surprise!" shouted Andrew, bolting from his mother's lap onto the floor. He danced around Grace, his arms flailing in the air.

"I said *maybe*, so don't get so worked up, Andrew. Grace, y'all stay in the house while I'm gone, you hear me?"

"Yes, ma'am."

"You got specially to keep an eye on your brother. I mean every minute. He's liable to run off down to the river or something. You've got to watch him."

"I can watch him. He's no trouble."

"Now you can get out the checkerboard and play checkers in the front room."

"Andrew can't play checkers. He don't know how."

"Well, you can teach him. Time he learned."

"I *can to* play checkers, Mama," said a sad-eyed Andrew, his feelings injured by his sister's censure.

"Or play jackstones."

"I'll teach him how to play checkers," Grace said, with a shrug.

"All right, that's good. I'll fix y'all some dinner directly and then I'll walk over to Lanford's. We'll feed the animals when I get back. Now you two go on back out to the garden and finish up with the tomatoes."

She was anxious to get started. She did not much like leaving the children alone, although she knew that Grace was responsible beyond her years and would take care of Andrew. She would be back home as soon as she could. She put several sticks of wood in the stove and set a pot of water on it to boil.

With the sun high in a stark-blue, cloudless sky the children came through the back door with another basket of tomatoes, which they placed on the floor beside the small corner table.

"That's all the ripe ones, Mama. Not many green ones left either," Grace said.

"The season's about gone. There won't be many more this year. You and Andrew go wash up. Dinner's ready."

Judith ladled warm beans over the rice in each of the three plates on the table. After filling their cups with milk, she took one of the large ripe tomatoes from the basket, its firm but pliable skin still warm from the late morning sun. She sliced it into thick, red disks which she placed on the plate in the middle of the table. When the children came back into the kitchen they all sat down, and after the blessing, began to eat.

Fighting back a vague anxiety which puzzled her some, she picked at the food but ate very little, not tasting it. She watched the two hungry children devour their meal, not greedily but with the simple manners she had taught them. Her maternal feelings were strong and she was almost overcome with the deep feelings that washed over her. A slight but distinct shiver caused her to look away. It was almost noon.

"I have to get going now. Grace, you wash up the dishes best you can. You help her, Andrew."

"All right, Mama."

She went into the bedroom and took out a cardboard shoebox from the bottom drawer of the chifforobe. She removed the top of the box and took out the contents. It was a pair of yellow doeskin moccasins. Actually more boot than moccasin, as the leather came up just over her ankles. At the end of the leather laces were small tassels, each attached by a narrow, decorative band of hammered silver. She ran her fingers across the soft, supple skin of the shoes. The leather felt warm, almost silky to the touch. It seemed almost alive to her. The inner sole of the moccasins was lined with a thicker skin-like material, probably beaver, which made them more practical for walking over rough ground and in the cold. The moccasins had been a wedding gift from her mother, who had made them with her own hands.

It was with a sad sweetness that she remembered her mother approaching her shyly that day with the shoes wrapped in brown paper. She had seemed so small and frail and old beyond her years. She thought then that her mother was embarrassed by the simple, hand-made gift. But in looking back many times, she had come to believe that what she had mistaken for reticence was instead a humble pride in both the moccasins and her daughter.

She loved the moccasins. Just now they seemed more precious to her than she had ever realized.

CHAPTER 7

Instead of the main road, she took an old deer trail that ran from up just back of the farm yard and along the lower slope of Jones Mountain. The trail was a little rugged in places, but it would reduce the distance to Lanford's store by nearly a mile. Saving the time would be worth it. She could do it easily wearing the moccasins. It would have been more difficult in her leather shoes, and, besides, the soles were nearly worn through. Anyone at the store would notice the moccasins and would exchange quick, knowing glances and nods, but they would not say anything, at least not to her face.

So she was vaguely relieved that no one other than Lanford was in the store when she got there. He was pleasant enough, and they chatted amicably while she picked out the things she had come for. He was glad to get the eggs and gave her a fair appraisal for them in exchange for the items she needed. He did not mention the past due credit balance; that was business between him and her husband.

On leaving the store, she decided to take the county road back home. She loved walking the deer-trail but Lanford had mentioned someone seeing a bear and with two cubs somewhere in the vicinity of the creek where the trail crossed. She had seen nothing on her way there, but still felt uneasy about the possibility of encountering a female bear with young.

The county road was tar and gravel, with not much of a shoulder on either side. There would be little, if any, traffic so she could walk mostly on the pavement. She would hurry so it would not take her that much longer to get home than by the deer-trail. A slight breeze brushed her cheeks as she started the trek with the grocery items in the cloth sack slung over her shoulder. I must look like a real rambler. She smiled at the thought.

With Lanford's store well behind, her thoughts were mostly of Ezra and the children and the special evening meal. And the mountains all around her. Oh, how she loved these mountains. The rhythm of the days and the seasons. Of her life here. She knew there existed worlds other than her own, and she wondered if she might ever be someplace else.

Silly to think such, she thought. But still it caused an indistinct apprehension in her if she thought about it too much. This confused her some, so she did not dwell on it.

As she continued her trek, she became aware that the moccasins did not do as well walking on the hard paved road. She could feel the loose, sharp-edged gravel through the padded soles, and the midafternoon sun had warmed the road, softening the tar. The shoes were hot on her feet, but it did not matter to her. She loved the long-ago gift from her mother. She loved the freedom of the wild, beautiful afternoon and she loved the solitude.

The mountain road curved slightly and then spread out before her. Up ahead, it curved back again before disappearing into a dark canopy of ancient hickory trees and chestnut oaks hanging over the road. As she neared the cavern of trees there was an alien incongruous sound, something mechanical, approaching from behind. She glanced back over her shoulder to see a black automobile rounding the curve. She shifted the sack to her other shoulder and walked on.

As the car approached, she rightly sensed that it was slowing down. It then pulled up beside her, moving slowly, as she continued walking.

"Well, now Mrs. Burke, what are you doing out walking this road by yourself?" the driver asked, leaning slightly across the front seat of the automobile to the passenger-side window nearest her.

At first she did not recognize the raspy voice. She hesitated and looked at the driver but did not stop walking. The car crept along beside her. She finally glanced over at it.

"Oh, it's you, Mr. Tanner. I am on my way back home from Lanford's store."

"Got some things for supper, did you?"

"Yes."

"Won't be no need to hurry with fixin' it, I reckon," said Tanner with a short chuckle, almost to himself.

"Why do you say that?"

"Because I sent Ezra up to Asheton to deliver a load of lumber. Don't see him getting back 'til well after dark. That is, if that old truck of mine don't break down before then."

"I see. I was sure hoping he would be home for supper."

"Well, sorry about that, but he has to run his job. You certainly understand that don't you, Mrs. Burke?"

"Yes."

"And besides, he's the only man I got what stays sober enough to drive a load that far."

"He doesn't drink."

"I know it. That's my point."

"I've got to get on home, Mr. Tanner. Nice to see you," she said, as she looked away and increased her pace.

"Why don't you just get in? I'll be happy to drive you home. Won't take but a jiffy." He reached over and pushed open the passenger door."

"That's good of you, but I think I'll just walk the rest of the way. I like to walk."

"Now don't be foolish, Mrs. Burke. It's warm out today and you got that load of groceries. I bet them kids of yourn are waiting on you, too. Ain't that right?"

"Yes," she said, intuitively visualizing Grace and little Andrew at home.

She was sure they were safe and things were all right, but it was still at least a half-hour walk to the farm. She did not want to get in the car with this man, a man she did not know very well, a man she neither liked nor trusted.

"Well, come on, get in," Tanner said, smiling slightly.

"I'll just walk."

"I don't bite, Mrs. Burke. Just being friendly. You know, the Good Samaritan and all that. It's just a ride."

"All right," she finally said, not knowing what else she could do to tactfully refuse his offer.

She reluctantly got into the car, and immediately regretted it as she pulled the door shut. The car accelerated slowly.

"How do you like my car?" he asked, looking away from the road ahead and directly to her. She caught the foul, sour smell of alcohol from his breath.

"It's nice," she said softly, not looking at him, but at the road ahead.

"It's a new Ford. Well, not brand new exactly. Newer than any other buggy around Waverley. That's for sure."

She said nothing. She was extremely uneasy at how slowly the car was moving.

"Them's real Indian shoes you wearing, ain't they?"

"Yes."

"They're real perdy. Don't see shoes like that around here. Not no more, anyhow. But they're real perdy. 'Course you're real perdy, too. But I reckon you know that, don't you?"

She did not reply, but continued to stare straight ahead at the road as they approached the dark trees ahead, which seemed to swallow the road in their sustained blackness.

The car rounded the shallow curve and Tanner continued to drive purposefully, much slower than what seemed normal to her. He had pulled his felt hat down low across his forehead and turned his head slightly away from her. He steered with his right wrist draped over the top of the steering wheel. His left arm rested on the edge of the door; its the window was rolled down. Even with the windows down, the air was hot and stale in the automobile. She felt a small trickle of perspiration trail down the nape of her neck beneath her cotton dress. Her hair was damp beneath her straw hat.

Suddenly the car jerked with several quick sharp jolts as if it was going to stall. She stiffened, pressing her body hard against the seat back. She looked over at him.

"Damn it all! Thing seems to be running hot. Must be a leak in the radiator. Damn it all!"

He pulled the car over on the shoulder of the road and quickly got out. She did not move. She felt strangely weighed down by her own body and the oppressive heat. The inside collar of her dress was soaked with sweat. The damp fabric clung to her skin as she breathed.

Tanner's head and shoulders disappeared briefly under the raised hood of the automobile, as he appeared to be tinkering with the engine or with something she could not see. Just as quickly, he slammed the hood shut and got back into the car.

"Eh, seems the radiator's a little low. No problem though. There's a creek just off the road up yonder." He pointed to a small rise in the road just ahead. "I'll pull in there and fill 'er up. Won't take a minute. I got a jug in the boot. I'll have you home in a jiffy, just like I said. Just can't ever tell about these damn cars, even if they are near new."

Before Judith could respond, he pulled the car back onto the road, accelerating sharply.

He drove a short distance, then turned the Ford sharply onto a narrow unpaved road, an abandoned logging trial. It was barely visible and was grown over with saplings and vines, which slapped against the windshield and the sides of the car as it moved through.

"Mr. Tanner, where are you going? Where is this?" she asked, surprised and now frightened.

"Now settle down, Mrs. Burke. No problem. There's a clearing up ahead along the creek. I'm getting water for the radiator. Nothing for you to worry about. Nothing at all."

"I want out of the car. I can walk home from here. Please stop and let me out."

"Now don't be foolish, Mrs. Burke. This won't take a minute," he said, as the car bumped along the rough trail.

She thought maybe she *was* being foolish. She did not like Tanner nor did she trust him, but maybe all he was doing was what he said, filling the radiator. She took a deep breath and gripped the fabric of the car seat with both hands. Maybe she *was* being foolish.

They came into a small grassy clearing, just as he had said. She glimpsed to see the edge of a small, swift stream in the woods to the left. He stopped the car in the middle of the clearing and switched off the engine. He gripped the steering wheel with both hands and did not make a move to get out of the car. He just sat there looking out through the windshield.

"Mr. Tanner, the water. Get the water so we can go."

Tanner seemed almost startled at her voice. He shook his head a couple of times as if coming out of a shallow trance.

"Please, Mr. Tanner, I need to go."

"Oh, sure. I'll get right to it," he said, sounding almost dazed. "You just sit here. I'll be right back. Be done in a jiffy."

He got out and went around to the back of the car and opened the trunk. She exhaled deeply and tried to relax her body. She wanted to get this over with and be home with her children. She was just being foolish to be so uneasy. She had let the fear almost overtake her. Just a foolish woman. She gazed out at the clearing. The air was cooler here and felt good against her face as a slight breeze drifted across the clearing, into the open window of the automobile. The stillness was absolute. The only sound was from the creek where swift water ran, and splattered over stones worn smooth by the flowing water.

Suddenly, she felt open space beside her. The car door was jerked opened. She gasped loudly as he roughly pulled her out of the car. She tried to scream but his small, bird-like hand was strong, and it covered her mouth instantly. She could see the thin scar that ran from the corner of his mouth. It shone white against his stretched and saturnine skin. Her thoughts raced. I am dead. He is going to kill me here.

Strangely, it suddenly occurred to her how fruitless her screams would be. They were deep in the forest, a wilderness. No one was there to hear.

Tanner gripped both her shoulders. She felt his bony fingers dig into her. He pulled her up close to him.

"Now don't you go and act all scared and surprised. You knew all along what this was all about, now didn't you, you perdy little squaw?"

"You're wrong, Mr. Tanner. This is wrong. Please let me go," she pleaded, her breath in short gasps. "Please!"

"Oh, I'm going to let you go all right. Soon as I give you what you been wanting. Like you didn't get into this here car with me with the same idee I was having. I bet you're wet already down there," he snarled, his face now a strange red color, the mouth-scar a luminous line.

His body was shaking. The smell of his hot breath in her face was thick with whiskey and stale tobacco. A wave of nausea swept over her as she struggled hopelessly against his grip. He was stronger, much stronger than she was. Her struggling seemed to heighten his excited agitation.

"You've got to let me go. I don't want this. I thought you were just being nice, offering me a ride home. I didn't want to get in the car with you. I shouldn't have done it."

He eased his grip on her shoulders, no resistance now. Maybe she could reason with him.

"But you did, didn't you? I reckon that tells me all I need to know."

He tried to pull her to him and kiss her. She pulled back with all the strength she could muster. She turned her face away from his advance and his obnoxious smell. Her stomach churned with fear and revulsion.

"No!" she cried, trying again to pull herself out of his grasp.

"Oh, I think you do want it. Bad as me, I expect. You might be just a half-breed but I hear tell Indians' all hot blooded. Ain't no one man can satisfy 'em, they say. I know one thing, I sure want me some Indian snatch and I'm going to get me some."

With that, he pushed her backward into the car, onto the front seat. He stood in the doorway of the automobile and glared down at her. His breathing was rapid and heavy, almost labored. He bit his lower lip then wiped saliva from his mouth. He bent over and reached under her dress and clumsily yanked her under garment down over her thighs and ankles, and tossed it to the floorboard.

"Don't do it, Mr. Tanner! Please don't do this!"

She was sobbing. He was by now beyond words, or hearing her pleas. He was beyond thinking about anything but his own lust and his power over her. She sensed this and lunged at him from her prone position in the car seat. She grabbed his face with both hands, digging her short nails into the flesh of his thin, leathery flesh. He pushed her back into the seat with a scarred smirk and ignored the deep and bleeding scratches she had inflicted on him. He held her down with his left hand while he fumbled with the buttons of his trousers.

As he lay on her, moving, coarsely gasping, almost panting, she turned her face away and buried it as best she could into the rough fabric of the seat back. Her body remained rigid, her only defense at this point. She felt hot tears as they fell from her eyes and soaked into the cloth. Her fists were clinched to whiteness at her sides. There was no pain, no feeling at all. Just nothing. She felt somehow outside herself, floating in an unreal and light ether.

***

With a loud, hoarse, guttural groan, Tanner finished and collapsed onto her, but did not touch her with his hands. He quickly pushed himself off of her and, standing, began fastening his trousers. She had not moved.

"Now that wasn't so bad, was it?" he asked, his voice hoarse, his breathing still rapid.

He placed his hands on the edge of the car roof and lowered his head to look in at her.

"Shouldn't have scratched up my face like you did, though. But hell, I like a little fight in a woman. Sure expected it from an Indian, maybe a little more than you gave."

"Ezra will kill you," she said, as she pulled herself upright in the seat.

"Yeah, I expect he'd try if he found out. But then he ain't ever going to know, now is he?"

"When I tell him, he will kill you."

"Now, woman, let's just think about this a spell. You tell him and he comes for me, well, I might just kill him first. You wouldn't want that, now would you?"

She did not acknowledge him as she reached down to retrieve her undergarment from the floor of the car and held it close to her breast, almost shivering. She had been violated and felt nothing but shame and disgust. She sat looking through the windshield to the dark woods beyond the clearing.

"You go ahead and put them nice little under britches back on while I walk over to the creek and wash this blood off my face. I won't be looking," he laughed hoarsely, and walked from the car. He disappeared into the bushes beside the creek.

She dressed herself as best she could and smoothed out her dress with trembling hands. She ran her fingers through her long, thick, ebony hair and reached for her things in the backseat. As she got out of the car, she was trembling almost uncontrollably and could hardly stand. Nausea flooded over her as she made her way to the rear of the car, leaning on the cool metal of the automobile.

She fell to her knees without intent and vomited until she was retching. Her mouth was dry and parched, and she longed desperately for water. She could not get the odor of Tanner out of her nostrils nor out of her mind. Could she survive this? She did not know.

She finally managed to pull herself up, leaning uneasily on the rear fender. He appeared from the woods, wiping his face with a dingy red handkerchief.

"Now like I was saying, ain't no point in anyone knowing about all this. Couldn't come to no good anyhow. How would your husband feel about laying with a woman what's been with another man? A man like me. You might say I forced you and I might say I didn't. So who's to know for sure? And then you got them young 'uns. What you going to tell them? Might not be too easy to explain to them exactly what happened. Yes, it's best we just keep this between you and me."

"You are an evil man. If you ever touch me again, I'll kill you myself. I swear before God; I'll kill you myself."

He chuckled at this and smiled at her.

"Yeah, I expect you would at that, if you could. Anyway, it's done with. I got what I wanted and you don't appear none the worse for wear. We'll just forget it."

Another wave of nausea came over her, but quickly passed. She felt something go cold deep inside her. Her eyes were dry. She realized that this creature before her represented all that was evil in the world, all that was dark and not good. Was there anything left good in the world, her world? Images of her children, her husband, her mother flashed before her like shimmering mirages. There was *some* good but there was much bad as well.

She now knew what pure, objective hatred was. It frightened her. It frightened her because she had not realized that she was capable of such a thing. This was something different. It was without emotion or affect. Without expectation. She knew that without question she could kill Tanner or watch him die without the slightest hint of feeling or remorse. This hatred was not human, she thought, and she did not like it in herself, but she embraced it just the same.

She looked at his face and into his dead eyes. Shameless and without emotion, she repeated the words, "I'll kill you."

The stupid grin fell from Tanner's face. She picked up her things and took the trail leading out from the clearing onto the county road.

***

She walked past the vegetable garden and approached the house. There was nothing but silence and the children were nowhere to be seen. But that was a good thing, she thought, because she had instructed them to stay inside the house until she returned. As she climbed the steps to the front porch, she felt as if a great weight was upon her. Her shoulders ached where Tanner had so violently gripped her. Her dress was stained with perspiration from him and the walking. She had stridden steadily and purposefully from the clearing in the woods. The clearing of shame.

She slowly opened the screen door, expecting the children to run to her, glad to see her after her rare absence from them. But no one ran to meet her. Still shaky and edgy from Tanner's brutal assault, for a moment she felt her heart flutter with panic. But walking into the kitchen, she saw the two children asleep on the floor, with jackstones scattered around them. Grace had made a pallet by spreading a thick quilt on the floor, probably for Andrew to nap, but they had both fallen asleep. Her small thin arm lay light as a twig across her little brother's chest. She still held the small red rubber ball, from the game, in one hand.

Judith spread her hand across her chest in relief and love as she gazed down at the children. Tears streamed down her face as she wept bitterly and uncontrollably.

She did not wake the children, but rather slipped off the doe skin moccasins and placed them on the floor beside her bed. She then moved noiselessly across the room and out onto the porch. She breathed deeply. The sweet fragrance of honeysuckle from the river filled her nostrils, but she could not forget nor relinquish the vile odor of stale tobacco and whiskey.

Barefoot, she strode down across the open field to the river. It was low and sparkling as she walked just beyond the honeysuckle vines to the edge of the stream. She slipped the dress over her head and let it fall to the ground like an aimless leaf, without thought. She removed her undergarments and waded into the stream. The chill of the water startled her at first as it swirled around her ankles and the calves of her brown legs. But she embraced it. It felt clean and the wet coldness soothed her. She reached down into the stream with cupped hands and splashed the water on her face. The clear liquid was wonderful as it trailed down her neck and between her breasts. She must find a way to cleanse herself. Her violated body. The memory.

With the water of the stream swirling around her hips, she washed herself. She washed herself of his smell, of his touch, of his clumsy, disgusting probing. "Water has power", she said aloud, as it gently washed away the soreness and the pain of her body.

Out in the middle of the river was a large rock, a boulder really, where the water was deepest. She waded out a bit further and plunged into the water, completely submerging herself. Its life and coldness was a balm to her. She must somehow cleanse herself, she thought again. She must somehow cleanse herself of this horror.

***

When she thought back on this terrible time she knew it would always be there. There would be no escape. Ezra had come home late that evening, just as Tanner said he would. He tried to talk to her at supper but she had nothing to say. She was empty and could hardly look at his face. He eventually turned his attention to the children.

Later in the bedroom, she had undressed in the dark. In the bed, he had touched her arm. She remembered how light his fingers had felt against her skin. But she only turned away in the darkness, as the tears streamed down her cheeks, dampening the pillow.

CHAPTER 8

Ezra suddenly stood up and spoke, waking her from the worst of dreams.

"The way I see it it's pretty much as Tanner said, I got no choice." He shoved his hands into the deep pockets of his overalls.

He was still staring out toward the river, but she sensed that he had made a decision. A decision without knowing the truth, a truth he would never know.

"I'm going to work for Tanner, at the sawmill," he said, finally turning and looking up at her in the doorway.

"The sawmill? But how will you work the farm?"

"There's not going to be a farm."

"No farm? Where would we go?" She came out onto the porch and took the chair, looking at her husband.

"It's a job with wages. Three dollars a day. At least that's what he promised. His word, he said."

"And where would we live?"

She waited, but he said nothing.

"Oh Ezra, I know things have been hard, especially for you, but I love this place. *We* love it here, this place. The garden, the river. It's home, Ezra, it's home. And Mr. Tanner…"

"We can keep the house and the garden plot. Just not the land. Maynard Spearman will probably rent it and work it. I don't know or really care now when all's said and done. That's just what he told me."

"He likely wants his money, then?" she asked.

"He'll take it out of my wages."

Lost in a flood of their own thoughts with the events that seemed to be overtaking them, they did not speak for a while. He stared out at the river. The waters of the flooded bottom land had noticeably receded.

"It might be good to have wages. We have so little. Grace needs to start school. She have to have shoes."

"Yes, she needs shoes," she whispered, as tears welled up in her eyes, "I just meant…"

"I know what you meant, Judith, and you're right. We need a lot of things. All these years working this piece of dead rocky ground and nothing to show for it. I reckon that's what I hear you telling me. And, before God, I know it's true."

"We've been happy here. Made a life, as I see it."

"Of a kind, I reckon."

"You're a good man, Ezra Burke. The same one I took for a husband. We're a family. We'll get through this."

He turned and looked up at his wife. With a faint smile, he nodded. He knew then that she had always been, and still was, his soul and he was lost in her. This small beautiful creature of a woman with the bright, almost black, intelligent eyes. Her effortless way of making things seem natural and right. Her light step. Her even lighter touch. There was a sense of grace in her every movement, in everything she did. Not that she sought it, it was just there as a part of her. Being part Cherokee, he reckoned that her Indian blood provided her the capacity to be more than he could understand. How else to account for her resiliency, her wisdom, her wisdom beyond her years and experience. Indeed, her nobility. But how could this happen to him? How had she come to be a part of him, and he a part of her. But as unlikely as it seemed, it was true, it had happened.

Early the next morning, in a gray mist, he hitched the mule to the wagon and drove it across the mountain to Tanner's sawmill.

***

The sawmill was just off the paved state road in a large scrubby area that had long ago been clear-cut by loggers. Erosion had eaten away and made deep gullies of the drainage ditches that ran parallel to the road. A short gravel drive led from the road to an area in front of a small, unpainted clapboard shack—the yard office. A hundred feet behind the shack on a slight knoll was a single dilapidated outhouse which leaned precariously to one side.

To the right, just beyond the shack, was the mill or what they called the cutting shed. It was a pole building, a long open-ended structure, nothing more than a rough-hewn log frame with a roof of rusting corrugated tin. There were no walls, the sides were open. A raised platform in the middle of the building ran most of its length. Mounted at one end of the platform nearest the office shack was the saw, a huge steel-toothed disk taller than a man. The logs were loaded continuously at the opposite end of the building onto a slow-moving conveyor belt which fed them to the snarling, whirling saw.

Men moved languidly about the mill, some on the platform to keep the logs moving straight one behind the other, some at the end loading timber to feed the voracious, but insatiable appetite of the saw-monster. Others offloaded the rough planks the saw spat out as it chewed through the large round logs.

A couple of men squatted on the ground beside the platform, leaning against one of the support post of the building, chewing tobacco and spitting. One of them occasionally pulled a small flat brown bottle from his hip pocket and drank from it.

Ezra had known what to expect and was not surprised that not much had changed since he had last worked here briefly, a year or so before. Nothing had changed but the faces, and they all still looked pretty much the same. Because of the low pay, long hours, and the treatment by Tanner, the men drifted in and out of employment at the mill as frequently as the weather changed. Most were drifters looking to make a few dollars then to move on. They were hard drinkers, some just plain drunks. All, of course, were poor even by mountain standards. Tanner did not care. He took no interest in the men themselves or their stories. He just squeezed out his pound of flesh and sold the lumber that they cut. They were faceless to him, as interchangeable as the parts on his Ford.

He had arrived that first morning, numb with defeat and dreading the day. It was not just the fact that he was now working directly for the man, Tanner. With the debts he had built up in trying to make a go of the farm, he was already indentured to him anyway. His pride had defeated him, not Tanner. He had been driven. He had kept throwing good money, and years, after bad. He had been unable to accept that he must do something different, what was best for his family. He had been selfish that way. There was a price and now he was paying it.

"Well, looky yonder, would you. Looks like we maybe got us a new hand. A plowboy, I'd say," remarked one of the men in the group loitering outside the yard office door that morning when he had first arrived.

He did not respond as he rode past the men and pulled the wagon up in the field of weeds beyond where they stood watching him. He unhitched the mule and tethered it with a long rope to one of the wagon wheels. He walked back to the group of men.

"Tanner around?" he asked.

One of the men appeared to be seriously looking around the mill yard, shading his eyes with his hand.

"Don't see no shiny black Ford automobile, do you?" he asked Ezra. Some of the men chuckled.

"No, I reckon I don't," he said.

"Well, then, I guess he ain't here jis yet," returned the group's self-appointed spokesman. "You planning on coming to work here at the mill, are you? Looks like you might be figuring on staying awhile the way you went and tied off that mule."

"I am, going to work here, I mean. Tanner's hired me. I worked here before, but I don't recollect any of you fellas."

"That because none of us was here then, I'd say. Sawmill men don't tend to stay around too long. Always looking for new opportunities, I guess," said the spokesman, as he rubbed his fingers through the thick stubble of his chin. The other men laughed.

"Then where's the straw boss?" asked Ezra.

"Straw boss? Now that would be ole Burt, but he ain't here just yet either. Not right *here*."

"I expect he'll be in soon, won't he?"

"Soon enough, I reckon. He's in the outhouse," the man said, pointing his thumb over his shoulder. "He's got a bad stomach this morning so he might be a spell yet. I guess that raw onion and cornbread he had for breakfast didn't fancy that slug of liquor he had for dessert." The group roared with laughter.

"Come on boys, we'd better get to work. Old man Tanner's liable to drive up on us any minute. Don't 'spect he'd much cotton to us loafing here chewing the fat with the new man."

The loud-mouth spokesman and the other men sauntered on past Ezra toward the cutting shed.

Just then a large burly man came around the corner of the yard office absent-mindedly adjusting his belt buckle and whistling softly. He did not see Ezra standing alone in front of the shack.

"You Burt?" he asked, startling the big man who quickly glanced up.

"Damn, man, you 'bout scared hell out me. Yeah, I'm Burt. Whatcha want anyhow?"

"I'm here to work. Tanner hired me."

"He didn't say nothing to me about it. Not that he would anyway. I'm just the straw boss, not much more than anybody else around here when it comes right down to it."

"Well, I'm ready to go to work."

"Did Tanner tell you what he wanted you to be doing?" asked Burt.

"Lay off planks from the saw, I reckon."

"Suits me. Got Snake Loftis doing it now but he ain't worth a shit. Tanner told me he was going to fire his sorry ass. I suppose that's why he's hired you. Anyway, Snake laid out yesterday and I see he ain't here this morning neither. What's your name, mister?"

"Burke. Ezra Burke."

"Well, come on with me, Ezra Burke. Sounds like they done started the saw up."

The motor driving the saw had revved up with a low rumble and it had begun its high pitched whine.

"I'll get you to laying off some planks. Damn hard work. You'll sleep pretty good tonight. I'll guarantee that," Burt said, turning toward the cutting shred, with Ezra a step behind. Then he abruptly, threw a quick glance over his shoulder and said, "Want a snort before you get started, Burke?"

"No, thanks."

"Believe I will, if'n you don't mind." The straw boss pulled a flask from his back pocket and raised it in a mock toast as Ezra walked past him toward the cutting shed and the whine of the saw.

CHAPTER 9

The days grew shorter and cooler as autumn crept into the mountains. The work at the sawmill was steady and hard. He pretty much stayed to himself and did not mind the work. It helped keep him from thinking too much. Although the pay was low, there was now some money. This was a good thing. Grace had started school and finally had new shoes. There was adequate food in the house, much of it store bought, and he was paying down his debt to Tanner. He did not think much about the future other than to the day when he would be free from his self-imposed servitude.

But things had somehow changed at home, with Judith. He could not say exactly what it was but she seemed to have a certain melancholy about her now that he had not seen before. It was subtle, to be sure, and he could not put his finger on it, but it was there. He had asked her one night after supper as they lay in bed if something was the matter. She had only smiled wistfully and said no. He had told her that he loved her, and then turned off the lamp. They lay there in the darkness a long time, each knowing the other was not sleeping. Eventually he could hear only the soft rhythm of her breathing before he fell into the deep sleep of weariness. Early the next morning he left for the sawmill. She spent the morning, mostly alone, tending to her garden of collards and sweet potatoes.

***

He had not heard the engine as Tanner down shifted the Ford and turned off the state road, pulling up in front of the yard shack. The two men leaning against the post at the corner of the cutting shed, smoking, saw Tanner's arrival. They quickly flicked their half-smoked cigarettes to the ground and crushed them beneath their shoes. They disappeared like ghosts into the dusty interior of the mill shed.

Ezra looked up and saw Tanner go into the yard office across the dirt yard. He was glad that Tanner did not hang around the sawmill much. He arrived most days mid-morning, checking to make sure the crews were working and that the trucks, loaded with the newly sawed boards, were leaving out to make deliveries. Much of the lumber was sold to companies down in Corinth, mostly to the cotton mills there for their floors. The cotton mills were proud of their gleaming, waxed

hardwood or pine floors. There were also customers up in North
Carolina, up near Ashton.

But his visits were usually brief. He would come back in the late
afternoon to make sure the saw was shut down and the yard gate locked.
As brief as his visits were, Ezra hated to see him and always tried to
avoid him whenever he could. He kept to his work, off-loading the
freshly cut planks being filleted off the logs by the huge, screaming saw.

As Tanner stepped out of the yard office, the noise of the saw
blade that filled the air abruptly stopped. The drive motor bolted to
wooden beams on the floor just beneath the conveyor platform growled
and slowed under an unnatural strain.

"Pull the clutch back!" yelled one of the men on the platform to
the motor operator below, "she's binded!"

The motor groaned under the load. The operator froze and did
nothing, as if he had not heard the command from above. Sensing what
was happening, Ezra jumped to the ground from the platform behind the
saw. Roughly pushing the motor operator aside, he grabbed the heavy
clutch handle and pulled it toward him. The drive belt that powered the
saw went slack and the motor idled down, relieved of the resistance of
the stuck saw blade.

"Why you go pushing me like that for?" the operator
complained, as he regained his balance. "Weren't no need for it," he
continued angrily, almost in Ezra's face.

"The saw blade is binded on that big log. The motor was liable to
burn up. You didn't clutch it."

"I was going to," the operator slurred slightly, and Ezra caught a
whiff of alcohol on the man's breath.

"Too slow," said Ezra, and he climbed back onto the conveyor
platform to help the others unjam the log from the saw.

Tanner strode arrogantly into the cutting shed and looked up at
the men on the conveyor platform who had been guiding the huge log
into the snarling teeth of the saw.

"What the hell's going on, Burt?"

"Saw binded on this here big oak log. I told you last week that
saw blade was warped," Burt said.

"Ain't nothing wrong with that blade. Just dumbass operators,"
said Tanner, spitting a long brown stream of tobacco juice onto the saw
dust which covered the packed dirt floor. "Well, don't just stand there
like you was afixin' to take your dinner break. Get that saw going. We
got lumber to cut."

Tanner stood looking up at the men as they turned and began struggling to free the log from the hold of the saw. Its teeth had chewed several feet into the wood. It would not budge.

"Damn thing's stuck good, real good, Mr. Tanner," the straw boss shouted down. "Warped blade, I reckon."

Tanner shook his head and again spat tobacco. He then climbed up onto the platform, pushing one of the men aside as he inspected the saw.

"Hell, no wonder it's in a bind. The goddam log's canted. It ain't laying straight on the feed belt," said Tanner to the men, as he turned away from the stilled saw. "A fool could see it. Which appears to be pretty much what I got working for me. A log this big, 'specially oak, has to be laid on the belt straight and kept straight into the saw. Warped blade! You dumber than dirt, Burt."

Burt shrugged slightly and looked down at his shoes without reply.

Tanner directed two of the men to go to the far end of the log and try and move it over, aligning it with the conveyor belt. The log still could not be moved. Tanner called to Ezra who was on the other side of the saw, away from the others.

"Burke, go around and see if you can't help these two boys straighten this hunk of wood."

Ezra quickly moved back to where the other workers stood, sweating and leaning against the delinquent log.

"Now when I say heave, y'all push that end around, won't take much," ordered Tanner. "Now, heave!"

The three men, all with their shoulder to the huge log, pushed against it with all the strength they could muster. The end of the log shifted slightly.

"Whoa! That's enough. That should do it. Get back to your off-loading place, Burke. You other two, think you can feed this log to the saw like it's supposed to be done?"

"Yes, sir, I reckon we can," Burt responded.

"I ought to fire both of you, goddamn it," Tanner shot back. "All right, Cook, you can put 'er in gear."

The motor operator responded quickly this time and pushed the clutch handle aggressively forward. The saw blade leapt into motion and began chewing into the log, as Tanner bent close to the saw and viewed the whirling teeth cut almost effortlessly through the hard oak. He smirked and spat another stream of the heavy brown liquid that landed on the steel frame of the platform.

Just as he turned away from the saw to jump down to the floor he planted his right foot on the puddle of tobacco spittle he had just ejected. His foot slipped as he lost his balance and he fell back against the moving log. Knowing the imminent danger, he instinctively attempted to right himself, but he was too close to the saw. The sharp edge of the teeth of the whirling, serrated disk caught the sleeve of his flannel shirt. Almost instantly the force of the saw pulled him into it. There was nothing Tanner could do to save himself. All that was heard was a gurgling, muffled scream as the spinning blade of the saw, with the mindless focus of a predator consuming its prey, sliced through his torso. The force of the saw slung his mutilated body into the air. Limp and bloody it fell, slamming and lodging between the clutch handle and the hot motor below. The drive belt slackened as the clutch disengaged and the mindless lethal saw ground to a halt. There was no sound but for the low hum of the motor.

***

He drove the wagon around back and pulled up. Unhitching the mule, he led it into the shed and then headed back to the steps of the front porch. He had not seen his wife weeding the garden when she looked up as he passed by, somewhat startled.

"Ezra, you surprised me. Why are you home so early?"

It was just past noon. He stopped but did not reply, looking at her blankly as if she had woken him from a dream. He then turned away and sat on the steps, gazing out across the yard, the field, to the river. She dropped the hoe and went to him. She immediately saw the unnatural paleness of his complexion, his drooping shoulders. Dark red blotches stained the front of his overalls.

"Goodness! Are you all right? What has happened?" she asked softly, with rising panic in her voice "What is it?"

He sighed deeply, but did not look up at her.

"Tanner's dead," he said, finally.

"Dead. What do you mean?

"Tanner. Killed. At the sawmill."

"Are you all right?"

"Yes."

"There's blood on your clothes."

He looked down at himself as if he had been unaware of the still moist blood stains, and was seeing them for the first time.

"He got caught in the saw. Cut him near in half."

"But you're not hurt are you?" she asked, alarm rising in her voice.

"I got to him first. I reckon that's where all this blood's from. I pulled him off the motor to the ground but there was nothing I could do for him. Nothing anyone could do."

"And he's dead?"

"Yes. Dead."

She looked into her husband's face. He was distraught and she understood it. A horrible accident. Nothing he could have done. But it was her own thoughts of which she was most aware. She felt nothing, as far as Tanner's dying was concerned. Nothing but an emptiness. An emptiness to a degree that surprised her, but perhaps should not have. How many times had she lain awake or dreamed of this despicable man and what he had done to her? How many times had her hatred gripped her, frightening her so much that she had wished him dead? Her hatred of him had been cold and emotionless. It was never far away from her thoughts. She struggled mightily against it. This fierce abhorrence. She feared somewhere deep inside herself that such loathing could make her the same as him. That it gave him some kind of vague control over her. Maybe she hated herself more than she hated him. Now that he was dead, these feelings did not subside within her. She knew at this moment that there would always be a place in her that was cold and empty. In time, it would be better perhaps, not so raw, not so near the surface. But now she could almost touch it, as she might touch some part of her body. She had struggled. *Was* struggling. She must not let this thing destroy her.

He then spoke softly, as if he was speaking to someone in the distance, not to her.

"There was something funny happened. Not funny but strange, almost like it was not real. As I knelt over him, he was still breathing. Barely, but alive. His eyes were dark and wild, wide open. I didn't think he could see me or anything. But then he stared me right in the face. Then he just—I don't know—sort of grinned up at me. Like he knew or saw something. I don't know. It was the strangest thing. He grinned at me and died right there. I don't reckon I'll ever forget it. God help me, I won't."

With this, a wave of nausea swept over her. Leaving him alone on the front porch steps, she quickly retreated around the house to the garden where she began to vomit, and could not stop.

***

Not knowing what else to do, he returned to the sawmill the next morning to find the entrance to the yard blocked by a sheriff deputy's automobile. Several of the sawmill crew were milling around, blurry-eyed and hung over. Burt was leaning over the hood of the car. Beyond the barrier posed by the police car, where Burt was intently watching, he could see several other sedans parked near the yard office, all black and official looking. There was a group of men wearing ties huddled together, apparently in deep discussion. Several of them held submachine guns at their sides.

"What's going on, Burt?" he asked, ignoring the bottle one of the men extended to him.

"Feds. G-men, I reckon," Burt replied without looking back at him.

"Investigating the accident?"

"Started out that way, I guess. I mean with the sheriff's men coming in yesterday. After they questioned us. You talked to them didn't you."

"Yes," Ezra replied. "Is the sawmill going to open back up? Can we go to work today?"

"I don't know. I asked the cop who parked this here car the same thing. He just looked at me and shrugged. Said he couldn't say nothing yet. Said they'd been here all night. Then he walked back over there to the yard office and stood around with his hands in his pocket. The gents in the suits didn't seem to pay him no attention though."

Presently the deputy returned to his car.

"What's the scoop, chief? We going to be able to work any today? Thought maybe Tanner's brother might open the sawmill backup," Burt said, as he moved away from the car.

The deputy chuckled sardonically, "Looks like old Bud Tanner ain't going to be opening up nothing but a jail cell."

"How's that," Burt asked, as the other men gathered around, suddenly interested.

"Well, after y'all left yesterday the sheriff started poking around. That's the ways he is. Real suspicious, always looking for more than they is. Or maybe he had a reason to suspect, I don't know. Anyway, he told us all to spread out and search the property. We couldn't figure it, but well, he's the boss."

"What was you looking for?" one of the men asked.

"Like I said, at the time we didn't know. But the property goes all the way through them woods up to that ridge over yonder."

The deputy pointed to the hills and expanse of forest that began just beyond the leaning outhouse.

"Well, anyway, at near the top of the ridge two of the fellas smelled something, like a fire burning. Some smoke, too, I reckon. They snuck through the trees and saw ahead of them this here clearing. That's where the smoke was coming from. Sure enough, sure as I'm standing here, they walked up on a still. Drew their pistols and walked right in."

"A still? They ain't no still up there," said Burt incredulously, as several of the other men chuckled.

"The hell they ain't," the deputy continued, "and over under a hickory tree they say ole Bud Tanner was laying, passed out drunk as a skunk.

"No!"

"Yep, sure was. We cuffed him and drug his sorry ass back down here. Sheriff got on the horn and called the Feds. They's an office down in Corinth, you know. That's who them fellas are in the suits, Government agents."

All the men simultaneously looked beyond the deputy to the group of men in suits who were still in grouped in front of the mill office.

"What about the sawmill?" inquired Burt.

"Look, I done said way too much to you fellas already," said the deputy. He then walked to the rear of his car and pulled a heavy chain from the trunk.

"I got to put this here chain across the road. No one can come on this property. Can one of you fellas give be a hand? Need to hook it to them posts there."

The sawmill was closed down and the property was subsequently confiscated by the Government. The cut lumber was sold off to the cotton mills, mostly around Corinth, for their floors, as always. Soon weeds and kudzu claimed the cutting shed, the heavy vines leisurely, but inexorably, snaking across the ground, around the structure, up the posts, and over the tin roof until it became part of the forest itself. The vicious saw blade maintained its silence and dark stains, slowly rusting away in the cool, damp mountain air.

PART TWO

CHAPTER 10

Edmonds suddenly shot passed the car just ahead of him, swerved in front of it and pulled the car up to the curb. Ezra was relieved to be stopping and getting out of the heavy traffic and the automobile driven by this affable, though possibly deranged, young man who never seemed to stop talking.

"Well, Mr. Burke, this is where you and I part company. See that street on the left down the next block?" Not waiting for a response, "That's Galway Avenue. Named after the mill, Galway Mill. Mr. Allgood usually names his mills—he's got a slew of them—after one of the women or girls in the family. Let' see, there's the Edith Mill, the Emily Mill, and, well, you get the idea."

"So there's a woman named Galway?" Ezra asked.

Edmonds slapped the steering wheel with both hands and laughed.

"No, no I don't think so. Folks say—I don't really know—old man Allgood had a great grandpappy, or maybe a great grandpappy, who came over from someplace in Ireland called Galway. Who the hell knows? You can't ever tell about rich folks."

"I reckon not. Never knew any."

"Me neither, not personally. Anyway, the mill is about a mile or so down Galway Avenue over yonder. I'd drop you by there myself but I got an appointment you see. Way out in the country and I'm already late. Not too smart for a peddler to be late if he's trying to make a living."

"I reckon not. I don't mind walking," Ezra shook hands with him. "I sure appreciate the lift, Mr. Edmonds. You're some kind of driver. I never rode so fast."

"Think nothing of it. There's lots of folks hitchin' rides these days. I like to pick 'em up. Do it all the time. Gives me a body to talk to. Sometimes I practice my spiel on 'em. They seem to like it."

"Well. Thanks anyway." Ezra stepped out onto the sidewalk.

"Ain't you forgetting something, Mr. Burke? Your bag. In the back seat. Might be needing it."

"Yeah, I reckon I might at that."

He reached over the front seat of the coupe and retrieved his belongings. As he slammed the door shut, the automobile shot away from the curb and down the street, barely missing a pedestrian and an oncoming car. He was glad to be out of the car and on the sidewalk.

He walked down the block and crossed the busy street over to Galway Avenue. It felt good to be outside and able to move about again. The day was hot, but a slight pleasant breeze caressed his face as he walked. This part of the street was broad and lined with huge oak trees guarding large two-story white clapboard houses. The houses all had neatly trimmed lawns and were set back, well off the street.

Must be some mighty rich people living here, he thought as he walked on.

Occasionally he would see a black man working in a yard, planting flowers or trimming shrubbery. Negroes. He did not know of any living in the mountains around Waverley. Nor had he actually seen many in his life. Only at the sawmill and the few times he had come down to Corinth. The ones at the sawmill had been brought down from North Carolina by Tanner during the months he was cutting a lot of timber. They had all lived together in tar-covered shacks not far away from the sawmill. They pretty much kept to themselves.

After walking some distance, the large homes with the immaculate lawns gave way to a series of small brick stores and shops, and then more houses, row after row of them. But these were not like the big houses back up the street. These were small and had also been painted white at some point in time, but they did not gleam in the sunlight like the big ones he had passed. Most were dingy and low, their paint chipped and fading. But for the paint, they were not too different from his own house in the mountains. But never had he seen so many painted houses. He had never lived in one. In the narrow front yards there was no grass or shrubbery like the big houses, just bare earth–dirt. He could see patterns of thin, narrow parallel groves covering some of the yards where someone had methodically pulled a hand rake across them. And strangely, all of the houses seemed to be exactly alike, at least as far as he could tell from the street.

As he walked on, Galway Avenue ascended gently but steadily. There was a large two story red brick building up ahead on the left that appeared to be a school. A huge portico supported by four columns sheltered the two large oak doors of the front entrance. As he crested the hill where the school stood, the avenue sloped away, still lined by row after row of the small dreary repetitive houses. Then out beyond the houses, on a long rise surrounded by pecan and oak trees, he saw it. Galway Mill.

Shading his eyes with his hand, but still squinting in the bright sunlight, he could see it shimmering in the distance, a gigantic inanimate thing that rose above and dominated the village surrounding it. Like the school he had just walked past, it was of dull, red brick.

Four or five stories high and maybe a half-mile long, he figured.

He had never imagined it to be so massive and intimidating. The few times he had been to Corinth, in the distance he had seen the smoke stacks of the mills strung along the west side of the town, but he had never seen one this close up.

His confidence shaken momentarily, he considered the mill. It's just a building where a lot of people work making cloth out of cotton. Nothing more. Just folks, likely some same as me come down here to work. Nothing more. Shaking off the doubt, he gathered up his sack and trudged on up the gentle rise toward the mill.

From a few hundred yards away, as he approached the huge plant, there was a low rhythmic rumble emanating from the structure. Machinery running, he concluded. Smoke bellowed from the monstrous towering smoke stack, turning the blue sky high above him to a thick gray fog that seemed to hang in the air. The ground itself trembled, almost a palpitation, like the heartbeat of the mill itself. Rather than inanimate, the mill was an organic thing. It breathed and shook with life.

He finally crossed to the other side of the street, opposite the mill. Traffic was heavy, with cars and trucks surrounding and passing by the mill like bees swarming around a hive. There were people on the street hurrying someplace, only glancing at him briefly if at all.

A high chain-length fence encircled the mill, at least as far as he could see. His view of the far end of the building was obstructed by a grove of pecan trees. At the near corner, beside the fence, was a small low structure, a guardhouse maybe. Just beyond it was a large, steel gate which was the only entrance to the mill grounds that he could see. A short heavy-set man in a dark blue uniform stood just outside, leaning against the guardhouse door, smoking a cigarette.

On the corner where he stood was a trolley stop with a wrought iron bench. He sat down and lit his pipe. Upon until now he had been confident of his decision to leave the mountains and find work in Corinth. It was the thing to do. For a better life, or at least to provide better for his family. Some of the people he knew from the mountains had done the same thing over the last few years. Had come down to work in the mills. They had said they would return after getting back on their feet, after the Depression was over maybe. But it never seemed to quite work out that way. He could not recall knowing or hearing of anyone who ever returned once they left. It seemed almost as if once in the town and working, the mill just somehow consumed them and they did not exist anymore. They had become just another part of the mill. This would not happen to him.

He had been sure then, but now he hesitated. Now he was not so sure. It was not just the intimidating gargantuan red-brick structure before him or all the people, strangers, who seemed to be always hurrying someplace. For the first time, he considered how things would be changing. How different life would be, crammed into the mill village, people living in row upon row of identical houses like tombstones in a crowded cemetery. These were the houses he had strode past on his way here. He did not want to be one of those people. People with no connection to the land. People who, as he saw it, were in a way homeless. And what would the work itself be like? Machines linked to people only by necessity. Everything the same in a man-made world of endless and monotonous noise, motion, and people. No weather to be concerned about. No seasons to be considered. Just the machines. Nothing to be reaffirmed.

Just then an open-top Ford coupe whizzed by, filled with laughing young people. The driver honked the horn and one of the pretty girls waved and yelled out something to him. Above the noise of the traffic, he could not hear what she called out to him as the car sped out of sight. He gently tapped out his pipe on the steel bench frame and crossed the street.

***

A short street perpendicular to Galway Avenue ran in front of the mill. He would come to know it as First Street. Across First Street from the mill was a small, brick one-story building. Its red brick had long since been painted white, perhaps to distinguish it from the mammoth grossness of the plant across the way. It was set back from the street in an innocuous grove of mostly pecan and oak trees, and a few old elms.

He crossed Galway Avenue and approached the squat uniformed. The guard looked up at him when he was a few yards a way.

"Whoa, right there, buddy. Where you think your going?" the guard asked, flicking the cigarette away and adjusting his cap.

"I'm looking for work. Heard they're hiring here. That's all," Ezra relied, "thought you might could help me, tell me who to see about work."

"Looking for work, huh?"

"That's right. Are they hiring here?"

The guard rubbed his fleshy, unshaven chin, and then glanced over at the mill office across the street. He was going to have a little fun with this ole boy. Like he did with all the other mountain hicks who came by looking for work.

"Yeah, as a matter of fact they are. Good pay too. Just you go on over to the mill office there and tell 'em you ready to go to work. Tell 'em you want on the day shift. They'll fix you right up, my man."

"Well, I sure appreciate it. Just over there at that building, you say?"

"Yes, sir. Just go on over and walk right in. They'll be glad to see you. Always looking for good, strong, young men like yourself," the guard said, feigning sincerity.

"Much obliged," said Ezra, as he turned to cross the street.

He strode over to the low-roofed, narrow building. As he mounted the few steps up to the small concrete porch, he read the large block letters of tarnished brass on the door, *Mill Office*. He dropped the burlap sack on the porch beside the door and went in.

At a heavy oak desk, just a few feet inside the front office, sat a thin woman in a neatly pressed but slightly faded cotton dress. Her wire-rim glasses and pulled-back hair, streaked with gray, briefly reminded him of his grade-school teacher, Miss Milford. It was not a pleasant memory.

The woman, hunched over a black chunky Underwood, was focused intensely on her typing. The typewriter was on a side table and the she was facing the left wall of the room, away from him. He noticed a long dimly lit hallway behind her desk, to the right.

She did not look up as he came in. He stood there motionless for a long moment before removing his hat. He suddenly realized how worn and sweat-stained it was, so he held it low to his side against his left leg. Maybe she wouldn't notice it. She continued to type, banging mercilessly on the keys.

"Beg your pardon, ma'am."

She did not look up. He shuffled his feet slightly, and self-consciously cleared his throat.

"I'm not deaf. I heard you come in. I'll be right with you," she said curtly, without looking up from her typing.

"All right."

The woman typed a few more lines. She then gently pulled the sheet of paper from the machine and perused the words she had typed.

She placed the document in a wire tray beside the Underwood and turned toward him.

"Yes, what is it I can do for you?" she asked in a clipped, impersonal tone.

"Name's Burke."

"And what is it I can do for you Mr. Burke? As you can see, I'm very busy."

"I'm here to see about work."

"You mean you're looking for a job. Is that it?"

"Yes, I reckon it is. The man, the policeman, over at the gate across the street said all hiring was done at the mill office."

"He's not a policeman. He's the gate guard. He works for the company."

"He said I needed to see Mr. Jordan if I had any chance of working at, uh, getting a job here."

The woman chuckled haughtily and shook her head.

"You don't know much about cotton mills, do you Mr. Burke?"

"No, I reckon I don't," he said hesitantly. "But I'm a good worker."

"Yes, I'm sure you are, at least in some capacity. You see, Mr. Burke, Mr. Rufus Jordan is the mill Superintendent, which means he is over everything around here. He's the big man and works directly for Mr. Cates B. Allgood. Do you know who Mr. Cates B. Allgood is, Mr. Burke, do you?"

"I recollect hearing his name. I think he might be the owner of this here mill."

"Right you are, Mr. Burke. *This here mill*, as you call it, and five others like it, and a lot more than that. Mr. Jordan is his right-hand man and he sure doesn't do the hiring himself, not directly. There's no way in the world someone like you, off the streets, and I would guess fresh out of the mountains, is going to get to talk to him about a job or anything else for that matter. The guard was pulling your leg. He's a real character." Her tone was condescending and unfriendly.

"I see," he said, chastised and embarrassed. "Then who does *do* the hiring?"

"It doesn't matter. We aren't taking on any new help right now. I'll be glad to give you an application. You fill it out and I'll put it in a file. I assume you can read and write."

"Yes, ma'am, I reckon I can."

"Good. If something comes up, we'll let you know." The women slid a blank form across the desk to Ezra. He looked down at it.

"That's mighty nice of you, but that won't do. You see, I need to go to work now. I heard that the Galway Mill was hiring hands, even read it in a newspaper here lately. I've come down here all the way from Waverley."

"I guess you can't believe everything you read in the paper, now can you, Mr. Burke?"

She turned away from him and placed a carbon between two fresh sheets of translucent onion skin paper and proficiently fed the paper into the carriage of the typewriter. Realizing that he was still standing at her desk, she asked, without looking up at him.

"Is there anything else I can do for you, Mr. Burke?"

"I don't know, ah, it's just, say, if the mill was hiring hands who would I see about a job? That's all."

Seemingly exasperated, the woman sighed deeply and turned back to him.

"Look, Mr. Burke, you are wasting your time and mine. I've done all I can do for you. You can fill out the application and leave it with me or not. It's up to you. Now if you'll excuse me, I have work to do." She began typing.

"Do you have a pencil I can use?"

"Here," she snarled, handing him a sharply pointed pencil. "You can use the window sill over there."

He took the pencil and began filling out the form in a neat legible hand. He finished the form and placed it back on her desk. Again hunched over the Underwood, she did not seem to notice.

"I'm leaving it right here on your desk, ma'am. I thank you for your help."

"Sure," as she continued typing.

He left the mill office and headed back toward the street corner.

He had not known what to expect but he was not prepared for what the woman had told him. He had been certain of obtaining work right away. Maybe things down here were not as easy as he had thought they would be. Didn't have to be easy, exactly, but a man willing to work, and work hard, ought to be able to. At least it seemed that way. It seemed right.

The gate guard had spied him walking across the office yard and called to him.

"Hey, how'd it go? Did you talk to Mr. Jordan?"

Ezra hesitated. He was already feeling the fool and he did not want to talk to the guard or entertain him further by being the mountain hick come-to-town that he was.

"No," he said and walked on.

"Ah, come on. Don't be sore. I was just having a little fun, that's all. Job gets boring as hell sometimes. I do it with all the hillbillies. Don't mean nothing by it."

Ezra ignored him, but the guard persisted as he approached.

"Look, I knew you'd get the business from old Miss Wilcox. She's a bitch, ain't she? Bet she got real haughty and told you Mr. Jordan was a god, top dog around here. Right?"

"Something like that."

"Well, fact is, he is. Bet she told you the mill ain't hiring too."

"She did. But I filled out a piece of paper. Some kind of application, I reckon."

"A waste of time. She's likely already throwed it in the waste basket. Good old file thirteen. Anyway, she's lyin'. They're always hiring people for something or the other around here."

"Why would she tell me they're not?"

"Like I said, she's a bitch. Been here since Christ was a corporal. Thinks it's her job to keep people away from the boss men over there at the mill office, I reckon."

"Look, mister, I got to go." He turned away and continued toward the street corner.

"No hard feelings?"

"No, I reckon not," Ezra said, almost to himself.

"Wait a minute," the guard followed him to the curb. "Look, you seem like a good egg. Won't last long as a lint-head I 'spect, but I'll let you in on something."

"What is it?" Ezra was uninterested and anxious to be on his way. There were other cotton mills in Corinth. He did not have time to waste on a practical-joking guard.

"Ole Charlie Matheson is the man you need to see. Nickname's 'Bulldog' but he don't like it, so you can't call him that to his face. Anyway, he works for Rufus Jordan, the Super. He usually does the hiring, Bulldog Matheson, I mean."

Ezra was suspicious of this information, suspecting the gate guard was looking for another laugh at the expense of the rube.

"I appreciate it, mister, but I got to go."

"Wait a minute. Now just listen a minute, will you? I ain't ribbing you this time. Bulldog—Mr. Matheson—is over at the mill office sometimes but he's up in the mill right now. Problem in the weave room or something. Anyway, when first shift is over at four o'clock he'll likely be coming through that there gate," he said, with his thumb pointing back toward the mill gate that he was supposed to be guarding. "If you'd like me to, I'll spot him for you and you can talk to him. He ain't a bad egg, either. You got nothing to lose. Right? Hell, anyway, it's already after three."

***

Charlie "Bulldog" Matheson walked slowly but deliberately down the center aisle of the gargantuan weave room. On either side of him were banks and rows of motor-driven looms. The noise was deafening as the shuttles of the looms were sent flying back and forth between the web of threads of yarn being fed into the backside of the machines. The air was hot and thick with floating, brown-gray lint.

As he walked, he surveyed the entire weave room and seemed to be able to inspect each of the hundreds of moving looms simultaneously. His appearance and demeanor solidly confirmed his nickname. Physically, he was muscular but not a tall man. He looked almost square rather than squat. His large head, square like his torso, was topped with thick unruly brown hair. A renegade lock centered his forehead regardless of his constantly brushing it back with his meaty fingers. No neck could be ascertained, as the head seemed to be attached directly to his shoulders. The sleeves of his dingy white shirt were rolled up past the elbows, exposing thick muscular triceps. He chewed mechanically on the black stump of an unlit cigar.

He stopped at one of the looms where a man in greasy overalls squatted on the floor beside it. He stood silently for a moment watching the squatting man who did not look up from his work on the machine.

"What's the problem, Henry?" Matheson asked gruffly.

"Damn drive belt broke, Charlie, and I'm having a helluva time getting this here new one on the pulley. Just won't slip over the shaft wheel like it's supposed to."

"You been down there working on that loom since I came up here. If you can't fix it, I'll get another loom fixer on it. I can't have a loom sitting here idle."

"I think I can get it," said the loom fixer, as he pulled on the thick drive belt trying to stretch it just enough to slip over the lip and into the groove of the wheel. Sweat streamed down his face and dripped from the tip of his nose on to the floor. He gave the belt a yank but it did not budge. It slipped from his hand as his knuckles scraped against the black steel frame of the loom.

"Damn!" he said, shaking the pain from his hand. Matheson nudged him slightly on the shoulder.

"Get out of the way, Henry. Let me take a look." The man stood up and moved away from the loom. Matheson bent over the machine without squatting down beside it. He gripped the troublesome drive belt and with one swift motion pulled it onto the wheel.

"Need to eat your grits, Henry. It ain't that hard," Matheson said, as he pulled a handkerchief from the back pocket of his twill trousers and wiped the grease off his hands.

"Thanks, Charlie," said the loom fixer, shaking his head, staring down at the machine. "Don't usually have this kind of problem. Sometimes them new belts can be stiff as the dickens."

"Get back to work, Henry. Shift ain't over just yet."

Matheson continued his inspection walk through the weave room, occasionally nodding or speaking briefly, by shouting, into the ear of the weavers, all of which were men.

Some of those who worked the second shift were beginning to drift in. They congregated in and around the large bathroom area known as the waterhouse, smoking, chewing, and drinking Coca Colas in small, green, hourglass-shaped bottles. This popular dark amber drink was commonly referred to as "a dope" by the workers, in the belief that it contained a trace of cocaine; in an earlier time it may have.

Matheson walked past and approached the freight elevator at the far end of the weave room. Company rules did not permit mill personnel to use the elevator except to transport yarn or finished beams of cloth to another floor. All workers, including managers and supervisors, were required to use the stairs, even up on the fourth floor weave room.

Nevertheless, he pulled the small steel lever beside the elevator door and waited while a loud buzzer sounded, signaling the elevator was on its way up. It stopped abruptly with a dull thud, and he reached down and pulled the thick web strap that opened the steel, horizontal doors. Stepping inside, he pulled the doors shut and descended to the ground floor of the mill. Bulldog Matheson made his own rules. Sometimes.

***

Ezra had walked along the chain-link fence that surrounded the mill and stood thirty or forty feet down from the gate and the guardhouse. The guard had tucked in his shirt, donned and hastily adjusted a cap vaguely matching his uniform, in a futile attempt to appear somewhat official and on the job. It was shift change.

Although he was suspicious of the guard's motives, he was willing to risk being made a fool of again in the hopes that Mr. Matheson would speak with him and give him work. But he felt outside of himself somehow. Everything around him was alien. The giant red brick mill with its towering belching smoke stack, steel fences, people who could not be trusted. Except for the small patch of grass in front of the mill office across the street, the earth here seemed to be   covered in asphalt, or concrete or gravel. Everything was artificial. He was out of place here and he knew it. Maybe coming here *had* been a mistake all along. Maybe he had given up and come down here too quickly. A man got lost here. There was no connection to anything. No pull of the mountains or of the land. Nothing grew, it was just *made*. Even the air breathed differently. It was heavy with smells unfamiliar. It offered no hope. He felt lost.

As he waited for the shift change, and hopefully the guard's signal, he realized with a deep sadness that life could never be the same for him here. He had sworn to her that once they were back on their feet and had saved some money, they would return to the mountains. The farming would be better. He'd buy land. Good bottom land. It had sounded hopeful and good, but somewhere deep down now he knew that it would not happen that way. It never did. Folks like him had been coming down to the mills for years, always promising to return. But they never did. They just got sucked into the system and became like he was becoming, invisible.

Things would be different he knew, and it frightened him. He had lived a kind of a freedom that had been guided by the gentle rhythm of the land, the seasons, and family. Working hard, to be sure, but feeling a connection, a kind of belongingness, with the world around him. A world he knew. Knowing when things were bad but also when things were good; they were not *that* different sometimes. What lay on him most heavily, he thought, was the loss.

He shook his head in quick jerks, as if he was trying to dismiss the residue of a bad dream. His head cleared, he sighed deeply. All that he had been thinking was true enough, but he had to remember why he had come. He needed work. He needed to be able to feed and clothe his family. He had made the decision and there was no turning back, he knew. He was here and he could not think of going back to the mountains. At least, if he thought it, or dreamed it, it would be a dream he would not share or talk about, not even to her.

CHAPTER 11

At precisely four o'clock, the dull insipid noise surrounding him was drowned out by a high-pitched piercing sound. It was like a terrible loud scream, not human nor animal. Wild but measured, in a mechanical way. The very air seemed to deflect it back on him and vibrate the earth beneath his feet. It was the mill whistle. In time it would come to rule over him like a tyrant. It would dictate his waking in the morning, his leaving for work, when he took his meals, and when he went to sleep. It would always be there, reminding him that he did not really exist for anything but the mill, that he was and would remain, dispensable and invisible.

Inside the fence, across the concrete expanse from the guardhouse, was the large steel door to the mill itself. When the whistle blew, hundreds of workers—the first shift—streamed out through this door, squinting in the sudden sunlight of the afternoon. Most were men, but there with some women. The men wore overalls and brogans, or leather shoes. The women, except for a few who wore denim trousers, were in print dresses, mostly with muted and faded colors. Most all were covered in varying degrees, with cotton lint—it clung to their clothes and on the bare skin of their arms, neck, and face. It clung even more tenaciously to their hair. They were, indeed, lint-heads, as they were derisively referred to by townspeople. To the mill folks, at least to some of them, it was a term they embraced among themselves as a point of pride.

Some were chatting among themselves and many lit cigarettes or carved off chunks of tobacco from plugs pulled from their pockets. But most said nothing as they passed through the gate and dispersed in all directions toward their homes in the surrounding village. None seem to step lightly and many bore a somewhat haggard look.

One thing Ezra noticed immediately and was puzzled by it. Several of the workers in the crowd were very young, twelve or thirteen, some maybe even younger, he couldn't tell. The incongruity of these children in the mass of exiting adult workers was unexpected and struck him as inexplicable and in some way very sad, as he thought of his own children back on the mountain.

The guard, standing next to the gate as the workers filed past, looked over at him and shrugged. As the last of them passed through he motioned for him and he reluctantly walked back to the gate.

"He didn't come out with the shift. I guess he's still in the mill," the guard said, pointing to the steel door.

"Maybe you just missed him."

"Naw, naw. You see, he woulda gone across the street to the mill office. Always does. I couldn't miss him. You were standing over by the fence across from the mill office. Did you see anybody walk over?"

"No, but I really wasn't looking."

"I tell you he ain't come out yet. Just wait here. We'll grab him." The guard seemed sincerely trying to help.

"I don't know. I think we're probably just wasting our time, yours and mine. I better go." He turned to leave.

"Time ain't no problem for me. I don't get off until six and can't retire for another 20 years, if then. By the way, who might you be?"

"Name's Burke."

"What's your last name?"

"Burke."

"Okay. *What* Burke?"

"Ezra. Ezra Burke."

"You any kin to them Burkes from over near Jackson Crossing?"

"No."

"No, I guess you wouldn't be, coming from the mountains and all. Them Burkes been around here awhile. Anyway, they just white trash. Not much better off than niggers, but that ain't saying much."

He looked away from the guard's gaze, and again turned to leave.

"Look here, Burke, my name's Newton. Clarence is my first but everybody calls me Fig. You know, Fig Newton," the guard said, and guffawed at what he considered the humor of his nickname. He extended his hand to Ezra.

"I don't get the joke, but good to meet you Mr. Newton."

"No. Fig. Folks around here wouldn't know who you was talking about if you said Mr. Newton."

"All right. Fig."

Fig, still shaking Ezra's hand, laughed again at the sound of his name.

"That's it! Fig!"

The door to the mill swung open and Matheson stepped into the afternoon brightness and approached the gate. He seemed preoccupied and did not appear to be aware of the guard or of Ezra.

"That's him coming this way. I told you he'd be coming out, didn't I?" Ezra did not respond. "Just hold on a minute," said Newton, stepping away from him toward the approaching man.

"Afternoon, Mr. Matheson. Hot enough for you?"

"Hotter in the mill," Matheson mumbled grumpily. He did not pause, but walked past the jocular guard, basically ignoring him.

Ezra had remained standing just outside the gate watching and hearing the exchange. Matheson walked by him without acknowledging his presence. He hesitated as this square chunk of a man walked across the street toward the mill office. After his earlier fruitless encounter with Miss Wilcox, he suddenly realized that this might well be his only chance to get work at Galway Mill. The man he was watching walk away was the one who could hire him. He called out.

"Mr. Matheson!"

Matheson looked back over his shoulder at the voice and stopped just at the low steps of the mill office. Ezra approached him with long, swift strides.

"Mr. Matheson, can you spare me a minute? I'd be much obliged."

Matheson folded his thick arms impatiently. "What do you want?"

Ezra instinctively stopped several feet from where the much shorter man stood. Any closer and he would have towered over him. But it was a useless gesture. There was no doubt whose turf this was.

"Name's Burke." He stepped closer and extended his hand, which Matheson ignored. He quickly withdrew it, dropping it to his side. "I'm looking for work. Mr. Newton said you did the hiring here."

"Mr. Newton?" Matheson asked, genuinely puzzled.

"Yes, sir, the guard over at the gate. Said you were hiring people."

Matheson chuckled softly, "You mean ole Fig?"

"Yes, sir."

"Well, Fig talks too much. He ain't got much to do around here other than sit on his fat ass all day gossiping to anybody who'll listen to him. He's sure not much of a security guard, more of a security risk in my book. Don't matter anyhow, we ain't hiring."

"Look, Mr. Matheson, I'm a real good worker. I'm willing to do about any job you might have. I come all the way down from Waverley to find work," he pressed, desperate and undeterred.

"Where the hell is Waverley?"

"Up near the state line. Not much of a town, more a wide place in the road. Up in the mountains."

"I reckon I'm aware where the mountains are in this county. 'Course ain't no hiding the fact you come down from the mountains. Ought to know a hillbilly when I see one, by now. Hired enough of them."

"Mr. Matheson, I really need to work. Want to work. This is a mighty big operation you got here. There must be something I can do useful. I'll make you a good hand."

Matheson sighed, maybe a little impressed with the man's persistence and seriousness.

"I suppose you never worked in a cotton mill before."

"No, sir. I'm a farmer. Was a farmer. I've worked in a sawmill some too."

"Up around, huh…"

"Waverley."

"Up around Waverley, huh?"

"I know it's not cotton mill work, but work is work."

"Look, Burke, I like your grit. You look like a nice young fellow and I'm sure you're a hard worker, but I just ain't got anything for you right now."

Ezra looked away. Across the mill office yard, the cars on Galway Avenue whizzed by in an almost continuous stream. Matheson shook his head slightly.

"I'll tell you what, Burke. You go on in there to the mill office and fill out a job form. Mrs. Wilcox there will take care of it."

"I already did that. A couple of hours ago."

"Well, I will say one thing for you. You're sure a go-getter. I tell you what. Check back with me in a few weeks, in the fall. Maybe something will come up. We just don't have anything right now. That's just the way it is, Burke. It's the times."

"I don't have a few weeks. I got a wife and young 'uns. I got to find work now."

"Sorry, I can't help you. Look here, there's at least a dozen mills and plants in and around this town. Maybe more. Just look for the smoke stacks."

Matheson gestured down the hill toward Galway Avenue, in the direction Ezra had come when Edmonds had dropped him off earlier that morning. He could see four, red-brick smokestacks in the distance, although none towered over the landscape like the one here at Galway Mill.

"Reckon that's what I'll do, though I sure wanted to work at the Galway Mill. Best one from what I heard."

Matheson looked down at the ground and remained silent.

"Well, anyway, Mr. Matheson, I surely appreciate your time and for talking to me," he said, and again extended his large right hand. This time Matheson met it with his own.

"Good luck, son."

Matheson turned and climbed the steps to the mill office, but hesitated on the porch. Ezra, with his hands jammed deep in the pockets of his overalls, had headed off toward Galway Avenue when he suddenly heard the gruff voice call to him.

"Wait a minute, Burke. I just thought of something. Get back over here."

Ezra trudged back up to the mill office. Matheson stood on the porch looking down at him.

"I plum forgot something," Matheson said, matter of factly, with no hint of enthusiasm, but with an expression that indicated he might be slightly pleased with himself.

"There might just be something after all, come to think of it. Arthur Ferguson's boy, Perk, been working here at the mill just a few months but he's up and joined the Marines. The Marines, of all things. Anyway, he's a sweeper on the third shift, which is low man on the totem pole around here for sure. But I got to replace him. I might can work something out for you, Burke, if you be interested."

"I would, Mr. Matheson, I purely and surely would," he answered, his voice rising with guarded enthusiasm and hope.

"Only problem is he don't report for duty for another three weeks yet. From what you been saying you can't wait that long. Is that right?"

Ezra's shoulders slumped in spite of his instinctive determination not to show his disappointment.

"No, sir. Don't reckon I can. I'm near broke. I hate to say it but it's the truth."

"There is one thing we might can do to bide the time until 'ole Perk leaves. That is, if your pride don't get in the way."

"I about lost what pride I had," he said softly, almost to himself, but which he knew deep down was not quite true. Not yet anyway. "Like

I said before, I'll do just about anything as far as work goes. Long as it's not against the law, naturally speaking."

"Mind working with colored folks?"

"Never have. Don't know any, but I reckon I could. I surely could for wages."

"It's like this, Burke. Coloreds can't work in the mill. Not just this mill, not any mill around here. But we hire them on to fill the coal bins for the boilers mostly. By filling, I mean shoveling coal and it's hard, dirty work."

"The work don't bother me."

"No, I guess it wouldn't. Anyhow, you don't have to associate with them, just work alongside of them."

"All right."

"Another thing, and you need to hear the rest of it, though I 'spect it won't matter to you none. The work don't pay much, dollar and half a day. For a white man, that is. Shift is from seven in the morning to around six at night. You'd work week days and half a day on Saturday. It's the best I can do for you, Burke. Take it or leave it."

"Reckon I'll take it and I'm much obliged to you, Mr. Matheson."

"Can you start work in the morning?"

"Yes, sir"

"Okay, good. Come here to the mill office in the morning. I'll take you round back to the coal yard and get you started. The lead man is Yates. He's colored and he's mean. He ain't going like it much to have a white man on the crew. But he can't do anything about it so just do the work and do what he says, and things will be okay. He'll know you won't be around long. We don't normally work white people in the coal yard."

"All right."

"You do that and it'll work out just fine. By the way, Burke, where you staying? You got people in Corinth?"

"No, sire. No people here. To tell you the truth, I hadn't thought much about it. Just been thinking about getting here and finding work. I got a bedroll in that tow sack over there under the bench across the street."

"Well, to start with, I wouldn't be going and leaving my things unattended. You ain't up in those hills of yours. Some of the people down here around town ain't quite as trustworthy as you might be used to. They'll steal your stuff for sure. You'll be lucky if it's still there."

Ezra glanced across the busy street and could see his bag still stashed securely under the bench near the bus stop.

"I reckon I need to be more watchful."

"You'll get used to it. I mean the way things are down here. Look here, see the high school over yonder, that big brick building on the hill?"

He remembered walking past the school earlier in the morning. He remembered the large doors and the porch with white columns.

"Yes, sir, I see it. I came passed it this morning. The brick looks a lot like the mill brick."

"It ought to because it's the same brick. The company built the high school, at least they paid to get it built. Used the same brick they used to build the mill. The Allgood's take care of their folks."

"Their folks?" he asked, not quite understanding Matheson's reference to the mill owners.

"That's right, the people who work at the mill. They're all Allgood employees. Got a good new schoolhouse. Good houses on the mill hill. The Company Store. Like I said, they take care of us, their people."

"I see," he said, although he did *not* see. Matheson continued.

"Anyway, what I was telling you was that over by the school on Seventh Street is Mrs. Aintry's boarding house. She'll put you up for fifty-cents a night or three dollars a week. Breakfast and supper are included but not dinner. She expects everybody to be out working at dinnertime, not loafing around her place. It ain't nothing fancy, but it's pretty clean. She changes the sheets every week, or so I heard. Food's good though. I can vouch for that myself. How's that sound to you? Be a roof over your head until you can get settled in a mill house."

"All right," he answered.

"You got any money?"

"A little. A couple of dollars."

"Well, that ain't much to be traveling around the country on. Tell you what, just let Mrs. Aintry know that I sent you over there and tell her you're working at the mill. She'll likely let you ride 'til pay day."

"All right, thanks, Mr. Matheson," he said, shaking Matheson's hand again.

"One other thing, Burke," Matheson said, an ever so slight glint in his eyes, "don't ever call me Bulldog."

"No, sir, I won't."

Ezra, with a slight smile, turned away to cross the busy avenue and retrieved his bag under the bench at the trolley stop.

CHAPTER 12

The new high school of which Matheson seemed so proud stood on the corner of Galway Avenue and Seventh Street. Walking to the mill that morning Ezra had noticed that, oddly, all the streets intersecting Galway Avenue did not have names, but rather numbers. I reckon, he had thought, it's easier to keep up with things that way and not get lost.

Turning onto Seventh Street at the high school, Mrs. Aintry's boarding house sat halfway down the block. There was an overgrown vacant lot behind the house, beyond which was the high school's new football field, with wooden bleachers on one side of it. The mill could be seen in the distance.

The appearance of the house was unlike that of the surrounding mill houses which, with their four rooms and narrow stoops in front, all had the dreary sameness without significant exception. The boarding house was somewhat shabby in appearance too, needing paint, but it was much larger than the mill houses. It had almost a certain rambling grandiosity by comparison. Across the entire front of the house ran a porch with a low, shallow pitched roof. The steps leading up to the porch were wide and there was a huge front door painted red with a tarnished brass knocker. Several weathered cane-back rockers, facing the street, were lined in a straight row across the expanse of the porch. Except for the front door, everything had been painted white, but not recently.

He hesitated momentarily then climbed the steps onto the vacant porch. Ignoring the brass knocker, he tapped on the windowless door with his knuckles. There was no response from inside. He tapped again, this time more forcefully. Still no one came. After knocking a third time without response, he hesitantly twisted the large black knob. It turned freely and the door seemed almost to open itself. He stepped inside.

Standing just inside the doorway, he peered down a long dark hallway. There were several doors on either side as far as he could see into the shadowy interior. A large room, a parlor, opened up to his right. The red and brown velvet that covered most of the furniture was worn and faded. None of the lamps in the room were lit but slanted rays of the late afternoon sun streamed through the side window at the far end and reflected dully off the hardwood floor. Particles of weightless dust flashed and floated like fireflies in the golden light. No one was in the room.

"Hello. Is anybody here? Hello," he called out, but his voice seemed muffled and insignificant, absorbed by the house's silence. No one answered, as he looked around. Then he had heard something.

Across the hallway to his left, opposite the parlor, was another large room. Set in the middle of the room was a long table, a dozen straight-back chairs around its parameter. Porcelain plates, all chipped in several places, and unpolished silverware had been placed on the table at each plate. Unlike the parlor, there were no curtains covering the windows. The sunlight poured in, giving it a bright, pleasant appearance. He stepped across the hall into the room.

The noise that he had heard, and which continued, came from behind a large, closed door at the back and far end of the room. There was the aroma of food cooking and he realized that he was very hungry. He walked over to the door and it suddenly swung open, barely missing his face. Startled, he jerked his head and shoulders back just in time. The woman coming through the door shrieked.

"Whoa, son. You 'bout scared me to death!" she said as she crossed her hands across her chest. "I didn't hear you come in."

"I'm real sorry, ma'am. I knocked on the front door, more than once. The door was open so I just stepped in. I called out, too. I'm real sorry I scared you."

"Well, no harm done. Back there in the kitchen you can't hear much of anything going on out here. Just getting supper ready," she said, still standing in the doorway.

"Sure smells good," he said, looking past her into the steamy kitchen.

"What can I do for you, young fellow?"

"Would you be Mrs. Aintry?"

"I am. One in the same."

"My name's Burke. I'm looking for a place to stay. I reckon for a few days. Not really sure yet."

"Burke your Christian name or your given name?"

"My last name is Burke. First is Ezra."

"Well, I sure am sorry, Mr. Burke, but I'm plumb full up. I don't believe I can help you. Wish I could."

He looked down at the floor and then glanced again into the kitchen. He hoped she had not heard the low growl in his stomach.

"It's just that Mr. Matteson up at the mill said you might have a room. That's all. Sorry again about scaring you," he said, as he turned to leave.

"Bulldog Matteson sent you, eh?"

"Yes, ma'am."

"You know Bulldog?" she asked with interest as she stepped into the dining room, leaving open the door to the kitchen.

"Can't say that I rightly know him. You see, I just met him today. He hired me."

"Hired you, did he, that old buzzard," she chuckled and shook her head. "Ever work in a cotton mill, Mr. Burke?"

"No, ma'am."

"Then I guess you'll be starting out sweeping. That right?"

"No, ma'am. Not starting out. I reckon I'm going to be shoveling coal for a spell."

"Shoveling coal? Good lord, that ain't mill work. Not for a white man, anyway. How'd you let Bulldog talk you in to that?"

"I need the work, and it's just for a few weeks. Until the sweeper on the third shift leaves for the service. Then I reckon I move up to sweeper."

At this, Mrs. Aintry laughed out loud and continued to shake hear head.

"Well, now if I ain't heard all! Move *up* to sweeper. How does a body move up to the bottom, Mr. Burke? Why, I never!"

"Well, I reckon in a cotton mill going from shoveling coal to sweeping floors is moving up," he offered, laughing with her.

"Third shift sweeper joining the service? Hmm, guess that'd be Perk Ferguson. Sorriest white boy on the mill hill. Bulldog's likely glad to be rid of him. Only got the job on account of his daddy anyhow. Did Bulldog tell you who shovels coal at the mill?" she asked.

"Yes, ma'am. I'll be working alongside some colored folks I reckon."

"I reckon you will at that."

"Don't bother me, though. I just need the work."

"You look big and strong enough for the work, Mr. Burke. I just hope you big and strong enough to deal with Josh Yates. Even his own kind's scared of him. I know one thing, at least I heard it often enough. He don't like white folks. And Mr. Burke, you sure are white."

"I'm not looking for trouble. Just need the work," he replied.

"Well, trouble might be looking for you if you go messing around with those colored boys' jobs. And I wouldn't count too much on Bulldog Matteson neither," she warned.

"I'm just going do what they pay me to do. That's all. Look, Mrs. Aintry, I got to go. Do you know anywhere else around here that might put me up?"

With short stubby fingers the woman massaged her chin as she looked away from him. She seemed to be deep in thought as if she was not listening. He turned away from her and walked toward the front door. He had not eaten since early morning and he suddenly realized how tired he was. Newton was right, he thought. I'm just a dumb hillbilly. I just didn't figure on it being this hard, this different. He was alone, and he felt it.

"It doesn't matter, ma'am. Not your problem anyhow. I apologize for bothering you," he said, looking back at her as he pulled open the heavy front door. When he spoke she looked up at him as if she were coming out of a trance.

"Say you only need a room for a few days?" she asked.

"Like I said, I'm not sure exactly how long. I expect to be able to get a mill house as soon as the sweeping job comes open. Maybe before. Anyway, that's what Mr. Matteson told me."

"I got me an idea, Mr. Burke, I might can help you out some. But first tell me why you, being a single fellow, need a mill house. Why you need all that room?"

"Mrs. Aintry, I'm not a bachelor. I have a wife and two young 'uns. So you see, I have to get a house. I just need a place to stay until I get the house and bring my family down here."

"From the mountains, I guess, like a bunch of these other lint-heads. No offense. You ain't a lint-head yet but you soon will be. Probably your wife, too. Maybe your kids. Anyway, I worked in a cotton mill twenty years so I know what a lint-head is and what it means to be one."

"You said you might could help me some," he said, his voice slightly tinged with hope.

"Look here. I got this mudroom on the back porch just off the kitchen. Keep yard tools and paint cans and such stored in it. Things I never use and don't plan on starting anytime soon. Anyway, I'd be willing to let you clean it out and sleep there. I could make you a quilt pallet on the floor. You'd have to come inside for the toilet and to wash up, but all my renters on the first floor share the bathroom anyway. The mudroom don't have a window, and you might be cramped and the roof leaks when it rains, but it's the best I can do for you right now."

"All right," he said, relief evident in his gray eyes.

"I won't charge you nothing for sleeping here, just for meals. I fix a hot breakfast and supper for my renters. How about a two-bits a day for your board?" she smiled broadly.

"All right. I reckon I can afford a quarter a day. I sure appreciate it, Mrs. Aintry. It's generous and I purely and surely appreciate it." Although he still felt himself to be stranger in a strange world, his mood brightened noticeably.

"Good, then, we got us a deal," she smiled and held out her right hand palm up. He looked at the fleshy, pink hand with the stubby fingers quizzically. "A quarter, Mr. Burke," she said good-naturedly, looking up at the tall young man from the mountains. "You said you had a quarter, didn't you?"

"Oh, yes, ma'am, I reckon I did." With embarrassment, he withdrew several silver coins from his pocket and placed a twenty-five cent piece in her still-outstretched hand.

"Atta, boy. By the way, Mr. Burke, when was the last time you had a hot meal?"

"It's been a spell, I reckon," he said.

"That's what I figured. Supper's cooked and on the stove but we don't eat until six o'clock. After my renters all get in from work or from whatever it is they do days. But you sit down here at the table and I'll fix you a plate now. After you eat we'll take a look at the mudroom. Maybe you can start cleaning it up while the others eat supper. After I'm done with the dishes, I'll find them quilts for a pallet."

"All right," he said, and faintly smiled down at her.

***

He switched on the bare bulb that dangled from the ceiling by a worn, braided wire, and lay down on the pallet. Mrs. Aintry had folded quilts length-wise and placed them carefully on the floor of the mudroom. After a generous supper of meat loaf, potatoes, green beans, and cornbread, it had taken him the better part of an hour to clean and sweep out the small room.

Along with the thick quilts, she had placed a small straight back chair in the corner. Three wooden crates were stacked next to the door. They would do for a table. His clothes hung loosely on nails along the inside wall. He placed the pocket watch his grandfather had left him as a boy on the floor beside him. His pillow was the rolled up burlap bag in which he had brought his things from home.

Lying in the darkness, he could hear the soft, measured ticking of the watch. It was reassuring and it soothed him. He just then realized how utterly exhausted he was. The day almost seemed like a dream. He thought how he had left her that morning, about the people he had encountered during the long day, and the mill. And how he had somehow ended up here in a small, dark room, in a strange place, helped by strangers.

He liked Mrs. Aintry, even if she was a little rough around the edges. She's down to earth, he thought. Straight forward, like folks in the mountains. My folks. A little more cynical maybe, but she must be a good person to help him the way she had and not take advantage. He was thankful to have a roof over his head and food in his belly. As his thoughts turned back to Judith, Grace, and little Andrew, he drifted off into a deep, dreamless sleep.

***

The inside wall of the tiny room separated it from the kitchen. This accounted for his being awakened by the dull rattling of pots and metal utensils, and by the strong aroma of frying bacon. He sat up briefly and pushed a quilt away from his body. He stood and reached to switch on the light hanging just above his head. He looked at the watch. It was almost five-thirty. He hurriedly dressed and pulled his brogans on and tied them snuggly around his ankles.

Stepping out on the back porch in the coming dawn, he could see the mill in shadows off in the distance, beyond the rows of mill houses. It looked hard and forbidding in the thin, gray light. Not like anything he had known before. Nothing like the mountains. They were natural and eternal. The mill was not. Thin, wispy clouds on the horizon far beyond the mill were taking on a pinkish tint, an incongruous backdrop against the lurid reach of the mill's towering smokestack.

Suddenly a loud, prolonged, screaming whistle penetrated the quiet of the early morning. The high-pitched sound seemed to come from the direction of the mill. He had heard that sound before. Then he remembered being at the mill yesterday when the shift changed and the workers spilled out of the huge red brick plant. It was precisely five-thirty when the mill whistle blasted and he thought he could feel the ground itself vibrate beneath his feet. It was the mill's own voice. He turned away and stepped through the back door into the kitchen.

"Up and at 'em I see, Mr. Burke," said Mrs. Aintry, not looking up from the stove where she was turning the bacon over in a large, black skillet with a fork.

"Yes, ma'am."

"It's a mite early. What time you got to be at the mill?" she asked, tending to her cooking.

"Seven's what Mr. Matheson told me."

"I don't generally put breakfast on the table until about that time. Some of my boarders ain't even up by then. I clear the table at seven-thirty, so if they miss it it's their own damn fault. But, hey, they know the rules."

"I think I might have an apple left. That'll do me fine," he said, still standing just inside the doorway. He had closed the door behind him.

"No, you sit down here at the kitchen table. Won't take but a minute to fry up some eggs to go with this here bacon. You didn't know my rules and I can't hardly send you off to work with no food in you, now can I?"

"I certainly do appreciate it." He pulled back a chair from the small table and sat watching Mrs. Aintry. At the stove, she hummed softly while she tinkered with the thick strips of bacon sizzling in the skillet. "Can I ask you something, Mrs. Aintry?"

"What?" She did not look up from the stove.

"About the mill whistle. I was just wondering why it blew at five-thirty?"

"Oh, that's just the mill telling folks what to do. The mill figures it's time we all be up and about. You can hear it all over the mill hill. In town, too, I expect. Wants us to know they looking out for us."

"Who wants us to know?" he asked, genuinely puzzled.

"The owners. They're like your daddy, see. They want you to know who's in charge."

"In charge of what?"

"I can see you told me the truth about not working in a mill before or living on a mill hill," she said. She stopped cooking and looked hard at him. Grease dripped from the fork onto the floor.

"It's the truth."

"Well, from the looks of you, and with your ways, I'd say you are a farmer. That right?"

"I reckon it is. At least I *was* a farmer."

"My daddy said that once a fellow was a farmer he would always be a farmer. Can't get the dirt out from under his finger nails," she chuckled.

"Is your daddy a farmer?" he asked.

"Was a farmer—like you. He came in to work in a cotton mill, too, just like you. Hated every minute of it though. Hated it for thirty years. Finally drank hisself to death, so I guess it don't matter much now." She removed the skillet from the flame of the burner and ladled out the bacon on a pale yellow porcelain platter.

"But I reckon you had a good life."

"You don't know much, Mr. Burke, but you'll learn, and learn quick I'll bet. Good life? Me? If you call a good life going to work in a goddam cotton mill when you turned eleven. Had to stand on a crate to reach the spinning frame. If you call a good life hiding behind a door every Saturday night when your daddy staggered in drunk, snarling, and cussing as he beat your ma. If you call a good life getting paid in mill script that you could only spend at the Company Store. If all that sounds like a good life, Mr. Burke, then I sure as hell had a good life."

Her eyes glistened, as small tears trekked down her cheeks. She quickly wiped her face with her apron.

"Here's your food, Mr. Burke. You go on and wash up. Bathroom's down the hall," she said, placing the plate of food on the table before him.

CHAPTER 13

Coal was delivered to the mill by rail, in hopper cars. Located on the floor of each car were three, sharply-angled chutes. When the hatches of the chutes were opened, the coal poured out of the cars into cavernous, open concreted bins located beneath the tracks. From the concrete bins, wide conveyor belts, with steel scoops attached, lifted the coal to large, three-sided concrete bins above ground, near the boilers.

Men, not machines, hauled the coal from the open bins to the screw pit, which fed the insatiable appetite of the boilers. With shovels, they filled wheelbarrows manually and pushed their loads across the coal yard, dumping them into the feed pit. The feed pit was a twenty-foot long concrete structure built into the ground. Its v-shaped sides formed a kind of long-edged funnel. At the bottom of the pit, twelve feet below, a huge slow-turning auger ran the length of it. Thus was the coal fed continuously into the firebox of the boilers.

The Galway Mill usually employed six men, all black, to work the coal yard. That is, to feed the screw pit with wheelbarrows of coal. It was dirty, backbreaking work. Recently one of the men in the crew, Josh Yates' brother-in-law, had been stabbed to death during a Saturday night craps game. Ezra Burke had been hired to replace him, at least temporarily. No one could recall a white man ever working on the coal yard crew.

***

After a hurried breakfast, he walked from the Mrs. Aintry's to the mill. Mr. Newton, Fig, was already on duty at the main gate. Somewhat unsure of himself, he hesitantly approached the guardhouse.

"Well, howdy do, Burke, 'morning to you. Figured I'd see you this morning. Heard ole Bulldog hired you on," Newton said with a sly grin, as he pulled down a clipboard hanging from a nail on the doorpost. He scribbled something on the paper form.

"Gotta sign you in, you know."

"All right, but I think I'm supposed to get with Mr. Matheson first. He said yesterday."

"He ain't here yet, so don't worry about it. Besides, he left word, so you're going back to the coal yard, I reckon?"

"That's right. Don't know where it is though. Can you show me?"

"I can *tell* you, sure thing, but it's a ways from here. Come on through the gate. You gotta walk around to the back of the mill. Back to the far corner. Back where the smoke stack sits. Don't reckon you could miss that," laughed Newton.

"No, don't reckon I could," he said, and strode off toward the far corner of the mill, nearly a quarter of a mile away.

"Keep an eye on Josh Yates, he's the biggest one of 'em—the blackest and the meanest," Newton called out. Ezra walked on, not acknowledging the unsolicited caution.

As he turned the corner to the back of the mill, he saw before him the coal yard and the parked hopper cars on the tracks beyond. A small group of black me were gathered around an unpainted wooden shed. He walked across the yard toward the shed, feeling the crunch of coal and gravel bits beneath his feet. He approached the men.

"Morning, I'm—,"

"I know who you are," said one of the men, a big man, as he stepped forward toward Ezra. "You a white man come to work in the coal yard." All the others laughed and looked defiantly at him.

"Name's Burke. I've been hired to shovel coal. Same as you."

"Same as us?" The large man smirked and looked over his shoulder at the others standing behind him. "Why you want to come back here for? Don't you know this is coloreds-only work? Little enough work for us as it is. Don't need no soda cracker taking away our jobs, the few we get."

"Mr. Matteson—," Ezra started, but was again interrupted.

"Look here, Burke, I know all about you. I knew you was coming back here to work for a while. That is, until they give you a real job, a white man's job, in the mill. Matteson came by here yesterday evening and told me all about it. And I don't like it, you hear. Not a bit. I doubt you'll last long at it anyway. That's what I told Matteson. Work's too hard and dirty. People going to be laughing at you, back here working with us niggers."

"I reckon you must be Mr. Yates," he said to the big man, who did not reply. He continued, "I don't care much what people say or think about me, Mr. Yates, and that includes you. I been hired to work on this crew and I aim to do it."

Yates turned to the other men.

"You boys get to work."

The four men went into the shed and quickly exited, each with a shovel and wheelbarrow.

"Look here, Burke, you here at the coal yard and they ain't nothing I can do about it. I don't like *it*, or you, so we'll leave it at that."

He disappeared into the shed leaving Ezra standing alone. He came back out of the shed holding a coal shovel and handed it to the white man.

"This here is your shovel. You use the same one every day. You won't have trouble recognizing it because it's short-handled. You won't like it. You have to bend way over to shovel the coal. Going to be hard on a tall drink of water like yourself," Yates chuckled. "And another thing, Burke. I don't have a wheelbarrow for you. You'll work with Sugar Joe. That's him over there, that light-skin boy."

"All right."

"Ain't nothing to this work but hard. Fill up a wheelbarrow with coal and dump it over there in the feed pit. That's what we do, all day long, six days a week. You won't like it much. But then, who would?"

"I can do the work."

"Well, I guess we'll see soon enough," replied Yates, doubtfully. "Go on, get to work. And Burke, one other thing. You best watch your step around the feed pit when you dumping coal. You slip and fall, you liable to get chewed up and fed to the boiler. Lost a man like that one time, bad way to go." With this, he walked off in the direction of the other men filling their wheelbarrow with coal from the bins. Ezra joined Sugar Joe loading the wheelbarrow.

His presence was not acknowledged by his workmate or any of the others. He was, at least for the moment, a pariah.

The hard work, the short handle shovel notwithstanding, did not bother him. Nor did the immediate castigation of the black men on the crew. He, in fact, understood it to some extent, an understanding that allowed him a quiet acquiescence.

***

So he shoveled coal and fed the feed pit with wheelbarrow loads like everyone else on the crew. He more than kept pace with the strongest of them, Yates. He was the first to arrive at the yard each day and the last to leave. But by the end of that first week he was beginning to win a grudging respect of the other men. A respect, of course, not expressed nor overtly acknowledged by the black men. Not even among themselves. But once it was seen that he was not malingerer, and could do the work, Yates treated him pretty much like the other men in the crew, no better and no worse.

They stopped work for dinner each day at noon which was—naturally—signaled by the ubiquitous mill whistle. Wrapped in a piece of oilcloth, he brought food left over from Mrs. Aintry's supper the night before. He did not ask her for extra but rather left food on his plate and took it to work with him the next morning. The meat and vegetables were cold, and the biscuits somewhat stale by dinner the next day, but he it didn't matter. He was glad to have the food.

The other men adjourned across the yard to the shelter of a large, low-spreading oak tree near the fence, where they sat in the grass and ate. After they finished their meal, they usually dozed in the soft grass for the last few moments of their break. He sat away from them in the gravel yard, resting against the concrete wall of one of the coal bins, eating his meal alone.

It was during the second week that Yates, taking a bite of cornbread, called across the yard to him almost, but not quite, good-naturedly.

"Hey, Burke, you too good to eat with us black folks?"

"No. I just don't go where I'm not wanted," he answered, after a moment's hesitation.

The other men sitting under the oak tree with Yates were occupied with their meals and did not seem to hear the exchange, or more likely, were just not interested.

"You part of this here crew now, ain't you?" Yates continued, as he wiped crumbs from his lips with the back of his huge hand.

"I reckon I am, as far as that goes," said Ezra.

"You over there sitting atop them cinders and gravel. Gotta make your butt sore," said Yates. A couple of the men heard this and laughed.

"I'm all right."

"Just better than us, is that it, 'cause you white and we ain't?" probed Yates.

"Makes no difference. At least not to me. I told you that before," replied Ezra.

"Well, seeing as you on this crew, you can eat your dinner here in the shade too. Ought to anyhow. The grass is soft and cool here. Ain't that right, boys?" None of the men replied, or seemed more than vaguely interested.

At twenty past twelve there was a short blast from the whistle and they returned to their work. But the next day, and for every day as long as he worked in the coal yard, he quietly sat with the five black men in the soft grass in the shade of the oak tree.

***

He did not mind working with Sugar Joe. He was a soft-spoken young man, not much more than a boy. He seemed almost shy, but his disposition was even and relaxed. Although he worked steadily shoveling the coal without complaint or grumbling, usually two-thirds of the coal in the wheelbarrow was loaded by Ezra.

On a day that was unusually hot and the work hard as always, he noticed Sugar Joe had noticeably slowed his pace shoveling.

"Been a hot one, eh, Sugar Joe?" he asked, with sweat dripping off his face. The young black man had stopped working and was leaning on his shovel.

"Sho 'nough. I'm dragging. Don't mind saying it," the young black man replied, as he wiped his face with a dingy rag that he had pulled from his back pocket.

"I sho need a break, but Yates'll kick my ass for sure if he sees me stopped."

"Just slow down a little bit. Get you some water," said Ezra, as he continued to scoop coal into the wheelbarrow.

"You 'bout the strongest white man I ever seen. You like a machine yourself."

He did not respond, but dropped his shovel and reached for the handles of the full wheelbarrow. Sugar Joe quickly reached over in front of him and gripped the handles.

"You done took the last three loads over to the feed pit. I better push this one over before Yates gets on me for loafing."

"All right," said Ezra, stepping aside. He was thankful for the brief respite as he watched Sugar Joe struggle to push the heavy load the short distance to the feed pit.

At the pit, Sugar Joe bent over to leverage himself in order to pull up on the handles of the wheelbarrow and dump the load of coal into the pit. As he heaved with all his might, the load tilted abruptly and unevenly. The young man lurched forward to try and gain control, but the wheelbarrow overturned and crashed to the ground beside the concrete lip of the pit. Sugar Joe lost his balance and tripped on the raised edge. Screaming horrifically, he tumbled into the twelve-foot deep pit, landing on the thin layer of coal at the bottom. The turning auger moved the coal, slowly but relentlessly, toward the firebox.

Ezra, who had seen Sugar Joe struggle with the wheelbarrow of coal, bolted for the pit. It was obvious that the man below was injured and in agony. He quickly lifted Sugar Joe's empty wheelbarrow, and dropped it into the feed pit. It fell between the injured man and the opening of the firebox. Ezra hoped it would jam the powerful, rotating auger. But instead, the wheelbarrow had wedged against the slanted sides of the pit. It was lodged, uselessly, several feet above the auger, the moving coal, and Sugar Joe. The black man was doomed.

Almost instinctively, Ezra stooped, grasped the lip of the feed pit, and lowered himself over the wall. Having braced himself just above the coal-moving auger, he was now between Sugar Joe and the firebox. He wedged himself securely by spreading his legs, and pressing his hands against the slanting concrete walls. The coal flowed beneath him. The grinding of the auger was deafening this close, but he could still hear Sugar Joe's screams for help. As the injured man was moving toward him by the turning auger, he reached down and grabbed a strap of his overalls. He was able to lift Sugar Joe a few inches to keep his body from banging against the twisting screw of the auger.

There was no coal in the pit by now, only the turning auger just below his spread legs. He did not know how long he could hold onto the injured man. Every part of his body ached with the strain of holding him, and of keeping himself wedged above the auger. His grip was becoming tenuous but if he let go, the young black man was as good as dead.

Yates, working way on the other side of the yard, had somehow heard Sugar Joe's cry and had run to the pit. As soon as he realized what was happening, he raced to the tool shed and retrieved a thick, hemp rope. Running over to the feed pit, he tossed one end of the rope over the side. It fell over Ezra's shoulder and lay against his chest, the end dangling just below his grasp on Sugar Joe.

"Hold on, boys, we'll get you out," Yates called down to the two trapped men. "Burke, can you tie the end of the rope to him?"

With all his strength, he struggled to keep hold of the man while keeping himself wedged above the rotating auger. Sugar Joe had passed out and was deadweight in his grip. He would have to use his other hand to loop the rope through the straps of Sugar Joe's overalls while balancing himself with only the lower part of his legs pressed against either side of the pit.

He quickly took the end of the rope in his left hand and looped it through the straps of Sugar Joe's overalls. Once this was done, he let go with his right hand and held him suspended by the looped rope. Somehow he managed a square knot while fighting against the man's weight, and his own pain.

"Okay, Mr. Yates, pull him up," he yelled up to Yates and the other men now gripping the rope. He guided Sugar Joe's body as he slowly ascended the pit dangling from the end of the rope. "Better be real careful with him. I think his leg might be broke."

"He ain't moving. Is he dead?" asked Yates nervously, as he gazed down into the pit and the dangly body.

"No, he's alive," Ezra shouted up. "Just passed out. Might have hit his head."

Sugar Joe came to as the men pulled him carefully over the edge of the feed pit and onto the safety of the ground. He was sweating profusely and was in pain. His left leg had been broken from the fall. The splintered bone bulged beneath a bloody patch of his overalls. He lay on the ground moaning but conscious.

Yates hurriedly untied the rope and tossed the end of it down to Ezra, and the men pulled him from the pit. He fell to the ground beside Sugar Joe and stretched out on his back trying to catch his breath.

"Go get Matteson," Yates ordered one of his men, "and hurry up about it."

The man sprinted off toward the mill office.

"You all right?" asked Yates, looking down at Ezra.

He did not respond, his chest rising and falling rapidly, his eyes closed. He had not heard Yates voice. It all seemed suddenly like a blur—what had just happened. For a few moments he felt nothing and welcomed the numbness, as if every ounce of strength had been drained from his body. He then sat up uneasily when one of the men handed him a tin dipper of water. He gulped it down without speaking. He was alive, and thankful to be so.

When he finally stood up, unsteadily, the other men just stood around him, staring at him, as if waiting for him to speak, to say something. He looked at Yates.

"Why didn't someone just shut off the auger?" Ezra asked breathlessly, still obviously shaken.

"What you thinkin', man? They don't allow no nigger to shutoff anything around here. Or *on* either, for that matter. The switch for the auger motor is way off in the powerhouse. Couldn't have got to it in time anyhow," Yates spat out as he looked away. "Here comes Matteson. Rest of y'all get back to work."

***

Matteson had the mill truck brought around, and it took Sugar Joe away, presumably to the hospital. After talking with Yates at length, he walked over to Ezra who was back shoveling coal.

"Why'd you go and do a thing like for, Burke. You looking to die young or what?"

"Had to do something. The boy was hurt bad."

"Well, it was a stupid thing for you to do. Could have killed yourself. I don't want nobody killed at my mill, you hear?" growled Matteson.

"Sugar Joe would have been killed for sure."

"Yeah, and I near lost *two* men, and one of them white."

"But you didn't."

"No, I reckon I didn't, but it was still a stupid thing to do," said Matteson, shaking his head. "Anyway, you'll be moving up to the mill in a week or so. Soon as the Ferguson boy quits. I got you a mill house lined up. Four rooms is the best I can do, but it's clean and got a good back yard."

"Thanks, Mr. Matteson," Ezra hesitated, then continued. "Plumbing, uh, I was wondering if it might have indoor plumbing. *Does it have indoor plumbing?*"

"Damn, Burke," Matteson chuckled, "Of course it's got indoor plumbing, with indoor bathroom to boot. Kitchen sink with running water. You in town now, son, not up in the hills. *Does it have indoor plumbing?* I swear, you mountain people! You seen any outhouses around here lately?"

"No, reckon not," Ezra said, embarrassed at the exchange.

"It's going to be a few weeks before you can move in, though. Doing some roof repairs or something. You can bring your family down then, assuming they're still up in the mountains."

"Yes, sir, they are. I might need some time off to move our things down here."

"We'll see," replied Matteson. "I've got to get back to the mill but, Burke, don't pull a stunt like this again. It just ain't worth it." He turned to leave.

"Mr. Matteson, one other thing on my mind."

"Yeah, what?"

"There ought to be a switch out here in the coal yard, near the feed pit. Yates needs to be able to stop the auger, in an emergency I mean, like what happened today."

Matteson looked down at the ground for a moment and said matter of factly, "Ain't gonna happen." He then spat on the ground and walked off back toward the mill.

The next morning an older black man appeared at the coal yard. He was Sugar Joe's replacement. He stood over by the tool shed talking with Yates. That is, looking at him, as the new man listened and said nothing. After a few minutes Yates walked over to Ezra.

"That there's James, the new man. Taking Sugar Joe's place."

"All right."

"I see you're still using that short-handle shovel. Where's Sugar Joe's?" asked Yates.

"In the tool shed, I reckon."

"Well, I'll be putting the new man with Jesse. You keep the wheelbarrow. Give me that shovel."

Yates took the shovel from Ezra's hands before he could respond.

"Go on over to the shed and get that long-handled shovel of Sugar Joe's. New man'll use this one." He took the shovel from him.

"All right," Ezra said, almost to himself. With a brief, slight smile he went to the shed for the shovel.

Yates never said anything else about it. He knew Yates would never much like white people, maybe with good reason, maybe not. But somehow he felt that after the incident at the feed pit Yates found it in himself to at least tolerate him. And that was something.

CHAPTER 14

When he had returned to the boarding, the sun was rapidly receding beyond the tree-lined horizon, and supper had long since been served. Several of the boarders, none of whom he had yet met, sat in the front porch rockers smoking in the waning light as he approached. He nodded as he walked past them, and entered the house. He strode back to the kitchen where Mrs. Aintry was washing dishes. She looked over her shoulder at him while she continued her work.

"Long day, huh?" she asked.

"Pretty long," he said.

"The coloreds give you a hard time?"

"Just Yates. But not too bad, I guess. Work's hard but I don't mind it much. Boring, though."

"Not quite like back on the farm, I gather," she asked, as she wiped off a wet plate and placed it on the stack beside the sink.

"No, not much," he answered softly.

"Well, anyhow, your supper's over there on the stove. Should still be warm."

"Thanks," he said.

"You can eat out in the dining room or here at the kitchen table. It don't matter."

"If it's all the same to you, I'll just eat here in the kitchen," he said.

Mrs. Aintry wiped her wet hands on her apron and placed the food from the stove on the table. He sat down and ate in silence.

"Just leave the plate there beside the sink when you finish," she said as she removed her apron and placed it on a hook beside the back door. "Guess I'll go sit a spell on the front porch and catch up on the latest gossip. Been a long day for me, too," she said wearily.

"Mrs. Aintry, can I ask you something? I mean a favor."

"All depends. What?"

"I need to, that is, I want to write my wife a letter. Do you have any paper, and maybe a pencil I could use?"

"Why don't you just call her? There's a phone in the parlor. It'll be long-distance but it won't cost much. 'Least you'll get to hear her voice that way."

"There's no telephones in Waverley, not where she is."

"Oh, okay, I see. There's writing things in the desk drawer in the parlor. Help yourself," she replied. "Just seal the envelope and leave it on the desk. I'll mail it for you in the morning."

"I'm much obliged. How much is a stamp?" he asked.

"Nothing extra. A stamp a week comes with the rent," she answered, with a quick wink. "Now you go on and eat your supper," she said, and left him alone in the kitchen.

There was no one in the darkening parlor later when he entered the room. He switched on the light and found paper and a dull lead pencil in the desk drawer. He began the letter to his wife.

Judith,

I got to Corinth without much trouble. Hitchhiking is not much to my liking after riding with Mr. Edmonds. I will tell you about him sometime. I have good news. I got work at a cotton mill. It's a big one, bigger than you can picture. Pay is not much to start with but it will get better. I am working in the coal yard for a few weeks before I go inside to work in the mill. Starting as a sweeper. Can you picture it, me sweeping floors all day long? The people here are all right, I reckon, but different from what we're used to. I got a room at a boarding house near the mill. It's cheap. Mrs. Ainty runs it and she has been nice to me. I reckon you can write to me here. I am pretty sure we will be able to get a mill house soon but I don't know when just yet. I reckon Grace and Andrew are all right. Tell them that I miss them already. I miss you too. I'll send you some money when I get paid. I am going to wash up now and go to bed so I'll close. I will write again as soon as I have news.

Ezra

He folded the letter neatly and carefully inserted it in the envelope, placing it on the dusty desktop. She would get it in a few days.

***

She got the letter four days later, the day after Maynard Spearman called on her. He had stood on the front porch and spoke in a low, almost inaudible voice. He seemed fidgety and self-conscious.

"I've come by to tell you, Mrs. Burke, that I bought the land from Widow Tanner. Just got the deed signed over yesterday. I thought y'all ought to know." He held a crumpled document in his hand—the deed, she suspected.

"I see," she said. "What about the house?"

"I went and bought it all, house and everything," he answered, looking away from her out across the now defunct cornfield.

"Thank you, Mr. Spearman. I mean, I appreciate you coming all the way up here to tell me yourself. We'll need to move out, I know," she said as her dark eyes glistened with moisture. Her lips involuntarily pursed.

"Well, there ain't no real hurry I reckon. I know you folks had some bad luck lately."

Bad luck, she thought, as she considered the irony. She did not believe in luck or quite understand what people thought that it was. It seemed to her just a way to dismiss things. Like no one can control what happens. Bad things, good things. Good people, bad people. Good weather, bad weather. Was it all just luck? She did not think so.

"I know your man's gone down to Corinth to try and get work and it's just you and the young 'uns here. How's he getting on, I mean looking for work?"

"I don't know. We haven't heard from him yet."

"Now don't y'all worry none, Mrs. Burke. Ezra's young and strong. And right smart, too. He'll get his self a good job in one of them cotton mills down there. I'm sure of it." She did not respond. "Have y'all got a place to go? I mean until y'all can move down to town and all?" He seemed genuinely concerned.

"We'll manage," said Judith.

"I reckon you will at that. I'll be back here next week." He hesitated. "To tell you the truth, Mrs. Burke, I'm going to have to tear the house down. Don't need it. I can use the extra land for crops." He hesitated, a then added needlessly, "Y'all going to need a place to go," he reminded her, needlessly.

"Just give me a few days, Mr. Spearman, we'll be out soon enough."

"Like I said, I hate it come to this but it's just business, you know," he said defensively and seemed to be waiting for a response from her, but none came. There was nothing left to say. They both just stood there, looking away rather than at each other.

"Well, let me know if I can help you anyway," he said, clumsily breaking the awkward silence between them.

"All right," she said, and Spearman turned and left.

For a moment, she felt weak and helpless as she sat down unsteadily on the porch steps and gazed out to the river beyond the bottomland below. Against her will, she wept silently for a few minutes, until the thoughts she had just had about the absurdity of blaming things on luck returned to her. She was stronger than this. Self-pity would solve nothing. She had children to look after. Her husband depended on her in so many ways, ways she could not quite put her finger on right now. Her family. They would be all right somehow, she knew. She could do this. But the cold feeling of being alone would not leave her. Not for a long time.

***

He would receive her letter days later. Without elaboration, she told him of Spearman's visit and the eviction. Her sister over in Wofford County had taken her and the children in. They were all right. There had been no way to take the furniture, but Spearman had sent word that it was stored in the back shed, and could stay there until arrangements were made to move it. She acknowledged no gratitude toward this gesture in her letter, although she felt deep relief for it. *The house is gone,* she had added at the end, without further comment.

He did not sleep that night. He lay awake on his pallet and stared above into the darkness. He could hardly bear the thought of having left his family alone as he had. He felt emasculated and weak. But he kept telling himself, half believing it, that he would make a life here, a good life here in this mill town. He would have them here soon and they would be together. He knew that he would never leave her alone again. No matter what. He would be moving to the job in the mill soon. Then a mill house. The mill village. He considered it all, and wondered how he could ever really be a part of it.

Just then the screech of the mill whistle pierced the cool dawn silence, signaling the start of the day, and to remind him of where he was.

CHAPTER 15

He finished his stint working with the black men in the coal yard and became a sweeper in the weave room at two dollars a day. Not only was a sweeper on the bottom rung of the job hierarchy, but he was also placed on the third shift, working midnight until eight in the morning, six days a week.

That evening, in the coal yard, he had emptied the last wheelbarrow of coal into the grinding screw pit as a gray dusk settled over the yard. He placed his tools in the shed, as always, and stepped back out into the waning light. Of the other men, only Yates remained.

"Guess you tired of breathing coal dust ain't you, Burke?" Yates asked, not with hostility, but still with an edge to his voice.

"Ah, it's not so bad."

"You work out here much longer around all this here coal you'll be as black as me," laughed Yates, and so did Ezra. "Going up on the floor Sunday night, huh?"

"I reckon so. Third shift, the graveyard shift I guess they call it. Going to be sweeping floors up in the weave room," he said and gestured toward the mill that hovered over them.

"Now ain't that something. Getting yourself promoted. Going from the coal yard to being a sweeper on the third shift," the black man chuckled.

"Don't seem like much of a promotion, I reckon. But the pay is a little better." The irony of Yates comment was not lost on him.

"Reckon you'll be getting yourself a mill house now?" Yates asked, his voice becoming more edgy with sarcasm.

"Reckon so. You know, Yates, I got a family."

"Yeah, I got me one too, but I ain't getting no mill house. Not in this life time."

At this, Ezra looked down at his shoes. Both men were silent for a long awkward moment.

Then Ezra spoke, "I liked working here, in the coal yard I mean." He extended his hand to Yates.

"Well, you worn't too bad. For a white man, that is. Not many would've, or could've, done what you done," said Yates, shaking his hand. "You made a good hand, Burke."

"I guess I better be going."

"Yeah, see you around, Burke. Don't take no wooden nickels."

"I won't," he smiled. "G'bye, Yates," he said softly as he walked off into the darkness.

***

On Sunday, the weather turned cooler. He pulled up the collar of his thin coat as he stepped off the porch of the boarding house. It was just after eleven when he walked toward the mill to be a sweeper on the graveyard shift. A car or two sped by on the otherwise deserted street. He encountered a few anonymous figures in the faded yellow glow of the streetlights, trudging up the sidewalk, against the wind. He rightly assumed that they, like himself, were headed for third-shift jobs at the mill. The graveyard shift seemed like a good name for it.

Only a short walk from Mrs. Aintry's, he was early for shift change. He sat down on the familiar bench at the bus stop, across the street from the mammoth plant which leered down at him. In the cold half-darkness, ill-lit by the dull streetlight on the corner, he felt alone as he had never felt before. But he *had* been alone here before. This was the same spot from which he had encountered the mill on that first day he had arrived in Corinth. Although it had only been weeks, that day seemed long ago and far away. He pulled his coat tightly around his body and waited. For what, he did not know, or wish to think about.

A few minutes before midnight there were many more people arriving at the mill. He watched them as they passed through the guard gate and were swallowed up by the red-brick monster. Some shuffled by him languidly, in pairs and small groups, mumbling inaudibly to each other. They did not seem to be in a hurry to cross the street to their work, to the long night ahead. He pulled out the silver watch from his pocket. Flicking up the cover, he could hardly see the hands in the dim light, but well enough to make out that it was ten minutes before midnight. As a small contingency of workers passed by, he rose from the bench and followed them into the Galway Cotton Mill.

The air in the crowded stairwell was faintly stale with the lingering odor of sweating bodies and cigarette smoke. There was a constant muffled kind of a roar, low and relentless, that grew louder as he ascended the concrete steps, which vibrated beneath his feet. The steel pipe handrail pulsed in his grip like a living thing. At the landing of the eight set of stairs, he stopped at a steel gray door, over which hung a sign. Its large red-block lettering faded, WEAVE ROOM. Several men pushed past him and disappeared through the door, as it slammed shut behind them. He grasped the handle of the heavy door and stepped inside.

Nothing that he had ever seen or had happened to him before could have prepared him for what he then encountered. The gigantic weave room was almost twelve hundred feet long. The three thousand looms seemed to be simultaneously screaming at each other, and at the workers tending them. The noise was deafening and merciless, as thousands of shuttles were batted back and forth on the looms by the slamming picker-sticks. He instinctively started to clasp his hands over his ears, but instantly realized that this would be useless and futile, in wake of the penetrating thunder created by the looms. Besides, no one else seemed to notice the racket.

The stifling heat in the cavernous room grabbed at him as he stood there. Immediately, perspiration coated his forehead. He felt the dampness of his skin against the cotton shirt beneath the coat. The hot dusty air was thick with what he would come to know as lint. It floated in an almost delicate suspension, like a soft snow, as it slowly twisted in the glare of the huge overhead electric lamps that hung from the low ceiling, along the length of the room. But it had a faint, almost pleasant smell, which he could not identify. Perhaps it was the smell of processed cotton. It was a strange thing to him. The lint, like a fog, hung over the entire hall, and the people and machines, just a few feet away, melted into faded apparitions in its grayness. He could not see to the far end.

In the almost overpowering heat and mugginess, he removed his coat and stood there with it hanging limply in his hand. He felt lost, and a vague sense of helplessness came over him. A feeling he did not know or like. None of the workers seemed to notice him or have any interest in his presence. They were too busy screaming at each other and making hand signals across the banks of looms in attempts to communicate above the din.

He had not seen the person approach from his left until he felt a hard tap on his shoulder. He shouted something to Ezra, which of course he could not discern above the noise of the looms. The man then shook his head and motioned for him to follow him, as he turned abruptly and walked away.

Walking a few steps behind him, he noticed that the man strode with a rocking motion, as if he were on the rolling deck of a ship at sea. He led Ezra to a door in the left corner of the weave room, a low-ceiled cube of an office.

As the door shut behind them, the noise, though still present, was muted enough to make conversation possible. The man picked up a clipboard from the cluttered desk and glanced briefly at the sheets of paper clamped to it. He then placed it back on the desk, turned toward Ezra, and leaning against the edge of the desk, thrust his hands into his trouser pockets.

"I guess you must be my new sweeper," he said with a sardonic half chuckle.

"Yes. Name's Burke."

"I know your damn name. You the one been working back there with them niggers, ain't you?" The man's voice was high-pitched and thin.

"I've been working in the coal yard, that's true enough," he replied looking directly into the close-set, unblinking eyes of the man.

"What you trying to prove by doing something crazy like that?"

"I needed work. Mr. Matheson hired me on until the sweeper job came open. Can't say it was bad work."

"You think I don't know who hired you? You figure me for some kind of dumbass, Burke?" said the man, smirking, in a thin nasal tone, his voice almost cracking.

"No, I don't reckon I know you," Ezra said softly.

"Well, you'll damn sure get to know me. So you don't know who I am?"

"No, I reckon I don't. A boss man I'd say."

"You goddamn right a boss man. Your boss man. I'm the second-hand for the third shift weave room. My name's Tuttle. Queasy Tuttle."

Tuttle shifted his weight to his left leg. A quick grimace shot across his squinched up, almost ferret-like face.

"Please to meet you, Mr. Tuttle," he said, extending his hand, which Tuttle ignored.

"No 'mister'. Just Queasy. You got that?"

"All right."

Ezra withdrew his hand and unconsciously rubbed his thumbs across the tips of his fingers several times, as if he was trying to remove something from his skin.

"I just can't understand for the life of me why Bulldog keeps sending me the likes of you. First, I got to put up with Perk's boy. He wat'n no good. Useless as tits on a boar hog. He won't last a week in the

Marines. I'll guarantee you that. Then you. I'm guessing you ain't never
seen the inside of a cotton mill before now. That right?"

"This is my first job in a mill," he spoke matter of factly, without
inflection.

"I'd say by the way you talk, you from the mountains," said
Tuttle, pleased with his apparent clairvoyance.

"I'm from up near Waverley."

"What'd you do up there, make shine?"

"I farmed," he replied, shoving his hands into the pockets of his
overalls.

"Couldn't make a go of it? Thought you'd come down here and
get rich in a cotton mill? That it, Burke?" Tuttle bore in, apparently
enjoying the needling.

"I came to work."

Tuttle pursed his lips with a slight sucking sound to show
disgust, and stepped to the back of the desk, where there was a chair but
he did not sit down.

"Enough of this bull crap, Burke. I got to get to work and so do
you. Ain't much to it. Even *you* might be able to do it," the small man
said, with the nasty sarcasm that was evidently part of his character.
"There's a closet down that first aisle, right of the main floor door you
came in. In it's your broom and a dust pan. Just keep the lint off the
floors. Bulldog's mighty particular about these floors. A lot more
particular than he is about the people he's been hiring here lately.
They're yellow oak, come from old man Allgood's land they say.
Anyway, keep 'em clean. Think you can handle that, Burke?"

He did not reply and Tuttle did not wait for one.

"No set breaks. You go to the waterhouse – that's the bathroom
– when you need to go. You can eat your supper whenever you want to,
but don't take more than twenty minutes doing it. You can't ever get
caught up sweeping, so you got to stay with it. If you ain't doing a good
job, the weavers and loom fixers will let you know and they'll tell me. I
don't want to hear no grumbling. You got any questions?"

"No, I reckon I don't." He turned back to the door behind him to
leave the office and the miserable second-hand. He stopped when Tuttle
spoke.

"One more thing Burke, and you need to understand this. I don't
like you. I don't like the way you got in here and I figure you for a
nigger-lover. You got two strikes against you right off the bat," Tuttle

chuckled at his witness pun. "Just do your job and keep out of my way, you hear?"

Ezra walked off to try and find the broom closet.

CHAPTER 16

He continued to live at Mrs. Aintry's boarding house. One of the boarders moved out and she offered him a room in the house proper. He politely declined and continued to sleep in the mud room off the back porch. Except for what he paid Mrs. Aintry, he sent his pay back to his wife each week and she was able to save some of it.

The mill house that Charlie Matteson had promised came available after he had been in the weave room six weeks. He was not able to get off work other than his day off on Sundays, but fortunately Judith's brother-in-law, Eugene, was somehow able to hire a truck to move his family to Corinth.

They had left Wofford County early in the morning and had stopped at the shed to collect their meager furnishings. The use of the pickup truck cost ten dollars, which was most of what she had been able to save. But that did not matter to them, even if Eugene pocketed a couple of dollars for his trouble. Late on a pleasant Sunday afternoon in early October, she and the children arrived at number Twenty, Fifth Street. The family was finally together again. There now seemed hope.

***

The mill owners had adopted many of the practices of their Northern counterparts, evolved many years before the cotton mill industry migrated to the South. One of these was the paternalistic nature of mill owners. There was no mistaking it for altruism. It was business. If the company provided cheap housing to its employees, they were likely to be more dependable workers and be tied to the mill, not move around as much. And the owners collected the rents; money stayed in the *family*.

Surrounding each cotton mill, the owners constructed houses for the workers. Grouped together, they were called mill villages, with the mill at the center—literally and figuratively. The streets typically laid out in all directions from the mill in neatly laid-out grid patterns. The white clapboard houses were built close together along either side of the streets. Some of the houses had four rooms, others five, but they all looked pretty much the same.

In keeping with the concept of a grid, the streets were typically not given names, but rather numbers, beginning with First Street. You could how determine how far a person lived from the mill by knowing the number-name of the street. Maintaining the villages allowed the mill owners to pose as compassionate and magnanimous benefactors. They were, in fact, only protecting their investment.

Ezra was considered to have been fortunate to get a house on Fifth Street, only five blocks from the mill. It was clean, and for some reason, had been newly painted, which caused it to stand out conspicuously from the others on the street.

He was standing on the high front porch of the house when the truck pulled up at the curb. He smiled broadly. Judith climbed down from the cab of the dilapidated vehicle. They embraced each other, naturally, without affectation. He kissed her face and brushed away the tears that glistened in her eyes and on her cheeks. The children, who had ridden to Corinth in the bed of the truck with the tied-down belongings, crawled over the low tailgate, squealing with delight as they ran to their father. For a moment, the small family seemed to meld into a single thing, before pulling themselves apart from each other and turning to view the house.

"Is this our house now, Papa?" asked Grace excitedly.

"I reckon it is. This is where we'll all be living for a while," he answered, glancing briefly at his wife.

"Where's the garden," asked little Andrew, "and the chickens?"

"Well, we don't have a garden. Not yet anyway. There likely won't be any chickens. It's different here, not like the farm," he explained to the boy.

"Mama told us you work at the mill now and get wages. What's wages, Papa?" asked the little girl, alive with her natural curiosity.

"I go to work at the mill every day and they pay me money for doing it. That's wages, I reckon."

"Are we rich now?"

"No, we're not rich. Just mill folks now."

"Maybe we *are* rich! The house is big and shiny white. We never had a painted house before but there's a bunch of them here. And you got wages. Surely, we must be rich, Papa. We must be!"

They smiled at the child's naïve appraisal of their new status. Andrew grew restless and pulled away from his father's hand, running to the yard back of the house.

"Go look after your brother, Grace. There's a right big yard round back."

He and his wife stood looking at the house. He held her hand tightly in his own.

"It's nice, Ezra. Really nice. Do you like it?"

"All right, I reckon," he replied. He was looking intently at the white mill house, but he did not seem to see it.

"We can make a home here. We *will* make a home here."

"I reckon we will," he said, his voice flat.

Eugene, the brother-in-law, had gotten out of the truck and stepped into the yard.

"Ez, let's get this stuff unloaded. I got to get this here truck back before dark, or old man Lawson will charge me another dollar."

"All right. We'll just set everything off here in the yard so you can be on your way. Can't afford to pay no more than I already have."

Eugene was already untying the ropes that had secured their belongings for the trip. Soon, every possession that they owned stood clustered in the yard. He then quickly jumped in the truck, honked the horn twice, and waved out the window as the he drove away.

Ezra walked to the edge of the yard.

"Grace, you and Andrew come on over here. Y'all need to help get things inside."

Judith was inside inspecting her new home. The children came running.

***

"Well, old boy, looks like you might could use some help."

Ezra turned and looked at the source of the voice, which came from a man sauntering toward him from the adjacent house across the dirt yard.

"Reckon I might."

The man walked up and extended his hand.

"I'm your new neighbor. No, that ain't exactly right. I guess you're my new neighbor, if you want to be exact about it. Name's Melvin. Melvin Jackson."

"Pleased to meet you, Mr. Jackson."

"Whoa, now. Mr. Jackson was my pappy. I'm just Melvin," he jibed good-naturedly.

"All right, Melvin. Name's Ezra."

"Oh, I know *who* you are. Everybody on the mill hill knows who you are. Didn't take you long to get famous around here."

"I don't rightly know your meaning," said Ezra.

"I mean you the one's been working in the coal yard with them colored boys, ain't you?"

"Well, that's true enough. I *was* working with them but I'm in the mill now."

"Yep, know that too. You're the third shift sweeper in the weave room. That true about your saving that boy's life?"

"You talking about Sugar Joe?"

"That's the one."

"I just helped him. It was an accident. Don't know that I saved his life. Maybe I did," he replied.

"Ain't the way I heard it. Anyway, we can talk later. We'd better get this stuff into the house. Looks like it might be coming up a cloud."

He then grasped one end of the kitchen table and lifted it while Ezra took the other. The two men worked steadily, and in a short time the yard was cleared.

Melvin sat down on the front steps and wiped his forehead with a handkerchief.

"Now that weren't too bad, Ez. Not exactly a day's work. Looks like the clouds passing north of here. We could use some rain though."

"What for? Don't see much growing around here that needs rain. The yards are mostly dirt anyway. I don't see much point in needing rain. The mill don't need rain. Wouldn't know if it's raining or not anyway, the way I see it. I'm tired of worrying about needing rain," he said, with more than a trace of bitterness and frustration.

"Now, Ez, that ain't exactly right. Look over back of my house yonder at that stuff growing. We got us a little garden. Keep one 'bout-year round except in the dead of winter naturally."

"You can have a garden here?" Ezra asked, surprised with the revelation of the garden.

"Course you can. Why couldn't you? Chickens too if you wanted to fool with them, which I don't."

"Well, I just didn't know the mill would allow it. That's all."

"Sure you can plant a garden. I got sweet potatoes in the ground now, and collards coming up."

"I don't know, I just didn't think about it, I reckon."

"Y'all like sweet potatoes and collard greens?"

"Yes, we like them. I mean me and my wife. The children will tolerate them I reckon. They're used to them."

"You a farmer, Ez?"

"Was."

"Was a farmer, now a lint-head. Right, Ez?" Melvin chuckled.

"I reckon so. That's about it."

"Judging from the way you talk, I'd bet two bits you from the mountains."

Ezra smiled slightly, "I'd figure you already knew that. Seems you know everything else there is to know about me already."

"Well, not everything. Just *some* things."

"How's that?" asked Ezra.

He did not like other people knowing his business. He did not understand why anyone would be interested. In the mountains, people tended to stay to themselves and keep their own counsel in personal matters. If you were in trouble or needed help, neighbors might pitch in and lend a hand, but they did not ask questions or pry into your affairs. They were suspicious of strangers.

"*How*, you ask?" Melvin thoughtfully rubbed the stubble on his chin. "You see, Ez, down here things are different. You'll see soon enough. People are different too, I'd guess, from what you're used to."

"That's true enough," interjected Ezra.

"See, we all live here in this mill village. We all work at the cotton mill, just like our ma's and pa's did, and most of their folks before them. With people working and living so close together, it's hard *not* to know things about each other. Lots of gossip, though. Usually only 'bout half of it got some truth in it. That's on a good day."

"What difference does it make, I mean talking and knowing about other folks?" Ezra asked, genuinely puzzled.

"Oh, I don't know. Just gives 'em something to do I. Ain't much going on here on a mill hill like this one. Other than talk, mill's baseball team is near 'bout the only excitement we ever get. Like when folks heard about a white man working with the coloreds in the coal yard, now *that* was news. Couldn't wait to tell their neighbors, or chew the fat about it around the water- house on the floor. News like that breaks the monotony I s'pose."

"Don't seem like much," Ezra offered.

"Ain't much, but you'll get used to it soon enough. Be a part of it, like most folks here."

"I don't think so," said Ezra.

"Oh, it ain't so bad. Lot of good folks around here. Just keep your shades pulled down at night," said Melvin, again chuckling. "Yep, you're working for *the Man* now, Ez. He'll take real good care you. That is, if he don't kill you first."

"The Man?"

"That's right, Ez. The mill, or I guess the mill owner, to be exact. He's *the Man*. And you a Galway man now. We all are. Galway women, too," his neighbor said, with only a touch of sarcasm.

He thought for a moment but did not reply to Melvin's new and strange vernacular. *The Man. Being taken care of. Gossip.* He had a vague discontent about him, almost as if he were beginning to drift without anything to hold on to. He could not say what it was, but he did not like it.

Finally, Melvin rose from the steps and stuffed the handkerchief back into his pocket.

"I best git. Earline will have supper on directly. Likely she'll be bringing over a dish or two for y'all. She's a helluva cook. Works at the mill, too. In spinning."

"I'm much obliged for the help."

"Don't think nothing about it. That's what a neighbor's for, right? I'll be seeing you, Ez," he said and ambled back over to his house.

Ezra stood there staring at him as he walked away, thinking with a vague uncertainty about what he had said. Particularly what he had said about *the Man*. Curious.

CHAPTER 17

As things turned out, the Jackson's were good neighbors and became friends. Later that first day, Earline Jackson had appeared at their front door with a large wicker basket. Grace heard the gentle rap on the door and rushed to discover who had come to call.

"Why, hello there little girl. Now who might you be?" asked the tall, thin woman with the basket.

"My name's Grace," eagerly responded the child, her eyes wide with excitement and expectation as she looked up at the friendly stranger with the big basket.

"Well, now that's surely a pretty name for a sweet thing like you. I'm Mrs. Jackson. We live next door."

"I know Mr. Jackson. He helped Papa and me move the furniture in side. He's a nice man," offered the child brightly.

"Well, I can see right now you and Melvin—that's my hubby— are going to get along just fine. Grace, is your mother around?"

"Yes, ma'am. She's in the back room helping Papa put up the bed. I'll go fetch her." Before Earline could respond, the little girl disappeared back into the house. In a moment she returned, tugging her mother along by the hand.

"See, Mama, she's here. Mrs. Jackson. She's Mr. Jackson's wife." Judith looked at Earline and smiled, a bit embarrassed.

"I'm sorry, Mrs. Jackson. Please do come in. We are working on our manners but as you can see, we have a ways to go."

"Manners, poo. Think nothing of it. She's a sweet little thing. I like her spirit. She's a little sprite she is," laughed the neighbor as she stepped into the house. She extended her hand, "I'm Earline Jackson. Live next door."

"I'm Judith. The Burkes, but I guess you already knew that. House is a mess. I hate for neighbors to see it this way," she said, her voice soft and resonant.

"And why shouldn't it be a mess. The house, I mean. Y'all just moving in and all. It takes a while to get things settled," came Earline's kind and insightful reply.

"Thank you for saying that," said Judith.

She then spoke to Grace, who was still tightly gripping her hand.

"Grace, go see if you can find a chair for Mrs. Jackson and tell your Papa we have company. Andrew, too." The child disappeared instantly into the back of the house. "Andrew's our youngest. I'm afraid he's a mess, too."

"Oh, no, no, Judith. I'm not staying. Y'all got your hands full here with moving in and all. Don't need to be entertaining no neighbor. No, ma'am. I just thought y'all might be getting a little hungry after while. A body can't be expected to cook supper the first night you move in. I brought over some hot food for you. Just some things left over from supper."

"Oh, that's too much trouble, Mrs. Jackson, we—"

"It's Earline. We're neighbors now. No formalities. Anyway, weren't no trouble at all. Like I said, after me and Melvin ate, we got plenty left."

"That's awfully kind of you."

She glanced away as small tears welled within her and glistened on her black lashes. When they had left the mountains that morning, she had only been able to hurriedly pack away some cold biscuits and sorghum. She had also managed some apples that had already begun to go mealy. She had worried about feeding the children, although Ezra had assured her they could get what they needed at the Company Store in the morning.

The stay at her sister's had not been easy, nor had it gone well. Although she had sensed the intrusion and the imposition, nothing had been said between them. But she had felt the dull resentment of the burden she and the children presented. She was not used to the kindness and generosity of someone like Earline. She fought back the tears, not wishing to let herself be embarrassingly overwhelmed in front of a stranger. She could only guess that Earline and Melvin suspected just how poor they were. And she was tired.

"If you'll just take this basket, or tell me where to set it down, I'll be on my way. I know y'all still have lots to do." Earline presented the basket with both hands.

"Yes, of course," she said, taking the basket from her. "I can't tell you how much we appreciate it. I know the children must be getting hungry, and Ezra too."

"And Judith, too, I suspect," laughed Earline. "Well, I'll be running along now. Better eat it before it gets cold. There's some fried chicken in there and it ain't half bad, if I do say so myself."

"I'm sure it's delicious," said Judith. The two women looked at each other briefly and as Earline turned to go Judith said, "I am very glad to meet you, Earline. I'm glad we're going to be neighbor Earline laughed again, "We already are! But that is a sweet thing for you to say. We—me and Melvin—work the first shift so we won't be around tomorrow until late afternoon. You'll hear the four o'clock whistle sure enough. But anyway we'll come over after we get off work and help y'all get things fixed up. Bye, Judith."

"Bye, Earline."

Cupping her hands to her mouth, Earline playfully called out toward the back rooms of the house, "Bye, Grace." Then she was gone.

***

As the weeks and months passed, a fondness for Earline grew in Judith's heart. The vague, undefined sense of isolation she had sometimes felt those years in the mountains began to be slowly replaced by the closeness of community, people around her. The mill village was precisely as it described itself—a village. Although it was officially part of the city, it was more or less self-contained, not really a part of Corinth at all.

Everyone she would come to know worked at the mill, shopped at the mill-owned Company Store, and understood the hierarchy that existed to define the differences between the workers, bosses, and owners. To her, there was almost an attraction—a reassurance—with these implicit boundaries, the orderliness. These feelings surprised her.

She had not realized until now how much she had missed companionship, in the form of closeness with other people. People outside her small family. She knew Ezra's heart would always be with the mountains and the farm. Sometimes, though less often now, he sat on the front steps smoking his pipe, gazing off to the north.

A few weeks ago, she had sat down beside him there and asked what he was thinking about.

"Oh, nothing much," he said. "Just home. Farming. That's all. We're going back one of these days." She had smiled wistfully and placed her hand lightly on his arm.

She did not think that they would ever return to the hills—she was not sure that she even wanted to—but she never told him. She left him to the solace of his dream.

Earline came to represent companionship. Her kindness and openness had erased any fears of loneliness or alienation that might have come over her in this new place. As they became fast friends Earline, being older, became almost a mother figure to her. This feeling surprised and puzzled her some at first. She then realized the depth of the void that had been left by her own mother's death. It now seemed like so many years ago.

Since their yards were adjacent they—she and Earline—had expanded the garden in the spring following their arrival to Corinth. It ran along both backyards, and they shared in the work and the resulting bounty. As a young girl, Earline's family, like many of the mill people had moved from the country to work in the cotton mills. So the garden kept them in touch with the land and augmented meager salaries with fresh vegetables in the summer and autumn. There was even enough to can and store for the winter.

The best times for her were the long summer afternoons. Soon after the mill whistle blew at the four o'clock shift change, Earline and Melvin could soon be seen coming down the street, with their black and battered tin lunch boxes dangling from their hands. The mill whistle also woke Ezra, who slept in the darkened bedroom during the day. He appeared a little bleary-eyed in the kitchen, where he gulped black coffee. He usually took a nap after dark, before he went to the mill for the midnight shift.

But just after supper, they often joined Earline and Melvin in the garden, weeding and checking for ripe fruit, picking any that was ready. Earline and Melvin seemed to really like having the children around. They quickly became Aunt Earline and Uncle Melvin. Without children of their own, they laughed and played games with both of the them. They tried to show no favorites, but you could see that Grace had grown special to them.

As dusk settled over the mill village, they would sit on the front porch amidst blinking fireflies and drank Earline's iced tea, southern sweet, of which she was especially proud and to which Melvin seemed addicted. Talk was mostly about work at the mill and swapping gossip about co-workers or neighbors, which more or less were the same thing. Not working at the mill, Judith listened intently and laughed often at Melvin's stories. He had a talent for elaboration, if not actual fabrication. This likeable man, wiry and bandy-legged, had also become their friend. The only real friend as far as she knew that her husband had in the mill village.

With darkness came the yawning, and Melvin's delivering the benediction. "Well, folks," he would say as he rose from the porch rocker. "Been a long day. Drinking all that ice tea'll probably keep me up half the night. Come on, Ma, we got to rest up so we can give *the Man* his pound of flesh again tomorrow. Night, y'all. Have a good shift, Ez. See you tomorrow evening I reckon."

When everyone else had left for bed, she and Ezra often sat on the porch, wrapped in the soft warmth of the evening, not speaking much, but staring into the darkness beyond. She felt his closeness, and she knew that she was at last safe.

CHAPTER 18

Sundays are quiet in the mill village, sometimes almost eerily so. The mill whistle blows at midnight on Saturday, signaling the workweek is over. Most of the second-shift workers shuffle out of the mill and walk home, with their black tin lunch pails under their arms. A few spend the nickel it takes to ride the electric trolley to downtown Corinth to sip cold draught beer, and maybe dance a little, if the joint has one of those new music machines, a jukebox. Alcohol is not available on the mill hill, as bars are not allowed by the mill owners. Mill owners, of course, do not live on the mill hill.

But Sunday mornings dawns with a self-conscious silence. The mill, around which all life in the village revolves, stands unnaturally noiseless. A reminder of *the Man*, as resolute as ever, still hovers over them, motionless and silent. In this briefest of respites, the ground beneath their feet ceases to pulsate from the machinery for a few hours. No black smoke swirls from the red-brick smokestack to rise and mar the clear blue sky. It is as if the world, albeit briefly, stands still.

The early morning streets of the village reflect this interlude between the end of the boisterous, but monotonous work week, and the beginning of the next. Little stirs. Occasionally, with their parents snoring and sleeping off the weariness of the week, young boys lazily toss around a string ball, or girls play hopscotch in the street. Some of the older ones, who look to be twelve or thirteen, work at the mill during the week, but on Sundays they can become children again, if only for a few fleeting hours.

The pastors of the two small brick village churches—one Baptist, one Methodist—arrive a little later, but still early enough to unlock the doors of their respective chapels and perhaps take one last look at their sermon notes. They wonder, these days more than usual, what the collection plate might render. At a quarter to ten, clanging church bells abruptly split the silence of the village, calling the parishioners, those who have reluctantly roused themselves early enough, to Sunday school.

It was on one of these spring Sunday mornings that Earline stepped lightly off the steps of her front porch and crossed her yard to the Burke's. She tapped gently on the door with her knuckles. She waited, but when there was no response she tapped again. Finally, the door creaked open and there Judith stood, brushing her hair back, like black, thick silk, from her face.

"Good morning, Earline," she said softly, but pleasantly perplexed by the early morning visit. "Is anything the matter?"

"Morning, Judith. Oh, no, nothing's wrong. Sorry to be calling so early, but when I woke up this morning and was sitting on the porch sipping coffee, I just had this feeling. I don't know, like I wanted to have a special day. Do something. It felt good to be alive. Do you know what I mean? Have you ever felt that way?" Earline beamed with anticipation of excitement.

"Why, yes I have. Yes, of course I have."

"Yes, spring is here for sure. I think the cherry tree back of the house is about to bloom!"

"I was looking at your garden yesterday. Things are starting to come out."

"What do you mean *my* garden? Now you look here, Judith Burke, that there is *our* garden. We both have worked it, you probably more than me. I come home from work every day and go right out to it. I notice it's always just been weeded, and I say to myself, 'Why that Judith's been out here weedin' and straightening things again.' Best garden on the mill hill. It's *our* garden, you hear me? And I won't truck no arguing different."

"Yes, ma'am," replied Judith, seriously. Then the two women laughed.

Judith stepped out onto the porch, pulling the door closed behind her.

"Everyone is still asleep. Hard to get used to. Ezra's been up at four in the morning all his life. Now during the week, he sometimes doesn't seem to even know what day it is."

"Yeah," agreed the older woman, "working the graveyard shift in a cotton mill will do that to you. Me and Melvin both did it for five years. 'Bout near killed us. Me anyway."

"It's a long way from farming, I guess," Judith added thoughtfully, with a wistful sigh, the meaning of which Earline did not catch.

"Listen, the reason I came over is I thought we might have a picnic later on. The weather's so warm and wonderful. I bet the kids would love it."

"Yes, they would for sure."

"Then how about it?" Earline pressed good-naturedly.

"It's been a long time since we did anything like that. I mean we used to go down to the river. I would spread a quilt on the ground. We would eat our dinner, then sit and watch the children splash around in the water at the edge of the bank. It was nice. I haven't really thought of doing anything like that here. We just seem... so... so closed in here. I don't know."

"Well, it's time you did," Earline shot back.

"Where would we go? I mean for a picnic."

"To the City Park. In town. They got a big park, lots of grass. Not like here. There's a small creek runs through it. young 'uns could slash around in it. Shade trees all up and down it where us old folks can talk and relax a spell."

"Sounds nice, Earline. It really does," she said with a touch of hopefulness in her voice, her dark eyes bright in the narrow shafts of early morning sunlight that danced on her face.

"How would we get there? I wouldn't mind walking, seeing the town."

"Whoa, now girl. You a lot younger than me. And a country girl to boot".

"Mountain girl," corrected Judith.

"Country girl, mountain girl. Girl all the same. Anyway, don't forget these old bones are bent over a spinning frame all week. We'll take the trolley. Stops on the corner just across from the mill."

"Does it cost anything to ride the trolley?"

"Well, yes, but it ain't much. A dime there and back. Kids don't pay. Whatcha say? Let's do it! I got Melvin over there washing a chicken right now," she chuckled, pointing a thumb over her shoulder toward the house next door. "When's your folks getting up?"

"Anytime now. I'll see if Ezra wants to do it."

"You do that. It'll be fun. When y'all get ready, come on over to the house and we'll all head out for the trolley together. I better go get that chicken frying."

"It does sound like fun," she smiled broadly as Earline practically bounded down the steps.

That word—*fun*—seemed to hang in the air for her. *Fun*. Nothing much had been what you could call just plain fun here, so far. She felt her heart race a little with excitement. A picnic. Such a small simple thing. But, yes, they could have fun!

"See you in a little while," Earline called back over her shoulder.

"All right," she replied, too softly for her friend to hear.

She stepped back into the house, closing the door behind her. Her husband was up sitting at the kitchen table, still a little bleary-eyed from sleep, sipping coffee.

"Good morning, wife."

"Good morning, husband," she responded. She touched his shoulder as she walked past him and took the chair across the table from him.

"Been outside?"

"Yes, I was on the porch with Earline. I closed the front door. I didn't want to wake you."

"Time I was up, don't you reckon?" he asked without waiting for her to answer. "Way past time. I never thought I would be one to sleep in like this. Not natural. It's not like the farm, is it?"

"No, it's not like the farm. You work nights, Ezra. Sleeping in the daytime is what you do. Nothing wrong with it."

"I reckon not, but it's not exactly right somehow either. I don't know," he said, looking at her directly, into her eyes.

"You can forget about the mill today. It's Sunday and we have all day. Oh, Ezra, it's such a beautiful spring day."

"I guess old man Spearman's got the field all plowed and planted by now." His voice trailed off as he looked into the coffee cup on the table before him.

"Earline came over to ask us to go on a picnic with her and Melvin," she said, with the excitement of expectation." "There's a real nice park downtown she said. With a stream and grass and shade trees. I bet the dogwoods are in bloom. I'm sure there are dogwoods. It would be fun, Ezra. The children would love it. I just know they would. So would I."

"You sound all excited about it," he said.

"It would be fun. Don't you think?"

"I reckon there hasn't been much fun around here lately," he half chuckled, but there was an edge to his voice.

"Earline's frying chicken. Let's wake the children up and go. We'll all ride the trolley Earline said." She reached over and placed her small, brown hand over her husband's.

"All right," he said, with a wistful smile.

***

The day had brightened under the spring sun as they caught the trolley for the ride downtown. Earline sat on the slatted bench seat with the children. The electric trolley moved forward with a jolt, sparks flying as the spring-loaded trolley poles scraped along the electrified wires overhead.

Ezra, Judith, and Melvin sat across the narrow aisle facing them. Both children, filled with the excitement of adventure, knelt backward on the bench looking out the window and pointing with amazement at the things they saw. Very usual and mundane things to people of the town, but all new and sometimes perplexing to children from the mountains.

They were soon out of the familiar and repetitive surroundings of the Galway Mill village as the trolley passed another cotton mill with a village of its own, just as featureless and monotonous. The avenue then opened up into a boulevard lined on either side with large two story mansions, whose wide expanses of manicured lawns seemed to spread out like a smooth green sea before them.

"Is that the park?" asked little Andrew, without taking his eyes off the scenes moving past the bus.

"No, sweetie, that's not the park. That's just where the rich folks live. Some of them anyway," laughed Earline, as she gently patted the the thin leg knelling beside her.

The trolley moved swiftly through the affluent neighborhood. There was no one waiting for the trolley at the numerous stops along the way, as the maids and yardmen were off on Sunday.

After crossing a series of closely laid railroad tracks, low built stores and shops began to appear on either side. They were mostly closed and shuttered. This was Sunday in the South, and it would be far into the future before the prevailing blue laws would become a quaint and odd memory. On several corners were churches, seemingly an inordinate number of them. From several of them, people were streaming out through from their heavy wooden doors, down the steps, onto the concrete sidewalks, as the bells in the steeples clanged dissonantly to indicate that services were over. It was near noon.

"Look, Mama," Grace said, pointing. "Look at all the pretty dresses. Oh, those are such shiny shoes the girls are wearing! Do you see them, Mama?"

"Those are patent leather shoes, Grace," explained Earline matter of factly, as the trolley pulled over to the curb, just beyond a cream colored-brick church, its tall copper-covered steeple pointing like a needle to the sky.

Compressed air from the cylinder hissed as the front door opened, folding back on itself. A family dressed for church boarded the trolley. They walked past the picnic goers and took seats. Grace, who was very much absorbed by the boarding, quickly slid from her kneeling position to sit beside Earline. One of the children with the family was a little girl, not much older than her. She stared enviously at her shoes, which were gleaming black patent leather, as the little girl prissed by to take her seat. Silver diamonds of moisture rimmed Judith's eyes as she silently watched her daughter longingly stare at the shoes. But Grace never mentioned the little girl or the glossy leather shoes.

As they approached the center of the city, the boulevard curved eastward. The street sign on the corner read 'Main Street'. The trolley stopped frequently for traffic lights, as more people got on and off the bus.

At one stop, Ezra, who had appeared to be distracted during most of the trip despite Melvin's almost constant banter, watched as a black man and a very old woman boarded the trolley. The woman was stooped and walked with great difficulty, leaning on her cane. The man fumbled in his pocket for coins and dropped them into the clinking coin box next to the impatient driver. The man, perhaps her son, walked behind her gently touching her stooped shoulders and guiding her as best he could. They moved slowly and self-consciously past Ezra and the others. They took seats at the very rear of the bus while ignoring the numerous empty seats they passed by. As he watched them pass, he thought of Yates and the coal yard.

As the trolley rumbled through the business section, the street narrowed and descended down a gently sloping grade. Just past a gas station on the corner the street, lanes divided and curled around a small square, a low island of carefully cut and laid granite block. In the center of this small isle stood a statue, larger than scale, of a man. A wide brimmed hat sat rakishly back on his head as he leaned, ever so slightly, on his musket.

"Papa, what is that?" asked an animated Grace, as the trolley swept by it on her side of the bus.

"It's a statue," Melvin offered.

"What's it doing here, Uncle Melvin?"

"Why, it's a monument. It's for the Confederate soldiers who died in the war. "You know, the Civil War," Melvin continued to explain.

"But what's it for," the child persisted.

No one spoke as Melvin hesitated, thoughtfully.

"They put it there so we would remember. So we wouldn't forget, I s'pose," he finally responded.

"Oh," said Grace as she turned back to the window. The statue was left behind and had disappeared in the distance.

The park was only a few blocks further down the hill. Melvin yanked on the thin cord overhead, ringing the small bell up near the driver's seat. The trolley slowed and pulled to the curb. They stepped off the bus onto the sidewalk and then onto the thick grass of the park. Earline led them to a shady spot near the stream, under a tall sycamore tree whose mottled bark had flaked off in large chunks. She pulled a worn wool blanket from the basket and Judith helped her spread it on the ground. The two men stood by with their hands pushed into the pockets of their overalls, self-consciously watching the women.

"Not much we can do to help, I reckon," offered Melvin, fishing for an affirmative response from his wife.

Judith knelt in the grass and finished smoothing out the edges of the blanket. She gazed off to the nearby stream where Grace and Andrew had instantly bolted, as soon as they had escaped the confines of the trolley. They were squealing at each other with delight and happiness as they splashed in the shallow water.

"Ezra, would you mind going over to the creek and just check on them," she said.

"Eh, you don't need to fret about that water, Judith. It's wide but it ain't no more than ankle deep. Hadn't been no rain lately either," Melvin advised.

"Come on, Melvin, let's just walk down there. I'd like to get a better look myself," he said, giving Melvin's ribs a slight nudge with his elbow.

"Okay," the older man readily agreed and they strode off toward the stream.

"Hey, Papa. You and Uncle Melvin get in the water with us! You can take your shoes off and wade in," Grace said as she kicked up a spray of water on Andrew, who just giggled and tried unsuccessfully to return the favor to his sister. She nimbly dodged his counter attack.

Ezra sat down on the grassy bank and Melvin squatted beside him and began chewing on a small twig he had picked up off the ground.

"Me and Melvin will just sit here a spell and watch y'all play. How's the water?" he called out to the children, now out in the middle of the stream.

"It feels good, Papa," yelled back Andrew.

"Is it cold?"

"A little bit," said Grace answered. "But not as cold as our river."

"What does she mean by *our river*?" Melvin asked.

"Nothing, just when we lived up in the mountains. There was a river on the property a ways down from the house," he replied in an almost pensive voice.

"A real honest to-god river or just a creek like this one?"

"Oh, no, it was a real river all right. Deep enough to swim in. Lots of rocks and boulders, and fish. It was beautiful. Still is, I reckon."

He offered no more and Melvin did not pursue it, probably more out of disinterest than anything else. They just watched the two children splashing around joyfully in the stream.

"Heard you might be moving up in the world," Melvin finally said, after a few minutes.

"Might be," answered Ezra dryly.

"Heard Bulldog's going put you on that filler job."

"I reckon."

"Well, you don't seem too pleased. Most people would be jumping up and down and hollering to move up to filler from a sweeper. I know I would. Hell, I did, come to think of it"

He shook his head and laughed at his friend. "I reckon I *am* happy about it. The money, I mean."

"You going to be able to get off the graveyard shift?"

"No, I reckon not. No time soon anyhow."

"Damn, I hate that for you. Having to put up with Queazy Tuttle for a second-hand. Nobody much likes him, do they?"

"I reckon not. At least not that I know of. He's not happy with what Mr. Matheson did."

"Whatcha mean, Ez?"

"Giving me the filler job. Queazy says I haven't been around long enough to be moved up."

"Ah, to hell with Queazy Tuttle and the horse he rode in on!" Melvin said as he chewed the twig in two. Ezra just smiled and looked out at his children.

***

Earline and Judith emptied the contents of the basket and arranged them neatly on the blanket. Earline had packed fried chicken, potato salad, biscuits with jam, and of course a thermos of sweet tea.

"Oh, Earline, this all looks and smells so good. I feel bad, though, we didn't bring anything. You've been so good to us."

"Nonsense, girl. I invited *y'all,* didn't I? You're our friends, sure, but like company today. There, I'll hear no more about it. Sneak me over a drumstick, will you?"

Both woman laughed as Judith passed over the plate of chicken to her neighbor.

"You think we ought to call them to eat now?" asked Earline, chomping on the drumstick and lustily licking her fingers.

"It's so nice here and the children are having fun. It's a whole new world for them, and for me. Let's just sit for a while," she said, her voice soft and natural. So they sat for a while in silence.

"You look like a woman who has something on her mind," Earline finally said, breaking the silence.

"Oh, I don't know. This Depression we keep hearing about. It sounds bad, but I don't understand it. Do you?"

"No, not exactly, but it don't sound too good, I admit. Maybe it's just happening to folks up North. I don't know. Lot of people up there out of work. Least ways that's what the paper says. They keep telling us at the mill not to worry about it. The overseers, I mean."

"I *do* worry," Judith said, her face somber with concern.

"Me, too, a little I guess. But don't seem much we can do about. Long as the mill keeps running we'll all be okay. Maybe it'll just pass us on by."

"Yes, maybe," said Judith, staring pensively at the cool green grass beneath her feet.

"You appear sad sometimes, Judith. Is anything wrong?"

"No."

"I'm sorry. Have trouble minding my own business sometimes. Been on the mill hill too long I guess."

"Oh, no, Earline. It's all right. It's just sometimes I get to thinking too much. That's all. It's just silly," Judith said, brushing back her black hair from her face.

"It's not silly if it's bothering you. You don't like it here maybe?" Earline was casual and soft with the question.

"We—I like it here. I mean I like a lot of things about it. Farming in the mountains is a hard life. Hard on a family. No, I like the things that come with living here. We never had running water. Plumbing to the kitchen. An indoor toilet. Things like that. It's easier here in a lot of ways."

"My, I can't imagine!" exclaimed Earline, and both women laughed briefly.

"But things have happened to us, to me. I shouldn't dwell on it, I know, but sometimes it just all comes flooding back over me. I can't seem to help it," she said, and then looked away as tears welled up in her deep dark eyes. Earline lightly touched her hand. They again sat in silence for a while.

"Ezra talks sometimes about going back to the mountains. Not as much as he used to, but he still thinks about it. But, Earline, we won't ever go back to farming up there. Have you ever heard of anyone quitting the mill and going back?"

"No, I can't say that I have. The mill gets a hold on you somehow and won't let go. Some folks, like y'all, say they're going back some day but they never do. It's like a dream, I guess," Earline said.

"You mean a pipe dream, don't you?"

"Yeah, I reckon I do. But they stay here. Then ten, twenty, thirty years pass. The mill becomes home and the dreams, well, they just seem to fade away somewhere," sighed Earline.

"But you know something, Earline?" she posed the question with intensity, looking hard into her neighbor's eyes, and before she could answer, continued, "I don't want to go back."

"But you're okay? Things will be all right."

"Yes, I'm fine. Like I said, it was all just silly woman stuff," she said with an ever so slight shiver.

"Why don't you go down and fetch those men of ours and your young 'uns, too. It's time we ate. I'll keep the flies off the food."

"All right."

Both men were stretched out on the grassy bank, dozing as she approached.

"Wake up you two. Wonder where the children are?" she asked, with a teasing gleam in her dark eyes. Ezra roused instantly and bolted upright, trying to find his bearing from the light sleep.

"What? Where?" he stammered. Melvin had not stirred. Then he saw them squatting on a sandbar a few yards downstream, scratching around in the sand with sticks.

"Oh," said he relieved and slightly embarrassed, "they're okay."

"*They* are," replied his wife lightly, still smiling down at her drowsy husband. "I've been keeping an eye on them myself. I don't know when I've seen them so happy. Are you hungry?"

"Yes, I reckon I am," he replied and sharply elbowed Melvin from his slumber. "Come on, Melvin. Time to eat."

He called and motioned for the children who reluctantly withdrew from their play and ran up the bank toward picnic. They all sat on the grass as Earline passed out the fare. No one spoke as they ate.

The children, still effervescent in the excitement of the adventure downtown and the park, squirmed and fretted and were soon released to scurry off across the meadow to the far end of the park, to rope swings and a see-saw.

"Y'all stay away from the creek just yet."

"We will, Mama," Grace yelled back over her shoulder without breaking stride.

"Boy-hidey, them two's sure a bundle of energy. Never seen kids so worked up," laughed Melvin.

"This is all something new to them, Melvin," she smiled, "for us, too."

"Damn, if I ain't full as a tick," said Melvin, rubbing his stomach as he stretched out in the grass on his back, and closed his eyes.

"I wish you wouldn't cuss so much, Melvin," his wife scolded lightly as she was placing things back into the basket.

"Ah, I don't mean nothing by it. I don't cuss around the kids, least I try not to. Do you think I do, Judith, cuss too much?" Melvin asked lazily, without opening his eyes or moving from his reclined position.

"Oh, I don't think so, Melvin."

"I guess we'll know when one of them lets one go," Ezra offered, and they all laughed. "That was a mighty good spread, Earline. Sure appreciate it. Everything, y'all inviting us and all."

You're welcome, Ez, but don't say nothing else about it. It's a treat for us just to be around the young 'uns. Y'all, too, of course," said

Earline as she finished repacking the basket. "Y'all want to go for a walk?"

"Nah, let's just stay here and rest awhile," replied a drowsy Melvin.

"Rest from what? You ain't struck a lick at a snake all day," Ezra jibed and grinned.

"So what's your point?"

"All right," Ezra said, pulling out and filling his pipe.

"We've been talking about the Depression," Judith quietly interjected.

"What Depression?" asked the immobile Melvin.

"Oh come on, Melvin, you know what she's talking about," said Earline.

"Yeah, I know. I was just kidding around. Ain't nothing to worry about. Not for folks like us, anyway," he said, almost seriously.

"What do you mean, 'folks like us'?" asked Ezra, earnestly.

"We Galway Mill people, ain't we? Allgood's people. Won't nothing happen to no Allgood mill. You can take that to the bank."

"What difference can that make to people like us?"

"Well, I'll tell you. It's like this. Most of these other highfalutin mill owners, they ain't as smart as the Allgood's, at least not as smart as old man Allgood is. See, they all own their mills all right, but that's about it. They have to buy their cotton, pay to get it ginned, haul it in, and then send off the cloth to be dyed or bleached or whatever they're going to do with it."

"Don't the Allgood's have to do the same thing?

"Nah, you see that's what I'm talking about."

Melvin, still stretched out in the grass, had raised himself on one elbow as he held forth.

"The Allgood's own it all. They own cotton fields down in the lower part of the state and in Georgia, maybe a few in Alabama too. It gets picked by Allgood field hands, and it gets shipped to the gin by Allgood's own trucks. Owns the gins, too. After we make the cloth, like here at the Galway mill, he sends it to one of the bleacheries he owns. Owns a dye house too."

"But he still has to deal with the Depression some way or another," argued Ezra.

"No he don't. You see, he don't have to depend on other people. It's like the Allgood's figured it all out, a long time ago. Like they got a rope around it. Us Galway lint-heads going be just fine."

Melvin resumed his reclining position in the grass, with his hands locked behind his head. He closed his eyes and began to nap.

Earline stood up and smoothed out the front of her cotton dress lightly with her hands.

"Come on, Judith, let's go walk and watch the children play."

"All right."

As the two women walked away, Ezra sat in the grass smoking his pipe and staring at the stream beyond. With a certain uneasiness, he noticed that a lot of people, families mostly, had come into the park and were all around him.

CHAPTER 19

Despite Melvin's exuberant optimism, The Great Depression came to the South, and to Corinth, and to the other Southern mill towns like it. These towns' very life-blood flowed from the many cotton mills that saturated them and the rest of the region. You either worked in a mill or you worked for a company or store that supplied the mill, or depended on the mill workers to spend their money there. It was, in an economic sense, a closed loop. There was no diversity of industry or commerce.

Many of the mill owners had been considered brilliant men by some, geniuses even, during the boom years of the twenties. But they were, at the onset, oblivious to the encroaching inevitable devastation of the coming economic monolith. They continued to produce without regard to market demand for their goods, or for the market's ability to buy. If one warp of cloth was good, two were better, and three still better than that. But like a powerful mindless tidal wave, The Great Depression became almost a living thing that would not be denied as it swept Corinth and the world before it.

***

Cates B. Allgood had slept little, not an unusual thing for him lately. After a futile struggle with his insomnia, he succumbed to it by pulling a scarlet cashmere robe around his ample body and ambling down the long hallway to the kitchen. Dawn was a ways off, so Mattie the black cook, was not yet about her business. He fumbled through the pantry and finally managed to find the coffee. He filled the Farberware percolator and plugged it in to a wall socket. The Allgood's had pretty much all of the modern appliances and any new gadgets that implied affluence and status - especially status. The coffee maker quivered slightly and wheezed as the water in it heated up. Soon it settled into a low rhythm as the darkening liquid bubbled up into the small glass globe atop the lid.

Before the percolating of the coffee was finished, he impatiently poured coffee from it into a china cup, and with it, walked back up the hall to his study. It was a small, cozy walnut- paneled room just off the main parlor. He opened the polished roll-top desk and sat down, looking at a sheaf of papers he had pulled from a drawer. He read as he sipped the coffee.

Each week by ten o'clock on Monday mornings, all of his managers were required to deliver to him what he referred to as production reports. These reports were what he was now poring over, mainly those from his largest mill, the Galway plant. The report was divided into three sections – weekly production, inventory, and shipments – all expressed in yards of finished cloth. The language of mill men. He could readily convert yards-of-cloth to dollars, in his head.

None of the numbers he read and absorbed pleased him. All indicated trouble. Serious trouble. He reluctantly realized that he had ignored the impact of the Depression on his business far too long, thinking smugly that his vertical organization was somehow insulated from it. Let the others squirm and panic and scurry around like scared mice, he had thought. And they had. He was not yet ready to panic nor would he be likely to do so, but clearly things were not good, and he knew that something must be done.

There was a soft tapping on the study door as thin rays of the early morning sun slanted through the part in the curtains onto the Oriental rug.

"Yes? Come in."

"Good morning, Mr. Cates," said a small, thin, black woman as she opened and stood in the door, not entering the room.

"Morning, Mattie. You up already?"

"Why, it's past six-thirty, Mr. Cates. You know I'm always up this time. Miss Winky, she up, too. She sent me to check on you. Say you got up early. I made fresh coffee. Don't see how you drink that stuff you made," she chuckled to herself, then clicked her tongue against her white front teeth.

"No. No thanks, Mattie. I'm going to get dressed and go down to the mill."

"You going to want some breakfast, ain't you? I'm fixing omelets and fried potatoes."

"No, I don't have time this morning," he said.

"Here now, Mr. Cates, you ain't been eating lately like you supposed to, like you used to eat. You better eat something," the cook admonished him, good-naturedly.

"I'll have a cup of coffee with Winky, if you say she's up."

"Oh, don't you worry yourself none about that. Miss Winky's been up awhile yet herself. You musta forgot. This the big day."

"Big day?" he asked as he shoved the papers back into the drawer and pulled down the desktop.

"You know, Miss Winky's trip. They all leaving today."

"Damn, I *did* forget. Forgot all about it."

"Yes, sir. She's all excited. She about giddy, I'd say. Going to It-lee, my word. Her and all them friends of hers. Your friends too, I reckon, Mr. Cates."

"Yeah, I guess so. But I believe it's France and not Italy, Mattie. I don't know why she would be so worked up over it though. Been over there a dozen times it seems like. Buying all that junk. Shipping it back here. Just winds up in attic or basement. Most of it anyway. Cost me a fortune," he muttered, grumbling, almost to himself. Mattie slipped quietly away closing the door behind her.

He hurriedly dressed and joined his wife in the dining room. It was much earlier than she was usually up and about, but she was charged with the excitement of her travel preparations. He listened with forced patience, frequently glancing at his watch, as she prattled on, non-stop, about the impending trip abroad. How they were taking the express train, the Southern Comet, to New York. From there, the boat to Marseilles. Hired chauffeured cars, three of them, to Paris. How lucky they were to have the train station in Corinth. The Louvre. La Rive Gauche. On and on she went, interminably.

When he thought he could stand it no longer, he took one last look at his watch, feigned surprise, absentmindedly gave her a cursory kiss on the cheek and excused himself, mumbling something about seeing her off at the station at five.

"Yes, dear, see that you do," she said, and continued her animated monologue with Mattie, who was replenishing the silver coffee urn at the sideboard. The black woman responded with an occasional "mmm-mmm" or "my, my" but her thoughts were somewhere far away.

***

Rufus Jordan always arrived at his mill office before seven each morning, six days a week. He liked to be there at shift change and to poke around to see what had been going on during the previous second and midnight shifts He seldom went into the mill itself. There were always problems.

He had been Superintendent of the Galway mill for nearly twenty years and considered himself, in every respect, a company man. He was the one who prepared the weekly production reports for Mr. Allgood, for which he had seldom received feedback or a response.

Sometimes he wondered if they were ever actually read. But *he* read them and he knew things were not looking good. Production was steady all right, but inventories were bulging, shipments were way down—historically low. The men wearing the green eyeshades and sleeve garters in accounting were wary. Starting to point out cash flow problems, high expenses, especially labor costs. He knew this could not go on, even at an Allgood mill. But he had not tried to hide or cover up anything, or make excuses. He just gave Allgood the facts and figures every week and waited. But nothing ever changed.

He had just come in from the yard and sat down at his desk when his phone rang. Unusual, this early in the morning. He reached for the phone.

"Galway Mill," he said gruffly.

"Rufus. That you?" the voice crackled over the line. Jordan stiffened noticeably and slid his chair closer to the desk.

"Why, yes, Mr. Allgood, it's me.

"Where's Miss Wilcox?" asked Allgood.

"Not time for her. She doesn't come in this early. Be here around eight. Actually, exactly at eight. Set my watch by her coming through the door," Jordan replied, relaxing somewhat.

"Oh, yes. I suppose it is rather early. Didn't realize."

"Something I can do for you, Mr. Allgood." A phone call from Allgood was not a usual thing, and it was never social, especially this early in the morning.

"Yes, I want to get together this morning. First thing."

"All right." Jordan straightened himself in his chair.

"I'm calling from the drug store. Stopped by to get a Bromo. Stomach's bothering me. Indigestion or something. I don't know. I'll be at the mill in ten minutes."

"What's up? Don't recall having you at the mill early on a morning."

"Hell, it's my mill isn't it? I figure I can stop by anytime I want to." Allgood was irritated and spoke sharply. "Matter of fact, it appears I might be needing to spend more time there!"

Jordan expelled a deep breath. "Like you said, it's your mill. Love to have you."

"Drop the hogwash, Rufus. Look, I want you to get the boys together. Accounting, Charlie Matheson, Harley Jacobs if you can find him, and he's sober."

"So we're having a meeting?"

"Yes, a meeting. You been looking at the numbers lately?"

"Well, yes. I *do* compile the weekly reports."

"Okay. I'll see you in a few minutes," Allgood said, and hung up the phone.

In precisely ten minutes Allgood's roaring Packard turned off Galway Avenue and pulled to an abrupt stop on the grassy lawn beside the mill office. Jordan met him at the door and led the way back to his office. Allgood slumped onto the leather couch across the small room from Jordan's desk.

"Miss Wilcox will fix us some coffee. She'll be here in fifteen minutes."

Jordan knew that Miss Wilcox, who did not live in the mill village, would see the parked Packard when she got off the trolley, and would waste no time acknowledging Allgood's presence, and attending to him.

"Pardon me, Rufus, but this isn't a social call. Where are the others?"

"They're on the way over. I caught Bulldog going in the plant. He'll be here shortly. So will Buford."

As he was speaking, two men entered the mill office and walked briskly back to Jordan's office. The door had been left open.

"Good morning, Mr. Allgood. Good to see you," said Buford Kelly, the chief accountant for the Galway plant. His nervousness was betrayed by the red blotches glowing against the pale whiteness of his face. Under one arm he carried a worn leather portfolio stuffed with papers, which he almost dropped as Jordan motioned for him and Matheson to take a seat. To him, Cates B. Allgood was a great man; Buford Kelly was not accustomed to being in the presence of greatness.

"Good morning, gentleman," Allgood nodded, speaking as one does to those in the realm over which he exercises the power of life and death. Or at least of continued employment.

"Where is Harley Jacobs?" asked Allgood. The other men exchanged knowing side-glances. Jordan cleared his throat.

"I believe he's on the road, Mr. Allgood," Jordan offered. "Down at the state house. They're putting that new state prison contract out for bid later today. Sure like to get it."

"We'll get it, all right, but it will be because I'm going dove hunting with the Governor next month. It won't be because of anything Jacobs' done. I'll warrant you that," Allgood said, and the subject was closed. "Let's get down to business, shall we, gentlemen?"

He stood up, straightened his silk tie, pulled down the edge of his vest. For a moment or two he paced the floor, his head lowered and seemingly oblivious to the presence of the other men in the room. Then in a measured monotone, replete with the soft-drawn southern vowels of his class, he offered his version of the causes of the Great Depression in which, he assured them, they were currently in the middle. He then launched into a soliloquy about the history of the Allgood empire, alluding only obliquely to the near-aristocracy of his family and the importance of the Allgood name.

Bulldog Matheson scraped grime from his underneath his fingernails with the edge of the nail of his forefinger on the opposite hand. He wished he could take out his pocket-knife to do the job properly. Although he did not rock back in his chair, he was tempted to do so several times. Jordan was pulled up close behind his desk on which his crossed forearms rested. He kept his eyes on Allgood as he paced, and held forth. Buford Kelly sat in a straight-back chair clutching his papers, enthralled, almost mesmerized by the speech and mannerisms of the man before him.

"And, gentleman, that brings me to the point," Allgood finally said. "I need ideas. Things are bad! You know it, I know it. Oh, I don't think we're going under or anything like that. Not on my watch. But we've got to stop the bleeding. We're hemorrhaging cash."

He glanced sharply and inexplicably at Kelly, and then looked away.

"Now, I'm not blaming anyone. No one in this room anyway. Maybe myself some. I get the numbers every week. I just kept thinking we were going to pull out of it. And we will! But we have got to get through these tough times. It won't be easy." With this, Allgood took a deep breath and sat back down on the couch, loosening his tie.

There was an awkward silence, then Jordan said, "What do you have in mind?"

"We've got to cut costs. Simple as that," came the immediate response from the great mill owner, flat and passionless.

The other men in the room knew that he was not just suggesting a solution. An edict had just been delivered from on high.

"It's true," volunteered Kelly to no one in particular, as he shuffled through his papers. "We are experiencing negative cash flow."

Jordan cleared his throat. "Most of the other mills around here have already laid off workers. Some already gone to stretch-outs."

"Precisely," said Allgood. Matheson stopped cleaning his nails and looked hard at Jordan.

"We've never had a layoff at Galway."

"That's because we never had to. But like I said, gentlemen, things are dire and apt to get worse before they improve."

"Okay, say we lay people off. When? How many and for how long?"

"Mr. Kelly, if we let ten percent of the workers go, what would the savings be?" Allgood addressed the accountant, who immediately pulled a mechanical pencil from his shirt pocket and began scratching calculations on a piece of paper.

After a brief time, Kelly replied, proud of himself for coming up with the numbers so quickly.

"I would say approximately sixty-five hundred a month." Allgood frowned. Kelly shifted uneasily in his chair, with a look of dejection.

"Twenty percent? I suppose that would be near thirteen thousand," Allgood pressed, and Kelly again began scribbling.

"Damn, Mr. Allgood, that's a lot of people."

"Yes, and a lot of money," responded Allgood to Jordan's protest.

"Yes, at least that much," said Kelly, almost excitedly, as he pushed the paper across the desk to Jordan.

"All right, here's the plan, Rufus," said Allgood, leaning forward toward the Superintendent. "Call a meeting of all your supervisors and overseers, second-hands too, on Friday and make the announcement. Effective Monday, fifteen percent of those working for wages will be let go, indefinitely. We're going to stretch-outs in spinning and weaving. Anybody doesn't like it can quit. And I won't tolerate grumbling or unrest. You decide who goes and who stays, Rufus."

"Okay," said Jordan without emotion. "Is that it?"

"Yes, for right now. We'll see how things go. However, you need to keep in mind that if business continues to go south we'll be forced to take additional measures."

"Such as?"

"We may have to pay in script for a while. Labor's where the costs are."

Kelly smiled in agreement. Charlie Matheson bit his lower lip and looked out the window of the office at the shiny Packard coupe.

"Script!" a surprised Jordan exclaimed.

"Sure, if we have to. I wouldn't want to do it, but they can get everything they need from the Company Store. They have electricity and running water. Hell, man, we practically give them the houses they live for free as it is."

Allgood stood up, cinched up the knot of his tie, and donned his fedora. Jordan and Kelly also rose from their seats. Matheson did not move.

"I notice, Mr. Matheson, you haven't said much. Nothing at all, as a matter of fact. Would you mind letting us all in on what you're thinking?" Allgood asked, as he looked down at Matheson sitting there.

"Well, sir, I'm thinking you better have your pal, the Governor, send in the National Guard to protect you and Rufus here after Monday," Matheson quipped, not realizing how accurately he may have been predicting events to come. No one laughed. All color left the face of Buford Kelly.

"Maybe so, but I'm not a politician and I'm not in a popularity contest. My aim is to keep operating, and operating at a profit," Allgood shot back at Matheson. "On second thought, Rufus, I would suggest that you lay off the women first, as you are able to do so. And the younger people. I never liked having these children in the mill anyway. Any worker doesn't have a family to feed goes on the list, too. That's about as fair as I can make it."

"Sir, yes. That seems fair enough," replied Jordan. He did not look at Matheson.

Without any additional formality, Allgood left the building and sped away in the Packard, the spinning rear tires leaving deep ruts in the soft grass of the mill office yard.

***

Two of the nastiest and more dehumanizing practices that mill owners embraced during the Depression in the South were the issuance of company script, instead of money for wages, and the implementation of the stretch-out.

Script could only be redeemed, that is, exchanged for goods, at the Company Store which was owned, as the name implies, by the Company. The Company Store was much like a general store or a small department store. It stocked and sold essentials including food, but only as canned goods, rarely anything fresh. The workers could get by, to be sure. They had no choice. Items at the Company Store were always marked up; nothing was sold at cost. The Company Store was a profit center.

Once the cotton mills were deep into the Great Depression, many plants instituted the loathsome stretch-out. To the owners, this practice, naturally despised by the workers, seemed a perfectly logical solution. Although the number of employees had been reduced, the number of looms was the same, and they must be kept running at all costs.

First, after the layoffs, wages were reduced or piece-work requirements increased. Therefore, in order to maintain production, additional machines were assigned to each weaver. A weaver who was previously making six dollars a day now found himself making four-fifty. Where he had been responsible for keeping twenty looms running, now he might have thirty or thirty-five. Some mills as much as doubled the workload.

For the already hard-pressed textile worker, it was an almost untenable situation, met with the bitterness and anger that inevitably accompanies injustice. Unrest and dissension began to grow among the workers in the mill villages. At first, only in their minds, then within families and between friends, as they talked around the kitchen table, and finally on the mill floor itself. The Great Provider—*the Man*, the mill owner—began to be regarded as an avaricious despot with little or no feeling for his employees. They began to see the heretofore thinly-veiled charade. You come down from the mountains or in from the countryside, come in from the farms and work for me. I will take care of you. I will provide you with jobs, houses, churches, stores, doctors—all the things you need. You will enjoy a new kind of happiness. A life without worry. I only ask of you two things. Be a good worker and don't think too much. That's all. We shall then get along just fine.

But as the Depression engulfed America and the world, many of the cotton mill workers began to see the true nature of the relationship between them and *the Man*. They were important only to the level that they could produce cloth. They were valued as human beings only to the extent that allowed the owner to increase his wealth and maintain the socially mandated status quo. Nothing more. They had tricked themselves into believing that they existed in a vague self-contained bliss, albeit at the whim of the mill, when in reality theirs was a life of little more than obtuse servitude.

***

Superintendent Rufus Jordan made the changes that the Cates B. Allgood had directed. He did it efficiently, devoid of emotion. It must be remembered that he was a company man, and the company would endure.

CHAPTER 20

Ezra kept his job although Queazy had placed his name on the layoff list. As a matter of fact, it was the first name on the list that he handed to his boss. Matheson had taken the lined sheet of paper from the second-hand and thoughtfully scanned the column of neatly printed names. He then twisted the paper into a tightly spiraled fuse, took a match to it, and lit his cold stub of a cigar as it flared into a small flame. He exhaled a cloud of smoke into Queazy's puzzled, scrunched-up face.

"What'd you go and do that for? That's my list for the third-shift layoffs."

Matheson took a deep, exasperated breath.

"Goddamn it, Queazy, why can't you just do what I tell you for once? You just want to get rid of the people on your shift you don't like. I gave you the priority. You then go and put Burke's name at the top."

"Well, he ain't been here that long. I thought you'd want to …"

"I don't give a tinker's damn what you thought. He's the best filler you've got. Probably the best in the mill. Besides, he's got a wife and kids. We're not letting Burke go," said Matheson evenly, as he gently tapped ashes into the ashtray on his desk. Queazy was sullen and quiet as he continued.

"Anyway, I heard he can fix looms too. Is that right?" Queazy had folded his arms was looking down at the floor. He did not answer. Matheson continued.

"Okay, let me make sure I got this right. You got a man who comes to work every day and does his job, and does it well. When he gets caught up, he learns to fix looms on his own time. Well?"

"Yeah."

"You're short of people due to the layoffs and you got a man, who not only is doing his job, but helping out the loom fixers. And you're firing him. Is that right?"

"I guess so," mumbled Queazy, as he slumped further in the chair.

"That's pretty stupid, Queazy."

"You calling me stupid?"

"I'm not calling you anything. What do you think?"

"All right, I'm stupid," Queasy looked down again at the bare floor and made a sucking sound with his teeth. "Whatever you say, Mr. Matheson," he inserted, with mild sarcasm.

"Look, Queasy, I hate this crap laying off people. We got good people in the weave room. Always have. But I don't have a choice and I don't need you making it any harder than it already is. Now you get me another list together. One that makes sense, by the rules I gave you. And you best keep in mind that second-hands ain't above being let go either. Get back here with it in an hour."

Matheson propped his elbows on the desk in front of him and grasped one raised meaty fist with the other hand. Resting his chin on them, he thought that he did not much like this job anymore. In truth, he had never liked it much. He was not a company man. At least not in the sense that his boss, Rufus Jordan, was. They did not own him. Or did they?

He knew what the layoffs meant. The people without work would be reduced to depending on neighbors and friends. In their pride, they would see such help as handouts. But the mill village was a close-knit entity, like a family in some ways. They would help each other as they were able. The churches could usually be depended on. Most would make it, he tried to convince himself, and some would just move on. To where and to what, he could not answer.

***

Ezra climbed the stairs to the weave room floor and entered the low, cavernous room. He would never get used to the din, the vibration, and the floating ubiquitous lint, but he did not think of it much anymore. It did not matter. He knew that in many ways his life was better now. Things were easier on Judith, and that meant everything. He had seen the change in her and this made him happy. Not that she had ever complained during their life in the hills, trying to wrench a living from spent, rocky soil, but he knew it had been difficult for her. They now had conveniences beyond anything they had ever dreamed, or even thought much about, when he was farming in the mountains. The children were in school and doing well. There was finally enough money for some of the things they needed. He best forget about farming and the misty blue mountains. That was all in the past and there it would remain. It was not a dream anymore, only a memory.

He hung his coat on a wall peg beside the waterhouse and pulled the bobbin cart from its place beside the wall, where his second-shift counterpart had left it. The filler job was not much better than that of sweeper, just paid a little more. Sweeping had been a mindless endeavor, requiring little or no innate skill, certainly not intelligence. Each night he had pulled the heavy push broom from the tool locker and began guiding it steadily down the long aisles between the throbbing, clanking looms, seemingly without effort. The stiff black bristles of the broom soon built up a thick row of curled gray lint before it. He would scoop it up into one of the large metal bins scattered throughout the floor and continue his sweeping. He would empty the bins as they filled.

But the job had allowed him to quickly get to know the weavers and loom fixers who worked in his section of the weave room, and most liked him right off. Some of them had at first thought him aloof and perhaps somewhat backward. A frequent response to those not accustomed to new, or different people, in their midst. But they soon learned that he had about him a natural reserve and a quiet manner. But he also possessed a certain confidence that was not, at first, readily apparent. Past these things, they discovered he was a friendly, if not an outgoing, person. With his innate serious bent, they sensed a man who would say something when he had something to say, and a man who could be trusted.

To himself and those close to him, he too had changed. Almost imperceptibly at first. He blamed himself for what had happened. He had failed at farming. And against all his nature, had accumulated debt. Tanner's widow told him to forget what he owed; she did not need it. Her husband had died a rich man, at least by mountains standards. But each month he sent her money against the balance. It was part of his redemption, if there was any to be had.

He discovered that there were some things about the mill work that he liked. He had learned the sweeper job quickly, of course, and often got caught-up in his section of the weave room. With nothing to do for short periods of time, he would stand over the loom fixers and observe them closely as they repaired and maintained the looms to keep them running. As a farmer, mechanical skill had been a survival necessity. He liked working with his hands, always had. He easily picked up the workings of the looms and had actually showed some of the fixers better ways to repair the machinery.

The time came when he could soon fix a loom as good as any fixer on the floor. His natural aptitude for mechanics was apparent, and several of the fixers would occasionally ask for his help if they got behind in their work. With the stretch-outs, many of the loom fixers found it extremely difficult, if not impossible, to keep up with the allotted looms in their sections. His work load too, had been increased, but he was still able to get caught up some nights and help the fixers. Queazy Tuttle, the second-hand, occasionally observed this, and he did not like it.

CHAPTER 21

He turned onto his back and sleepily opened his eyes. The room was dark, pitch black. Judith had recently bought remnants of heavy black cloth from the Company Store and sewn them into curtains for the two windows in the bedroom. Working nights, it was often a struggle to sleep in the daytime, certainly for someone who for so many years had measured his workday by the rhythm of the sun's rising and setting. But the thick curtains blocked out the light and after initial restlessness, he was usually able to drift off to sleep.

He heard muffled sounds from the kitchen. The comforting and familiar aroma of food on the stove wafted into the room on the still dark air. She was cooking supper. He pushed back the covers and lifted himself slowly to sit on the side of the bed. Will I ever get use to this upside- down world of working at night and sleeping day, he wondered. No, he would not, he decided as he fumbled for the thin braided string that hung from the unshaded bulb above the bed. Light exploded into the room. He gradually eased the squint of his eyes as they adjusted to the glare.

After splashing cold water on his face at the bathroom sink, he ran his fingers through his dark hair. He examined his reflection for a brief moment in the small mirror over the sink, then pulled on the faded, clean overalls she had folded and placed on the low chest at the foot of the bed.

"Smells mighty good in here," he said smiling, as he entered the kitchen.

She was at the stove frying salmon patties.

"How did you sleep? she asked, without turning from her work at the stove.

"Good. Good enough, anyway. It's dark as a cave in there now with those curtains."

"I thought the milk truck might have woken you. He's bad about clanging the empty bottles."

"Didn't hear a thing. I reckon I was pretty much dead to the world. Where are those young 'uns?"

"They're in the front room doing their homework."

She had earlier closed the door from the kitchen to the front room so they would not disturb their sleeping father. The front room of the house would have, at one time, been called the parlor or sitting room, but most of the mill folks referred to it as the living room. It was an odd, uncomfortable name for a room to her, so she just referred to it as the front room.

"I'm mighty proud of their schooling. That's one good thing we get from the mill," he said thoughtfully, as his wife placed a mug of steaming coffee on the table as he sat down. "Better they be separated by grades instead of everybody being in just one room, like the school in Waverley."

"Yes, it's better here. Miss Weston sent a note home today. They're going to move Grace up to the third grade," she said matter of factly, but with a noticeable trace of pride in her soft voice.

"When?"

"Tomorrow."

"Well, that sounds right. Grace is smart as a whip. Always has been. Just fooled them at first I reckon, being as little as she is," he said, sipping the coffee.

"She's growing," Judith inserted quickly.

"I know she is, and she looks so much like you. I reckon I can look at you and see what Grace will look like. Two prettiest girls I know," he said without turning toward his wife, but stealing a glance of her from the corner of his eye.

"Well, she's sure pretty enough," she said. A wistful smile crossed her lips as she felt a slight, but pleasant warmth, move up from her body to her face.

"I don't get to see them as much as I used to. I mean when we..."

"When we lived on the farm," she said, finishing his statement.

"Yes."

"You work hard. You're a good father. They adore you. They're fine. They like it here."

"All right."

The two children heard their parents' voices and burst through the door to greet their father. Each had sheets of paper on which they had been doing their school work—Andrew his ABCs printed *almost* neatly on the three-lined paper and Grace with sentences, the subject and verb underlined without error. After looking over and properly praising each of them for their completed assignments, the family all took their places at the table and ate the fried salmon patties with grits.

After supper he helped his wife clear the table and stack the plates beside the sink. He watched her momentarily, as if he was remembering something, as she twisted the faucet and hot water poured into the sink, quickly filling it. He turned and wiped the oil cloth tablecloth with a damp rag and then pulled his pipe from his pocket.

"I reckon I'll go out and sit on the front porch for a spell. You coming?" he asked as he stuffed tobacco tightly into the briar bowl of his pipe.

"Melvin came by earlier and left his newspaper."

"It kind of bothers me some. Him paying for the paper, then bringing it over here when he's done with it. I told him I appreciated it, but that he oughtn't do it."

"He wants to do it," she said.

"I know, but I wish he wouldn't."

"He said he wanted to talk to you when you got up. I almost forgot. If you felt like it, he said."

"Did he say what about?"

"No."

"It's already dark, but reckon I'll go over there and see what he wants. Nothing probably, just wants to chew the fat."

"Maybe," she said.

"I won't be long. I want to see the children before they go to bed," he said as he took his hat from a wall peg. He stepped up close behind her and embraced her as she stood at the sink. She turned her face to him and brushed his lips with a kiss.

Melvin was dozing, cradled in the worn, over-stuffed fabric chair beside the radio. On nights when the weather was especially clear, he could pick up the *Amos and Andy Show* on WMAQ out of Chicago. Everyone with a radio tuned in. It was a pretty funny show, they all agreed, but Melvin was impatiently waiting for the day when baseball would be played at night and broadcast over the air. It was coming they said, but no one seemed to know when.

Amidst the cracking and static of the speaker, he was roused from his nap by the loud tapping at the front door.

"Just a minute, be right there," he said loudly as he shaded his eyes from the glare of the floor lamp, and fumbled around the floor for his shoes.

"Someone here, Melvin?" Earline called sleepily from the bedroom.

"I'll see. Go back to bed."

Melvin opened the door to find Ezra standing there.

"You asleep already, Melvin?"

"Nah, just dropped off listening to the radio."

"Judith said you wanted to talk. If it's too late, I can come by tomorrow."

"Oh, no, it's fine," said Melvin, his voice dropping to a whisper as he stepped out onto the porch, closing the door behind him. "It's a pretty night. Mind if we sit out here?"

"All right."

Melvin sat down in one of the wooden rockers on the porch. Ezra leaned against the rail of the porch bannister facing him, his arms folded across his chest. Melvin lit a cigarette and began.

"I guess you're fixin' to go to work, heh?"

"I reckon so."

"Third-shift's tough, ain't it?"

"I try not to think about it much."

"Yeah, right. I worked it a few years when I first hired on at the mill. Hated it. Damn near killed me, and I wasn't married then neither."

"Some folks like it," offered Ezra.

"Yeah, at least you don't have to worry about boss men and overseers being everywhere looking over your shoulder, like we do on the first shift."

"I reckon so," Ezra said, shifting his weight on the rail and thrusting his hands into his pockets.

"What do think about these stretch-outs, Ez?"

"I don't like them any better than anybody else does, I reckon. Don't see that there's much we can do about it though."

"It's killing me; I don't mind telling you. I ain't getting no younger, you know. I been working the same twenty looms for years. Making damn good cloth, too. That first stretch-out they bumped me up to thirty and we're going to thirty-five next week. I don't see how I can keep up with thirty-five." The tip of Melvin's cigarette glowed bright red in the dark as he inhaled.

"It's hard on everybody right now. Just got to do the best we can, I reckon."

"I reckon. But it must be hell on you, too. Trying to keep up filling them bobbins. What you got now?"

"They gave me another bank of looms. Maybe two-hundred now."

"Damn, Ez, two hundred! How you doing with it? I mean can you keep up?"

"Yeah, I'm keeping up now, but I don't know if I can if they put any more on me. The bad part is I can't get caught up enough to have time to tinker with the looms."

"Yeah, I heard you were helping out the loom fixers. Is that what you want to do, be a loom fixer?

"Maybe so. Fixing things comes right natural to me."

"That son of bitch Queazy mind you doing it?"

"I don't know that he knows about it. I don't see him on the floor much lately.

"I hear he's been going down to the spinning floor, sniffing around that new girl. They say she's a real looker. Ain't seen her yet myself. And old Queazy uglier than a dog's butt." Melvin laughed, but Ezra did not respond.

"Look, Melvin, it's good talking to you but I better get on back to the house. I want to see the young 'uns before they go to bed," he said, pushing himself erect off the rail.

Melvin took a deep draw from the cigarette and flicked the butt out into the dirt yard. The ash, caressed by a light breeze, suddenly brightened into an ember, then died away.

"I just wanted to ask you something, Ezra." Melvin leaned forward in the chair. He could just make out the silhouette of his neighbor against the dark sky.

"All right."

"Are you going to the meeting?"

"What meeting?"

"*The* meeting. The one at Tucker's Sunday night. Surely to hell you know about it."

"I didn't until now."

"Damn, Ezra, don't you ever talk to anybody at on the floor?"

"Not much."

"Well, I do. We've had about all we can take. Layoffs, now these goddam stretch-outs. Where's it going to end? I've heard we're going to get wages cut too."

"I *did* hear it that. Might be just a rumor though."

"Yeah, and it might not be. Look, Ezra, we got to stand up for ourselves. The Allgood's don't give a tinker's damn about us. Not as long as we keep making cloth and they keep making money."

"Seems like you're looking at the Allgood's different these days."

"Yeah, I reckon I am."

Hidden in the darkness, Melvin's face was flushed with emotion. His fingernails dug into the wooden armrests of the chair.

"Is that what the meeting's about?"

"Yes."

"I don't see what good can come of it, Melvin."

"You don't now, but you will. That is, if we all stick together. Look, Ez, there's some organizers in town. From up North and they know what they're doing. Mean sons of bitches though. Some of the boys been talking with them. They're the ones holding the meeting."

"Organizers?" he asked, his voice flat in the darkness.

"Hell, yes, organizers! union men. They're going to help us deal with the owners. All the lint-heads in Corinth will get help. We need help, Ez. If we all pull together, the owners won't have a choice. It's the only way they'll understand we mean business."

Melvin had risen from the rocker and was close to Ezra's face.

"I don't know, Melvin. Unions? I don't know."

"Just come to the meeting. Listen to these boys. Hear what that got to say. They know what they're doing, I tell you."

Ezra stepped away and turned toward the porch step.

"I've got to go, Melvin. It's getting late." He descended the steps and looked back up at the figure on the porch. "Night, Melvin."

"You'll come to the meeting won't you, Ez?"

"No, Melvin, I don't think I will," came the soft, but firm answer, as he disappeared into the night.

CHAPTER 22

The gray clouds were tinged with a trace of pink, as a reluctant dawn spread over the city and the rolling hills surrounding it. The train had already noticeably slowed when the conductor came into the coach car. He was sleepy and irritable as he switched on the dim interior lights and brushed flakes of dandruff off the shoulder of the black coat of his uniform.

Most of the eight or ten passengers in the car began to rouse from their naps. Some wiped the sleep from their eyes with the knuckles of tight fists. Others just moved about in their seats, trying to stretch away the stiffness incurred after the long period of confined riding.

In the far left corner of the car were two men, both slumped in their seat, arms folded across their chests, with hats pulled down across their faces. They had not stirred.

The conductor spoke loudly.

"Pulling into the burg of Corinth,_____. Short stop. Nothing's open in the depot anyhow. Can take a quick stretch on the platform if you've a mind to."

There was a low groan from some of the passengers, but most just shifted in their seats in attempts to attain at least some degree of comfort and go back to sleep. The conductor walked backed to where the two men dozed. He lightly tapped the back of the seat of the one on the aisle.

"Rise and shine, gents. We're pulling into your stop, Corinth."

The two men had boarded the train in New York City seventeen hours earlier, and were the only two passengers ticketed for Corinth. The train entered the limits of the rail yard and crawled to a stop at the platform of the station.

"Wake up, Ski. We're here," said the small swarthy man in the aisle seat, as he removed his flat cap. He combed back his thick curly hair with fine, almost feminine fingers. Then he stroked his goatee. Once awake, he appeared to be very animated. His sleepy companion was a much larger man, heavily built, having a Slavic appearance. Beneath his well-worn, brown fedora, his sandy-colored hair was close-cropped.

The smaller man was already in the aisle pulling two worn leather suitcases from the rack above the seats.

"Let's go, Ski. We got to get going," he spoke with a thick Northern accent, New England, North Boston maybe.

"Okay, already. Damn back hurts. Hate trains."

The big man slid across the seat and stood in the aisle beside his companion. Each took a suitcase, strode unsteadily down the aisle of the car, and stepped down from the train onto the deserted station platform.

"Geez, Leon, it's cold as hell. I thought it was supposed to be warm down here. Cloudy, too," Ski grumbled, looking around and turning up the collar of his corduroy coat.

"It's not exactly the tropics, you know. Let's get a cab and find the joint. Should be just in time for breakfast. I'm starved."

"Okay."

The two men left the station and walked out on to the street as a milk truck rattled by and a few shadowy pedestrians shuffled along the sidewalk. Streetlights still twinkled in the grayness of the coming day.

"That a taxi parked down the street there?" asked Leon, pointing to a dingy yellow sedan parked at the curb.

"Looks like it. Let's go."

The dozing cab driver, startled, shot upright when the man tapped on the window with the large gold ring he wore on his middle finger. The driver rolled down the window.

"Scared hell out of me. I guess I dozed off a little. Need a ride?"

"Sure do, chief. Know your way around town?"

"Well, I ort to, seeing as I was born and raised here."

The driver opened the car door as the two men stepped back. "Here, give me those suitcases. I'll put 'em in the trunk. Door's not locked, y'all get in the back," the driver drawled.

The two men glanced at each other and got into the car.

"Where to, downtown?" asked the driver, now wide awake, as he pressed the ignition pedal to start the motor. Leon, the smaller man, pulled a small leather notebook from his breast pocket.

"201 East Seventh Street. Do you know it?"

"Well, yes and no. Sounds like a mill hill street," the driver said to the face framed in his rear-view mirror.

"A mill hill?"

"Yeah, you know, a mill village. Problem is we got slew of 'em around here. Would you happen to know which one you got the address to?"

"It's near Galway Mill. The big mill."

"Oh, sure thing. Know exactly where it is. They say it's the biggest cotton mill in the world. In the world, mind you. Right here in little old Corinth,_____. I don't actually know if it is or not. Might just be them big shots at the Rotary Club talking, you know, so who knows?"

Neither man in the backseat responded. Then Leon leaned up toward the driver.

"Happen to know where Tucker's Pool Hall is, chief?"

"Sure. Jimmy Tucker's place. But it's in town, back the other way. I used to hang out there a lot. Got married, so my pool shootin' days is over," the driver snickered.

"Mind driving by it, show us where it is?"

"Sure," said the driver as he took his foot off the accelerator, "but he ain't going be open this early. Generally, opens about ten."

"That's okay. We just want to get an idea of where it is."

As the car slowed, the driver skillfully executed a U-turn on the empty street.

"Say, you guys ain't pool pros, are you?" the driver asked, with more than a tinge of curiosity.

"No, we just want to see the place."

After driving several blocks the cab slowed and turned down a side street. On the sidewalk, a few men, haggard and dark, shuffled along, hardly noticing the taxi. The driver pulled the car to the curb in front of a low, dingy-brown building. A thick, dark-green curtain was pulled across the large plate-glass window on which was painted in large neat gold letters, *Tucker's Pool Hall*. The house-rules underneath this lettering read like bullet points—*No Cussing, No Gambling, No Fighting, Shirts & Shoes Required, Whites Only*.

"Well, fellers, that's it. Ain't much to look at from the street but they got some mighty fine tables. Keeps 'em leveled too."

The two men in the back seat looked at each other and nodded, as if agreeing that the pool hall was the right place.

"Okay, thanks. We can get on now," said Leon.

The driver shrugged and pulled away from the curb and drove toward Galway Mill. His passengers rode in silence until he turned off Galway Avenue onto East Seventh Street. At the next block he pulled to the curb and stopped the car at 201, Mrs. Aintry's boarding house.

The driver pulled the suitcases from the trunk of the cab, and set them down on the sidewalk. He then leaned against the open door of the cab.

"Okay, boys, here you are."

Leon paid the driver with bills he slipped out of a thick, leather wallet and joined the Slav on the sidewalk. Both men stood staring at the rambling, white two-story house. Leon checked the address written in the small notebook he had taken from his coat pocket.

"201 East Seventh Street. This is it all right," he assured his companion, and himself.

"Don't look like much. I just hope it's not a flophouse."

"No, it's a boarding house. Looks okay. Anyway, they probably don't have flophouses down here. Nabors says it's an okay place. Clean rooms, down-home cooking and all that. He set it up for us."

"Who's this Nabors guy anyhow?" asked Ski.

"He's the local man. Mill worker. He sounded okay on the phone. He set things up for us down here," said Leon.

"I just hope he don't get in the way."

They stepped onto the porch and the big man knocked on the door. Mrs. Aintry, slightly irritated by interruption to her work, shuffled to the door and pulled it open and looked up at the two men.

"Morning, boys," she said, with no more than her usual affability, smoothing her apron. Her mouth was caved in with her lips folded back on her gums. She had not yet gotten around to putting in her dentures this morning.

"Good morning," said both men in unison.

She gave them a quick once-over. "You must be them two I'm supposed to be holding rooms for. Eugene Nabors a friend of yours?"

"An acquaintance," replied Leon.

"An acquaintance, eh? Come by here and told me y'all were coming into town. I got you a room a piece. Just had a renter move out."

"Perfect," said Leon. He glanced at Ski.

"A Mr. Deminici and a Mr. Dobinsky, he said you were. With those names I 'spect you ain't from around here?" She wiped her face with her apron. "Got to excuse me. I'm sweating like a field hand. Gets hot back in the kitchen. I'm Mrs. Aintry. Martha Aintry to be exact, but most folks just call me Mrs. Aintry. This here's my place."

"The rooms, Mrs. Aintry?" asked Leon, attempting not quite successfully to suppress his impatience.

"Look, boys, it's this way," she said, realizing these men, Northerners—Yankees, would not object to her directness. And she could be direct. "You're both welcome to board here. For as long as you pay on time and there ain't no trouble, that is. Eugene's a good man. I knowed him most of his life and he vouched for you, both of you. But there's a lot of things going on around here 'bouts. Troubles. I mean with the mills. I reckon y'all come down here for *something*." It was more a question than a statement.

"Were not exactly looking for anything, but we plan to help with the mills. The mill workers, I mean." Leon said, his accent sharp and clipped.

"Help with the mills, eh? I declare, something's got to give. The way the people's being treated. I know jobs is hard to find nowadays but it ain't right what they doing."

"You mean at the mills?" asked Dobinsky. Leon shot him a look.

"Yes, but I ain't blaming the managers much. They're just doing what they got to do to hold on to their own jobs. It's the owners is what's driving it."

"I couldn't agree more," smiled Leon.

"You boys Reds?" she asked bluntly.

"No, we're not communists."

"Well, they say there's some Reds mixed up in some of this organizing. I figure you two connected some way with organizing.

"That's true enough, Mrs. Aintry, we are. But we're not, as you say, Reds. We're just going to help the mill workers get what the law says they should be getting. Better working conditions, decent wages. Things like that. That's all."

"What the law says? I guess you mean all these new Roosevelt laws. Them's Federal laws."

"Yes, ma'am, it's the law of the land now," offered Dobinsky.

"Might be, but it didn't seem to work too good for those folks up in North Carolina awhile back now did it?" Neither of the men responded to her pointed question. "I don't want trouble. No meetings or nothing like that here at my place. I won't tolerate trouble."

"There won't be any trouble, Mrs. Aintry. Our work won't involve you," Leon said confidently. She noted that Dobinsky raised his eyebrows only slightly.

"Okay, that's good. Come on in and I'll fix you some breakfast. Y'all ever ate eat grits?"

CHAPTER 23

After Bulldog Matheson had chewed him out for placing Ezra's name on the layoff list, Queazy's irrational hatred and resentment of Ezra grew. He aimed to make his life as difficult and unpleasant as possible during the graveyard shift. But subtlety and nuance were not part of Queazy's makeup. It had not taken Ezra long to figure out how much the second-hand disliked him, as inexplicable as it had at first seemed. He was given an additional bank of looms to work, even though the increase had not been ordered by management.

Queazy would often stand off a ways, leaning against a post, usually with a half chewed toothpick dangling from the corner of his mouth. He watched Ezra at work in the distance, down the long aisle between the looms. Ezra was aware of his being observed, and of the passive   harassment by the little man, but did not spend much time thinking about him. He just went about his work and tried to stay out of his way. Besides, lately Queazy did not seem to be around as often.

During their infrequent breaks, the men working on the floor went to the waterhouse. Squatting on their haunches against the tiled wall, they smoked, gossiped and complained. They now spoke mostly of unions and organizing and the changes that were coming. Ezra sensed that they all pretty much agreed with what Melvin had suggested to his him that night on the front porch.

Whenever he could, Queazy slinked off downstairs to the spinning room. He was hopelessly and stupidly enamored with the new girl there, which was fine with Ezra. The nasty second-hand's absence permitted him to do his job and help out the loom fixers whenever he could.

***

That night he had seen Queazy step off the freight elevator and saunter toward him, hands dug into his pockets. But he turned and disappeared into the weave room office, as Ezra was finishing up with the last four looms in the line nearby. Then Queazy came to the door of the office and motioned for him. Entering the office, he found the second-hand leaning against the edge of the desk, picking his teeth.

"Looks like you a little behind tonight, Burke."

"A little maybe, not much. Expect to get caught up on the next line." Giving as concise a report as possible, he did not wish to engage this little man, but he was his immediate supervisor and had little choice but to respond.

"Best see that you do," smirked Queazy. Ezra did not respond but turned back to the door.

"Hey, Burke, seen that new girl down in spinning? She's a doll-baby!"

"No," answered Ezra, uninterested.

"She a looker, all right. Hotter'n a two-dollar pistol too."

"I got to get back to work."

"Yeah, she's going out with me Saturday night. What do you think of that?" Queazy smugly asked.

"Not much, Queazy, that's your business. I reckon it don't much concern me."

At this, Queazy squinted at him through the narrowing slits of his eyelids. The fingers of his left hand gripped the edge of the desk tightly. Ezra was aloof and uninterested. Damn mountain hick, he thought, probably thinks I can't get a girl like Ginny Lou.

Then Queazy relaxed, regaining his misplaced air of superiority, and with a thin crooked grin, looked away.

"Well, naturally, I don't guess you would now, at that. If I had that perdy little half-breed you got waiting at home for me, I don't guess I'd be looking around much neither."

Ezra did not reply. There was a tense silence. Queazy was too imperceptive and stupid to realize he had crossed some barrier, entered into some region of the other man's being, where neither he, nor anyone else, was permitted. A place non-negotiable. Before the second-hand could react or realize that he needed to, Ezra sprang, almost leaped, toward him. He grabbed Queazy by the throat, his powerful fingers nearly encircling his neck. He virtually lifted him from the desk and slammed him against the bare wall of the room. Queazy helplessly gripped the thick wrist of his assailant in a futile attempt to free himself, struggling to breath.

Inches from his face, Ezra looked into the surprised, panic-stricken eyes of his prey and spoke calmly, "If you ever mention my wife again I'll kill you, you little bastard. I swear it, Queazy, I'll kill you."

Queazy stopped struggling. As his body went limp, the grip loosened from his throat. He dropped to the floor, a miserable little pile of humanity gasping for air. He had thought that he was going to die. Ezra stood over him.

Coughing and holding his throat, Queazy spat out, "You tried to kill me, you mountain-trash son of a bitch! I'm getting you fired! Fired, you hear! I'm telling Bulldog about this in the morning. He'll fire your ass for sure. Now git out of here."

As he closed the door behind him, Queazy was still on the floor, raised up by one bony arm, screaming repeatedly, "You crazy son of a bitch. I'll get you fired!"

As Ezra strolled back into the din and lint haze of the weave room, he knew that whatever Queazy did or said did not matter.

CHAPTER 24

His wife had pulled back the front curtains after dinner. Thin shafts of light from the mid-afternoon sun angled into the room, dancing on the hardwood floor, warming the parlor, as the bright rays filtered through the slightly swaying oaks in the yard.

Rufus Jordan sat slumped in the well-worn leather wingback chair, *his* chair. His head tilted forward, slightly to the left, and his generous jowls rested heavily on his chest. His snoring was soft and rhythmic. The Sunday paper had fallen from his lap and lay fanned-out on the slick hardwood floor beside him. The quiet stillness that often comes with Sunday afternoons had settled over the house. Mrs. Jordan napped in the bedroom down the hall.

The stillness was suddenly shattered as the telephone in the hallway rang and echoed through the house. With the invading noise, Jordon seemed to rouse slightly, smacking his lips as he shifted in his chair. The phone continued to ring until Mrs. Jordan, in slippers, sleepily padded down the hall from her bedroom and picked up the receiver.

"Hello," she said, still groggy from sleep.

"Mrs. Jordan?" came the man's voice.

"Yes."

"Mrs. Jordan, I'm sorry to have to bother you on a Sunday, but I must speak to Rufus. Is he available?"

She hesitated a brief moment, but her head cleared quickly as she recognized the voice on the line.

"Yes, of course, Mr. Allgood. Just a minute and I'll get him."

"Thank you," came the terse reply.

She stepped down the hall into the parlor and gently shook her husband's shoulder. He woke slowly and reluctantly, and pulled himself erect in his chair, his eyes heavy with sleep.

"Wh...what is it?" he asked grumpily, not used to having his napping disturb.

She put her finger to her lips and said in an almost whisper, "It's Mr. Allgood. He's on the phone."

"Allgood? Oh, okay," he replied, removing the wire-rimmed glasses, and wiping the sleep from his eye with his thumb and forefinger. He gathered himself quickly and stepped into the hallway after nearly slipping on the newspaper on the floor.

"Hello, Mr. Allgood," he said into the receiver, after clearing his throat into the hollow end of his fist.

"We've got trouble, Rufus, at least I think we do. Can you meet me at the mill office this afternoon?"

"Why, sure thing, Mr. Allgood but I don't know of anything wrong at the mill. It's shut down today. It's Sunday."

"I'm aware of the day of the week, Rufus. It's not the mill. I understand there's organizers in town."

"Organizers?" Jordan repeated, incredulously.

"That's right. Goddamn organizers! Here in Corinth. Can you be at your office in an hour? We've got to nip this thing in the bud."

"Absolutely, Mr. Allgood. I'll see you in an hour."

"All right, Rufus." The receiver clicked in Jordan's ear. He turned to his wife who had been standing nearby at the parlor door.

"Got to go to the office. Allgood's all up in arms about some organizers he says are in town. Probably nothing. He's gotten pretty edgy lately with all that's going on at the mills. Thinks the unions might be trying to agitate and stir up the workers. Hell, I think they're all glad to just have a job in these days."

"Things have been pretty rough on those folks, Rufus," she said softly, but knowingly.

"Well, maybe so. But these stretch-outs and layoffs won't last forever. There's good times again down the road. My people know the mill will take care of them. I can't believe they'd go off and listen to some commie organizers. Damn rabble-rousing Yankees!"

"I don't know, Rufus."

He took the striped tie off the knob of the bedroom door where he had placed it after coming home from morning services. Absentmindedly, he placed it around his collar and tied it without the use of the dresser mirror. He pulled the knot tight up to his throat. The narrow end of the tie hung an inch below the front. He pulled on his suit coat and headed out the back door to the black Chevrolet parked in the garage.

Allgood's gleaming green Packard was already parked in the grass beside the mill office. Vaguely irritated, Jordan parked in the gravel space marked by a sign, "Mill Superintendent". There was also a space designated by a sign with Mr. Allgood's name on it, but no one, including Allgood, ever parked there.

It was Sunday and it was hot. It felt ridiculous to be wearing a coat and tie. He hastily removed his coat and tossed it onto the back seat of the Chevy. He loosened his tie and noticed a small gravy stain on his white shirt, which added to his irritation. He shrugged it off and entered the office building. The door to his office was open. Allgood sat, his legs gentlemanly crossed, on the cracked leather couch along the wall to the right of Jordan's desk. He had placed a fresh cigarette in a short Bakelite holder, the kind that had become popular with Roosevelt's election. He lit the cigarette.

"Good afternoon, Mr. Allgood," said Jordan, as he moved around to his desk chair. He liked having the large desk between them. Allgood nodded. Jordan leaned back in the swivel chair.

"Rufus, I have information from very reliable sources that a meeting is to be held tonight. A meeting led by outside organizers. And worse, I suspect some Galway workers might be participating."

"Are you sure about all that, Mr. Allgood? I haven't heard anything like that around here, and I pretty much try to keep my ear to the ground, if you know what I mean."

"Of course I'm sure. I know what's going on around Corinth and my mills."

"I guess you do, at that," Jordan conceded.

"Meeting in the back of some poolroom dive downtown, which I suggest is appropriate for this kind of riffraff. Tucker's, I believe is the name of the establishment. Tucker's Pool Room or something like that."

"*Hall*, Tucker's Pool *Hall* I believe it's called. Yeah, I know the joint. Rough part of town."

"I'm concerned, Rufus, deeply concerned. The unions up North, well, we've tried to keep them there and have done so for a long time now. But look what's happening in the Midwest. All the violence and corruption. We don't need that kind of thing here." Allgood, agitated and his voice rising, uncrossed his legs a leaned forward. "Already heard of some rumblings over in Georgia."

"Yes, I saw that in the paper a few weeks ago. Sounded like more than rumblings to me," Jordan interrupted. Allgood continued.

"That's my point. We just can't have it here. I won't have it!" Allgood said loudly. Appearing to realize this uncharacteristic emotional outburst, he settled back onto the couch and drew on his cigarette. "I won't have it," he said softly, almost to himself. "We can't have it."

Jordan wiped the sweat from his forehead with a handkerchief. He leaned forward in his chair and rested his arms on the desk, the fingers of both hands intertwined.

"What do you propose we do, Mr. Allgood? I mean at this point."

"We need information. That is, to start with. Find out what the workers are saying and thinking. Most importantly, we must find out who the Galway workers are that are involved. Root them out. Destroy them!"

"Destroy them?" asked Jordan, as he fell heavily back into his chair.

"Hell, Rufus, you know what I mean. Identify the troublemakers, fire them, and then put them on the union-supporters list."

"You mean blacklist them?"

"Of course that's what I mean," said Allgood impatiently. "They'll never work in a Southern cotton mill again, or at least have a hell of a time trying to find that'll hire them. This is my town and have I influence with all the other owners, most of them anyway. I mean to blacklist every damn one of them. To hell with them all!" Allgood snuffed out his cigarette, and placed another one in the holder and lit it. His pinched a small piece of tobacco from his tongue.

"But we need to find out who they are before this thing gets a life of it's own and spreads. It's like a cancer. Got to cut it out!"

"I agree with you. That's for sure. I didn't realize things were getting stirred up so here, though. How do you propose we handle it?"

"Look, Rufus, you're the mill manager. *You* figure out the details. Just get the information. Who the scum are that work for me and are planning to go with a union. I won't have it!" He stood up and flicked a few pieces of tobacco off his linen trousers. "Get back with me in a couple of days at most. I've got to run."

He turned and left the office. Jordan leaned back in his chair with his hands locked together behind his head. He heard the Packard start, and the low rumble of the engine, as his boss sped out of the yard.

He wiped the profuse sweat from his forehead and face again with the now damp handkerchief. His white cotton shirt, wet with perspiration, clung to his body. He hardly noticed it. He reached down and yanked on the handle of the large drawer of the desk, knowing from habit that it stuck and was difficult to open. He pulled out a bottle of bourbon. Good bourbon. He had been tempted to offer Allgood a drink but then thought better of it. Not quite a social situation. Anyway, he put the bottle to his mouth and took a long drink. Damn good bourbon, he thought, worth the price.

He placed the bottle back into the stubborn drawer and pushed it shut. He picked up the phone and dialed a number. He doubted there was be any late-night organizing meeting, at least one involving Galway workers.

CHAPTER 25

Jimmy Tucker was nervous as he pulled the heavy curtain across the front window. He placed the red-lettered, *Closed*, sign in the window and shut the door, but did not lock it. It would seem strange to his regulars, his being closed at nine o'clock. But, he told himself, Sunday nights were slow anyhow. Most of his patrons would be still nursing hangovers, or be in the doghouse with their wives for getting locked up Saturday night. Anyhow, Nabors had paid him twenty-five dollars. All he had to do was guard the door and admit only the mill people coming to the meeting. And they would only use the back room. Probably wouldn't mess it up much. Maybe he could sell them some beer. Men soon began to show up at the door.

"Y'all here for the meeting?" Jimmy asked.

"Yeah," came the low, muttered response.

"Okay, come on in and go to the back room. That's the door over yonder." He pointed to the black, heavily-lacquered door to the back room, where on any other night of the week he would have had several poker games going and a hot craps table—all illegal.

To the few regulars who came to the door, he told them the plumbing was busted and he couldn't open until it was fixed, probably sometime in the morning. This explanation seemed plausible and had they moved on. He just hoped a cop didn't come by. They might be curious and could cause him trouble.

By 9:45 p.m. the room was pretty well filled with men. Most stood around in small groups, talking in low voices. Others sat quietly, slumped in straight back chairs, with their arms folded skeptically across their chests. Some just leaned against the wall with their hands deep in the pockets of their overalls. A blue cloud of cigarette smoke hugged the low ceiling. Bright, shaded, overhead lights pierced the man-made fog with an almost eerie glow. Ventilation was poor, so the air in the room was stale and heavy. It was hot.

"Damn, when we going to git started? It's hot as hell in here and I ain't got all night," one of the men leaning against the wall grumbled loudly. Several of the men nodded and cursed, too.

"Eh, keep your shirt on, Henry. Eugene's got everything all set up. They'll be here any minute," shouted back Melvin Jackson, who had joined in conversation with a group of men across the crowded room.

Jimmy wanted the meeting over and done with. He could not care less about what he called bitchin' lint-heads. His business did not depend on them. They did not have money to spend shooting pool regularly. They sure never sat in on a poker game. His cousin, Benny Ray, came around some. He always seemed to have money, but then again he was not exactly a mill hand. Jimmy did not know exactly what he was. A tough customer though, when he wanted to be. Jimmy was glancing at his watch when Eugene Nabors came through the door with two other men.

"How you doing, Jimmy. This here is Leon and Ivan, they call *him* Ski," singling out Dobinsky.

"Okay," replied Jimmy hurriedly. "Looks like all your people are here. In the back room. I'm going to lock the front door now."

Before he could move, Leon extended his hand.

"Just want to thank you for letting us use your place tonight, Tucker. Did you get your money?" Leon glanced at Eugene.

"Yeah, sure. Eugene brought it by last week. Everything's good."

Jimmy reached passed the men and engaged the deadbolt lock of the front door. He pushed aside the edge of the curtain and peered onto the dark street. It was deserted except for a large, gray rat scampering toward a street drain. Jimmy sighed deeply and went behind the bar. He poured a glass of whiskey and gulped it down with a grimace.

Eugene Nabors opened the door to the back room and hesitated. No one had noticed him, and the low rumble of the chatting men continued. He then made his way into the room. The men roared with hoots and sarcastic applause as he pushed through them. Deminici and Dobinsky followed close behind. Once at the far wall, he turned to the crowd, raising both hands above his head.

"All right, all right, boys give me your attention!" The din receded somewhat but there was still low murmuring about the room. "Come on, men, settle down so we can get started."

"You're late, Nabors," shouted someone from the crowd.

"Yeah, did you bring breakfast?" another man responded, and they all guffawed in unison.

It would likely be a rowdy meeting. Leon and Ski glanced at each other knowingly. Nothing new here. They had been through it all before, and a rough-and-tumble gang of men was typical in organizing and union work. They liked it this way. Showed energy and potential for action.

Eugene, redheaded and pale-skinned, blushed. He lowered his hands to chest height, palms up, facing the group.

"Okay, so we were a little late."

"Your wife make you do the dishes and put the cat out before you could leave home?" Catcalls and laughter roared from the men. They were enjoying ragging Eugene.

"I'll get you for that, Rayford," Eugene shouted back good-naturedly. "But come on, boys, this is serious business. Sooner we get started, sooner we get out of here. I know some of you work third shift so let's get on with it." Several of the men nodded in agreement and the room fell silent.

"First, let me say, we all know why we're here," he said, his voice taking on a low, somber tone.

"Who put you in charge anyway?" asked Henry loudly, still leaning against the wall to Eugene's right.

"Shut the hell up, Henry, and listen for once in your life. You might learn something," Melvin shouted back. There was a ripple of approving laughter. Henry folded his arms across his chest and spat on the floor.

"Anyway, like I was fixin' to say," Eugene continued, "we're all sick and tired of how we're being treated at the mill. Not much more than a piece of property to the owners. And cheap property at that." The men all nodded in agreement. "We got to do something. We, me anyway, can't live like this. So what we going to do about it?"

"Yeah, what?" a man in the back called out.

"Well, that's why we meeting tonight. You might have noticed these two strangers followed me in." The men laughed as Eugene gestured to Leon and Ski standing slightly behind his left shoulder. "This here is Mr. Deminici and Mr. Dobinsky." Eugene stammered slightly, struggling with the pronunciation. "Did I say that right?" he turned, and asked the two organizers. Both nodded. "So I guess I'll turn the meeting over to them now."

Deminici stepped forward, facing the group.

"Good evening, fellas," he said. In low, self-conscious voices, several of the men in the crowd returned the greeting.   "First, let me clarify something. Although I appreciate Eugene's manners, my name's Leon. None of this *mister* crap." The men laughed in appreciation of the gesture. Leon was smart. "And there's no Mr. Dobinsky here either," nodding toward his associate, "this is Ivan."

"But everyone calls me Ski," Ivan spoke up.

"He's a big 'un, ain't he?" someone called out. More laughter.

"Yep, he's full grown," retorted Leon. Ski smiled broadly. Leon knew how to work a room.

"First, let me say, and I mean this seriously, you ought to appreciate Eugene here." Eugene stared down at his shoes, his hands in his pockets.

"He's stuck his neck out for you people. Setting up this meeting and calling us to come down here to work on organizing. He would be fired tomorrow if the bosses knew. He's not out for glory or anything like that. He's just tired of being treated as you all are, well, like a piece of shit." The room exploded with applause.

"Another thing. You heard me use the word *bosses*, right? Well, that's what they are. They like to think of themselves as managers. Hell, they couldn't manage a troop of Boy Scouts." Applause and profane shouts of agreement. "They can do only one thing - boss you! Nothing more. So, we're just dealing with two nasty animals here – bosses *and* owners. These are the enemy and they're both the same."

Leon went on to inform the men of the status of the current union movement in the South, as he saw it and knew it to be. He talked about what it took to organize against stubborn, and literally militant, opposition from mill owners. He related ordeals he, and others, had experienced up North and in the Midwest as union organizers. He then pulled up his shirt to show a scar. It was from a thirty-eight caliber bullet that had entered his chest just below the heart. He told them that, being inoperable, it was still lodged there. And other scars on his face and body imparted by baseball bats, knives, and blackjacks wielded by malicious policeman and mill thugs.

By this time, the gathered group of mill workers was silent and intent on what this diminutive, goateed man had to say. There was always the chance of violence, but that was not his way. Violence was the weapon of *the Man*—the bosses and the owners. But you had to be ready for it, and protect yourself and your family as best you could. The men were listening now. A somberness fell over the hot, smoke-filled room.

"Okay, that brings us to the present. The here and now you might say. To the Galway mills and the other mills in and around Corinth."

"So what can we do?" someone asked.

"First of all, there's talk of a general strike throughout the entire Southeast next month, maybe sooner. That means everyone, at least in theory, walks off the job or doesn't report to work."

"What's that going to do but put us in the poor house?" Henry asked sarcastically, but this time several of the men nodded in agreement.

"Good question," responded Leon quickly, seizing the opportunity to lay out what could be done, and perhaps win over the recalcitrant Henry, and others like him, in the process.

"We want to avoid a strike. Going on strike is the last resort. But it's the only ace that you, the worker, got up your sleeve. What I propose is that we first draw up our grievances and present them to the owners. That is usually the first step."

"They ain't going to give us nothing. They won't budge an inch, I tell you."

"Well maybe, maybe not, but this is how we get started making things better. This is how we get started improving our lives. Anybody here like being a slave? Because that's about what you are? Anybody?" Leon bore down, knowing it was time to push. "I didn't see any hands go up. That's good."

"So where do we go from here?" asked Melvin who was now sitting on the floor, his back to the wall.

"First, join the Allied Union of Textile Workers, the AUTW, and try and get as many of your coworkers, those people who aren't here tonight, to join. Ski, pass out the application cards. Give each man ten."

"I don't know about all this. I don't want to get fired," the man beside Melvin spoke up. Leon smiled, thankful for the comment.

"What do you do in the mill? What's your job?" asked Leon, and everyone looked at the man.

"I'm a weaver and damn proud of it!"

"As you should be. How long have you been a weaver?" asked Leon.

"Near 'bout eighteen years."

"How much do you make a week, if I might ask?"

"Ain't no secret. Weaver makes ten dollars forty cents a week or thereabouts."

Leon moved toward the man.

"Ten dollars forty cents a week or thereabouts," he repeated for effect. "I come from a little town in Massachusetts. Got a textile mill there, or at least *had* one. My father worked there. Funny thing, he was a weaver too. Know what a he made for a forty-hour week?"

"No, I reckon I wouldn't know that."

"He started, and I said started, at twenty-five dollars a week."

"That's mighty good money," someone offered as most of the men looked at each other in disbelief.

"You damn right it's good money," said Leon, stepping back to the center of the group.

"And he worked same as you, same looms, same cotton, so why should he make two and half times a week what you do, my friend?" The question was rhetorical, and Leon did not pause for a response. "I'll tell you why. It's because of the union. He belonged to the AUTW."

"But ain't all them jobs moving down here?" someone asked dully.

"Of course they are. Most already have. Now, why wouldn't a greedy mill owner move to the South? Answer, no unions. Almost free labor."

The men shifted uneasily in their seats or where they were standing. Nearly everyone took the cards Ski was passing out.

"What about these grievances you been talking about? We puttin' it in writing?" came a question from the wall.

"Exactly! Here's the way I see it. You boys chime in and we'll do this together. First of all, these stretch-outs have to go. Next, no more pay by piece-work. Hourly pay only. Then, every worker gets a scheduled break and time to eat his dinner. And finally, they have to reduce the number of bosses, especially those who do nothing but walk around and make sure you don't slow down, take a break, or go the waterhouse to take a wiz. That's it. Anything unreasonable about those demands, gentlemen?"

"All sounds good, but what about pay raises?" asked Melvin.

"Good question, again. Pay increases come next, after we get a foothold in the mill. Once we get the union established and strong, they'll *have* to deal with us."

"Okay."

"Here's the thing, boys. You got to stick together, especially if there's a strike. Our strength is in numbers."

"Hell," said Henry, "they's a hundred men just waiting to take my job. Bosses wouldn't do nothing but fire me and hire one of them. Probably at less wages."

Leon listened to Henry and smiled, "Say, I like you. You like to give the opposing view—devil's advocate. What's your name?"

"Henry. Henry Duncan."

"You're right, Henry, there are a lot of people on the street out of work. And if one or two of you get fired the bosses can easily replace you. That's why you all have to stick together. Most of you are skilled workers. Those bums on the street aren't. Mill can't replace everyone at the same time and keep up production. It's all in the numbers, men." Everyone in the room was listening now.

Leon explained that he would draw up a paper, listing the grievances. He would be meeting with workers from the other mills in Corinth over the next several days, but Galway Mill was the key. It was by far the largest cotton mill in the Southeast. If it went union, the others would follow for sure.

The union rally was planned for Friday at noon at the park downtown. After maybe a few speeches and a push for membership signups, the entire group of attendees would march the two or three miles to the Galway Mill office and present the grievances. The newspapers would be properly notified and maybe a press conference was in the offing. A lot of pressure would be on the mill owners. They could avoid a strike only by complying with the very reasonable and legal demands of the workers, who were only asking for what was fair. Everyone would see it that way for sure.

It sounded rather straightforward and logical to the men in the room that night. They were just looking for hope, a decent workplace. This might even work out, be easier and less painful than they had first thought. Leon knew differently.

CHAPTER 26

On Monday, Charlie Matheson arrived at the mill early, but he noticed Jordan's Chevrolet was already parked beside the office. He couldn't recall ever being called at home on Sunday by his boss. He had not told him anything except to be in his office first thing in the morning, before shift change. There were no other cars in the parking area, so he assumed they would be alone. He hated this kind of stuff.

He closed the office door behind him and walked down the hall to Jordan's office. Jordan was at his desk, but was turned toward the window which looked out at the mill across the street. He seemed preoccupied and did not notice Matheson's entrance. The office door was open, but he stopped and tapped gently a couple of times with his knuckles.

"What's up, boss?"

"Take a seat, Charlie," replied Jordan as he turned in the swivel chair.

"Okay."

Matheson sat down in the straight back chair across the desk. He dropped his hands to his lap and waited.

"Look, Charlie, we got problems. Maybe big problems, I don't know. Old man Allgood had me in here yesterday raving about outside organizers in town."

"Ah, I wouldn't worry too much about that. They're always drifting through here. Starts when times get bad. Most of 'em Reds. Don't know their ass from a hole in the ground. Cops usually run them off."

"No, this may be different. Allgood said there was going to be a meeting. Seems a group of workers might have met with a couple of union men down at Tucker's Pool Hall last night."

"How does he know that?" asked Matheson.

"Hell, I don't know! Says he has sources. I guess he does. He's a powerful man."

"Okay, so what? People got a right to meet. Got nothing to do with us."

"Ah, come on, Charlie. You know there's talk. These stretch-outs and layoffs aren't the most popular thing around, you know. Lots of unhappy folks. People are restless."

"I'm guessing you called me in here for a reason," Matheson finally said, and shifted his body slightly in the uncomfortable chair. He pulled a fat cigar from his breast pocket. He placed it in his mouth, and rolled it back and forth thoughtfully with his thumb and forefinger as he lit it, his first of the day.

"You're not going to like this and neither do I, but Allgood wants information."

"What do you mean, *information*?" asked Matheson. He exhaled a huge plume of blue-white smoke that floated to the ceiling and hung there in a motionless cloud.

"According to him, there were Galway Mill people at that meeting last night," Jordan paused, letting his statement sink in before continuing, "Allgood is adamant, and I mean damned determined, to squash anything even resembling a union. And I can't say that I blame him."

"Might have been some of our men at the meeting, but I doubt it. That is, if there was a meeting at all. Anyhow, I can ask around," Matheson offered.

Jordan leaned forward on his desk. "And just what the hell do you think they're going to tell *you*? God almighty, man, you're management. You're the enemy!"

"Yeah, I suppose you're right about that. But I'll keep my ears open on the floor. You never know what might turn up."

"Forget it, Charlie, that's not enough. Allgood wants inside information. You know, what the boys are saying, who's going to the meetings, who's on the floor talking up this union crap. Somebody *is*, that's for sure."

"Well, there's a few of them that I could pretty well guess might be tied up in this here organizing, if you want to call it that. You know, there's a few the hotheads and malcontents who are always complaining and running their mouths. Never seems to come to much."

"I've got to come up with a plan and do it quick. Allgood's going to be back in here in a day or two. Bottom line is, Charlie, we got to get somebody on the floor on our side. Someone who'll tell us what's going on and who's involved."

"Whew, good luck with that one," said Charlie, shaking his head.

"Well, you're going to do it. Find somebody, I mean. You've got to. Allgood puts it on me, I put it on you. Crap flows downhill. You know how it works, Charlie."

"Don't I," Charlie chuckled sarcastically, as he leaned over and tapped a long, gray ash from his cigar into the large, amber-glass ash tray on Jordan's desk.

"Look, Charlie, think. Is there anybody on the floor that you trust or can be trusted? Anybody?"

Jordan leaned back in his chair. The man across the desk grew serious and thoughtful. He rubbed his chin, looking down at the patterns in the dusty and faded rug.

"Well, like you said, I don't like it either. All this under-the-table stuff."

He hesitated.

"Well?" asked Jordan impatiently.

"Thinking about it, there might be someone on the floor that can be trusted. At least, I trust him."

"Great," said Jordan enthusiastically, "let's get him on board."

"Only thing is, I doubt he'll do it. I'd be real surprised if he did. Just ain't the type."

"Hell, fire him if he won't," ordered Jordan.

"Come on, Rufus, that's no way to handle it. Only make things worse with the people. Besides, he's a damn good hand. Way to do it is to maybe sweeten the pot, maybe get him beholden to us in some way. I still doubt he'd do it. Just ain't the type, like I said." He took a draw of the cigar. "God, I hate this crap."

"You going to talk to him?" pressed Jordan.

"Just hold on, boss. I'll work something out and see how it goes. You know, like I said, sweeten the pot."

"Okay, I don't care what you do, just get him working for us on this thing. And hurry up about it. Let me know something by the end of the day."

"Whoa! Not that quick, no way. Rufus, I know Allgood's pushing, but I'm going to need a little time with this. Going to take more than a day or two. Otherwise, we can forget it."

"Okay, I'll see what I can do to hold the old man off. He can be fairly reasonable once he settles down a little. You think we can have something working by Friday? That's five days."

"I'll give it a shot, Rufus, that's all I can do."

Charlie rose from his chair and started to leave. At the door he turned briefly to the man behind the desk. He said nothing, but thought to himself, God, I hate this crap.

***

As Matheson exited the office, the mill whistle blasted and cut through the still morning air, a reminder of who was in charge and that it was eight o'clock. Across the street the third-shift workers poured out of the mill, pale, lint-covered, and carrying the proverbial black lunch box. He walked to the curb and waited.

When he spotted Ezra passing through the gate, Matheson whistled loudly through his fingers and beckoned him over to where he stood.

He's talked to Queazy already. Probably going to fire me right here on the street, thought the tired and bleary-eyed mill worker as he crossed the street.

"Good morning," said Matheson.

"Morning," returned Ezra as he placed the lunch pail under his arm, freeing his hand to fill his pipe.

"How was your shift?"

"It was okay, I reckon."

"Yeah, I know it's been pretty rough for you boys on the floor, but these stretch-outs won't last forever. Just got to get through hard times."

Ezra looked past him at the mill office behind him and did not respond. Matheson continued.

"And third shift on top of that. Didn't much care for it when I started out. Hell, that seems like a hundred years ago. Couldn't hack it now, I don't expect."

"It's all right."

Ezra impatiently shifted his weight, still holding the unlit pipe. He was tired, and looking forward to the short walk home, but he sensed Matheson was getting around to something. He hoped he would do it soon.

"Yeah, these stretch-outs and pay-cuts hurting near everybody I guess. But the mill will take care of its own."

"I reckon."

"I don't think we need to worry any about any of this union stuff. Not like they're having with that mess over in Georgia."

"I reckon not."

"People talk, though. Never seems to come to much."

Matheson eyed his charge carefully, waiting for a response that did not come. There was a brief, almost awkward silence, before he spoke again.

"Wife and kids doing okay?"

"Yes, they're doing all right," replied Ezra, looking down at the lint covering his clothes and shoes. He absentmindedly, out of habit and self-consciousness, brushed lint from his hair and sighed.

"Look, Burke, I know you're about worn out but I just wanted to talk with you for a moment. I think you'll like what I got to say."

"All right."

"Thing is, we've had our eye on you. I mean me and some of the other overseers. Even the Superintendent said something in a meeting the other day. Good, loyal, hard workers are not easy to come by, not like they're falling out of trees."

Yes, they *are* falling out of trees, Ezra thought, as he visualized the line of men that lined up every morning at the mill office looking for work. A few were already gathering around the big oak tree beside the office, waiting for it to open. In a few minutes the guard would come over and tell them the mill was not hiring and that they would need to vacate the premises.

"Anyway," Matheson continued, "you've gotten pretty good at fixing looms, haven't you? At least, that's what I'm hearing."

"I know I'm not supposed to be working on looms, Mr. Matheson, but I only do it after I get caught up and to help out on account of these stretch-outs."

"No, no, it's okay. Not a problem. Shows initiative. Man trying to get ahead. We like that. That's one reason we been watching you, like I said."

It was obvious to him that Matheson did not know of the incident with Queazy in the weave room office.

"I wouldn't want do anything that would cost me my job, but I need to tell you something, Mr. Matheson. I need to tell you now." He slid the unlit pipe back into the bib pocket of his overalls.

"Tell me what?" Matheson asked, somewhat annoyed at having his train of thought and his plan interrupted.

"I got into it with Queazy tonight. I mean this morning, during my shift."

"Got into it about what?"

"I grabbed him, assaulted him, I reckon."

"Good god, man! Y'all got into a fight on the floor?"

"Not a fight exactly. He spoke to me in a way I can't—won't—put up with. I grabbed him with my hands and near about choked him. It happened in the weave room office."

"Anybody else see it?" Asked Matheson, now interested.

"No, not as I know of."

"Look, Burke, don't worry about it. Queazy's a squirt, an idiot. I'd get rid of him if I could. I'll talk to him. Anyway, what I was going to tell you will get Queazy out of your life. You'd probably like that, wouldn't you?"

Ezra half smiled and suppressed a chuckle, but he did not respond.

"I need a loom fixer on the first shift. They won't let me hire any new people. I'm moving you to the day shift to take the job. You'll be getting a raise in pay, naturally."

Ezra looked hard at his boss. What is this all about? Could be just good luck. Sure been little of that in my life, he thought. He instantly felt the guilt of this thought as Judith and his children flashed in his mind. But a first-shift loom fixer. There were men he knew had been at the mill much longer than he who would be in line for this job. It did not add up. But maybe it was luck. Just plain good fortune.

"Well, what do you think? You don't seem overly enthusiastic, I might say. I thought you'd appreciate it."

"Oh, I do appreciate it, Mr. Matheson. I do and mightily. It's I just I don't understand why me. There's other…"

"Don't worry about why. We just think you're a cut above. That's all."

"What about people been here a lot longer than me?"

"That's not your problem. We just want the best man for the job. No such thing as seniority here. We hire and fire pretty much how it suits us. You let me worry about all that. Anyway, I run the weave room and I'm going to do it. Simple as that."

"All right."

"Good. I'm glad you understand. Now, you take tonight off and report to me in the morning."

"I'm much obliged, Mr. Matheson, but I couldn't afford not to work my hours tonight. Things are too tight."

"I'm going to pay you your hours for the third shift tonight."

"Pay me for not working?"

"That's right. Consider it kind of a bonus," Matheson said, and reached out to shake hands.

Almost hesitantly, Ezra extended his hand and immediately he was not sure what had happened here this morning, on the curb, across from the mill. As he walked home in the light of the bright morning sun, he continued to consider it. She would be happy. Life with his family would be more normal, working days like it's supposed to be. Maybe expand the garden in the back yard. But still, something was there. Something worrisome. Or maybe not. Hard times had made him skeptical and a little cynical. That's all it was. Maybe good fortune had finally smiled on him, like the warm sun he felt on his back. Yes, maybe that was it. Could be just plain good luck.

***

Queazy was exiting the mill as Matheson turned to go back into the mill office.

"Charlie, hey, Charlie, got to talk to you," he yelled out shrilly as he passed through the guardhouse gate, almost at a run. Matheson stop and, annoyed, waited.

"What are you still doing here, Queazy? Not like you to be hanging around after shift change?" Matheson asked as he approached.

"I got to talk to you." Queazy was almost gasping for breath. He stopped and placed both hands on his hips and bent over.

"Better layoff those cancer sticks, Queazy, you look like you about to die right now. What do you want?"

"I need to talk with you about that goddamn Ezra Burke," he spat out, his chest still begging for air.

"What about him?"

"I want the son a bitch fired! He about killed me last night. Up on the floor."

"Yeah, he told me about it awhile ago," said Matheson.

"You kidding me, he told you?" Queazy asked, stunned. "What did he say?"

"Pretty much what you just did. He about killed you," Matheson said lightly. There was nothing about Queazy that he liked.

"Well, he did. He did for sure. I ought to have him arrested. Just fire him, that's enough. I want him out of the mill! Just look at my neck." He pulled open his shirt collar to display the dark red imprints on his skin.

"What provoked him, Queazy? Can't see Burke as the type to pick a fight."

"I don't remember, not exactly. We're just shooting the breeze. About women, I guess. Told him I sure admired the way his wife looked. Something like that. You know, didn't mean nothing by it. He just went crazy and grabbed me. Near about choked me to death."

Matheson knew Queazy and he knew him to lie for his own purposes. He was not to be trusted. Anyway, it did not matter at this point.

"I'll take care of it. Now you go on home and put some ice on that throat. It'll keep the swelling down. Still going to bruise some I expect."

"You going to fire him, ain't you?"

"Well, no, Queazy, as a matter of fact, I'm not."

"Why not, Charlie? It ain't right."

"Thing is, I expect you goaded Burke, probably on purpose, but running that mouth of yours anyway you cut it. I'm not firing him. As a matter of fact, I'm moving him to first shift, fixing looms." Charlie delivered the news with more relish than he would have liked to have had.

"No!" exploded the shocked Queazy. "That just ain't right, Charlie! I'm going to tell—"

"Tell who, Queazy? Tell who?" Matheson's face reddened and veins in his neck stood out like thick red cords. Knowing he had gone too far, Queazy looked down at the ground and said nothing. "Something else, Queazy. This thing ends right here. You got that? Say you got it?"

"Yeah," Queazy mumbled, "I got it."

"You just remember I'm not the one you've got something on just because I know about it. One of these days Jordan's going to get fed up with all your crap, with you, and it won't be good. You got your little boss-job on the third shift. Now if you want to keep it, you best keep your mouth shut and go on about your business. And stay away from Ezra Burke."

"Anything you say, Charlie, but it ain't right."

Matheson left Queazy standing in the grass yard in front of the mill office. He went to his desk, lit a fresh cigar and wondered where all this was going to lead.

CHAPTER 27

By Wednesday morning, after the meeting at Tucker's Pool Hall, the local paper, the Corinth Gazette, had obtained enough of what it considered reliable information about the union rally, to print the story. Although he had presented it to the papers as being an *impromptu* gathering of disenchanted cotton mill employees, Leon had leaked the information. The rally would be a big deal in Corinth, the entire state maybe, and that was good thing. That was what he wanted. However, there was no mention in the frontpage article of worker grievances being formally presented to Galway management. From experience, Leon knew when to play it close to the vest. This was one of those times.

The Sunday night meeting had gone well and the enthusiastic responses he was getting from the people at the other mills encouraged him. There had even been a few women at a couple of the subsequent meetings. This was progress, a *sign of the times,* he told Dobinsky over a cold beer late one night after one of the gatherings.

***

Deep in paperwork at his desk, Rufus Jordan absentmindedly reached for the unsolicited coffee Miss Wilcox placed in front of him. She returned quickly to her desk to answer a clanging telephone.

"Good morning. Galway Mill. Miss Wilcox speaking," she spoke into the receiver with her usual clipped monotone.

"Miss Wilcox, put me through to Rufus, please."

"Yes, sir, Mr. Allgood. Just a second." She clicked on the intercom. "Mr. Allgood on the line." Same clipped monotone revealing neither emotion nor urgency.

"Good morning, Mr. Allgood."

"Have you seen the paper this morning, Rufus?" Allgood asked calmly.

"No, can't say I have. Don't usually read it until the evening when I get home." Jordan sat forward in his chair, sensing trouble.

"Well, it seems there's going to be a rally in City Park on Friday. A mill workers' rally."

"That's news to me. Of course, I haven't been out of the office this morning. What do you make of it?"

"The article in the paper didn't give much detail, but it did make a reference to union organizers. Looks like the AUTW is in town. Pretty much what we thought. At least what *I* saw coming."

"I wonder how they got a permit from the police department without you—uh—anyone knowing about it."

"I already talked to Chief LeCroy. First call I made this morning. He doesn't know anything about it. He said they probably won't need a permit if they don't advertise or promote the rally. As long as there's no trouble, the city won't do much about it, at least according to LeCroy. He's going to have some of his men scattered around the park. Don't know how that helps us though."

"How did the paper get hold of it, I wonder?" Jordan asked, almost to himself.

"The article mentioned an *unnamed* source, so who knows?"

"Well, I suppose there's not much we can do about it either."

"Look, Rufus, I want you to have some people at this so-called rally. I don't want trouble, but I want to know of any Galway employees there. Have them take down their names. They'll be fired and blacklisted immediately. That goes for any worker not reporting for work on the first shift Friday. Make an announcement and post it in the mill right away."

"All right, Mr. Allgood. No problem."

"Do you have men we can place at the rally? I mean who can be trusted."

"Yes, sir, that's no problem. I've got..."

"I don't want to know who they are," Allgood interrupted, "just get the information."

"Yes, sir. I understand."

"All right. By the way, have we recruited anyone yet to report back from the floor?"

"Charlie Matheson is working on it. I believe he's got a man on board. I'll check with him when we hang up."

"Good. We've got to fight this thing. I'll probably want to meet with you and your people in a day or so. Tell Charlie to have his man ready."

"Will do, Mr. Allgood."

"Goodbye, Rufus. I'll be in touch."

There was a click from the receiver before Jordan could respond. He pushed away from his desk and stepped across the hall to Charlie Matheson's office. Matheson was not there, so he returned to his desk and dialed the weave room. There was no answer. The phone continued to ring. He finally returned the receiver to its cradle and rolled down the sleeves of his starched, white shirt, re-inserted the gold cuff links, and donned the dark-blue pinstripe suit coat.

As usual, Newton was leaning against the post of the guard-house door smoking a cigarette. He took a deep draw and looked up as he flipped the butt onto the gravel yard.

"Holy shit!" he said to himself, as he began tucking in his sweat-stained, blue shirt. "Here comes the old man! He's going in the mill for sure." He virtually snapped to attention as the Superintendent approached.

"Good morning, Mr. Jordan. Perdy day, ain't it?"

"Morning, Newton," Jordan said, as he unexpectedly stopped and spoke to the guard directly, a rare occurrence. "I need to speak with Matheson. I can't get him on the mill phone. He's probably on the floor somewhere. I want you to go up and tell him to come to my office directly, right away."

"Yes, sir, Mr. Jordan."

Jordan almost expected a salute from the stupidly erect Newton who continued to maintain his soldierly posture. Both men stood there.

"I mean *now*, Newton," Jordan ordered sharply. The indolent guard turned away and almost trotted to the mill door, and disappeared behind it.

Damn bigshot, Newton thought, as he breathlessly struggled to climb the myriad of stair-steps that would get him to the weave room. He coulda come up here his self. He'd a rode the freight elevator. He just didn't want to get lint all over him. Didn't want to mess up that nice blue suit. Damn big boss man, can't remember last time he come in the mill. Runs a cotton mill and don't like lint. Now ain't that something.

By the time he got to the top of the stairs and to the door to the weave room, Newton was sweating profusely. His shirt, wringing wet, bled dampness into his serge uniform coat. Gasping, he leaned red-faced over the deep stairwell, gripping the steel-pipe railing with both hands. Finally catching his breath, he stood erect and unbuttoned the coat, but it still clung to his short, stout frame. He loosened the tie he had cinched up tightly to his collar to impress Jordan. He pulled on the heavy steel door and stepped into the lint-filled and hazy hell of the weave room.

He immediately spotted Matheson between the rows of clanging looms. He was shouting to a loom-fixer who was struggling to hear him above the roar of the machinery. Apparently frustrated by the difficulty to make himself understood, Matheson just shook his head and walked away. When he saw Newton beckoning to him, he pushed opened the door and both men stepped out into the stairwell.

"Damn, Fig, you look like hell."

"Well, I feel like hell. Must be two-hundred stair steps up here."

"Should have taken the elevator."

"Yeah, should've. Didn't want to break the rules. Not with the old man prowling about."

"Jordan in the mill?"

"No, not likely. He sent me up here to tell you he wants to see you. Couldn't get you the phone."

"Okay."

"He said right away. I think he wants you down there now."

"Damn!" said Matheson. "Come on, Fig, you can ride down with me. Might save you a heart attack."

Matheson went directly across the street to the mill office, leaving Newton at the guardhouse where he collapsed in a straight chair, still breathless and suffering from the most physical exertion he had endured in recent memory. He lit a cigarette.

Walking past Miss Wilcox's desk without acknowledgement, he tapped on Jordan's office door.

"Sit down, Charlie. More crap going on, I'm afraid."

Matheson sat, pulled a dead cigar from his shirt pocket and re-lit it. Something was up. When he had gone to the waterhouse earlier in the day to relieve himself, the usual chatter of the workers waiting for shift change had abruptly given way to silence when he walked in.

"I'm not surprised, Rufus."

"Have you heard about the rally?"

"No, what rally?"

Jordan related his morning phone call from Allgood. When he mentioned the firing and blacklisting of workers, Matheson ran his hand through his hair and sighed deeply.

"Can you have a couple men at the rally?" asked Jordan.

"Well, the only two that come to mind is Queazy Tuttle and Benny Ray Tucker. They're thicker than thieves and sleazy enough for the work, that's for sure."

"Sending Tuttle is all right, he's an employee and can be controlled. Just needs to keep out of sight. I don't know about Tucker, though. He's mean and might just enjoy getting something started. Allgood doesn't want trouble, least not on our part. Just information. You think we can trust those two jokers?"

"I think so, as far as it goes. They're both on the payroll, one way or the other. Benny Ray's done side jobs for us before. Remember those colored boys coming in here that time?"

"I remember. Didn't have to be as heavy-handed as it was though. We just can't have any trouble. Just need information. We got to keep the union out of Galway Mill and Mr. Allgood's other holdings."

"I understand all that, Rufus, but this can be tricky stuff. Lot of folks unhappy with things. These stretch-outs—"

"No use discussing stretch-outs. You're wasting your time. We have to do whatever it takes to make a profit. That's the only way to keep the mill running until we get through these hard times. I think we might eventually get some help from the Government."

"Well, I reckon I'd rather see Roosevelt bail us out than push our own people like we're doing."

"Don't get too close to your people," Jordan warned. "You get paid by the owner. And paid pretty damn well, I might add. Remember that, Charlie. You got to do what's best for the mill."

"That's what I'm trying to do, Rufus." Matheson noticed that his cigar had gone out.

"Anyway, you get those two to do the work at the rally for us. By the way, you got anybody looking out for us on the floor, yet. We need that inside man."

"Yeah, I think so. I've worked on one. Pretty much set up, I'm figuring. Moved him from third to first. And a pay raise."

"Who is he? Do I know him?"

"I don't think so. Name's Ezra Burke."

"Burke? Name rings a bell. Say, isn't he that hillbilly who worked with the niggers in the coal yard when he first hired on?"

"Yes, he's the one."

CHAPTER 28

He decided not to think too much about it as he turned off Galway Avenue onto his street. Things pretty much have a way of working out, he thought. And they do. He breathed in the warm, heavy morning air and if his step was not lighter, his stride became longer and rhythmic. He pursed his lips, but he did not whistle although he might have felt like it. He was anxious to share the news with his wife.

She was kneeling in the garden as he crossed Melvin's front yard to his own. She was working with the vines of the tomato plants, gently tying them with string to the narrow, wooden stakes she had driven into the soft soil beside each one. She blew a wisp of hair from her face as delicate beads of perspiration, small and diamond-like, glistened on her forehead.

"Staking the tomatoes?" he asked as he approached.

"They're growing like crazy. See the buds? The dirt here is good. I wonder what was here before the mill came. I mean all this land where the houses are now. It's good dirt. Real good dirt. Are you tired?"

He stood near her and she looked up at him.

"No, I reckon I'm not," he said.

"Breakfast's on the stove. I bought some more of that canned salmon at the Company Store. From Alaska it says on the can. I fried up some patties with eggs and grits. It's real good. Andrew didn't care for it much though."

"Never had fish for breakfast before," he chuckled, rubbing the short stubble on his chin.

"Go on in and get you some coffee. I'll be there in a few minutes. I got two more plants to tie off." She brushed her hands together to shake off some loose soil.

"I got some news," he said.

"What kind of news?" she asked, not looking up from her work as she resumed tying the vines to the stakes. Her small fingers work skillfully and effortlessly with the tender, green plants.

"Good news, I reckon," he said, shoving his hands into the pockets of his overalls, the lunch pail under one arm.

"Good news? What?"

"Mr. Matheson caught up with me coming out of the mill this morning. Said he wanted to talk with me." He hesitated.

"Yes?" she said, with a trace of impatience.

"Well, it looks like they're moving me to day shift."

"First shift?" She stopped her tying and looked up at him.

"That's right, first shift."

She stood up and brushed the rich dark soil from her dress and shins. She hugged him tightly.

"I am so happy for you. For all of us. Folks work for years waiting to get on the day shift. I can't believe it." She was excited. "The children will be so happy."

"That's not all. There's more," he grinned down at her. "I'm going to be fixing looms too. What do you think about all that?"

"It just seems like a dream. What's happened? It just feels, I don't know, unreal somehow."

"Well, I reckon it's real enough. I get the night off this evening and go back to work in the morning fixing looms."

"You're not going to the mill tonight?" she asked, stepping back from him.

"No, Mr. Matheson said he'd pay me for tonight anyway and to just come in tomorrow on the new job."

A seriousness came over her, her brow furrowed slightly as she looked down at the turned soil of the garden.

"I don't know, Ezra."

"What do you mean?"

"I'm not exactly sure. It just seems too much. Just out of the blue," she said.

"Well, I've been working real hard. Doing more than I'm obliged to do. Mr. Matheson said they'd been watching me. Keeping an eye on me, I believe is what he said."

"Yes, but...uh...I just don't know. Do you feel right about it, Ezra? Does it feel right to you? Deep down?" she asked as she placed her hand on his arm.

"It didn't at first, I admit that. But the way Mr. Matheson laid it all out it came to sounding right, I guess."

He thought back to the conversation with Matheson at the curb. He thought about the incident with Queazy, of which she would never know. It had felt a little off-center, like maybe there were some things he did not know. But then of course there would be things of which he was unaware. He was only a shift hand. Mr. Matheson was the overseer. Management. And, anyhow, maybe this was the way good fortune happened when it came your way. He did not have much to compare it to.

"I guess we'll see," he said.

"Yes, I guess we will at that," she agreed. "Go on in and get your coffee. I'll go with you. I'm through here. But look at the dirt. It's real good dirt for growing things."

Ezra looked at the freshly turned soil of the garden.

"Yes, it sure looks like good dirt," he agreed. Fleetingly, he wondered if things might have been different if he had ever had soil like this to farm—rich, black dirt. Might have been farms here one time. Right here on the mill hill. Maybe even where the red-brick mill stands. He then quickly moved his hand across his face as if he were brushing away the thoughts. He turned and followed his wife into the house.

***

Full of grits and eggs and fried salmon that came in a can from Alaska, he crawled into bed, exhausted, and fell into a dreamless sleep. In the quiet house, she went about her normal tasks mechanically and absentmindedly. The low hum of the nearby cotton mill was in the background, but she no longer noticed it. Good fortune seemed distant and unfriendly. Underserved good fortune did not seem like good fortune at all, but rather somehow a debt that would eventually have to be repaid. Ezra had seemed to embrace it, but he would need to have a sense of its rightness. It would come to him. She was confident of it.

When the children came home from school that afternoon, their father was sitting on the steps of the front porch. This was unusual. He almost always slept until suppertime and then went to his job at the mill long after they had gone to bed. But he had woken rested, and was anxious to start experiencing the routine of normalcy that his recent good fortune would bring.

They both ran to him from the street, Grace squealing with delight at seeing her father, and her brother waving a colorful, Crayola drawing of stick people for him to see. They sat with him for awhile and related the adventures of their school day. They both were doing well, learning quickly. Grace was even helping some of the slower children in her class with their reading and spelling words.

Without detail, he told the children his good news and that perhaps another picnic at the park might be in order on Sunday, or at least soon for sure. It had been awhile since they had done such a thing.

"Can Melvin and Earline come, too?" asked Gracie excitedly.

"Who?" quizzed Ezra.

The girl blushed slightly and said, "You know who I mean, Papa, the Jenkins."

"We'll see. Have to talk things over with your mama first." With this, both children sprang from the steps and ran into the house to spread the exciting news with their mother. He remained on the steps and lit his pipe.

"Howdy, neighbor." Ezra turned at the loud voice to see Melvin with his lunch pail crossing the yard toward him. "What you doing up at this hour? Couldn't sleep?"

"No, I slept. Just got up a while ago. Wanted to see the children."

"Young 'uns home already?"

"They're in the house."

"Ain't none of my business, Ez, sure ain't, but I got to ask you. What happened between you and Queazy on the floor last night?

"Nothing."

"Come on, Ez, that ain't what I heard. You know they ain't no secrets on the mill hill."

"I reckon not," returned Ezra as he tamped and relit his pipe, "but I'm not going to talk about Queazy Tuttle. You know him good as I do."

"Piece of shit is what he is," Melvin retorted and spat on the ground.

"It's not important. But I probably ought to tell you about my talk with Mr. Matheson this morning, or his talk with me, to be more like it. Or do you and everybody else already know about it?"

"No, ain't heard nothing. What?"

He related to Melvin his encounter with Matheson at the curb. About the shift change, the new job, more pay, but he made no reference to the incident with Queazy. Melvin listened intently, looking out across the yard as Ezra spoke.

"Holy shit, Ez. That's downright unbelievable. Ain't nothing like that ever happened at the mill that I know of, and I been making cotton into cloth at Galway a long time. What do you make of it?"

"I don't know," he said as he tapped the pipe against the edge of the porch. "I reckon it does seem out of the ordinary in some ways."

"Look, the Allgood's always run their mills a certain way. A man works his way up. Hell, it ain't been that long ago you was out shoveling coal with them coloreds."

"Yeah, I know."

"I hate to tell you this, Ez, but something's up. Got to be. I swear, I hate to tell you; I swear I do."

"I don't get your meaning, Melvin. What?"

"I don't know, least ways, I can't say for sure. I know you tend to stay out of things, Ez, and mind your own business, but they's a lot going on."

"What do you mean, all this union talk going around?"

"Ain't just talk. I reckon you recollect me trying to get you to come to the meeting at Tucker's?"

"I do."

"Well, we had the meeting. Eugene Nabors had it all set up. Did a real good too. Had two ole boys, Yankees, down from the AUTW. Had a good turnout from the mill. We put together a list of our complaints that we going to take to management—the owners. They's going to be a rally on Friday at City Park. Union men in charge. We going to leave there and march back here to the mill and give 'em what for!"

"You'll lose your job, Melvin."

"Not if we all stick together. Can't fire and blacklist everybody, now can they?

"I don't know, they might can."

"No, we just got to stick together. The union boys say Galway's the key. If we can get them to go along, all the other mills around will fall in line. That's the stuff what's going on, Ez."

"What if the Allgood's won't go along with it? I expect they won't?"

"Things could get a little rough, I guess," Melvin said, as if he had only now considered the alternatives to the organizer's plan. "Point is, Ez, something's up. Bulldog Matheson wouldn't have just singled you out and done what he did on his own. This had to come from the top."

"You mean from Mr. Jordan?" asked Ezra.

"Mr. Jordan, hell. I'm talking about old man Allgood hisself. Got to be," Melvin said, convinced.

"I don't know, Melvin, why they would give me a better job and more pay. I can't do anything for them except work my job."

"I don't know either, but just be careful, Ez. Might be some kind of set up. Sounds crazy I know, but you got to watch 'em."

"I will," said Ezra.

"You ought to come to the rally, Ez. We need every man we can get. Women, too. You can't be happy with the way we been worked and treated. More of those goddam stretch-outs, getting paid in script, piece-work. I've had it, I tell you, I've had it with those bastards! Them all getting richer by the day, us not much more than slaves. That's what the union man said and he's right, too. Don't you hate it?"

"I don't like it much either, Melvin. It's just I'm not good with those organizers here from up North telling us what to do. I've always worked on my own, done things my way. Tried to do them right. With this union stuff, I don't reckon I got a dog in the hunt."

"It's a different world here," argued Melvin. "You ain't up in them mountains no more, up some holler by yourself, trying to farm hard ground. It's all machines here, and men running them and working on them. And bosses cussing and hollering at you. Pushing you. All closed up in that brick mill like a tomb. Ain't nobody can work by hisself anymore, Ez, they just can't."

Melvin took off his cap and wiped sweat from the headband with a soiled rag he pulled from the back pocket of his overalls.

"I'll think on it, Melvin. Talk to my wife, too."

"You do that, Ezra, you do that. Just be careful, you can't trust 'em."

"All right."

CHAPTER 29

A long blast from the mill whistle signaled the end of his first day on the day shift. He pushed against the heavy, steel door and stepped out from the dry, stagnant heat of the mill into the waning afternoon sun. A different kind of heat. A hot breeze briefly caressed his face. He breathed it in. He stopped to brush the fine gray-brown lint from his hair and face with his hands. His faded blue overalls, damp with sweat, were covered and almost colorless with the small, fluffy flakes. He chuckled to himself and thought ironically, Reckon I *am* just a lint-head after all. Like everybody else here—nor more, no less.

The burst of sunlight had almost startled him. Always before, when he had exited the plant after the graveyard shift, the rising sun was still low in the sky, just peeking over the trees and houses. The air then had the cool freshness of morning. But leaving the mill after the first shift—his first day—was different. Today he had come to the mill when ordinarily he would have been punching out and leaving for home. It felt strangely unfamiliar.

Instead of shuffling down the sidewalk toward Galway Avenue with the other workers and heading home, he turned right, round the corner of the mill, toward the rear. Back where the coal yard was.

Across the yard, Yates was dumping a load of coal into the pit. He then deftly pirouetted the empty wheelbarrow with one hand and headed back toward the never-shrinking mound of coal. Across the thin grass, which skirted the building, he caught the movement of an approaching figure, in the shadow of the mill, in the corner of his eye. He looked up sharply and suspiciously. He shaded his squinting eyes from the white streaks of the afternoon sun with a closed palm as he set the wheelbarrow down. Suddenly he dropped the shading hand, relaxed with recognition as the apparition, with a wide grin, strolled toward him.

"Well, I be damned. Look what the cat drug in."

"Howdy, Yates, how you been getting along?"

"What the hell you doing back here? Miss having coal dust up your nose?"

"Might be better than lint," Ezra returned the banter.

"Might be at that. From the looks of you, you sure got plenty of it to breathe." Ezra looked down at his overalls and self-consciously flicked lint from the bib. "I guess you know now why them town folks call y'all lint-heads."

"I reckon I do."

"Good thing about shoveling coal. It's dirty all right, but they ain't no lint. Us niggas are called a lot of things by you crackers, but you can't call us lint-heads. Got to look on the bright side, right?" Yates' laugh came easily from deep within him. He liked his joke and he did not miss the irony.

"I don't recollect calling you anything," Ezra said, seriously.

"No, I guess you never did at that."

"Looks like pretty much the same crew," he said, looking beyond Yates into the coal yard.

"Yeah, same old sorry bunch. Got one new man, but he sure ain't nothing to write home about."

Ezra noticed one of the men as he emptied his wheelbarrow in the pit and turned back toward the coal pile. He was slow, with a decided limp.

"Looks like Sugar Joe over there," said the white man.

"That's him, all right. Moves real slow but he's got work here as long as he wants it on account of the accident."

Yates called out to the man.

"Hey, boy, recognize this here cracker?"

Sugar Joe stopped for a moment and looked up, shading his eyes.

"Sure looks like Mr. Ezra. Why, I believe it is." Sugar Joe limped over to where the two men stood and extended his hand. "How you doing, Mr. Ezra?"

Yates set his jaw hard and looked away. Although he had grown to accept and respect Ezra, a white man, in his own way, he resented the deference shown to him by Sugar Joe.

"Been doing all right, I reckon. How's the leg?"

"Damn near came close to losing it. Now what good would a one-legged nigger be? Not much around here I tell you. That's for sure. Still hurts some, but I can work. I see—"

"Don't need your life story, Sugar Joe," Yates interrupted.

"Go on back and tell the boys to take a break."

Sugar Joe turned and hobbled away, smiling because Yates was letting him call the break.

"Never took a break when I was working here. Except for dinnertime," Ezra said.

"Well, it's like this. Even with these long summer days, we still got to work 'til near about dark. We ought to get paid more. I talked to Bulldog about it and told him it just ain't right. Us working these long days for the same pay. I didn't figure anything would come of it, but what the hell, couldn't hurt none neither. Askin', I mean."

"What did he say? Get more pay?" asked Ezra.

"Yeah, when pigs fly! Bulldog says, 'I see your point, Yates, but I can't increase y'all's pay none. I'll tell you what I can do though. You and the crew can take a twenty-minute break in the afternoon. Get you some water. Rest in the shade. Best I can do by you.' Now what you think about that, Burke?"

"I don't know. Time's hard all over."

"Harder for some folks than others," said Yates, almost bitterly. My grandpa was a slave. We ain't slaves no more, but we ain't too far from it, way I see it."

At Sugar Joe's directive from Yates, the four other men of the crew had put down their wheelbarrows and shovels. They sauntered over to the water-can that was on a small raised wooden platform by the tool shed. In turn, with the dented, tin-dipper, they each took a drink of the tepid water and retreated to the shade of the old oak tree. They lounged in the dry grass, or sat leaning against the huge trunk, with their caps pulled down over their eyes.

"Come on over and sit a spell," Yates offered.

"All right."

The two men strode across the gravel yard. Yates turned off to the left toward the tool shed.

"Let's get us a drink. Water's not too cool, but it's wet and near 'bout clean."

He filled the dipper, and handed it to Ezra who gulped down the water from it and handed it back empty to Yates.

"You know, Burke, I never knowed a white man who'd drink after a colored one. Like them water fountains they got in the mill and in them fancy stores downtown. One for your folks and one for mine. Bathrooms, too. Seems a funny thing to me, having two of everything. But folks, black and white, just go on about their business, like it's the most natural thing in the world. But you know something? Ain't nothing natural about it. Least not to me. It's just a way to keep us down. You different from me, Burke? I mean as a man?"

"I reckon not. We all just working trying to make a living. We all poor," replied Ezra.

Yates stared in the face of the other man as he spoke, and when he had finished speaking, he still stared. He looked hard into Ezra's face, like he was trying to understand or figure something out.

"Let's go sit in the shade," Ezra finally said, self-consciously. Yates shook his head slightly as if he were waking from a trance or a dream. He said nothing as the two men walked side-by-side to the oak tree.

CHAPTER 30

A picker-stick is a finished wooden slat, located on either side of a power-driven loom. It propels the shuttle at relatively high speeds, from one shuttle box into the opposite shuttle box, between openings in the warp. More specifically, a picker-stick is a flat bat crafted from dense, very hard and polished hickory. It is approximately three feet long and one and a half inches thick. The wide end, approximately three inches, tapers to approximately one and a half inches at the opposite end. Because of the speed and constant stress on them, picker-sticks were replaced and discarded frequently, often within days of being newly installed on a loom. Although manufactured to be an integral and necessary part of cotton mill machinery, when taken from the loom as a separate entity, a picker-stick was an adequate substitute for a bat in a pickup game of street ball. Also, the tapered end of the picker-stick generally fit a man's hand comfortably, thus making it an effective weapon when swung aggressively.

***

In the waning darkness of early Saturday morning, the Ford van drove slowly through the deserted streets of Corinth. Occasionally, at a corner, the driver pulled to the curb, the engine idling. The young man in the front seat beside him scrambled out and ran to the back of the vehicle. Opening the metal doors, he yanked a tightly bundled stack of newspapers and flung them onto the sidewalk. If the delivery boy was not already waiting, sleepily leaning against a lamppost, for the papers he would be along shortly. Either way, the young man hopped back into the van as it drove away to its next stop.

After untying the bundle, the boy folded each newspaper with quick and efficient expertise. He then packed them neatly and snuggly into the wire basket mounted on the handlebars of his bicycle. Adjusting his tattered baseball cap, he mounted the bike and pedaled to the wide, neat, tree-lined streets of his route. The best paper route in town.

***

Cates Allgood was already up making coffee. Mattie was off on Saturdays. Just as well, thought Allgood, she wouldn't be up this early anyway. He heard the dull thud of the tightly folded newspaper as it bounced off the front door onto the tiled porch. Best damn paper boy in Corinth, Allgood said to himself.

He felt pretty good this morning, after ensuring the night's sleep with a couple of extra drinks after Rufus' phone call. He'd drive over to the mill in a little while, kick some butt, and then maybe get in nine this afternoon, if it wasn't too hot. Might just play alone, sharpen his game. Scooter would be drunk by then anyway. Maybe have supper at the club, with the wife gone and all.

He shuffled down the carpeted hallway, his leather slippers sliding noiselessly along the plush oriental runner. He opened the front door and reached down for the newspaper, which he carefully unfolded standing in the doorway. With an almost audible gasp, he read the headlines which leaped up at him in large block letters, *RIOT AT GALWAY MILL: STRIKE IMMINENT?* Underneath was a photograph of a policeman holding a man on the ground with one hand and a nightstick raised in the other. Damn, no wonder Rufus had sounded so shaken on the phone last night. Allgood admitted to himself that the reporter had even somewhat unnerved him when he had arrived home.

Last evening, he had been preoccupied and annoyed with himself as he turned into the circular driveway, pulling the Packard up in front of the white-columned mansion. He had played terribly and lost a two-dollar Nassau to Scooter.

I should have known better, he thought. Scooter plays at least seven rounds a week. Damned bankers. Must have lost my concentration thinking about mill troubles.

Tired and sluggish from the golf and the rounds of drinks afterwards, Allgood opened the car trunk. Jasper came out the front door and grabbed the bag of clubs before Allgood managed to lift them out of the car.

"Afternoon, Mr. Cates. You hit 'em good today, did you?" asked the black man cheerfully, as he hoisted the golf bag, with effort, to his shoulder.

"Like hell I did, Jasper. Couldn't hit one in the ocean today."

"Oh, I'm sure that ain't so, Mr. Cates. They's bad days and then they's good days. In golf, just like in life."

"If you say so, Jasper," said Allgood disinterestedly, "anybody call?"

"Oh, yes sir," replied the servant, without elaboration
"Well, who? From the mill?"

"Don't know, but don't think from the mill. Jis wanted to talk to you. Wouldn't leave no message. But some good news!"

"What?"

"Got a telegram from Miss Winky."

"Is that right? What did it say?" asked Allgood, as Jasper followed him onto the porch.

"Oh, I didn't read it, Mr. Cates. Wouldn't never do that."

Allgood turned slightly, raising an eyebrow to the black servant, and thought, Like hell you wouldn't. Jasper grinned and looked down at the golf bag.

"My, these clubs is a mess. I best go on out back and scrub 'em up. You need anything else right now, Mr. Cates?"

"No. You go on out and clean up the clubs. I left my shoes at the club so you don't have to bother with them." Jasper stepped back off the porch and disappeared round back of the house.

As Allgood pushed open the front door, someone called from the street.

"Mr. Allgood, Mr. Allgood. Can I speak with you a minute?" It was the reporter. He was accompanied by a photographer. They had been standing on the corner opposite the house, waiting for the mill owner to arrive. The sun had fallen behind the trees this late summer evening. The street was in shadows.

"Who are you?"

"We're with the Gazette. Just wanted to know if you're planning to keep the mill open or not." The two men had stridden swiftly across the thick immaculate grass of the lawn.

"What the hell you talking about?"

"Don't know about the riot today?"

"What riot?"

"Well, maybe not a riot, precisely speaking. But I'm talking about the demonstration and police mess at Galway Mill this afternoon. Three or four hours ago."

Allgood stepped away from the door, leaving it ajar, and back out onto the porch.

"Oh, it was probably just a bunch of malcontents stirred up by a few on those Yankee Reds. Not much to it. I know what goes on at all my mills."

"Well, I see you been golfing and likely ain't heard. Police came in and busted it up. Busted a few heads, too. Saw it all myself. Arrested about twenty people, maybe more."

The color seemed to temporarily vanish from his face, but he quickly regained his composure.

"Like I said, I am aware of what goes at my mills. However, I have no intention of talking to you about it. So, good day gentlemen." Allgood turned to enter his house.

"I guess we can't print you didn't know anything about it?" the reporter called to him.

As Allgood turned back to the reporter the camera flashed, catching him red-faced and angry, squarely in its frame. He hesitated and then disappeared, slamming the gleaming white door behind him.

"Are you going to keep the mill open?" shouted the reporter pointlessly to the closed door. He then shrugged, scribbled something on his pad, and he and the camera man walked away.

Allgood had pulled a handkerchief from his back pocket and wiped sweat from his face as he slowly climbed the carpeted stairs to his study. He picked up the heavy, black receiver and dialed a number. After ten rings, he slammed it into its cradle. Almost instantly the phone rang, but only once before he yanked it off the hook.

"Hello."

"Mr. Allgood, finally got you," came the exasperated, but relieved voice on the line.

"What the hell's been going on, Rufus?"

Jordan took a deep breath and settled back in the leather desk chair and related the day's events to Allgood. Uncharacteristically, he listened to the Superintendent's account without interruption.

When he had finished, Allgood asked, "What about the other shifts?"

"Not many showed up for the second. Of course we don't know about the third yet, but expect it will be about the same. I called in all the overseers and second-hands too."

"Yes, *that* should produce some really high quality greige," Allgood said sarcastically.

"Well, that's about all we can do until this thing blows over, unless you have some ideas."

Jordan was tired and responded to his superior somewhat more truculently than he had intended, but it didn't much bother him.

"Damn reporter here when I got home. Wanted to know if I was going to keep the mill open. Stupid bastard, why would he think we'd close the mill?"

"Yeah, they've been here today, too. I suppose we'll be able to read about it in the morning paper. Not much we can do about it," Jordan said wearily.

"I don't give a damn about all that, but I have no intention of closing down anything. Not for one day, not one shift, not one hour. You hear me, Rufus? Not for one hour!"

Jordan leaned forward in the chair, "Sure, we'll keep running. I'll keep everybody over for the midnight shift, just in case."

"You do that. And pay time-and-a-half to those who stay over. No, double-time. You got that, Rufus?"

"Yes, sir."

"We've got to fight fire with fire. I'll be coming to the mill in the morning. Have Matheson there and this man he's recruited. We need information. Should have already gotten it. I'm tired of fooling around with this thing, Rufus."

"Yes, sir. I know you are. Me too."

"And come to think of it, have that young man there, what's his name, the one that does things for you from time to time, the surly one."

"You mean Benny Ray?"

"Yes, him. Might need him on this."

"Okay," said Jordan. There was a loud click and then a dial tone in his ear, as Allgood had abruptly hung up.

***

Late into the night on that Friday, in the heavy, warm air beneath a sky black and moonless, men had crept about in shadows around the mill property. More bricks and stones crashed through the mill office windows. Windshields of bosses' cars imploded under the force of picker-sticks expertly swung by dark, stealthy figures. Trash barrels were overturned. In back of the mill, the chute levers of parked coal cars were pulled, the chunks of coal cascading to the ground, covering the railroad tracks.

Newton, the security guard, holed up and nearly suffocating in the small brick guardhouse, had fled as soon as the police had cleared the crowd late that afternoon. His night-shift replacement did not show up for work. Jordan, after speaking with Allgood, had taken a long slug of whiskey from his desk drawer cache. He then gave instructions to the overseers and left for home, wondering if things could get any worse.

***

Sitting at the dining room table, absentmindedly dipping and replacing his spoon into a bowl of limp corn flakes, Allgood began to read the article. Not only unflattering, it was almost scathing in its account of the mill's management and Jordan's inept handling of the situation on Friday. The union rally and the subsequent march from downtown to Galway Mill had started out peacefully enough. One of the union organizers, a Mr. Deminici, was quoted extensively, several times emphasizing the peaceful aims of the group.

But the mill owners had responded violently and recklessly, unleashing scores of armed policeman on the workers. The Superintendent, Mr. Rufus Jordan, had responded to the group with disdain and profanity. The article went on to recount, in detail, the attack by the police, described as being brutal, unprovoked, and heavy-handed. It ended by stating that Cates Allgood, head of the family that owns the mill, refused comment.

A shorter article below the fold gave a summary of union activity at other mills in the region. It spoke of the intransigence of management and the deterioration of working conditions and wages. By posing pointed questions, the article implied that strikes, perhaps a general one, loomed likely in the very near future.

Believing in maintaining his composure at all times and in the inherent rights—and righteousness—of property owners, he folded the paper neatly and placed it on the table beside the cereal bowl. He then wiped his mouth with his napkin and went to his room, and dressed for the day.

***

As he turned off Galway Avenue onto First Avenue, he saw that Jordan's car was already in its space beside the office building. He also noticed that several windows had been smashed and pieces of glass lay scattered beneath them in the wet, morning grass. It was the only visual indication that betrayed the quiet peacefulness of the still-silent mill and the shaded grounds of the mill office. He pulled the Packard into the gravel parking area and inexplicably into the space marked, *Reserved: Mr. Allgood*, something he had never done before.

This meeting will be short and sweet, he thought. Won't be a doubt who's in charge. Lead by strength. I want no one's opinion or ideas. I just want followers. That way, they'll see I'm confident and determined and maybe, by god, some of it will rub off on them. There will never be a union in an Allgood plant!

They were waiting for him in the front room, Miss Wilcox's office. Jordan sat at her desk, leaning forward on it with clasped hands facing the door. Matheson stood against the open hallway door, behind and to the right of Jordan. He bit off the tip of the day's first cigar and spat it into the painted metal wastebasket on the floor beside him.

Two men were by the wall, to his left, as Allgood stepped into the room from the small, concrete porch. The shorter of the two leaned against the wall, with muscular arms folded across his chest. His cap was tilted rakishly to one side of his head, almost touching his left ear. The short-sleeves of his thin, cotton shirt were rolled up tightly to accent his biceps. A matchstick dangled from the corner of his mouth and his eyelids seemed to droop precariously over dark eyes, mistakenly giving the impression that he might be drowsy and not alert. He appeared bored and uninterested, but this again, would have been an inaccurate assumption.

The other man, dressed in patched overalls, was much taller and perhaps a bit older. He stood almost erect, away from the wall, with his large hands at his side. A shock of dark, thick hair, not quite unruly, fell across his forehead. He brushed back his hair with a hand, and stared self-consciously at the bare wooden floor.

Except for some initial inane small talk, there had been no conversation as the four men waited for the owner to arrive. None of them knew what to expect. Two of them did not know why they were there at all. The room was filled with an uneasiness, just short of a foreboding. They were there because they had to be. It might well have been mistaken for a wake.

"Good morning," Allgood said to no one in particular, and removed his hat without smiling, placing it on the edge of the desk.

Jordan pulled back slowly and sat erect in the swivel chair. The other men, more or less self-consciously, shuffled around somewhat, but then returned to their previous postures. Matheson lit the cigar.

"Good morning, Mr. Allgood," said Morgan, as he rose from the chair. "Do you want to go back to my office?"

"No. No, this is fine. More room in here anyway." He pulled a gold cigarette case from the breast pocket of his coat. He removed a cigarette and inserted in into his Bakelite holder. Matheson stepped over with a lighted match. "Thank you, Charlie."

"Mr. Allgood, I don't think you know these two men, at least not personally," Jordan said, as he gestured to the men by the wall to his right. Allgood glanced over at them. "This is Benny Ray Tucker." Unfolding his thick arms Tucker touched the bill of his cap in greeting. Jordan continued, "And this is Ezra Burke."

"Ah, Mr. Burke," said Allgood, dropping the 'r' in Burke, displaying his best patrician Southern accent. "I have been made aware of your work here in my plant. Awfully good of you to come."

He extended his hand and Ezra stepped forward with his. As the two men from worlds apart shook hands, Allgood was unaware that the other had just finished working a double shift in the weave room. If he *had* known, it would have mattered little to him, if at all.

"All right, Rufus, give me a run down," Allgood said, turning to his plant Superintendent.

"Charlie, would you get Mr. Allgood a chair."

"No, I'll stand. I don't think this will take very long."

"Sure, thing," responded Jordan, as he sat back down in the desk chair.

The sun was well up by now and the room was warmed by it. A thin, blue haze of tobacco smoke drifted up and hugged the ceiling. Of the men in the small room, only Allgood seemed not to be perspiring. Matheson reach up and gently yanked on the bead-chain to the ceiling fan above the desk. The wooden blades began to whirl instantly, but no one felt any movement of the air in the space about them.

Jordan cleared his throat. He was not intimidated by Allgood's presence. He had worked for him many years and felt he knew how to handle him. But this time he was not sure how much his boss knew or what his reactions might be, though he might have guessed. He knew the man standing before him could be tough and capable of subterfuge, even perverse at times. But it would always be subtle and mildly superficial—with taste—in keeping with the expected and inbred manners of his class.

"Well, the mob arrived here around two o'clock," Jordan began.

"Excuse me, Rufus, but I read all about the incident yesterday. Excellent coverage by our local journalist," Allgood said sarcastically, with a tight smile from his thinly formed lips, interrupting his subordinate. "I want to know what we're doing at the mill, operationally. That is, our plans to keep producing cloth."

"Oh yes, the mill," said Jordan. "After the, uh, disruption yesterday we had a lot of people not show up for second shift. I kept most everyone on first over to work second, including folks like Mr.

Burke here. Overseers and second-hands too. I don't know if people were scared to come in or what, but we kept the looms running."

"Did you make production?" asked Allgood, softly but pointedly.

"Not quite, but close. Like I said, we kept things running. We just needed to make it to the end of second shift last night and then close for the weekend. I think we did all right," Morgan spoke matter-of-factly, not defensive in anyway although he was choosing his words carefully. He knew where this was probably going.

"What about next week?" Allgood bore in.

"Ah, I'm not too worried about it, are you, Charlie?" Morgan looked up at Matheson who shrugged slightly.

"I really can't say. Things seem a little out of whack. Oh, we'll keep running, Mr. Allgood, one way or the other."

"Quite right," the mill owner said.

"Uh, this will all blow over. These folks got to work, so where else are they going to go?" Morgan said, with what he felt was a simple and rational explanation. The people would continue to come, work their shifts, and collect their wages. What choice did they have? "Economy's bad," he added, overstating the obvious.

"This thing, this so-called union movement, is spreading all over the Southeast. Rabble-rousers from up North everywhere. I don't think that it will just vanish and go away on its own, Rufus."

"Maybe not, then."

"As we discussed previously, Rufus and I that is, we need information. Good information about what's going on with this organization stuff. What about it, Rufus?" With this question, Matheson cut his eyes to Ezra.

He had been standing almost motionless during this entire exchange. He was tired and a little bleary-eyed. He had had no rest, working twenty hours straight, except for the supper break when he had talked with Melvin. He wondered why he was here. Judith had expressed misgivings about it. Things had moved too fast. The move to loom fixer, to first shift, to more pay. Now he, nothing more than a worker on wages, summoned to a meeting early on a Saturday morning with the mill owner himself, not to mention the Superintendent, neither of whom he had ever seen until today.

"Charlie," Jordan said, looking back at Matheson. Matheson tapped the long, gray, cylinder of ash from his cigar on the edge of the ashtray and cleared his throat.

"I guess this brings us to why you're here, Burke."
Ezra thrust his hands into the pockets of his overalls.
"Any idea?"

"No, I reckon not," answered Ezra, glancing briefly at Allgood.

Jordan interrupted, "Benny Ray, mind stepping out on the porch for a minute. Close the door behind you."

Benny Ray, with a bored smirk, sauntered across the room and stepped out onto the office porch. I don't give a rat's ass what y'all scheming, he was thinking. All just big shots. All except that big, dumb hillbilly. Don't matter none to me though. They want me for something, some dirty little job. And I'll do it. I'll do anything for the right money.

"Go on, Charlie," said Jordan.

"Well, it's like this. As Mr. Allgood said, we need to know what's going on. I mean what the people, the troublemakers, are up to. There's got to be talk on the floor. Around the waterhouse. Always is. Most of it rumors, I suspect, but some of it might be information we can use to head off trouble. You get my drift here, Ezra."

"No, sir. I reckon I don't," came the loom fixer's laconic reply.

Allgood moved toward the desk and sat on the edge of it facing Ezra. He asked in a low voice, "Mr. Burke, have you joined this outlaw union?"

"No, sir."

"Do you intend to do so?"

"No, sir, don't reckon I do."

"Good. Yes, good indeed," Allgood said and seemed to relax some. "Please proceed, Charlie. Let's get on with it."

"The long and short of it, Ezra, is we need you to help us out. Don't have to do anything. Just keep your ears open and let me know what you hear. That's all. Nobody has to know, just the men in this room. Not much to it, really. We need you in on this, Ezra."

Matheson re-lit his cigar, but never took his eyes off Ezra. Okay, thought Matheson. There, I've done it. My yeoman's service. My ounce of flesh for *the Man*. Dirty business, all in all. I never should have dragged Burke into this. He's not like the rest of us. Anyway, who was I kidding? He won't do it and I'm glad he won't, damn it. God, I hate this crap.

Silence, heavy as the hot smoky air in the room, fell over the small group. Everyone looked at Ezra.

Jordan leaned back in the desk chair and swiveled around toward where Ezra stood.

"Well, Mr. Burke, can we count on you?"

Ezra hesitated for a moment, then said slowly, but distinctly, "I reckon I need to tell you what I am hearing and what I am thinking right now."

"That would be a good thing for you to do, Mr. Burke," Allgood said, misinterpreting Burke's implications.

"Mr. Matheson, if I am hearing you right, y'all want a spy on the weave room floor."

"I wouldn't call it a spy, not exactly," interrupted Jordan, glancing at Allgood.

"Yes, that's precisely what we want, Mr. Burke, a spy!" said Allgood forcefully, purposely overruling Jordan's reticence.

"I wouldn't feel right doing something like that. It's not my way. I do my job. I try to do the best I can. I don't aim to get messed up in any of this union organizing. I just want to work."

"Damn it, Burke, we have taken care of you!" Jordan exploded.

Allgood held up his hand coolly, quieting the Superintendent. In his soft draw he spoke to Ezra.

"But Mr. Burke, you, all of us here, *are* as you say, messed up with what's going on. Can't you see that?"

"No, sir, I don't see it that way at all. You see, where I come from folks pretty much tend to their own business. Of course we're obliged to help a neighbor out when he needs a hand."

"Okay, Burke," offered Jordan impatiently, "We're your neighbors. We need, uh, a hand."

"No, sir, Mr. Jordan, I don't see it that way either. You're not my neighbor, you're my boss man. I work at the mill for wages. I won't spy on people. I wouldn't do that."

Jordan rose with both fists pressed against the desktop.

"Look here, Burke. You owe this company. We were counting on you. How do think you jumped over twenty men been waiting years to get on the day shift, no longer than you've been working here? Think we just liked the color of your overalls? Put you on as a loom fixer so we could pay you more money. Ever think about how all that came about? You owe this mill—Mr. Allgood here—and you'll do what we tell you to do!" Jordan sat back into the chair, glaring.

At this, Ezra glanced over at Matheson, who stared back at him, shaking his head slightly.

"I owe you an honest day's work for a day's pay, Mr. Morgan, and I don't mean any disrespect. To you either, Mr. Allgood. Things are rough, I reckon I know that. Most of us working on the floor just trying to do what we can to get by until things get better. That's all. I just want to work and take care of my family."

He looked around the room and then just stared at the floor. There was nothing else to say.

"So, you won't help us out with this, Mr. Burke?" asked Allgood pointedly.

"No, sir, I won't."

"You look tired, Mr. Burke," said Allgood, after a tense silence. "Why don't you go home and get some rest."

Jordan looked up at the mill owner, the puzzlement apparent on his perspiring face. Ezra crossed the room without comment and left the conspirators behind him in the hot, stale office.

"Fire him Monday morning," Jordan said to Matheson. "Ungrateful son of a bitch."

"No, no, let him go," Allgood broke in. "No use alienating him. That would just add fuel to the fire for these union people. Besides, I suspect you're going to need all the hands you can get on the floor come Monday morning."

Monday morning, thought Bulldog Matheson, they'll be hell to pay around here. How I hate to see Monday morning come.

Allgood took his hat from the desktop and placed it on his head, careful not to muss his immaculately-groomed hair.

"That went well," he said sarcastically, his drawl articulate, soft and controlled.

"About what I expected," offered Matheson unapologetically, momentarily removing the cigar, now but a stub, from his mouth.

"Forget it, it doesn't matter," Allgood said and shrugged slightly. He then looked at Jordan coldly, almost with a glare. "Rufus, I want this mill up and running Monday morning. Do whatever you need to do, but see to it. And another thing, I don't want the police involved. Avoid another mess like we had yesterday."

"I can't see it being much of a problem. Folks will be back on the job come Monday for sure," said Jordan unconvincingly, despite the bravado.

Allgood turned and opened the door to leave. He paused and repeated to Jordan, "See to it." He then left the building, shutting the door behind him.

"Whew," Jordan exhaled. "What do you think, Charlie?"

"You saw the paper this morning. There's bound be some scrubby demonstrators on the street out there."

"You think there will be enough of them to picket?"

"Who knows?" Matheson shrugged. "But I don't think this thing is just going to go away. It's in the air now and folks are breathing it."

Jordan leaned backed in the chair, his hands interlocked behind his head. After a moment, he suddenly leaned forward, almost lurched, slapping the desktop.

"Okay, you may be right, Charlie. Get Benny Ray back in here."

Matheson opened the door and motioned to Benny Ray. The young thug came in and assumed his position, leaning against the wall.

"Here's the plan, Benny Ray. Get some of your boys together. Might as well use the same ones that helped you clean out those ramblers and hobos down by the railroad tracks awhile back."

"No problem with that," replied the young man, dryly.

"Get them all picker-sticks. I am assuming there's a slew of them discarded somewhere, isn't there, Charlie?"

"Sure, there's a pile in the bin out back near the coal yard."

"I know where they are," said the young man impatiently, taking the match from his lips.

"Yes, I suppose you do at that," Jordan smiled cynically, with an almost derisive curl to his lips. "Anyway, first thing Monday morning, and I mean first thing, before the eight o'clock whistle blows, I want y'all here at the mill. Be around the main gate. And I want you to post a couple of men around the office building here. Miss Wilcox was scared to death when she left here last night.

"Then what?" asked the young man.

"You make sure the first-shift people don't have any problem getting in the plant to go to work. I doubt there will be a picket line or anything like that, but there might be. Just make sure the gate's not blocked."

"And what if it is?" the young man, asked as he warmed to the assignment, rubbing the knuckles of his right hand with his left.

"Look here, Benny Ray, we don't want any trouble if it can be avoided. Make sure your boys understand that. I believe these union boys will see the picker-sticks and know that we mean business."

"And if they don't?"

"Well, obviously you would need to take steps. After all, that's why you'll be carrying the picker-sticks."

"Got it. Anything else? I ain't had no breakfast."

"I suppose not. You got anything, Charlie?"

"No."

"That's about it, then," said Jordan.

Benny Ray Tucker was already heading for the door. Matheson followed him and flicked the cold cigar stub into the yard. He stepped back into the office, shutting the door behind him.

"This ain't good, Rufus," said Matheson. He slumped into a chair.

"What the hell am I supposed to do? You heard Allgood. I got to make sure we're weaving cloth come Monday morning. I'll knock heads if I have to."

"Okay, you're in a tight spot, or may be. I guess we'll see." Matheson leaned forward in the chair. "Is that all for now?"

Jordan glanced up at the large clock hanging on the wall behind Matheson.

"It's almost nine. The Company Store is open by now. I want you to go over there and post a sign."

"What kind of sign?" asked Matheson, irritated slumping back down in the chair.

"Put it on the message board out front. As a matter of fact, take down all that other crap that's up there. Nobody reads it anyhow."

"The sign, Rufus?"

"Yes, the sign. Just have it say that any Galway employee that took part in the demonstration on Friday will be allowed to return to work on Monday, no questions asked. You better add that they will be placed on probation and fired if they participate in any further union activity.

"Anything else?"

"No, that should do it"

"Yep, that should do it," returned Matheson as he stood, hesitating a moment, and then left the office without comment.

Morgan walked down the hallway to his office. From his desk, the mill across the yard was framed by the shattered window to his left. The green leaves on the oak tree limbs danced lightly in the morning breeze, hot and misleading. This early on Saturday morning the traffic on Galway Avenue was sparse. The air, heavy with summer, was almost noiseless. He missed the low hum that emanated from the mill when it was running, but now there was only silence. He reached down and pulled the bottle from the desk drawer.

***

Ezra had descended the few steps from the mill office porch and walked across the yard to Galway Avenue, and home. A bus slowed at the stop across the street and then accelerated, as no one was waiting there to board.

I'm pretty much a damn fool, he thought. Must look like the hick that I am. Judith. I should have listened to her. She has a feeling for things like this, when they're not right.

Then he thought about the things Melvin had said. About the bosses and how the workers must stick together. And about the stretch-outs and piece-work. Many of the people in the weave room, especially the older hands, were struggling to keep up, and some of them just could not do it. They were either let go or had their already-low wages reduced. Even wages were now sometimes being paid in script. None of it seemed right to him. Just then he thought about the land, the mountains, but he dismissed the image immediately. He had let go of all that. It did not exist anymore for him. He would be at the mill on Monday. Just wait and see how things went. But for sure, he thought, she had been right.

Exhausted, he trudged on purposefully, his hands deep in the overall pockets, thinking. Maybe Melvin's right. These are not good men. Never thought Mr. Matheson would connive like this, but he did. He's one of them. I missed it that too, I reckon.

With an uneasiness that was nameless and abstract, he turned onto his street, tree-lined and shaded from the bright morning sun.

CHAPTER 31

The day before, on Friday, the sky had dawned almost colorless and cloudless. The sun would soon turn its pale blue tint to a glaring white, promising a hot and humid morning. It was late August and summer had its death grip on the South. Like a dreary, visitor who stays on long after his welcome has worn thin, the languid summer hung in the air patiently, as if it had no intention of ever moving on. High billowing thunderheads, capped in black, would later build in the west in the afternoon. Rain would be hoped for and would sometimes come, but more often it did not. The clouds would pass and fade away, teasing the hot dry ground and the people pushing against it, trying to overcome the inertia of the heat.

Word of the rally had spread to all the greige mills around Corinth, like Galway, but also to the spinning plants and the bleacheries. All the workers, though with jobs such as they were, shared the hardships of the deepening Depression—cut wages, oppressive bosses and conditions, piecework with unobtainable quotas, and the loathsome stretch-outs. They were frequently paid with script instead of money, redeemable only at the Company Store. Many had attended the organizing meetings, signed union cards joining the AUTW, and talked up the rally with their friends and fellow workers. They had had enough, and knowing that they risked losing their jobs and being blacklisted, they would band together. Surely, they thought, the owners would listen this time and understand their grievances. Things would get better.

The early morning had found City Park quiet and almost deserted except for a few elderly people walking dogs before the inevitable wet heat wrestled the day from them. By ten o'clock, a few men milled around the large gazebo which sat on a grassy knoll in at the center of the park. Some squatted in the grass, backs to the trunks of oak trees, spitting long streams of tobacco juice, darkening the grass in streaks in front of them. The sun was well up by now as the shade of the trees shrank upon itself. On the sidewalk to the north, overlooking the park, two policemen stood, bored and impatient, no doubt discussing, or cursing, the heat.

More people arrived, mostly men, but there were a few women among them who stepped off the bus at the stop at the far side of the park and walked in small, quiet groups toward the gazebo.

***

Sitting in the back booth at Bill's Good Eats, Leon looked at his watch and closed the small leather notebook. A large manila envelope lay on the table. It was hot in the restaurant, the air heavy with the smell of burnt grease and coffee. A squeaking ceiling fan rotated slowly above, offering no relief from the heat, but spreading the acrid aromas from the grill, mixing them with cigarette smoke across the room.

"Time to go, Ski. You ready?"

"Sure, let's go," replied the big man as he drank the last of the coffee from the heavy mug. "We've done about all we can do, at least until we get more help."

"Jake's sending down more people. Should be here in a day or two."

"We're going to need them, that's for sure."

"A lot depends on what kind of turn-out we get at the rally today. We got to get Galway Mill under our thumb. That's all there is to it," Leon declared.

"Well, you saw the report from the committee. They got a tough owner. Controls a bunch of plants. Big name in this town."

"That worries me some. I mean his influence. I just hope we don't have any problems with the police. At least not until we get help."

"Jake'll send good men; he always does. We did all right in St. Louis, didn't we? Wasn't easy though."

Leon placed two quarters on the table, picked up the notebook and envelope, and eased himself out of the booth.

"Okay, it's eleven-thirty. It's about a fifteen-minute walk to the park from here, right?"

"Yeah, I walked it yesterday. Fifteen minutes exactly."

Leon pushed open the heavily smudged plate-glass door and Dobinsky followed him out onto the sidewalk. They headed for the park. The traffic was heavy and moved sluggishly past them. They walked briskly, sweating in the heat. No one on the street appeared to notice of them. Finally arriving at the park, they turned down the sidewalk and saw the two policemen ahead. Several police cars had also pulled up to the curb. Then both men looked across the grass to the gazebo.

"God Almighty, Leon, there must be five hundred people down there. Workers too. Most all in overalls."

"At least five hundred," Leon agreed, and turned onto the gravel walkway that led to the gazebo and the throng of people gathered there. There was the low hum of hushed conversations.

"There they are. That's them, ain't it?" called out one of the men sitting on the railing of the gazebo above the crowd, as he spotted the two union men approaching.

Faces turned and several voices confirmed the sighting. An uneasy silence fell over the large gathering as they turned to see Deminici and Dobinsky striding toward them. The sudden quietness of the assemblage and the peaceful surroundings of the park itself struck Leon as odd and strange, almost surreal in its image and impact. He was used to rowdy, boisterous gatherings sometimes out of control or nearly so. But this was almost an acquiescence to something he did not quite understand. But then it occurred to him that this kind of thing— organizing, going against *the Man*, maybe even your neighbor—was foreign to these people. They were waiting on him. Someone to show them the way. How it's done. They were operating in a vacuum. A vacuum of leadership. Well, by god, that's why he was here.

What a great turn out, he thought, as he felt the rush of adrenalin course through his body.

As he and Ski pushed through the sea of people, they started to move about and chatter, many of them patting the shoulders of the two men as they pressed through. They felt the intoxicating and wonderful feeling of power.

"Now we'll show 'em!"

"Gotta all stick together!"

"Only way we going to get relief!"

"Go get 'em, boys. We're with you!"

"Damn the owners. Damn the bosses. Damn 'em all!"

The two organizers mounted the steps of the gazebo and stood facing the crowd. Applause and cheers went up. Ski caught a glimpse of the policemen, now ten or twelve strong, fanning out several yards behind the crowd. Thick, black nightsticks swung from their wide patent leather belts. He had expected it. He had seen it all before. He knew the drill.

Below, near the steps of the gazebo, a reporter scribbled vigorously on a note pad. A man stood with him fiddling with a camera, adjusting the lens and twisting in a flash bulb. The reporter put down his pad and glanced up at the two men on the platform. Ski nudged Leon, nodding in the direction of the newspaper men.

"Want to come up and get some shots of the crowd, boys?" he called down to them.

"You bet!" said the scribbler as he and the photographer scrambled up the steps.

Leon raised a hand to quiet the gathering. He had noticed the policemen too. A flash bulb flared as the photographer aimed and clicked the shutter. No one seemed to notice.

"First, let me tell you boys, and I see a few gals out there too, this is a great turn-out. Must be five hundred of you here today." An instant roar of hoots and applause went up. With another hand raised, they gave him the silence he needed to be heard.

"We all know why we're here."

He pulled a document from the manila envelope, and held it high for everyone to see. It was now something *real* to them. It was on paper. The owners would read it. They had something tangible, something that gave them hope.

"This is the list of grievances you guys have. All legitimate and legal. You're only asking for what's fair and just. You have the right by law to organize, to join the Allied Union of Textile Workers, the AUTW!" The crowd again exploded with approval and acknowledgement.

"We will do this peacefully. We don't want trouble. Not with the owners, or with the police, not with anybody."

Leon glanced over the crowd at the policemen beyond them, several of which unconsciously shifted their weight as they stood there watching him lead the rally.

"Okay, enough talking. We're all going to march down Main Street and out to the Galway Mill office. When we get there I'll ask, no, demand to see Mr. Allgood and present this letter of grievances."

"What if he ain't there? He ain't usually," someone yelled from the crowd.

"Doesn't matter," responded Leon. "We'll meet with the mill Superintendent. He represents the owner. Same thing." He paused and looked out over the crowd. "Eugene Nabors, you here?"

"Sure as hell am," came the response.

"Good, I was sure you were. Most of you know Eugene. Works at Galway. He's done a lot of work, mostly behind the scenes, trying to get organized. Eugene, I want you out front with me and Ski leading the march." More cheers.

Leon and Ski then stepped down, and with Eugene, passed through the crowd of workers to lead the march. Main Street bordered the park on the west, beyond them and the policemen. The leaders started across the green expanse toward Main Street. The crowd, the excitement of anticipation building, followed, nearly surrounding them. As they approached the line of cops one of them stepped forward to confront Leon. The organizers held up their hands and movement stopped.

"I'm Sergeant McAnarney, and you folks need to stop right where you are. There's not going to be any march down Main Street. Not today."

"What's the problem, Sergeant? We have a right to march," said Leon.

"You got to have a permit," replied the policeman.

"According to who?" ask Dobinsky.

"City ordinance, Mister. Looks like you Northern boys ain't done your homework," the Sergeant smirked and looked around at the other men in uniform.

"What if we march anyway?" asked Leon.

"You'll be arrested," came the response.

"All of us?" one of the workers near the front called out.

"These three up front here for sure and as many of the rest of you we can get a hold of," the Sergeant shouted for all to hear.

The other policemen had closed in a bit toward the crowd. Leon knew that this confrontation was not winnable. He also knew that a permit to march on a city street was required. But he knew that if they had applied for a permit it would have been denied. Allgood had that kind of power. So he had decided to just take a chance on the march and see what happened.

"Okay, Sergeant. We want to obey the law and the law says we can't march on the street without a permit," Leon said.

"That's right," Sergeant McAnarney broke in. "You folks need to go on back home or to work or wherever you came from." He glared at Leon and Ski.

"Okay, Sergeant, just one more question," said Leon.

"What is it?"

"Any law against walking on the sidewalks?"

"Of course not, so long as you ain't doing something that's breaking the law," answered the Sergeant.

"Such as?" Leon pressed.

"Well, such as public drunkenness or lewd behavior," answered Sergeant McAnarney, somewhat puzzled by Leon's questioning, "or spitting on the sidewalk."

"Do you see anybody here, Sergeant, drinking or appearing as if they might be drunk?"

"Not that I can tell."

"See any lewd behavior?" someone yelled out, followed by guffaws from the crowd.

"Just what are you driving at, mister?" asked the Sergeant.

"If we can't march on the streets to Galway Mill it appears to be perfectly legal for us to walk there on the sidewalk. You know, like taking a stroll. It's two or three miles away, but I believe there's sidewalks most of the way. Any legal problem with us doing that, Sergeant?"

The policeman hesitated and looked away from Leon, who sensed the tension of the moment passing. The Sergeant then straightened his shoulders and assumed a stance to demonstrate his command of the situation. The dozen or so subordinates had their eyes on him.

"No, anybody can walk on a sidewalk. But let me tell you something, buster, it better be a peaceful walk with respect for other pedestrians and the like."

"Okay, Sergeant, it will be," Leon said, and ignoring any further conversation with the policeman, turned toward the crowd and gave directions.

So the large group of workers moved across the park to Main Street where they split into two roughly equal groups. They began their trek to Galway Mill, a group taking the sidewalk on either side of Main Street.

During the altercation with the sergeant, Dobinsky had noticed two men standing away from the crowd, near a stand of trees, at the far edge of the grassy open area of the park. He had slipped away from the rally and approached them.

"You joining the march?" asked Ski.

"What's it to you?" responded one of the men who looked directly at Ski. He was much shorter than the organizer, but his biceps, accented by the rolled up sleeves of his white shirt, were taunt and chiseled. His body did not move as he spoke, but leaned arrogantly against the tree trunk. His companion thrust his hands into the pockets of his trousers. He held his head down and nervously scraped his shoes in slow traces in the dirt.

"Just asking," returned Dobinsky. "I've watched you standing here the whole time."

"Free country, ain't it?"

"You guys mill workers?"

"I can't see where it's any of your business who the hell we are. Do you, Queazy?"

His diminutive companion cut his eyes up at Ski, but did not lift his head.

"No, I reckon it ain't."

"You a tough guy?" Dobinsky asked the muscular one.

"All depends on what you think a tough guy is, I guess," he answered with a sardonic smile, unintimidated.

"Most tough guys I know are stupid. You stupid?"

Ski's voice was calm, matter of fact. The muscular man stood erect from the tree, his feet apart. Ski noted that he was flexing the fingers of both hands, making quick fists then releasing them. Tension filled the hot humid air around the men.

"You calling me stupid?" The man's body seemed to tighten like a steel spring wound on itself.

"I'm not calling you anything. Just don't *do* anything stupid. It would not be wise."

For a moment the two looked into each others' faces, not exactly glaring, but neither blinking. The small thin man, head still down, continued to scuff his shoes in the dirt. Finally, the fight-ready tenseness of the muscular one seemed to abate as he realized one-on-one combat with the huge union man might not be to his advantage. He would wait for another time. A time when he had an edge, fighting fair did not mean much to him.

"Come on, Queazy, that's get the hell out of here." Both men walked past Ski, across the grass, to the street away from the crowd of mill workers.

***

As the mill workers moved through the city, two abreast on the sidewalks, they were met with jeers and insults. From passing cars, people called out to them.

"Get off the street, lint-heads!"

"Hey, lint-head. Yeah, you, go back to the mill hill!"

"Goddam lint-heads. You can smell 'em from here!"

The marchers, shy and slightly embarrassed despite the momentary excitement of the rally, did not respond. Most of them just looked straight ahead and followed mechanically the men in front of them. They remembered what the union man had said—no trouble. Pedestrians avoided them, preferring to step off the curb onto the street rather than brush by them on the sidewalk.

It was a strange parade, to be sure. They strode through town self-consciously and almost noiselessly. Many had begun to realize the seriousness and gravity of their demonstration. It felt alien to them, this organizing, these unions. They were, by nature, not joiners but conformers. Just work, make a living, make a life around their families. That was what they knew.

But they had now come to realize that the mill owners, with avarice and contempt, had no interest in them as people. Working conditions were getting worse, not better. This is what they were thinking and telling themselves as the group moved inexorably toward Galway Mill and whatever fate might await them there. Only the force and strength of these thoughts, and the people around them now, could maintain them and bolster the courage they would need.

As they moved out of the downtown business section of the city and onto the main road that led to the industrial neighborhoods, the marchers no longer formed tight groups. The crowd was strung out in small bands but all still strode toward their objective.

As the first segment of walkers finally reached Galway Avenue, with the mill in sight, Deminici realized that many of the marchers had straggled and had become strung out along the way. He halted the group at a vacate lot. The avenue was tree-lined here so the people welcomed the respite as they sat in the shade, cooling themselves as best they could in the oppressive heat, and waited patiently for the others to catch up.

He instructed Dobinsky to stroll down to the mill, now only a few blocks away. He was to check things out. See if the police were there or anything that looked unusual, or that might be a problem. Just get a feel for things and report back.

Interestingly, the reporter along with the photographer, had stayed with the marchers. He had tried to interview some of the people as they walked but his questions were mostly either ignored or given sullen, single word responses. When Leon halted the marchers to let the stragglers catch up, the reporter moved up to the lead group and to Leon. He found him standing alone in the sun near the curb.

"What's going to happen when you get to the mill, Deminici?" He was writing in the notebook as he asked.

"I don't know. We'll present our list of demands to the management."

"How do you think they'll respond?"

"No idea."

"Will you strike?"

With this question, Leon hesitated and looked over at the nearest group of workers resting in the shade. He knew whatever he said would be in print the next day.

"Not if we can help it. We just want decent working conditions. And recognition of the AUTW. That's all."

"That's all, huh? Have you led strikes before?" pressed the newspaperman. Leon looked at him but did not answer. The questions continued. "Is the AUTW affiliated with the American Communist Party?"

"Hell, no! Not in any way!" Leon retorted, glaring at the reporter, but he was glad for the question. It was now on record.

"What are the specific grievances y'all making?

"Here, read it yourself," Leon said as he pulled the letter from the manila envelope. "Try not to sweat on it." Perspiration dripped from the reporter's chin. He wiped it on the sleeve of his dingy blue-stripped seersucker coat. After perusing the single page statement, he passed it back to Leon.

"Thanks," he said. He scribbled more notes in his pad.

Finally, all the marchers caught up and were assembled in the vacant lot. At this point, with the heat and the exertion of the walk from downtown, they were tired and restless, and doubt began to creep in. There was some sporadic grumbling. Some reclined on the ground, resting, others squatted next to trees, but most just stood there, waiting. Leon knew that action—movement—would revive them. He made his way to the center of them.

"Okay, people, listen up," his sharp distinct Northern accent cut through the heat and carried across the throng of workers.

"Get ready to move out. We're almost there. We're going to go into the street. No sidewalks this time," he gestured toward Galway Avenue. "We'll be stopping traffic, but don't worry about it."

"What about cops?" It was Melvin Jenkins.

"Screw the cops!" someone else returned.

Blood was up. Leon smiled. Then Ski strode up and made his way to where he stood. The people waited.

"What's it look like?" asked Leon.

"Cop cars parked on the street in front of the mill office."

"How many?"

"Three. Six or seven uniforms standing around the cars," he said. Leon nodded and turned again the crowd.

"Okay, let's move out into the street. It's only four or five blocks to the mill. Just follow me and Dobinsky and Eugene. You ready, Eugene?"

"I reckon so," responded Eugene, who was standing near Leon.

As Leon knew it would, movement and action invigorated the tired and sweat-soaked workers as a certain tension and excitement swelled within them. The reality of their intentions set in. He held them up at the curb as a car drove by, the driver slowed down, gawking at the assembled mass of workers. Another car approached and whizzed by, honking its horn. Momentarily the avenue was clear of traffic as Leon and Ski and Eugene stepped out into the street. The group behind them seem to move as one as they filled the tree-lined street. They moved forward, inexorably, toward the gargantuan red-brick structure—Galway Mill. Cars approached, slowed and pulled to the curb as the leaders held up their hands, signaling them over. Automobiles approaching from behind the crowd slowed to the pace of the walkers. Car horns barked with frustration.

The assemblage soon reached the mill and Leon turned them onto First Street, between the mill and the mill office. The people quickly and quietly filled this space. They spilled over onto the parched grass of the mill office, and like a living tide, engulfed the parked police cars. The policemen, momentarily overcome by the mass of workers, retreated to the steps of the office porch.

"Everyone sit down. Sit on the ground or in the street where you are," shouted Leon.

They all sat. Only the leaders were standing. Leon and Eugene walked toward the mill office and halted near the steps where the policemen had posted themselves.

"We are here to see the owner, Mr. Allgood, or Mr. Jordan, the Superintendent, if Allgood isn't here."

"You people are breaking the law," said the cop nearest them.

"We have the right to assemble peacefully," said Leon.

"You're blocking traffic and access to the mill. Break this up and leave. Now," the policeman said calmly.

"I don't believe we can do that, officer."

As Leon spoke, one of the sitting workers in the midst of the group stood up. Then another, and another rose. Quickly and quietly, all the workers were standing in solidarity.

"You can't go in the office without an appointment or permission from the manager," said the policeman nervously. The other cops had moved closed to each other near the porch. "And you're on private property. Called trespassing, I believe."

"We just want to deliver this document to the owner or to the Super. Mr. Nabors, here, is an employee of Galway Mill. He's allowed on company property.

"I don't give a damn who he is or you neither, mister. You ain't going in this office. Mr. Allgood's not here and Mr. Jordan's busy, so forget about it," snapped the policeman.

"Come on, Eugene," said Leon, and the two men turned and walked back to the workers.

"Jordan's here but he won't see us," shouted Leon.

"So what now?" came the question from one of the few women workers.

"We wait. Here in the street. We just wait."

So they all sat down again where they were, most of them in the street, some squatted against the high, chain link fence that ran along the front of the mill. The afternoon sun was still bright. The heat had not abated, the still air, thick and heavy. The people, by this time, were tired and thirsty but they all just sat and waited. For what, they were not sure.

Then someone, again a women worker, began chanting.

"We want Allgood. We want Allgood. We want Allgood."

The solitary voice floated eerily over the throng of workers. They turned and stared blankly at her. Then someone else, near her, took up the chant. Then another. They were together again, just as before in the park, united. They all took up the chant, "We want Allgood," over and over until at five-hundred strong, it rose to a crescendo and remained there.

CHAPTER 32

Inside the mill office Miss Wilcox banged away at her typewriter. She detested the workers and their despicable demonstration. Like her bosses, she was going to ignore it, at least as long as she could. The chanting from the yard, though muffled somewhat, was clear and still loud: *We want Allgood, we want Allgood, we want Allgood.* She wanted to scream, she wanted to kill them all. Who did they think they were anyway? Ignorant lint-heads, ensconced in this mill village. Why, they weren't worth the consideration or acknowledgement of Mr. Allgood or Rufus Jordan. They should be thankful for the generosity shown them. They had jobs. In some vague, uneasy way, she felt that they were threatening her. She was a professional, an honor graduate of Vaughn's Business College for Women. Her work was her life. Damned if a mob of stupid and disgruntled mill workers would intimidate her. Why don't they just shut up and go away. They had better, or there'd be hell to pay, she had no doubt.

She looked up from her typewriter and glanced at Jordan's closed door. No one else was in the office. The chanting continued and grew even louder as shift change neared and other workers arriving for the second shift joined the rally.

"Goddam it, I've had enough. Why don't the cops do something? Useless bastards!" Jordan said loudly as his door flew open, banging against the heavy brass doorstop. He stomped up to the front area near Miss Wilcox's desk, but stood clear of the window overlooking the hot ragged workers in their chanting.

"See if you can get hold of Charlie and tell him to get over here. I wonder where the hell he is anyway," he said gruffly to the secretary. She immediately dialed the weave room office. No answer.

Matheson, having watched the scene unfolding from high above at the weave room windows, had already taken the freight elevator down from the weave room. But when he stepped outside the building, the sea of chanting workers was between him and the mill office. He made it to the guardhouse where Newton was holed up, the small, closed room a virtual sweatbox torture chamber. From the small side-window, he could observe the seated throng.

Although he was *management,* he had earned a grudging respect from most of the rank and file over the years, and was not intimidated by the crowd. He then left the guardhouse and approached the rear echelon of the huge group.

"Come on, boys, let me through," he said as he threaded his way through the workers who, like ragged Buddhas in overalls, sat, chanting mindlessly.

"Boss wants to see me," he said, occasionally lightly touching a shoulder as he brushed against someone.

He tried to take note of any of the Galway workers in the crowd. There were too many to count. He made progress through the multitude and bounded up the steps and into the office building. The chanting, *We want Allgood*, had not ceased.

"Hell of a mess, Rufus."

"Yeah, we'll see. I just got off the phone with the police chief. He's sending out more men."

"That a fact?" returned Matheson, with a sarcastic edge in his voice. "Talked to Mr. Allgood yet?"

"Not yet. Couldn't get him off the back nine," Jordan said, with his hands jammed into the pockets of his trousers. He did not look at Matheson, but out the window at the chanting workers. He was nervous and seemed to be shaken.

"What'll he say, you think?"

"What'll he say?" repeated Jordan, turning to Matheson, "he'll say, tell those goddamn Reds to go to hell, and fire as many as you can. Just keep the mill running. That's what he'll say!" Jordan said, agitated.

"So I guess he won't be out here right away?"

"No, I guess not," Jordan glared at him.

"A bunch of them are our people, Rufus. Too many to fire maybe."

"We'll see."

Jordan went back to his office and yanked the double-breasted suit coat from the mahogany rack. He donned it, cinched up his tie knot, and buttoned the coat. He walked back to the front where Matheson stood beside Ms. Wilcox's desk, peering out the window.

"You going out and talk to them?" asked Matheson.

"Yes, I am and you're coming with me. This hollering or chanting or whatever you call it is driving me nuts. Let's go!"

Jordan stepped out on the small concrete porch of the mill office. The sea of workers, all still seated, spread out before him. There were onlookers standing around the perimeter in the distance, hot with anticipation and curiosity. The chanting grew louder as the two mill bosses appeared. Jordan just stood there looking over the crowd, into the faces of the workers seated in the grass nearest him. Finally, he lifted his arms high in the air, gesturing for silence. None came.

"We want Allgood!" came the response.

Then Leon, who had been sitting near the front of the demonstrators stood up and held both his arms high, as he turned back toward them.

He shouted, "Quiet, quiet. Let's hear what he has to say."

The chanting subsided and faded in waves until there was silence. The union leader motioned for them to stand up and the mass of workers responded again as one giant organism, living and breathing of its own accord. He stepped forward.

Jordan cleared his throat as he wiped sweat from his forehead with a starched linen handkerchief, pulled from the breast pocket of his suit coat. He glanced at Matheson standing slightly behind his left shoulder, and then back out to the crowd.

"I don't know what you people want or what you're doing here. Those of you on the yard and against the fence are trespassing," he said to the crowd, nearly yelling.

A few these people edged back onto the street.

"I see there's a lot of Galway hands in this mob so I'm going to give you a warning. Break this mess up right now and you'll keep your job. If you don't, you'll be fired. After we fire you, you won't find work, at least in a cotton mill anywhere around here. I mean to do it! Do you hear me?" he continued to shout, red faced and sweating profusely beneath the serge suit and white shirt.

Leon motioned for Eugene, and both men stepped forward onto the grass lawn of the mill office.

"We have grievances," Leon held up the manila envelope, "and we aim to present them to Mr. Allgood."

"And just who in the hell might you be?" came Jordan's angry reply.

"My name is Deminici, Leon Deminici. I am a representative of the Allied Union of Textile Workers. These here," he paused and gestured to the throng, "are union members now, most of them."

"I don't really give a damn who you are. Just a commie rabble-rouser as far as I'm concerned." Random boos came from the people as Jordan shaded his eyes with his hand from the late afternoon sun. "Nabors, you're with this bunch of hoodlums?"

"Yes, sir, I reckon I am and I mean to stay with 'em," Eugene spat on the ground and then said calmly, but loud enough to be heard

over the crowd, "and we have here a list of things we want fixed. We'd
like to see Mr. Allgood, too."

Jordan turned and spoke softly to Matheson.

"Fire his ass!"

"All right."

"Well, you're not going to see Mr. Allgood, so forget it. I want
you people dispersed and off this property immediately!" Jordan turned
to go back into the office. Leon nudged Eugene and both men advanced
to the edge of the porch. Leon pulled the grievance document from the
envelope.

"Wait, Mr. Jordan," called out Leon. "Here is the list of the
unfair working conditions that these people are being subjected to, and
want addressed. Our demands are not unreasonable."

"I am not interested in your demands!" Jordan shot back.

"You best listen to what these people have to say," said Leon.

"You threatening me?" Jordan's blood was up. Where the hell
are those police?

"No, not personally but we demand our grievances be
addressed."

"Or what?"

"You figure it out," said Leon. Eugene glanced at him nervously.

"So you're threatening a strike. You must be crazy, mister.
Galway people are not going to strike. Never have, never will. Company
takes care of them."

The crowd had begun to move forward, pressing against the
backs of Leon and Eugene. The low hum of murmurs was constant, as
the situation grew more tense. Many of the workers who had just joined
the AUTW figured they had nothing to lose. Their jobs were gone
anyway, even if they backed down now.

"These people deserve to be heard," said Leon, to cheers from
those near him.

The chant began again, "We want Allgood."

Leon stepped up closer to the porch, holding the document up to
within Jordan's reach. After a brief hesitation, Jordan nodded to
Matheson who reached down and took the sheet of paper from the
organizer. He turned and passed it to the Superintendent. Jordan snatched
it from his hand and held up for the crowd to see, waving it. He did not
look read it.

"Okay, folks," he called out hoarsely to the gathered workers
before him, focusing directly on Leon and Eugene. "Here's your list of

bitches and gripes. You see, I've got it. Am I going to read it or pass it on to Mr. Allgood?" He paused over the silent crowd. "Hell no, but I will show you what I think about it."

He then began tearing the thin sheet of paper into pieces. Over and over again until it was nothing but confetti, which he tossed into the heavy still air. Before the astonished people could react, he spoke down to Leon.

"And you, Mister *Demchi* or *Devinci* or whatever your wop name is, can go straight to hell!" Jordan followed Matheson back into the office, slamming the heavy door behind him.

The people were angry with the insult and the utter contempt heaped on them by the Superintendent. Their hopes of being heard had been, they realized, embarrassingly naïve. They began to mill around, talking in low angry voices. There was some meaningless plotting, but mostly there was just inane chattering.

But to the two veteran organizers things had pretty much gone as they had expected. Management never listened, or came to the table, until they were forced to. *Hardball* was what they played and understood. Leon moved through the crowd, encouraging those he passed, searching for Dobinsky.

Suddenly, the sharp crash of shattering glass split the air, as a thrown fragment of brick crashed through the window of the mill office. It skimmed across Miss Wilcox's desk and landed harmlessly on the floor in the corner of the room.

With the exploding window, many of the workers cheered. Others picked up chunks of gravel and began shelling the office building. Most of the wildly thrown missiles hit the side of the building or the front door with dull thuds, but a few hit their mark—the office windows. A large knot of men across the street began pushing and pulling on the heavy chain-link fence that encompassed the mill itself.

In places, between the steel posts, the fences gave way some, and began to sag inwardly. Newton, the guard, who had been watching the workers as he leaned against the door of the guardhouse smoking and amused, suddenly realized his position. He was not a mill worker. They might consider him allied with the bosses. He flicked away the cigarette hanging from his mouth and locked himself in the hot, airless, red-brick room.

As the unrest grew among the workers—all hot, tired and thirsty—their fatigue was offset by the heightened excitement of the moment. No one but Leon noticed the five black vans that had pulled up at the curb on Galway Avenue. As the vehicles stopped, the double back doors swung open, disgorging dozens of uniformed policemen. Jordan's reinforcements had arrived.

They quickly fell into formation and formed a line, shoulder to shoulder, on the lower flank of the rioters. Gripping shiny, black nightsticks in their sweaty hands, they began to move forward into the crowd. They waded into the people, like infantry in a medieval battle, and began relentlessly swinging the clubs. People fell to the ground, in the street, in the mill office yard, wounded and bleeding.

There were screams and moans from those wounded and hurting, as the surprised workers tried to run from the mêlée. Eventually, they were dispersed and the policemen dragged several of the now-disabled victims, arrested and bleeding, to the vans.

Leon had found Ski. The two men managed to slip through the crowd, vanishing it seemed, into thin air when the nightstick-wielding cops arrived. The reporter and the photographer rushed downtown to file the story and to interview Allgood, if they could.

Suddenly, came the inevitable shrill scream of the mill whistle, announcing shift change. The sound seemed inexplicable, and now incongruently paternal, against the events of the day.

CHAPTER 33

Down on one knee as he worked intently on a loom, Ezra had hardly noticed the people striding by him—some brushing his back and shoulder—as his large, skilled hands tightened and loosened bolts, reattached springs, and replaced small greasy gears. He looked up, almost absentmindedly, to see them crowded at the huge windows that lined that side of the weave room overlooking the yard, street and mill office. Most of the looms were left running unattended. Even the bosses—overseers and second-hands—joined the others at the windows.

He stood up slowly, but effortlessly, and wiped his hands on a rag he had drawn from his back pocket. He looked down the aisle at the rows of humming unmanned looms, many still banging away, weaving cloth. Some had already expended their beams of yarn and sat clanging and vibrating, noisy and useless. The changeover men had joined the weavers at the windows. Suddenly, from behind, someone hurriedly passed him, striding toward the workers crowded at the windows. It was Matheson.

"Goddamn it, what the hell's going on?" he shouted as he pulled the unlit stub of a black cigar from his mouth. "You people crazy, or what?" The workers were crowded three or four deep along the row of windows as he waded into them. "Get back to those looms, boys! What do you think you're doing?"

"Better take a look for yourself, Charlie. Looky down there if you want to know what's going on," responded one of the men Matheson had jerked aside by his arm.

Matheson cleared his way to the window. Below him were hundreds of people, mill workers mostly, crowded tightly on the street and yard between the mill and the mill office. The throng had spilled over onto Galway Avenue.

"What the hell!" Matheson exclaimed loudly to no one in particular.

By now he knew of the rally earlier in the day downtown. He had workers who had not shown up for work today. He assumed that they were at the union rally, and would all be summarily fired. But he had not expected anything of this magnitude. This was trouble.

He was finally able to pull aside all the overseers and second-hands, and got the people back to their duties. Anyone caught at the windows would be sent home immediately and would forfeit pay. He did not realize at that moment he would soon need every person he had on the floor, and then some. They would not only complete *their* shift, but would have to work the following shift, and maybe some of them the midnight shift as well, before being allowed to leave the mill for home.

He walked up and down each aisle, banks of looms on either side, shouting orders and making sure everyone was back on their respective jobs. Production was behind now. They would need to catch up.

In the far corner of the cavernous room, the phone in the weave room office continued to ring. Miss Wilcox frightened, infuriated and imprisoned by the mass of union workers outside, kept trying to get Matheson on the phone.

Once Matheson was convinced that a semblance of order had been restored to the weave room, he headed for the elevator. Ezra, stuffed the rag back into the pocket of his overalls and was moving toward a loom that had been flagged for repair. Matheson almost ran over him, causing the tools in the tray he was carrying to spill onto the lint-flecked floor.

"Sorry, Burke," he said hurriedly, "glad to see at least somebody's working, or trying to." Both men squatted to retrieve the tools.

"What's going on down there?" Burke shouted, trying to be heard above the din of the looms.

"You didn't see from the windows?"

"No."

"Come on down to the office," said Matheson, standing. Ezra followed him to the small office at the far corner of the weave room.

"I suppose you knew about the union gathering downtown this morning?" he asked.

"I'd heard about it, I reckon."

"Well, it seems they had a pretty good turnout from the looks of the mob out in the yard."

"Is that what's going on?"

"Looks like they marched from downtown to here, at the mill. Hundreds of them. Notice many hands laying out of work today?"

"Some, I reckon."

"It's a problem. Looks like half the second shift's down there all mixed up in this thing. They planning anything, Burke, I mean the organizers?

"I wouldn't know about that, Mr. Matheson."

"Don't matter. I'm going to need you to work over tonight. May have to work double shift for a few days."

"All right."

Matheson looked at his watch. "About six o'clock this evening you can go home and get you some supper, then come on back to the mill."

"All right."

"Look, I better get down to the mill office before Rufus does something stupid. Likely as not he already has, if he's nursing that bottle he keeps stashed in his desk drawer."

The phone on the desk began ringing again. "That'll be Miss Wilcox. I'll be back after while." He did not pick up the phone.

He jammed the cold stump of cigar into his mouth and headed for the nearby freight elevator. Ezra walked back out onto the floor, preoccupied, biting his thumbnail. He then brushed the floating brown specks of lint from his face, picked up the tool tray, and disappeared into the pounding rhythm of the looms.

***

By five o'clock Judith was worried. She had heard the brief wail of sirens from the departing police vans. Grace and Andrew had tried to sneak out the back door to go up to the mill and see what the excitement was all about. She caught them just in time and brought them out to the front, where they sat with her, restlessly, on the porch steps. Her lips pursed slightly as she abstractly smoothed the cotton dress across her lap. She had not seen Melvin as he came running from the mill with his hand pressed against one side of his head. He had entered his house by the back door.

"Grace," she said finally. "Go over and see if Earline is at home. If she is, ask her is it all right if we come visit."

"All right, Mama," the child responded as she, with her pent-up energy, instantly sprang from the steps and raced across the yard. Her brother, like a shot, was not far behind. She tapped on the front door and waited. It creaked open.

"Why if it ain't my two favorite young 'uns," said Earline, standing in the doorway, smiling as she peered down at the children. "What can I do for y'all?"

"Mama wants to know if we can come visit. I think she's worried about Papa 'cause he's not home from work yet. He's always home by now," said Grace.

Earline hesitated, as an ever-so-slight shadow seemed to veil her face for an instant. She glanced over her shoulder back into the house. She then stepped out onto the porch. She could see Judith sitting on the porch steps.

"Hey, Judith," she called out, waving. "I'll be over directly." She looked down into the faces of the two children.

"Tell your mama I'll come over and talk in just a minute or two. I got something on the stove I need to set off. Y'all run along now."

Grace and her brother bounded down the porch steps and ran back to their mother, and relayed Earline's message.

"All right," said Judith.

In a short time, Earline strode across the yard, wiping her hands in her faded cotton apron. She seemed to always wear an apron, even working at the mill, not an unusual thing on the mill hill.

"Hello, Earline. I didn't mean for you to have to come out. I just wanted to see if everything is all right, what with all that's gone on today. Ezra's not home yet."

"Well, things ain't all right, I can tell you that much. I don't mean with Ezra. I 'spect he's still at the mill working."

"What's wrong?" asked the younger woman anxiously.

"Plenty it seems. They had a mess of folks at the organizing meeting downtown. Melvin was there."

"Melvin was?"

"Yep, he's all jacked up over this here union organizing. Got him in trouble too. Anyway, they all come from way downtown. Can you imagine them walking all that way in this heat? Fools, all of 'em. But they did it. Gathered at the mill office wanting Allgood, or somebody, to listen to 'em. Fix the way things are at the mill since this here Depression hit us full hard."

"What kind of trouble is Melvin in, Earline?"

"Don't know just yet. Naturally, Allgood wasn't at the mill, so Rufus Jordan had to handle it and you know what a moron he is. Cussed 'em all out, I hear. Anyway, he or somebody called the police and they came in and busted it up. Took a bunch of 'em to jail, they say."

"Is Melvin in jail?"

"No, he got away, but just barely. He got knocked in the head, but he was able to run. Ran down the alley between Second Street and back of the mill. He's in the house. Scared him so bad he snuck through the back door. I put some ice in a hot-water bottle and he's lying on the bed with it against his head."

"How badly is he hurt?" asked Judith, her voice sharp with concern.

"Oh, I think he'll be all right. Just got a big blue-looking knot on the side of his head. Take more than a billy-club to break that gourd open," she chuckled lightly, "but it sure scared him."

"What about the mill, I mean his job?"

Earline frowned, her brow wrinkled.

"I reckon he's gone and got his self fired. I can't see it any other way. But he says he don't care. 'We got to stand together with this here union.' I said, they going to feed us? He says don't worry about it. But then you know Melvin. He's kind of a fool anyway, like the rest of 'em."

"You left work?" asked Judith.

"I was already out of the mill when all this happened. Good luck, I reckon. You know that female trouble I was talking about a while back?" She glanced down at the children sitting on the step below their mother.

"Yes."

"I got off work after dinnertime and went to the doctor. I missed the whole thing, lucky for me."

"Is everything okay? I mean are you all right?"

"Doc seems to think so. Just my time of life, the change. Woman's got a lot to put up with, I reckon."

"I reckon."

"Better get back and see about Melvin. Don't worry too much about Ez, he'll be all right. We'll talk later."

***

Melvin rose slowly and sat on up on the edge of the bed, steadying himself with both hands. He then lightly touched the bandage wrapped snugly around his head. The sweet oily smell of liniment filled his nostrils.

That woman sure takes care of me sometimes, he thought. He stood up slowly, gripping the bedpost to make sure of his balance. I'm okay, I reckon.

He heard her in the kitchen as he shuffled from the bedroom.

"What are you doing up?" she asked, glancing over her shoulder then returning to the dishes in the sink.

"Ah, I can't lay in that bed. There's still plenty of daylight."

"How's your head?"

"It's all right. Don't hurt much now."

"You probably don't need to be laying down anyway, not with a lick on the head. Might go to sleep."

"I reckon not," he said, and sat down at the table.

"You hungry? I put you a plate on the stove."

"Naw, not right now. Believe I'll wait a while."

The afternoon events were on their minds but both avoided bringing it up, as a delicate silence settled over them. She finished washing the dishes, wrung out the cloth and draped it over the faucet. He rolled a cigarette and lit it, the match shaking slightly between his fingers, which were stained yellow.

"Judith's worried about Ezra. He's not come home yet."

"Ah, Ez'll be all right. He didn't take no part in any of it. Probably got him working over. Likely a lot of folks not showed up for second shift."

"Likely not."

"Think I'll go out and sit on the stoop. Might be a breeze, with the sun going down." He snubbed out the cigarette in the tin jar-lid on the table.

"Sun ain't down yet. It's still plenty hot," she said.

"Don't matter. Come on out and sit with me."

"Not right now. I got some sewing to do."

"All right," he said as he ambled to the front door.

                              ***

Ezra wiped the handkerchief across his mouth and pushed back from the table. "That was good. I reckon I need to get back to the mill."

"Are you tired?" She had sat at the table with him while he ate, but there had been little conversation.

"Some," he said, looking into her face.

"What's going to happen, Ezra? It scares me."

"I don't know. They'll close the mill down for the weekend this evening at midnight like they always do, I reckon. Open back up when the whistle blows Sunday Midnight."

"Do you think Melvin and the others will be fired?"

"Seems likely they already are, according to the bosses."

"Earline says there might be a strike."

"Don't know. There's sure plenty of talk about it. I reckon we'll see." He hesitated, looking into her dark eyes. "I better be getting back to work. Be home when the whistle blows," he said. She smiled wistfully and turned away, busying herself clearing the table.

He stepped out onto the porch and into the dull airless heat of the slowly approaching evening. The sun had dipped below the trees in the distance. He strode across the dusty yard toward the street.

"Yo, Ez, where you headed in such a hurry?" Melvin called to him from the porch steps. Ezra turned and walked over to his neighbor.

"Back to work, but I'm in no hurry to get there." He noticed the bandage.

"Been a hell of day, ain't it?"

"Just work, same as usual," said Ezra dryly.

"I mean with the march and everything. That mess at the mill this evening." Melvin touched the bandage.

"You hurt much?"

"Naw, not bad. Damn cops waded into us slinging them billy-clubs left and right. I run like hell, but I slipped in the gravel and one of them caught me right up side the head. Hurt like the devil, but I sprung up and run like a rabbit. Cop just turned and started beating the crap out somebody else. A gal I think maybe. I didn't stay around to see."

"That's a bad thing, Melvin."

"I figured y'all were up there in the weave room looking down at it all from the windows.

"Some did, I reckon."

"But not old Ezra. Just kept right on working, I'd wager. Whole world caving in around him and he just kept right on working. That about it, Ez?" Melvin laughed.

"I reckon so. I sure didn't want nobody to get hurt."

"This is just the start of it, Ez. Likely going to be a heap more trouble. I'm fired, I know it. Don't really give a damn, to tell you the truth. But we ain't giving up over a few bumped heads and a night or two in jail. Them union boys bringing in reinforcements from up North this weekend. We got rights."

"I hope there's no more trouble."

"Wake up, man! After what happened today? They's *going* to be a strike. That's all there is to it. All the mills. A general strike, I tell you, we'll close 'em all down, by god!"

Ezra did not respond.

"What are you going to do, Ez?"

"Nothing. Go back to work, I reckon."

"Come on, we need to stick together. Join the union on Monday," Melvin implored.

"Don't reckon I'll be doing that, Melvin. I hope you don't get hurt again."

"I ain't worried about that," he said, and then paused. "What is it, Ez, that makes you against us? Looks like you standing up for the owners and bosses. I just don't get it."

"I'm not against y'all. I know you doing what you think you need to do. Me, too."

"What do you mean?" asked Melvin, a seriousness in his voice.

"I don't know that I can exactly put it into words. It's that I never been much on joining things. I don't feel right letting other people tell me what to do or what to think. The hillbilly farmer in me, I reckon."

"You don't seem to mind letting them bosses tell you what to do or think."

"See, that's different. It's just a job they pay me to do. It's all the same. Doesn't matter if I'm shoveling coal twelve hours a day with those colored fellas back of the mill or fixing looms eight hours on the fourth floor. They pay me wages, so they can tell me what to do, but they can't tell me what to think."

"How about the way they been treating us. These goddamn stretch-outs nobody can keep up with, much less make production. They ain't been paying for overtime, either. We just about slaves, seems to me. Can't hardly take a break to go pee. You okay with all that, Ez?"

"No, I'm surely not, but with all these new laws Mr. Roosevelt's pushing through I think things might get better pretty soon."

"Roosevelt!" Melvin was almost shouting. "Damn, Ez, he's one of *them*. He's richer'n they are! They passed them laws about working conditions and hours and wages, and he just looks over at 'em and winks. You ever know a politician you could trust?"

"I never knew one at all," Ezra replied dryly. "Look, Melvin, Mr. Allgood owns the mill and he pays people to work there. I don't have to do it, but I do. For the wages. If I can't put up with it, I can leave. He's got no say in it."

"That sounds real good, neighbor. Where would you go? Back up in them mountains?"

"No."

"Oh yeah, you can always go down to South Georgia and pick cotton with the coloreds for two-bits a day. Even that ain't going to be there much longer. That got machines now starting to do it. Do more in an hour than a hundred men in day's picking."

Melvin was not smiling as he looked at his friend, standing, almost a gray shadow in the dying light of the evening.

"I got to get back to work, Melvin, it's getting late."

"Back to *the Man*, huh, Ez?"

"I reckon so, if you want to put that way."

"I guess they closing down at midnight?"

"Yeah, I reckon they will."

"Any of the bosses talking about Monday? I mean, worried about what might be happening or anything?"

"Not heard anything," said Ezra, taking his pipe out as he turned to leave. Then he hesitated as if something suddenly occurred to him, something he had forgotten which might now be significant.

"Funny thing though, Melvin. Just before I left for supper, Mr. Matheson told me to come to the mill office in the morning. In the morning at eight o'clock."

"Hmm, that don't sound right, now does it?" Melvin asked, almost rhetorically. "Better watch yourself, Ez. They all slick, slick as glass, including Bulldog Matheson. Stop by the house in the morning when you get back and let's drink some coffee."

"All right," he said as he absentmindedly placed the unlit pipe back in the bib pocket of his overalls. Melvin sat and watched him disappear into the shadows of the street.

CHAPTER 34

That Friday afternoon, Leon Deminici and Ski Dobinsky had made it back through the alleys and side streets to the safety of Mrs. Aintry's boarding house. With her back in the kitchen preparing supper for the boarders, Deminici later slipped noiselessly from his room, down the stairs and into the parlor. The musty room was warm and dim, lighted only by the low afternoon sun that shot flat rays of white sharp light through the narrow openings in the pulled curtains. The telephone was on a small table in the corner. He picked up the receiver and gave the operator the number.

"Pete, Leon," he said softly into the receiver.

"Yeah?" came the terse response, mixed with intermittent static, from the other end of the line.

"We got problems down here. Things went pretty much south today, quicker than planned. These damn mill owners are real bastards."

"Yeah, I just hung up talking with the boys in Georgia. They got their hands full, too. Leadership's meeting tonight up here."

"You got to get me some people down here and I mean quick!" There was urgency in Deminici's voice as he glanced through the door into the hallway to make sure no one could hear him. Other than the muffled movements of Mrs. Aintry back in the kitchen, the house was silent. He was alone. "All hell's going to break loose Monday morning, which I know is a good thing, but we're going to need back up."

"Dobinsky okay?" asked the voice.

"Yeah, he's fine," answered Deminici impatiently. "Look, Pete, we got to move quickly. This Galway Mill is the key to everything around here. Just like you said. The people are riled up and ready. We need to have a picket line in place Monday morning.

"All right. Sounds good. Probably will go ahead and call for a general strike. I'll have to get the okay tonight, but it'll be a go. You and Ski spread the word to the mill workers. How's your locals?"

"Pretty good, I think. A few of them in jail after the cops busted up the rally this afternoon. I'll bail them out in the morning if we need to. They don't really have anything to hold them on."

"You got money?"

"Yeah, we're fixed."

"I'll get you some people down there right away, but I want that mill shut down come Monday. You got it?"

"Sure, Pete, that's the plan. No problem."

"One more thing. There's going to be some NTWU people coming with ours."

"I don't give a damn. Let's stir the pot. We just need men."

"They're a rough bunch, I mean the commies, but I think we can work together on this. At least for a while. Couple of boys from *The Times*, too."

"Okay," said Deminici.

By noon the next day, Saturday, two rented buses pulled out of New York City and soon picked up US 1 headed south. They were mainly filled with hired men, many of them goons and thugs. Except for the communists in the National Textile Workers union, they were desperate men, by and large, with no philosophical or emotional investment in their work. Many had experienced the recent union violence in the Midwest. They were glad to get the work, jobs were scare and hard to come by. The Depression had struck the Northeast hard. None had ever been inside a textile mill. They were big-city men mostly, street hardened and quick tempered. The thought of going South, and maybe busting a few redneck heads, created a subdued excitement in them. Some smoked, some napped, and some just stared blankly out the windows of the buses as they pushed past the slower traffic, and finally moved into open country. The buses, like large shiny metal bullets, sped inexorably toward their targets. In twenty hours they would all be in a land they did not know and would not understand. The phalanx was awakened and had begun to move forward.

***

All through the rest of Saturday and Sunday—glaring, windless, Africa-hot days—word of an impending strike spread like a veritable wildfire through the mill villages and the towns of the Southeast. On Sunday morning, in sparsely attended churches, the preachers, many on strongly-worded suggestions from the mill owners and bosses, pleaded from the pulpit for patience and forbearance. If they were selling the good fortune of having jobs at all and the benevolence of the owners, the subdued parishioners were not buying. The word in the air was *strike* and the more the workers repeated it to themselves and to others around them, the easier it rolled off the tongue. Under the seemingly almost impossible burden of labor placed on them by the mills, the word itself gave them, somehow, a lightness of being, of hope, a vague sense of power.

***

As the early morning darkness began to lighten into a thin still grayness on Monday morning, more people than usual loitered about the streets, small groups on corners speaking in whispers. All-night diners, usually empty of patrons at this hour, were filled with men sipping coffee, and too frequently, glancing at their watches or the clocks on the walls.

At five-thirty, the compliant mill whistle obliviously blasted its usual refrain, signaling the people it was time to wake up, get out of bed and get ready for work. The workers who were already on the street looked uneasily toward the direction of the mill, and at each other. Others, in the village, sleepily pulled on their clothes and departed from their mill-owned houses into the vanishing darkness. *The Man's* whistle, it is a consistent omen of his inexplicable dominion over us. He will not let us forget. Nothing has changed.

The union organizers, whose reinforcements had arrived from the New York late on Sunday afternoon, moved among the growing crowd of workers along Galway Avenue, near the mill. They had taken charge and were giving instructions on where and how to line up, what to expect, what to say and not to say. The picketers would form a line, hopefully three or four people deep along the chain-link fence and the entrance gate of the mill, facing the mill office across the street.

The entrance to the mill, the red-brick structure standing like a single gargantuan but unmoving phalanx itself behind them, would be blocked by this human barrier to anyone, other than the mill bosses, attempting to enter. The objective—clear and simple to them all—was to prevent the mill opening after its normal weekend shutdown. Once the mill was sitting silent and inept, and their resolve certain, they would surely be able to talk to the owners, to negotiate. They would be able to express their concerns and demands with clarity and logic. The owners and bosses would not like it, but they would listen and realize that things must change. The union men had assured them this was the way, the only way, to a better life. The union men, though strange to them with their dark faces and clipped Yankee speech, must know what they were doing. Surely.

***

Near daybreak the first city bus of the day pulled up sharply at the stop on Galway Avenue, catty-cornered from the cotton mill. The nervous driver yanked the steel handle, opening the two narrow panels of the door, unloading its cargo of men, almost none of them locals. They streamed crossed the street and gathered with the others in the mill office yard.

The low, but rising sun pushed back the night with its soft yellow light, dancing on the tree tops, and sparkling in the damp grass below. The air was still, warm, but without the usual, not unpleasant, smell of cotton yarn and processed cloth. Groups of men are huddled together all along Sixth Street and near the mill office yard, waiting uneasily for commands from the union boys. Workers and union men continued to arrive.

Earlier, at the five-thirty whistle, Deminici and his colleagues had begun to form the picket line by moving workers up to the fence and spreading them out, side by side, along it. As more arrived, they deepened and extended the line of human stanchions all the way to the far end, blocking the narrow road that led to the rear area of the plant. They then produced large cardboard signs nailed to narrow planks. The signs expressed various messages in neat black lettering: *Stamp Out Stretch-Outs; No More Piece Work; Decent Pay for Decent Work; Put Children in Schools, Not in Mills; God Bless the AUTW.* Several of the signs that the communist organizers had slipped in, read, *Workers of the World, Unite!*

The signs were passed out randomly to the men on the picket line. They took the signs, most without reading them, and waited. One of the men, taking a sign jammed into his hand, read it aloud.

"What the hell does this mean?"

"Look comrade, I am here to help you. To help all of us. Just do as you're told." The man shrugged and took the sign.

Leon did not like the communists but they were enthusiastic and were willing, even anxious, to do any dirty work that might come up. They were okay as long as you didn't have too many of them around. They just talked gibberish no one understood or cared to, and felt a certain superiority to the other union workers. I'm just using a few of them though, he thought to himself.

Across Galway Avenue from the mill, a compact man with rolled-up shirtsleeves that strained against muscular biceps, watched as the union men organized the picket line. He recognized and knew some of the men from the Galway Mill village, but most were strangers.

Don't really matter much, he thought. Just lint-heads. None of 'em going to fight. They'll run like wet paint. He lightly fingered the picker-stick that he held at his side. Little dose of picker-stick will cure what ails 'em. Better round up the boys.

He adjusted the wooden match at the corner or his mouth and strode confidently up Galway Avenue in the growing light.

***

At precisely seven o'clock, Rufus Jordan turned the black Chevrolet sedan slowly onto First Street and came to an abrupt stop. Driving down Galway Avenue on his way to the mill office, he had noticed many more pedestrians on the sidewalk than was normal for this hour, but had uneasily shrugged it off.

A motley human barrier stretched across First Street, just up from Galway Avenue. It was this barricade of these people that had forced him to come to a sudden stop. The men shuffled nervously in the line, shoulder to shoulder.

Someone shouted, "Hey, it's Mr. Jordan!"

Another voice from somewhere back, "Who's he?"

"The Super," came the reply.

"Let him through."

The men standing in front of the automobile stepped aside, creating an aisle for Jordan, who drove slowly past them. Along the street, the deep picket line formed his left flank. All the men were either in the line, or loitering in the street. None was yet on the grass of the mill-office yard.

As he turned right and eased the automobile onto the gravel parking lot, a wave of angry disbelief spilled over him. What he had thought, and said would never happen, came into sharp relief before his very eyes. This was a strike, to be sure, and they were here to shut down the mill. His mill. He sat in the car for a moment gathering his thoughts and attempting to garner his emotions. He would need to let Allgood know what was going on, of course. He would need the police, as bungling and inept as they had been on Friday. Where the hell were Benny Ray Tucker and his hoodlums? Miss Wilcox would be scared to death.

With a determined tenseness, he gripped the steering wheel with both hands, his heart pounding.

The he thought, goddamit! No gang of Red riff-raff and a bunch of ignorant disgruntled misfits are going to keep my plant from running. We'll put this crap to rest in short order. Kick some ass!

He yanked open the car door and strode the fifty-feet to the mill office. In his angry determination and indignation, he was oblivious to the insults and cat-calls emanating from the picket line across the street. He unlocked the office door and disappeared inside.

***

Four men, all nattily dressed in the fashionable golf attire of the day, strode with confidence and expectation from the club house to the nearby first tee box. They were followed closely by four black men in green cotton smocks, each with a leather golf bag slung over his shoulder.

"Still some dew on the fairway," observed C. Jameson Phelps. With a coin toss, he had won the honor for the opening hole.

Shading his eyes from the morning sun as he looked down the fairway, Cates Allgood said, "We should be okay. They're working on the greens now."

"I'm not sure I'm up for this, gents. Feeling kind of poorly this morning," said a bleary-eyed Scooter Pinckney, leaning forward slightly, his hands interlocked atop his driver.

"I suggested a Bloody Mary. You should have had one," quipped Allgood.

"I did," mumbled Scooter.

"Do you boys always talk this much? Are we going to play golf today or what?" J.B. Peters asked good-naturedly.

Phelps stepped up, bent over and pressed a wooden tee into the soft earth. He then placed an immaculately white ball on the tee and asked for his driver, which the caddy presented to him almost instantly. He glanced into the ebony face. The dark eyes, seemingly pupiless, momentarily looked back at him, but then averted to the grass beneath his shoes.

He stepped back up to the tee, waggling the club head. "All right, gentleman, I shall show the way." Peters sighed. With that, Phelps proceeded to hit a long arching drive down the middle of the fairway.

"Nice shot, old boy," said Allgood, followed by slight groan from Scooter.

Allgood planted his tee, gripped the leather of the club handle and prepared to swing. Then someone in the distance called out. The golfers turned to look back toward the club house to see one of the stewards running toward them, waving a yellow piece of paper. Breathlessly, he ran up to Allgood.

"I'm sorry, Mr. Allgood, but I jis got this here message for you. On the phone. Man say it urgent. Say I got to git it to you right now!" He handed the yellow paper to Allgood who read it quickly, then angrily slammed the club to the ground in the direction of his caddy.

"Is there a problem, Cates? Winky okay?"

"No, it's not Winky or anything like that. It seems I've got a damn strike on my hands."

"There's been a lot about it in the papers, Cates, but I thought your plants were okay."

"Damn Yankee agitators. Got this whole thing stirred up. Sorry, boys, I've got to go see about this. Could be a real problem."

"Me too, gents," said Scooter, whose face had turned pale, his hands shaking on the grounded club. "I'm sick as a dog."

Allgood abruptly left the group. By the time he had changed back into his business suit, one of the stewards had already brought the Packard around and parked it in the circular drive in front of the gleaming white club house.

He sped away, passing the overly-groomed lawns of the neighborhood, and slipped the Packard into the traffic headed downtown. He was in his office in fifteen minutes. He brushed by the receptionist and his secretary without comment or acknowledgement as he passed into his office. Standing at the massive polished oak desk, he picked up the phone and dialed Rufus Jordan's number.

***

The police soon arrived, the black vans pulling up to the curb on Galway Avenue, just below the mill office where they had parked on Friday. As they lined up and came to some kind of pseudo-military attention ordered by the Captain, many of them gripped their holstered nightsticks. The Captain pivoted toward the office and the mill in a sloppily executed about-face, his back now turned to his men. Instantly, he realized that the situation was different this time. They were not facing the same muddled, disorganized mob as they had a few days ago.

By now the picket line was orderly and well organized. Other strikers were posted in the street and in front of the mill office yard in small tight groups. The organizers shuffled around, from group to group, continuing to calmly give orders and instructions.

No, the Captain thought, this is different. And there's a hell of a lot more of them.

As no command was forthcoming to move forward, the cops began to grow restless, shuffling their feet at the edge of the grass where they stood, looking at each other blankly, with an occasional shrug.

"What's the holdup, Captain?" someone called from the front of the line. Ignoring the benign question, the Captain called over his shoulder.

"Johnson, get up here!"

"Yes, sir," came the response as one of the police officers broke rank and strode purposefully up to where his boss stood.

"Johnson, I'm going to give you a chance to use that new-fangled contraption you call a two-way radio. Think you can get it to work this time?" the Captain said with a hopeful smirk.

"Yes, sir, I'm sure I can."

"Okay, go back to your van and give it a try. Call headquarters and tell them I said we need more men out here."

"How many do you want me to say?"

"At least twenty. They'll need to call in some of the off-duties. Whatever, I don't care, but just tell them I want those men here quick, pronto. Get back up here as soon as you get through. Turn to."

"Yes, sir," replied the young policeman, as he resisted the temptation to salute his superior.

Johnson turned and trotted back down the gently-sloping yard to his vehicle. Several of the others, still in formation, but no longer at any resemblance of being at attention, asked him what was up. He ran by them offering no response, determine to follow orders and not be dissuaded from the important mission of trying to get the first mobile two-way radio in the Corinth Police Department to work; so far, it had been hit or miss.

***

Benny Ray Tucker had come to the same conclusion as had the police Captain. By mid-morning he had gathered his hooligans behind the shrubbery, which separated the bus stop across the street from the yard of the Galway Baptist Church. Leaving them huddled there smoking cigarettes and clowning around, he strode up the block and unassumingly crossed Galway Avenue.

He approached the mill office from the rear, away from the mill. With his street-wise judgment, he decided to stop short of the office, and instead, leaned against a large pecan tree. From here, he could view and coolly assess the situation. What he saw in no way convinced him to change his plan of violence and combat. His blood was up for sure, but nothing about his countenance or manner was altered.

Got to figure something out, he thought, them damn organizers got 'em tucked in tight and spread out, too. A bunch of 'em.

He rolled the match stick in the corner of his mouth back-and-forth with his fingers. He stood there beside the tree for a moment more, then withdrew, crossed the avenue and went back to his charges.

He pushed aside the limb of a large shrub, revealing the clearing where his boys were now squatting or kneeling, rolling dice in the dirt. They sprang to their feet as he kicked at the dry, red dust with the toe of his shoe, deliberately sending a spray of the fine powder covering the dice.

"What's up, Benny Ray? We ready to mash a few lint-head skulls?" asked one of them as he held a picker-stick in one hand, slapping it in the palm of the other.

"Well, yeah, sure thing, but we going to have to do it different. Different from what I first figured."

"Whatcha mean, different?" one asked. Gripping their picker-sticks, they looked at each other.

"What I mean is, there's too many of 'em to just go wading into and start knocking heads. Damn picket line's four or five deep. Got a bunch of extras standing around, too. Just too many of 'em. Cops all over the place too, but I ain't worried about them."

"You ain't scared are you, Benny Ray?" asked another, slapping his picker-stick against his palm.

With the mindless quickness of a cobra striking its prey, Benny Ray punched him hard and solidly in his relaxed, unsuspecting gut. He went to his knees groaning in agony as the picker-stick fell in the dirt. The others were wide-eyed and silent.

"Ah, git up, Smiley, you ain't hurt," said Benny Ray.

"Damn, Benny Ray, you didn't have to go and do that. I was just kiddin' you," said Smiley, as he got up on one knee, retched, and spat several times on the ground. "I think you done busted something inside. Damn, Benny Ray. I swear."

"Git up. You'll be all right."

One of the others helped Smiley to his feet. He stood there unsteadily and stared blankly at Benny Ray, his hands pressing against his bruised gut.

"Look here, boys, it's like this. These strikers aim to man that picket line around the clock. But a lot of 'em are Galway scum. I figure they'll be drifting off home to get something to eat or rest up before they come back to the line. Once they leave the line, we'll jump 'em, one by one, and beat the shit out of 'em. Pretty soon they're bound to git the picture. Ain't none of 'em going to like a picker-stick upside the head or in the gut. Are they, Smiley?"

There was a general guffaw at this, and even Smiley, still holding his stomach, managed a weak grin.

"We'll break up and meet back here this evening, just before dark. From here we can see 'em good when they drift off toward home. All right, let's git the hell out of here and go git a cold beer."

"Tucker's?"

"Damn straight Tucker's."

***

As the long summer day wore on, the workers rotated on and off the picket line. Leaving the line after standing for hours in the intense airless heat, they rested in the shade beneath the trees along Galway Avenue or in the vacant lot a few blocks away, where the organizers had set up camp for the non-locals. Wives and children appeared occasionally, frightened and uncertain in the strange unfamiliar crowd, bringing water and Spam sandwiches to the strikers.

More police arrived and formed a line across from the picketers on the opposite of the street, as if guarding the mill office. The Captain, after meeting briefly with Jordan, sensed the tenseness and potential explosiveness of the situation. Allgood had made it clear that he wanted no heavy-handed action by the police, such as had occurred on Friday. That is, he said, if it could be avoided. The Captain was uneasy about it all. His men were greatly outnumbered, should trouble arise.

"Gotta to talk this thing down," he said softly, to himself. Though armed, not much thought had been given to the use of firearms, should there be a flare up or a physical confrontation. At least not by him. Among his men though, several had lightly and nervously fingered the curved wooden grip of the thirty-eight revolvers holstered at their sides.

The Captain had stepped into the street several times facing the picket line. Shouting into a large red megaphone, he had demanded the strikers disperse immediately or face arrest and prosecution. From the line, his exhortations were met with a hot silence, some of the workers shifting about, nervously glancing at each other. It was not in their nature to ignore or flaunt authority. But they remained solidly together as one organic phalanx, following the instructions of the union men, hoping they knew what they were doing.

The day wore on, mostly uneventful, as a tenseness, bleak and dry as dust, settled over the streets of the mill village. It was apparent that the strikers were determined to stay. It was a standoff. The mill was shut down. The Captain, tired and frustrated, a ring of dried sweat staining the starched stiff collar of his shirt, dismissed most of the men for the night. He posted a few of them around the grounds—tired and apathetic sentries—in an ineffectual display of being in control.

Rufus Jordan, alone in his office, took a long slug of whiskey. He placed the nearly empty bottle back in the desk drawer and pushed it closed with his foot. He picked up the phone and made the final report of the day to Allgood, who seemed strangely collected about the whole affair. He then left the office building and strode calmly to his car and, without so much as a glance at the sea of strikers surrounding him, drove home.

***

Like the light of a new day, the strike, partly planned, mostly spontaneous, spread quickly to almost all of the surrounding cotton mill towns. Automobiles filled with volunteers and union men—Flying Squads— zipped around the countryside spreading the word. The strike was on.

The alliance between the union organizers and the mill workers was, to be sure, a curious and unlikely one. It was fraught with the suspicion bred by unfamiliarity, and fed by the apprehension of cultural misconceptions. Stranger bedfellows would have been difficult to imagine. The dependence and trust that the workers had placed with the owners over the years had evaporated, ending in their feelings of hopelessness and emasculation. Perhaps most devastating and disappointing to them had been the action, or rather inaction, of the recently- elected Roosevelt, and the National Industrial Recovery Act (NIRA) he had bullied through congress. This was to give them the right to form unions without harassment. It guaranteed them better and fairer wages. It would limit their work hours. It was to give them hope.

But so far, the NIRA had turned out to be just another piece of toothless New Deal legislation, lost in a government bureaucratic morass. The mill owners ignored the new laws and continued to do as they pleased. The stretch-outs continued and increased. Wages were abominable. Men were fired and blacklisted if there was even an inkling of suspicion that they harbored sympathy for the union. The President? Well, he appeared to be more concerned with maintaining his political alliances via the *good ole boys* network. After all, there was another election in thirty-six to be considered. These hick Southern lint-heads existed in another world, a world unfamiliar to him. They were, to be sure, a long way from Hyde Park.

Alas, with little hope and with only the prospects of continued oppression and ill treatment, they had turned to the alien *outside*. Against their exceptional and conservative natures, with a certain wariness, they aligned themselves with a most unlikely ally from the once-contemptible North – union men.

CHAPTER 35

He came through the back door carrying tomatoes in a burlap sack. He placed it beside the sink, nodding to the two women sitting at the kitchen table. They stopped talking when he came into the room. Earline glanced down and tapped a long ash from her cigarette into an inverted Mason jar lid. She then stood and smoothed the front of her apron with her hands, and crushed the cigarette into the lid.

"Well, I guess I better be getting back to the house. Got sandwiches to make for the men on the line," she said to Judith.

"I reckon Melvin's still up there?" he asked, as he began washing the ripe tomatoes at the sink.

"Yep, 'course he is. After what happened on Friday, there's no turning back now. Not for him anyway," said Earline pointedly. There was a strained silence. The two women exchanged quick glances.

"I'll walk you to the door," offered Judith.

"Not necessary. I'll just take the back door here if you don't mind."

"All right," Judith said, pushing open the screen door for her departing friend, who stopped in the doorway and turned to Ezra.

"Ez, I guess you heard about the mill. They going to try and open it tomorrow morning, first shift."

"I heard," he said without expression, not looking up from his tomato washing.

"Of course I can't go in. Not with Melvin being on the line and all. I'll likely lose my job too."

"I hope not," he said.

"I hope not, too, Earline," said Judith, placing her hand lightly on her neighbor's shoulder.

"I guess will see soon enough," replied Earline, "Heard tell they're bringing the army in here sometime this evening."

"National Guard, I believe."

"Same difference, I guess," she hesitated and then asked him, again pointedly," You going in, Ezra?"

He looked into her face briefly and then returned to the tomatoes. "Reckon I will," he said, almost to himself.

"Well, bye, y'all."

"Bye, Earline," said Judith softly. She watched her friend leave and then stood beside her husband at the sink. "She's awfully worried about Melvin."

"He'll be all right."

"He's out of a job for sure. They'll lose the house, too." He did not reply. He placed the washed tomatoes beside the sink and wiped his hands with a frayed towel.

"Do you want some coffee?"

"All right," he said and sat down at the table, his face serious and preoccupied.

"What's bothering you?" she asked, not looking at him while she measured out coffee from a large ceramic jar.

"Nothing, I don't reckon," he said, gazing out the back screen door and pinching his lower lip between his thumb and forefinger.

"Something is," she said knowingly.

"Ah, I don't know. I just, uh, I'm just thinking about all this mess. The mill, the strike, I mean. I don't know as I'm looking at it right. Don't know as I'm doing the right thing about it all." He did not look at her.

"You are doing what you think is right. What's best for your family. I never doubted that. Never have." She turned the burner on beneath the metal percolator.

"I just don't know another way. There might be other ways that are right, too."

"Might be," she said.

"The mill's hard on us, can't argue about that. But things have been hard on everybody. I reckon it's just that we, us, you and me, know what *hard* really is. Our life's been better here in most ways. Sure easier on you. I just think things have got to get better at the mill once we get through this Depression. The Government's doing some things, or trying to. This won't last forever."

"No, not forever."

They were both silent for a while. The coffee was percolating, so she walked to the stove and removed it from the flame. She poured the liquid, black and scalding, into a think ceramic cup and placed it on the table beside him.

"I reckon I'll go on in in the morning and see what happens. Not much, I hope."

She placed her hand hard on his forearm. "I guess I'm a lot like Earline. Ezra, I'm worried. I mean, you'll be careful?" she asked earnestly. It was more an exhortation than a question.

"It'll be all right. I just want to go back to work." He sipped the coffee. She wiped the dampness from her dark eyes.

"I think I'll walk out back and look at the garden," she said, rising from the table. She walked out, uncharacteristically letting the screen door slam against the wooden frame.

***

The morning sun had just topped the trees when Ezra turned onto First Street from Galway Avenue. The red-brick mill ahead of him was bathed in the sunlight, but the mill office across the street was still in the shadows beneath the trees. A line of young, clear-faced National Guardsmen stretched out along the fence in front of the mill. They awkwardly shouldered their Springfields. The five-round clips remained secured in the pouches attached to their wide web-belts. A lone NCO stood a few paces out front. He appeared to be much older than his charges. With a weathered face, brown and cracked from the sun and age, his uniform creased and immaculate, he moved about confidently. He carried no weapon other than the Colt forty-five semi-automatic pistol that rested securely in a highly-polished holster strapped to his side. Likely a veteran of the Great War.

More poignantly, a detachment of Regulars had been dispatched from Fort Benning. They had arrived shortly after the National Guardsmen. They were commanded by an officer, a Major, displaying an impressive military bearing. He disregarded the Guardsmen, considering them nothing more than civilians in uniform which, in fact other than the NCO, they pretty much were.

The strikers had been forced back across the street without any significant violence. Many were lined listlessly along the curb opposite the Guardsmen. Some were in groups under the trees. A few were asleep in the damp grass of the mill-office yard. They were a motley and haggard bunch by this time. Unshaven in soiled shirts and overalls, many had not slept since Sunday. Still, in their eyes was a hungry determination to see this thing through. They had come too far. Maybe the Feds would step in, some hoped. The showdown had come quicker than they had anticipated; many of them had naively not expected it at all. But it was upon them. They would not back down.

As Ezra approached the guardhouse and the gate, someone, a striker, threw a large piece of gravel at the opposing Guardsmen. With a dull clang, it bounced off a steel helmet. Then another rock was thrown and then another. The mob of strikers seemed to come to life. Almost instantly the citizen-soldiers were under a barrage of stones. They were ducking and bobbing their heads in an effort not to be struck. One rock slammed into the pink cheek of one of them. He fell to his knees in pain and blood. Then another.

"Hold the line!" shouted the NCO, who had been struck several times. His right hand felt for the slick leather holster at his side.

All of the strikers, those sleeping had been roused, were up to the street and spread out along the curb. They outnumbered the frightened and ill-prepared Guardsmen at least ten to one. As they melted into a tightly-banded phalanx, they began to slowly, almost like a swelling wave, to move, to surge into the street and toward the line of uniformed men.

The NCO, reacting instinctively, drew the pistol and held it pointed at the sky, the elbow of his bent arm pressed tightly to his side. With close-order drill commands, he ordered his men to withdraw at double time, which they did. As the Guardsmen vanished before them, the strikers surged across the street, only to be met by the steel chain-link fence protecting the monster red- brick building before them.

Ezra stood close to the corner of the guardhouse, the sun warm on his face. He shaded his eyes with this hand and watched the scene before him unfold. The wave of workers filled the street and the surge pressed against the high, steel fence. Those at the front edge of this human wave, those at the fence, leaned and pushed their shoulders into it. The fence began to sway, almost imperceptibly at first, but the angle advanced in degrees. As the workers felt the steel webbing of the fence give to their power, their excitement and determination grew. The shouts of the men blended together into a roar. A concerted and guttural sound—a yell—like ancient warriors attacking an entrenched enemy, filled the air as the phalanx moved slowly, but inexorably forward.

***

The exterior brick walls of the mill extended about three feet above the tarred, flat roof, thus forming a low parapet, as it were, around the parameter of the rooftop. Such a location would of course present a strategic position by which to observe the activity below and perhaps to control it as well.

The officer of the Regulars had seen this almost immediately upon arrival and had asked Matheson if there was access to the roof. Matheson hesitantly acknowledged that there probably was. With a quick investigation, a black steel ladder, bolted to an interior wall, was located.

Above, was a hatch that opened onto the roof. The officer would command from there, atop the mill. With him was a detachment of his best men, along with a machine gun team. He ordered the men to line along the parapet facing the street below, the mill office, and the strikers. They were to remain crouched or stooped, out of sight, until ordered to do otherwise. They jammed five-round clips of bullets into their rifles, but did not engage the bolts that would force the live cartridges in the chambers. That would be done only on orders from the Major. They were trained and ready to follow orders without hesitation or question.

The Major, standing back toward the middle of the huge expanse of black, hot roof eyed his men. They mostly sat facing him, their backs resting against the low wall. The Corporal was assigned the duty of peering over the wall and reporting the goings-on below.

A Regular Army officer, he had total control of his men and wished to avoid having to engage the power at his command. But he was concerned about the four or five civilians placed with him and scattered among his men. These were the mill owner's hired men, and they were armed with rifles. They looked to him to be nothing more than thugs, low-lifes, who were too eager for action. It was agreed that they were under the auspices of his command, but he was not assured. They were civilians. He didn't know them and he didn't trust them. He didn't want trouble. They made him, and his men, uneasy.

***

The round steel posts supporting the fence began to take a more severe angle back toward the mill as the force of the strikers increased. All were at it now, concentrated at the point that had given way most. Their fingers gripped the heavy wire mesh like the claws of an animal digging into its prey. They worked the fence back and forth, each time it gave a little more.

Precariously, the fence began to lean away from the constant pressure; its giving away was imminent. Ezra spotted Melvin against the collapsing wire in the wad of men. Sweat poured from his face. His clothes were torn and on his forearm was a wound—a deep, bleeding scratch. The narrow bandage was still wrapped snugly around his head but was now soiled and stained with perspiration. He could hear Melvin and the other men closest to him grunting and cursing with each surge against the steel barrier.

The fence finally gave way and fell, a steel-webbed mat, almost noiselessly to the ground. With this, the men exploded into a roar of shouts as they surged into the breach. Other sections of the fence soon disappeared as the strikers, now nothing but a mob, became a torrent of moving bodies gushing across the two-hundred feet of ground separating them from the red brick building. *The Man's* mill.

Suddenly, before the wave of workers could reach the building, the loud and distinct of machine gun fire split the air. About thirty feet ahead of the surge of men, bullets hit the ground in a straight line, sending up clouds of dust and gravel fragments before them.

The strikers were stunned and stopped motionless and helplessly where they stood—out in the open. Everyone looked up. The low wall of the roof bristled with rifle barrels. The machine gun rested on two small sandbags atop the parapet. The small dark shapes of helmeted heads, the men aiming the rifles, could barely be seen from below in the bright sun light. For a minute, silence hovered over the scene like a paled insignificance.

"Anyone crossing the mill yard risks being shot. Disperse immediately," the Major, standing in clear view, yelled down hoarsely from the rooftop. Silence. No one moved.

"Bull shit. He's bluffin'. They ain't going shoot nobody," someone shouted from the rear of the mob.

"Hell, no. They bluffin'," someone echoed.

"Let's go!" called a man at the front and he moved forward. The surge began again, edging across the ground toward the mill, more cautious now, and less assured. They all kept glancing up at the line of rifles barrels along the edge of the rooftop.

Again, about half way across, the ground erupted in front of the men as the machine gunner sprayed the ground before them, the bullets much closer this time. Ezra had squatted down from where he stood at the guardhouse, slightly rocking back and forth on his heels with apprehension, but peering at the scene unfolding beyond him. His fingers gripped the sharp edge of the brick corner. With the second spray of machine-gun fire, the strikers turned and ran back to what they hoped would be the safety of the street and the mill-office yard. He saw Melvin fall.

A bullet from the machine gun had struck a large piece of gravel just in front of Melvin as he turned in his retreat. The rock exploded, sending hard pieces of it, like shrapnel, in all directions. One of the larger fragments tore through his overalls and ripped into the muscles of his right calf. He fell to the ground and grasped his leg. The machine gunner fired another spray of rounds needlessly, but harmlessly, across the ground, ten or fifteen feet from where Melvin lay on the ground.

"Help me! Somebody help me! Please, somebody!" Melvin pleaded as he raised up on one elbow.

Almost before he heard Melvin's screams for help, Ezra sprang from the sanctuary of the guardhouse and sprinted across the yard toward his wounded neighbor and friend lying on the ground, Ezra assumed that he had been struck by a bullet. He felt neither fear nor panic. His body had responded automatically. He seemed almost to be gliding, effortlessly, to where Melvin lay.

"Ezra, git down," called a grimacing Melvin when he saw him running in the open yard toward him.

As he approached Melvin, high above, the barrel of a rifle glinted in the sunlight briefly as it slanted downward. There was a fleeting puff of white smoke in the high breezeless air. Spinning tightly and flawlessly, the bullet found its mark and struck Ezra just above his left temple. For an instant he staggered, his eyes blue and wild. Then to his knees, as he fell across his wounded friend's chest.

For a moment there was an indescribable silence, eerie and surreal, in the heavy, late morning air. Nothing, no one, stirred as the blood of a good man spread like a thin, scarlet shroud across the sterile hard, ground of the mill yard.

PART THREE

CHAPTER 36

The governor was quoted in the newspaper. He said, "... the shooting of the mill worker was most unfortunate." Funny, how *shooting* sounded so much more sterile and esoteric than *murder* or *killing* would have. He had also actually been contacted by one of the President's lackeys; Federal troops had been involved. Over the phone he had assured him everything was under control, just a few disgruntled lint-heads stirred up by union agitators. Yes, there had been a few Reds hanging around. No, he did not think he would need more Federal troops. But you tell your boss that we are mighty appreciative of his interest in our little ole state. You tell him everything looks good down here. Thirty-six shouldn't be a problem; he's good as reelected already. No, siree. He's our man down here.

There would be an inquiry. Of sorts. The black Ford police car would pull up in front of the house on Fifth Street days later, after the funeral. Standing at the screen door, just inside, she would read the inscription on the back fender. *To Protect and Serve.* Fleetingly and bitterly, she would say to herself, "Protect the mill owners', serve...," and then instantly dismiss the thought as small and shallow, a futile cry from the depths of her pain and loneliness.

She would step out onto the porch and wait as the policeman slammed the car door and strode across the yard. She would not want him in her house, so she met him on the porch. Would she answer some question? No. Was Mr. Burke involved with any of those Yankee organizers down here causing trouble? No response. Did your husband belong to the Communist Party? No response. Did your husband.... She would turn and step back into the house, shutting the door almost noiselessly behind her and then lean against it, sobbing uncontrollably.

The policeman would scratch his head with the erasure end of his pencil, fold up his notepad and get back in the black sedan. He would file his report in the morning. Nothing would come of any of it, nor did she wish that it would. She would ask herself, to what purpose? And the inescapable answer would be—none.

***

It was late afternoon and the westerly sun bathed the mill houses in a yellow haze of light, making them appear less dingy and bleak than they were. The shadows of the oak trees across the narrow street were lengthening by the moment and would soon bathe the houses in an illusory sense of dark twilight, long before the sun actually fell beyond the horizon. The four o'clock mill whistle had screeched precisely on time of course and, from a few blocks away, the low drone of traffic on Galway Avenue might have given an outsider the reassurance of a peaceful and routine normalcy.

There had been no acknowledgement, much less enforcement, of the new Federal laws. In the total absence of sagacious debate or consideration, under the powerful and relenting force of the status quo, personified by the mill owners themselves, the strike had ended. The union fervor had melted away like a light snow on the grass in early spring, warmed by the morning sun. It was as if it had never occurred. The strike, such as it was, was over. *The Man* was back in charge of the show. The mill was up and running full tilt. The workers returned to the monotony of the mill, to the whistle and to their jobs.

Perhaps things were once again as they had been. But also, perhaps, one could detect a sadder, but accepting, inevitability etched on their faces. And as they trudged past the mill gate to be swallowed up alive by the humming red-brick goliath before them, perhaps they strode a bit slower now with shoulders only hunched over, almost undetectable, a degree more.

***

A small, but continuous stream of people, mostly women, entered and exited the house. They moved quietly and gravely, carefully letting the screen door fall noiselessly against the palms of their hands before closing it, as they entered and departed. All were carrying something—a basket or a platter or a bowl—usually covered with a thick cloth. In that gracious and timeless tradition of the Southern wake, the women were bringing food and drink to the bereaved and to any of the visitors, those paying their respects, who cared to eat.

These dishes of food, always prepared from the best recipes of the benevolent cooks, would accumulate quickly on the days surrounding the funeral. There would eventually be such an enormous quantity that there would not be a square inch of space in the kitchen in which to place another incoming dish, no matter how miniscule. It was not the food that was significant. By this gesture of giving and empathy, friends and neighbors expressed without words their desire to share the grief and to demonstrate the caring in their hearts. It accomplished these things magnificently. It was all they could do. It was enough.

She sat almost motionless in the rocker, little Andrew on the floor at her feet, his doleful face expressing a sadness beyond tears. She absentmindedly touched him, on the small shoulders or softly caressed his hair. Occasionally, with the tips of her fingers, she would lightly rub the polished walnut cabinet of the radio that rested on the small oval table beside the chair. A reluctant wistful smile came across her lips as she remembered it now. The radio. It was the most, maybe the only, precipitous thing she had ever known Ezra to do. One of the weavers at the mill had bought a new radio and offered to sell his old one for ten-dollars, less than a quarter of the price new.

He had paced the kitchen floor, back and forth, as she prepared supper that evening, talking and wrestling with himself. He knew they couldn't afford it. Well, actually they were putting a little money back. Had done so since the beginning. Oh, but ten dollars was a lot of money. But this was a real chance to get a great deal. It's a Philco; of course it is. Model 45c. Nothing fancy, I reckon, but a good one. Maybe Homer would take eight dollars. Hmm, that's still a lot of money. He continued to pace and to talk, seemingly to himself.

She continued to peel potatoes at the sink, her back to his pacing. She was happy, and smiled broadly at her husband's self-imposed dilemma. His agony. She listened and peeled until finally he stopped his pacing.

"What do you think I should do?" he asked earnestly.

"What do *I* think?"

"Yes. Sure would be nice to have a radio. Listen to those new shows they got. A bunch of music, too. Good music, they say. You can even listen to the President. Can you imagine listening to the President of the United States just like he was talking to you face to face? That would be something!"

"That *would* be something," she echoed pleasantly. She had seldom seen him so animated.

"But, then again, I don't know," he argued with himself. He slumped down in a chair at the table.

She knew that he was just as upset with struggling with what he considered to be impulsiveness as he was with actually spending the money.

It's just not in him, she thought, but he doesn't know it.'

Finally, she said, without looking up from her work, "Ezra, go get the radio." And he did. Funny, she thought now, the things you think of.

Some of the women, with Earline's guidance, deposited their dishes wherever they could find space in the kitchen. They gathered and visited, speaking in subdued voices, their soft Southern drawls creating a soothing murmur about the house. They were scattered in small groups on the porch and throughout the house, except in the front bedroom where the casket had been placed. They chatted in low tones and exchanged the latest gossip about the shooting, the strikers, who still had jobs and who didn't, but mostly they wondered aloud what Judith would do now.

As soon as word had come that her husband had been killed, Earline took over. She had been with Judith and the children virtually every moment since then. She was with her when she told the two children. The sorrow was unfathomable, but they had shared it. She had helped bathe them, responded to their sad unanswerable questions as best she could, and sat up with them until sleep finally came. She touched them often, as she did their mother. She had stayed with them yesterday while Melvin accompanied Judith to the mortuary to meet with the undertaker.

Late in the morning a shiny black hearse, a Buick, had pulled to the curb. The four *living* occupants were large somber men, all dressed the same in dark brown suits with muted, silk ties. They alighted from the vehicle almost simultaneously and formed a formation at the rear from which they ceremoniously removed their cargo. Judith, with her children on either side of her, sat on the edge of the bed in the front bedroom, the room she had shared with her husband. Facing the window, they observed the ritual on the street. The men worked together, carefully and expertly, to keep it level as they slowly advanced across the yard and up the steps with their burden.

Melvin, leaning on a cane, stood helplessly watching as Earline met the hearse at the curb. She spoke briefly with the driver, and directed the men where to take and place it—the casket. It was a polished wooden thing, with neatly crafted dovetailed corners.

"Just a pine box, after all," she whispered to herself.

It was placed in the bedroom, at the foot of the bed, on a crudely constructed wooden stand that the mortuary had furnished. Judith, Grace, and Andrew stood back by the window as the men entered the room. The children watched, but their mother's eyes were closed. No one spoke as the men followed Earline's hand gestures. Finally, they nodded to each other, and to Earline, and left. She then left the room herself, gently shutting the door behind her, leaving the young family alone in their sadness.

Judith stepped over slowly, instinctively and inexplicably crossed herself, and placed her hand gently on the wooden container that held the body of Ezra Burke, her husband. She held Andrew's small hand with the other.

Gracie, with hot tears stinging her eyes and cheeks, knelt on the floor and tightly hugged the corner post of the wooden structure upon which the coffin, her father, rested. Despite her mother's urgings and reassurances, she would remain there until long after dark. Later when finally asleep, Earline would lift the child into her arms and place her gently in her bed.

***

Finally, a hush fell over the house as dusk gave way to darkness. The last neighbor had come and gone. She hated the silence and the inevitable darkness. The emptiness inside her seemed to press down on her, an almost unbearable weight.

My own soul has left me, she thought.

"Let me fix you a plate," said Earline, standing at the door of the kitchen.

"No, Earline, I'm not hungry."

"Andrew, you come on in here with me. Might be able to find some whipped cream to put on a piece of peach cobbler." Andrew looked wide-eyed at Earline, but did not move or respond.

"Go in the kitchen with Earline, son. I'll be all right here," she said, looking down at her son.

"All right," the boy said reluctantly, and rose from the floor and went into the kitchen.

"Where is Grace?" asked Judith blankly as if she had just woke from a deep trance and missed her girl child.

"She still in the bedroom. On the floor beside, uh, but I've been checking on her. She's okay."

"She's so sad, Earline. It breaks my heart."

Earline quickly turned and looked back in the kitchen. "Did you hear that?"

"No."

"Well, I think someone's knocking on the back door. I better go see about it," she said.

She gently brushed passed little Andrew and opened the back door. She glanced down instinctively to make sure the hook was latched on the screen door. A single, bare bulb hung from the porch ceiling, inexplicably swaying slightly in the still night air. Its light cast a pale yellow glow onto the porch and onto a small patch of the ground below, beyond which was the darkness. The constant muted hum of the mill could be heard in the distance.

The night caller had stepped off the small porch out into the yard after knocking. Standing at the edge of the dimly-lit circle of light, he cast a vague shadow behind him that touched the darkness.

Earline flicked open the latch and stepped out onto the porch, holding the flimsy screen door open behind her. The night air was still and heavy from the heat of the departed day. The shadowy figure moved more into the small circle of light. She emitted a short, quick gasp as she looked down at the large black man standing below her.

"What do you want? You 'bout scared the life out of me," she spoke sharply, gripping tightly the doorframe behind her.

"Sorry, ma'am, didn't mean to," he said, looking up at her and fidgeting with the brim of the felt hat he held in front of him with both hands.

"Who are you? What do you want?" she asked again, her voice tense but controlled.

"Name's Yates, ma'am, Josh Yates. I work at the mill. In the coal yard."

She relaxed her grip on the door and let it close gently behind her. She knew of the men who worked back of the mill shoveling coal and she had heard his name before. She remembered Ezra had worked in the coal yard when he had first come to Corinth.

"Okay, Mr. Yates, what can I do for you?"

He continued to fumble with the hat and glanced back over his shoulder into the darkness behind him. He cleared his throat and shifted his weight.

He's sure nervous, she thought.

"I know this ain't proper. It ain't the way things usually done, but I come to pay my respects to Burke—to Ezra."

"Why didn't you come around to the front door like everybody else instead of sneaking 'round back here in the dark?"

"Oh, I ain't sneaking around, no ma'am. But you know I can't come to the house like, uh, same as white folks."

She nodded, acknowledging the accuracy of his statement, "That may be, so what can *I* do for you?"

"Are you Miz Burke?"

"No, course I ain't. She's grieving. Her husband's layin' acorpse."

"I reckoned that," he replied. "I sure would like to speak to her."

"Well, forget it, Mr. Yates, you ain't going to. It's late and, anyway, what would you have to say to her at a time like this?"

"I ain't naturally a humble man, ma'am. I am what I am, that's all. But I'm asking you to please let me speak to her. If she'll just come to the back door for a minute. That's all, just for a time. I won't be long."

"And if I won't?" Earline folded her arms across her breast.

"Well, then, I'll just walk off and head back over to Free Town. You know, what y'all call *nigger town*."

"I don't call it nothing, Mr. Yates."

"If Miz Burke would come to the door just a minute, I'd sure be obliged."

Earline hesitated as she looked down at this dark apparition standing below her in the eerie, low, yellow light. Finally, she spoke.

"All right. I'll go see if see wants to talk to you, but she probably won't. You hear me, she likely won't come back here."

"Yes'm. I understand, I do. I'll just wait here," Yates said softly, and she disappeared back into the house, latching the screen door behind her.

Andrew had been sitting patiently at the kitchen table. She abstractly mussed his hair as she passed by, going into the front room.

"What is it, Earline? I heard voices," she asked, looking up from where she sat.

"Nothing's wrong, it's all right. Look, there's this big colored fella out back. Says he knows, uh, knew Ezra from the coal yard at the mill. Says he wants to pay his respects. I told him you likely wouldn't come to the door, but he just kept on asking. I'll just send him on his way." Earline turned to leave the room.

"No. No, I'll speak to him," she said, rising slowly from the chair.

"You sure? I don't mind sending him—"

"I'll speak to him."

"Okay, then. I guess I better go fix that young 'un of yours his peach cobbler, but I'll be close by."

Judith stepped out on the back porch. The man was still standing in the pool of muted yellow light.

"I'm Judith Burke, Ezra's wife. You wanted to say something."

"Yes, ma'am, I'm pleased to meet you. I know you must be in a bad way, but I thank you a heap for coming out here like this. Name's Yates. I know'd your husband."

A silence fell between them, and the darkness beyond seemed to thicken. He could not see the tears well up in the young woman's dark eyes.

Finally, "Yes, Mr. Yates, I know who you are. He told me about the coal yard and the men there."

"Yes'm, you know he worked with us a spell. Worked right alongside us."

"Mr. Yates, won't you come inside? We can talk and there is more than a plenty food."

"Oh, no ma'am, I couldn't do that, no ma'am."

He again glanced back into the darkness.

"I wish you would," she said earnestly.

"No, ma'am. I just wanted to tell you, you know, face-to-face like, how much I thought of your husband. I never met a white man that was like him. That's for sure. He might be finest man I ever knowed, black or white. He didn't seem to see no color. It was like we was all the same to him. He even saved Sugar Joe's life one time. Could have hurt his own self doing it too, but it didn't matter seem to matter none to him." After he said this, Yates looked down at the ground.

"Thank you, Mr. Yates."

Tears tracked down her cheeks and fell silently onto the dusty, wooden planks of the porch floor. She did not wipe them away.

"I'm just sorry what happened. It wat'n right. I just wanted you to know I'm sorry what happened. I'm real sorry."

She did not respond to him and a brief, awkward silence passed between them. He then placed the dingy, felt hat on his head and adjusted the wide brim low over his eyes.

"I reckon that's all I come to say, Miz Burke. I thank you for coming out to let me talk. I'll go now."

"Good bye, Mr. Yates."

She stood there and watched him turn and fade like a phantom into the darkness. She could barely make out the outline of his large frame as he approached the alley that ran behind the house, beyond the yard. She could not be sure, but she was almost certain that as the darkness of the night engulfed him there was another person, much smaller, walking beside him who seemed to move awkwardly, perhaps with a limp.

CHAPTER 37

After speaking with Yates, she returned to the sitting room. The lone, but shaded, bulb hanging from the ceiling cast a gloomy, dull light about the room, leaving the corners dark and the walls shadowy. Melvin, in one of the darker corners, slumped in a chair, snoring rhythmically, but softly. Both of the children were asleep in their beds. A slight but warm breeze stirred the trees along Fifth Street and a few dark figures could be seen moving along toward the mill as midnight drew nearer.

She sat motionlessly by the silent radio, her face relaxed but sad, her eyes dry. Earline, in the kitchen, finished sorting the mountain of food that had been brought in. She placed as much as she could in the small refrigerator, and emptied scraps into a pail on the floor beside the back door. After wiping the cleared table, she folded the damp rag and placed it beside the enamel sink. Standing in the doorway, she looked over at Judith.

"Why don't you at least try and eat a little something, Judith?"

The widow looked up at her friend and smiled ruefully. "No, I'm all right."

"Let me make you some coffee then."

"All right."

Earline withdrew to the kitchen and began filling the coffee pot with water. With her back to the sink, she was not aware that Judith had followed her into the kitchen.

"Earline."

Earline, startled, dropped the pot into the sink with a clank. "You 'bout scared the life out of me, sweetie. You and that colored man that came by after dark."

"I'm sorry."

"It's okay. The racket didn't seem to bother old Rip Van Winkle there in the sitting room none. What can I get you?"

"Nothing. I just want to ask you something."

"What is it?"

"Earline, is there a church, a Catholic church in Corinth?"

"A Catholic church? Why you want to know that for?"

"Is there one?" she repeated, ignoring her friend's question.

"Not many Catholics around here. Plenty of them 'round Charleston and Savannah they say. But, yeah, there's one downtown, I reckon. Why?"

"I might go into town in the morning. Do you know where it is?"

"Yeah, but I'm awful with directions. You know that about me by now, I reckon. I can't even recollect what street it's on."

"What the name of the church?" the younger woman asked. Earline started filling up the pot again with water from the spigot, thinking hard.

"Hmm, let me see. Kind of a funny name. I mean for a church. I'm a Holiness you know. At least raised one. But you can't smoke and be a Holiness. Drink neither. Reckon that leaves me out in the cold, or the heat," Earline chuckled.

"Do you remember the name of the church? It's important."

"Oh, yeah, the church. I believe it's called, uh, I don't know. Lady of Peace, or something like that. Might be wrong, but I think that's it."

"Our Lady of Peace," Judith instinctively breathed the words softly, almost to herself. "It would be Our Lady of Peace. Thank you, Earline."

"You not a Catholic are you?" she asked as she placed scoops of coffee into the pot.

"Yes, I am, or I mean I was. Much like you were a Holiness, I guess. It's been a long time."

"You planning to go in to town sometime and go to that church?"

"Yes. I'm going tomorrow. In the morning."

"Geez, Judith, I don't know if that's such a good idea. I mean with everything and all."

She placed the coffee pot on the burner and sat down at the table. She pulled a pack of Camel's from her apron pocket, withdrew a cigarette from it and lit it.

"Will you mind the children while I'm gone?"

"Sure, but... look, if you bound and determined to go into town tomorrow, Melvin will go with you. He'd be glad to do it."

"No, I'll go alone. I want to go alone. I'll take the bus or maybe just walk."

"You sure about this?"

"Yes, I'm sure."

The pleasant aroma of brewing coffee filled the small kitchen. Earline filled two thick, porcelain mugs and placed them on the table. She sat down and pushed one of the steaming cups across the oil cloth table top to Judith.

"Cigarettes and coffee, like old friends," said Earline.

The younger woman smiled, stared into the cup and placed her hands around the heavy mug as if she were trying to warm them.

"Look, Judith, I know it's none of my business, but I just got to ask you why you'd go into town tomorrow. I mean, the funeral's at four. Maybe you're just not thinking too clear. Who would be, with all you been through? Do you know why, honey, do you *really*?

"Yes, I know why. Of course, I do. My mind has never been so clear." She pursed her lips and blew across the cup, and then sipped the hot coffee.

"Can I go with you? Melvin can watch the kids."

"No, Earline, but thank you for offering and for your concern. I appreciate everything you've done for us. I don't know what I would have done without you here."

"Just trying to be a good neighbor, that's all," Earline said with a short chuckle. She flicked ashes from the cigarette into the jar lid, then leaned toward Judith with her elbows resting on the table.

"Tell me, Judith, does this Catholic Church business have anything to do with the funeral or burying Ezra or anything like that?"

"Yes, it does. And more."

After a pause, Earline spread her open palms toward her grieving neighbor and asked impatiently, "Well?"

"It's nothing really. At least not to anyone but me. Me and Ezra. I want a priest at the funeral. That's all."

"Oh, I see," said Earline as she sat back in her chair, not seeing at all. She reached over and crushed out what was left of the Camel. She ran her hands through her thinning and graying hair. She lit another cigarette and both women sat in silence. Finally, Earline spoke.

"Well what do you want me to tell that nice young Methodist preacher you talked to this morning? We got to let him know."

"Oh, no, I still want him to read the Bible passage and pray. None of that has changed."

"I'd not be too sure of that. We don't get many priests on the mill hill. What you want him here for?"

"He won't be *here* and probably won't come at all. But, you see, I've got to ask. Maybe he will," Judith replied.

"You think so?"

"It's possible," said Judith, who then folded her arms on the table and, as a pillow, lay her head upon them and closed her eyes.

***

As she turned the corner, she saw the church just up the block on the opposite of the street. She glanced back at the policeman who had looked hard at her and brusquely gave her directions at the trolley stop. She crossed at the light and then stood on the low, concrete steps of the church, facing the huge, ornate black doors, which reflected the morning sun like two giant, dull mirrors.

She pushed open one of the heavy doors and stepped into the narthex and waited a moment, letting her eyes adapt to the dimness. The coolness engulfed her and she felt herself suddenly and unexpectedly overcome by the comforting air of the church. The smell of lingering incense mixed with old prayer books and candle wax flooded her senses and her memory. It *had* been a long time. She had been not much more than a child. Suddenly, and inexplicably, she felt safe.

Dipping her fingers lightly into the basin of holy water, she crossed herself and walked slowly down the aisle of the nave. Halfway down she genuflected effortlessly, but self-consciously, and slipped into a pew to her left, the Gospel side. Then she knelt and repeated the Lord's Prayer slowly in a whisper, but which seemed loud to her, in the quietness. Despite the traffic outside, it was quiet here, the silence of the church muffled and overcame the noise outside. It was as if she were immersed in the silence. She felt as if she had been swallowed up by another world. Strangely, for a moment it seemed real to her, while a slain husband, children, the mill, the mountains did not. The feeling frightened her at first. It quickly vanished as a strange, but not unpleasant shiver ran through her body.

Seemingly out of nowhere, a nun appeared and began fiddling with a flower arrangement on the chancel rail, way down in front of her. No one else was in the church. She rose from the pew, adjusted the faded, red scarf covering her head, and approached the nun. She softly cleared her throat so as not to startle the black-clad Sister. If the nun heard her, it was not evident as she continued to move the white and yellow lilies around in a beautiful, large cloisonné vase.

"Sister," she said distinctly. Though spoken quite softly, her voice seemed to explode in the silence, and echo within the nave.

"Yes," returned the nun. Her voice, too, was soft and it had a soothing kindness to it, but she did not turn from her flower work.

"I would like to speak with the priest. Is he here?"

"Well, that depends, dear. You see we have more than one priest here."

"It doesn't matter. Not really. Any of them will do."

"Any of them will do," repeated the nun, smiling, with very light sarcasm and a breathy chortle. "They would be happy to know that: You will do, Father Casper. Or, you will do, Father Donovan. Or, you too, Father Ripken, will do." She pulled out a yellow lily and replaced it with two white ones.

"I'm sorry, Sister, I didn't mean to be disrespectful. It's just that I must see a priest. I don't know anyone here, you see. Is there a priest here, now? It's very important. Important to me, I mean."

"Well, I think there might be one or two of them *loitering* around here someplace," the nun said pleasantly, finally turning to look at Judith. She then pointed to a dimly-lit alcove beyond the chancel, behind Judith.

"Just go through that door and down the hallway. You'll find Father Donovan in his study, third door on the right."

"Thank you, Sister."

"You're welcome," she said, and returned to the flowers.

As Judith moved to the alcove door she hesitated, then stopped and looked back into the church with its high vaulted ceiling and pleasant, musty smell. Golden, almost white sunlight illuminated the great stained glass windows. With their iconic figures of the Bible and the Church, the colors were brilliant and dazzling. It was a beauty she perhaps had not really seen before, or at least not remembered. But now it was imprinted indelibly in her brain. She would not forget it.

The door to Father Donovan's study stood open. With a slight reticence, she tapped the polished oak jamb lightly. He looked up from his reading and surveyed purposefully the young, serious woman before him. He was instantly taken by her bright dark eyes, and her straight ebony hair that just touched her shoulders, burnished as it caught the thin rays of light from the window behind him. In the finely-etched features of her brown face, he saw instantly an alien beauty, but there was sadness in her countenance. Father Donovan was a sensitive man.

"Please come in," he said as he rose from his chair behind his desk.

As she stepped into the study, she was aware of the heavy, almost moist, odor of old books and wood polish. It was a small room and she had a strange feeling of being cloistered. She liked the feeling and the room. He motioned to a chair which was across from him, just beyond the corner of the desk. She sat, removed her scarf, and began to speak softly.

***

The simple coffin, pine and deeply varnished, rested on four small blocks of granite placed beneath each corner. It was set near the edge of a neatly dug rectangular pit. A mound of red-clay soil lined the edge of the pit opposite the coffin. The smell of newly turned earth struggled to linger in the hot, still air. The sun hung in the sky, motionless and merciless, with its unconscionable white heat. It seemed as if it would pierce the coffin. The reflected light gave it an unnatural translucence in the heavy breezeless air.

Nothing stirred in the shimmering stillness. The noise from the traffic on the highway a quarter-mile away was muffled and inconsequential. No birds sang or flew. The sky was a blank, faded haze of blue, an appropriate backdrop for the pitiless sun. It was as if nature itself was overcome by the oppressive heat and would permit only the most necessary languid movements of its charges, whether human or animal.

Behind the coffin she stood with the two children. The fingers of one hand lightly caressed the smooth, gleaming wood. With the other she held the hand of her younger child. The children, filled with sadness and confusion, stood motionless beside their mother, staring blankly and without comprehension at the coffin, or perhaps at the pit in the earth just beyond it.

The minister, young and close-shaven, stood at one end of the coffin. His black tie was cinched tightly. The starched collar of his white shirt was soaked with perspiration and was hot around his neck. He seemed to be gasping for oxygen. With moist hands, he nervously held an open, black Bible. He read aloud in a thin, measured, but distinct voice. Sweat dripped from the tip of his nose onto the delicate onion-skin page. The page became translucent, darkening the small, printed words, as the wetness spread across it. He finished the Twenty-Third Psalm by memory and closed the Bible. After a short prayer, he stepped back from his place near the coffin and stood stiffly straight, like a soldier at attention.

She glanced up as an older man in a clerical collar replaced the minister beside the coffin. Huge, hot tears welled in her eyes and streamed just as hotly down her cheeks as Father Donovan offered a blessing to Ezra and to her and the children. As he began the Lord's Prayer, she lowered her head and a solitary tear fell onto the heavily-lacquered wood before her. For an instance, it was like a bright diamond exploding on the warm surface of the coffin in the sunlight. Then it was gone, evaporated by the heat from the very source that had given it brilliance only a second before.

There had been no church service. She had allowed no obituary to be printed in the paper, which confused the mortician and the reporter from the Gazette, and the people of the mill village. Other than Earline and Melvin, she had invited no one to the graveside, but still there were people who had come—a few.

Beneath a small copse of trees on a knoll well beyond the grave, a small group of black men stood solemnly in the hot shade. All wore overalls and held their hats and caps respectfully in hands stained blacker than their skin, as the prayer was said. No one seemed to have noticed them, or if they did, just thought them to be the gravediggers. Gravediggers are always niggers, they would have thought to themselves. Everyone knew that. No one else would have the job. Even in hard times. Judith had seen them when she first approached the grave from the car to begin the burial service. She knew they were not gravediggers.

Earline and Melvin, he leaning on a cane, and a seldom-worn hand painted necktie tied uncomfortably around his collar, stood just behind their widowed neighbor and the children. A few people from the mill were grouped together a few yards beyond. But most of the mill workers had stayed away, confused by the violence and the irrational fear of being associated with the union. Like Ezra, the unions were dead now. Nothing mattered but the job, the work, the mill, *the Man*.

There was a moment of awkward silence when Father Donovan finished the prayer. As the few people there began to move away, the young Methodist minister walked over to where Judith stood. He gave his condolences and left. She just stared down at the coffin.

"I am sorry for your loss," came a voice. Father Donovan stood beside her. She looked into his face.

There was sadness in her now-tearless eyes, but a certain indescribable peace had settled over her. Much like the strange peace that had overcome her earlier that morning in the church. Maybe it had come from that. She did not know.

"Thank you for this, I mean, coming here. The blessing, the prayer…everything," she said in a soft, but composed voice.

"I could have done nothing less," the priest replied as he reached down and touched both children.

"But thank you. It meant everything."

"Perhaps we will meet again," he said kindly, without expectation.

"Yes, maybe," she replied, with a smile that was slight and rueful. She then looked away. He said nothing more and then, he too, was gone.

"Come on, Judith, let's go to the car," Earline said, placing an arm around her friend's shoulder. Melvin had already hobbled on down toward the automobile provided by the mortuary.

"No, I'm going to stay here for awhile."

The gravediggers had appeared and stood a few yards away. They held coils of thick, hemp rope and shovels. Earline glanced over at them knowingly.

"Now you don't really want to do this. Let's get out of this sun. We can go to the house and sit on the porch. I'll make us some ice-cold lemonade. How about it, sweetie?"

"No, I'm going to stay awhile. Would you mind taking Grace and Andrew with you though? I'll be home directly." Andrew, who was standing close to his mother, quickly wrapped his arms tightly around her waist.

"I want to stay with you, Mama," said Grace, her cotton dress wilted by perspiration and her short hair, limp and damp, sticking to her forehead.

"No, I want you to go with Earline and Melvin. I need to be by myself a little while." Andrew's grip tightened. She looked at Grace, her dark eyes pleading, "Please."

"All right, Mama. Come on, Andrew. You'll be okay, won't you Mama?"

"Yes, of course I will."

"Come with me, Andrew. Let's go with Aunt Earline and get some lemonade." The child gently pulled her brother away and, with her arm around his shoulder, followed Earline to the waiting car.

She watched them go and felt a vague guilt and trepidation sweep over her as she considered Grace, having placed such responsibilities on her so young. There will be more to come, she thought. It was time, or would be shortly, to come to terms with it all. She had lost her love, he was gone. She had cried her tears. There would be more, she was certain. But only in her own grieving and in her own time. Perhaps what she feared most was that in her private pain and desolation, there would be no consolation.

As she turned back to the grave, she knew without looking up that the gravediggers were approaching. Only half their work was done. The hole in the earth had been dug; now it must be filled.

Although the small knot of mill people had melted away, one remained. He was a stout squarely built man. Hatless, he wore a white shirt, now almost gray with the dampness of sweat, and a tie loosely tied between his shoulders and head. He seemed not to possess a neck. His left hand, which hung heavily at his side, held a fresh but unlit cigar. He walked toward the grave as he futilely brushed a recalcitrant lock of hair from his forehead.

"Mrs. Burke, can I speak with you a minute?" he asked, and without looking at them, he held out his hand, palm up, to the approaching gravediggers. With his signal, they halted and waited, leaning on the handles of their shovels. Judith looked at him impatiently and disinterestedly, but did not respond.

"My name is Charlie Matheson."

"I know who you are," she said flatly.

"I'm real sorry about your husband." He hesitated and when she did not reply he continued. "I know this isn't a good time, but I just don't know when a good time would be."

"It's all right, Mr. Matheson. What do you want?"

From his back pocket he pulled a wrinkled, light-brown envelope. He fought hard with himself to keep from squeezing it or wadding it up in his thick, sweaty fingers.

"I've been told, ordered I guess you might say, to give this to you," he said. He extended his hand with the envelope.

"What is it?" she asked, making no move to accept it.

"Why, it's money. A good bit of money, that is."

"What for?"

"It's from the Allgood family. They felt it was the least they could do, I reckon."

"The Allgood's?"

"Yes, Mr. Allgood actually."

"I see," she said.

"It's a thousand dollars," he said matter of factly, in a voice with no intention or motive.

"Why would he give me money?" asked Judith.

"Well, for Ezra. I mean Ezra was a good worker, a good man. He stood up against the union. That's the way Mr. Allgood sees it, anyway. He knows you'll need help. So that's it, I guess."

"Ezra didn't stand up against anything. He just wanted to work. The union had nothing to do with it. Neither did the mill. He just wanted to go to work. He felt that was the right thing to do. It was a simple thing, Mr. Matheson." She looked at him directly without expression. Neither spoke for a moment.

Finally, Matheson said, "Will you take the money? You have kids to take care of and all. Please take it, Mrs. Burke."

She thought for a long moment. Of the children. About the house. The mountains. Ezra.

"No, Mr. Matheson, I'll not take your money. I don't want it. It doesn't make everything all right. You see, everything isn't all right. You keep the money, Mr. Matheson."

"But you have children to look after," he pleaded, almost halfheartedly by now, knowing it was pointless.

"We'll get by."

"Please—"

"No."

Inexplicably, Matheson was almost relieved that she had rejected Allgood's gift. Perhaps it was a salve to his conscience, or more likely because here was someone who would not be controlled by the Allgood's. It was something—a feeling—he could not explain nor quite understand. He stuffed the envelope back into his pocket.

"You should take the money, you should. But I think I understand, at least a little," he said to her. "Anyway, I just want you to know that there will be a job in the mill for your kids. I mean, when they finish school. Folks need an education these days."

With hearing his words, albeit well meant, she felt her spine stiffen and both hands squeeze into tight fists. Then she caught her breath and felt her body become light, but grounded, as the peace returned to her.

"My children will never work in a cotton mill, Mr. Matheson. Not yours, not any."

The words came out evenly and without emotion, with absolute certainty and assurance. It was as if she was confessing her faith before God himself. Matheson stood there awkwardly for a moment and he could see the eons of survival and struggle and courage in the deep pools of her dark eyes. He walked away without lighting the cigar.

She stood by the grave as the men ran the thick ropes under either end of the coffin. Gathering the length of rope in their huge, calloused hands they slowly lifted it. With her standing there, they took more than casual care with the coffin as they began to lower it, letting the hemp line slid over their shoulder loosely, but controlled.

When it was done, one of the black men picked a shovel up off the ground. He stepped to the mound of earth, but before stabbing the piled, red soil with the spade, he looked to her and lightly touched the brim of his hat. She nodded slightly to him, and with a damp thud, the first of the red dirt fell on the varnished pine box.

CHAPTER 38

Norman Calicut sat in the waiting room, the *Anteroom* as it had been officially designated by the Company, bent over with an elbow resting on either knee. He occasionally would sit up suddenly in the chair and smooth down his hair or adjust the knot of his tie, yanking it tighter against his Adam's apple each time. He repeatedly pulled the ornate, gold-plated watch from his vest pocket to check the time, although there was a large round clock on the wall across the room. On the chair beside him was a thick, brown folder. It contained a sheaf of onionskin papers which he also kept trying, quite unsuccessfully, to straighten and align the edges. He was, in short, nervous.

Sure, I'm a little nervous, he was thinking, who wouldn't be? In the rarified air of the top floor. The executive suite, no less. A lowly, debit-route agent like me rarely, if ever, gets a personal interview with the boss, the real boss, the head honcho!

But he had been determined to do this, to get an appointment to plead his case. He did not care how much trouble it caused, it was the right thing to do. Might cost him his job, his wife had warned dryly that morning. It might, he admitted, but he was going to see it through. He had argued and fought tooth and nail, but he had finally done it. He had gotten an appointment with C. Jameson Phelps himself. He looked at his watch again. Almost noon. He had been waiting nearly an hour.

Finally, the door opened and a stylishly dressed young woman appeared. She hardly wasted a glance at him, but announced, "Mr. Phelps will see you now."

She's a real looker, thought Norman, pretty snooty though. Nice ankles.

He scooped up the folder, as one of the sheets of thin paper slipped out and floated to the floor. He reached down for it while still looking up at the woman, and stuffed it back into the folder, which he now grasped with both hands. As he squeezed past her in the doorway, she did not move aside to make way for him. His elbow unintentionally, and only lightly, brushed against the breasts that pressed against the blue silk crepe of her lizzie. She looked hard at him as he passed, not smiling, but making no effort to avoid the contact. She was used to it. Such things were part of working on the top floor of the Freedom Life Insurance Company.

As he entered the cool walnut-paneled office, Norman was astounded at its size. Almost as big as my whole house, he thought, and almost said aloud.

There were chairs and couches in various places, all covered in a luscious, almost succulent, maroon leather. Several large portraits of men, probably all dead now, hung on the walls. Beyond the large, ornate rug was the altar, Phelps' desk. Norman took a deep breath. Everything in here is made to make me feel small. And I sure as hell do.

Phelps stood up behind his desk and beckoned him to come in. He seemed a long way off. Is he shouting at me? Norman wondered.

He stepped quickly and quietly across the rug-covered floor. He felt he was almost tiptoeing. As he approached the desk, Phelps gestured to a chair. He took it and sat on the edge, hugging the folder to his chest.

"Good to see you, Mr. Calicut," said Phelps, as he lit a cigarette. The blue smoke curled and rose, rendered translucent by the light from the large window behind his desk. He leaned back in the luxury of the high-back, leather desk chair.

"I looked at your numbers before you came up. Excellent, I must say, quiet impressive."

"Thank you, sir."

Perspiration glistened on his forehead, as the sunlight from the window behind Phelps was like a spotlight on him. He felt he would melt at any moment.

"Sit back, Mr. Calicut, and relax. Can I get you anything? Some water or club soda perhaps?"

A real gentleman, thought Norman, disarmed momentarily by Phelps' suaveness and the acquired, unhurried ease of the Southern aristocrat. He sat back in the chair and placed the folder on his lap.

"I wish we had a hundred more men such as yourself out there, Mr. Calicut. The company can always use good men."

"Yes, sir. It's hard work, but I like it. Seems to suit me."

"Indeed. Your commissions have risen each month that you've been here. Shows initiative and drive. Good attributes for a young man these days. Shows me he's trying to get ahead. You *are* trying to get ahead aren't you, Mr. Calicut?" Phelps tapped the ash off the tip of his cigarette into a large, jade ashtray on the desk.

"Yes, sir, that's for sure. I do my best."

"I'm sure you do. That's evident in your numbers. Quite impressive," Phelps repeated.

"Yes, sir. Thank you, sir."

At this, Phelps cleared his throat ceremoniously and leaned forward, clasping both hands before him on the polished desk. He looked straight into the face of the young agent sitting before him, as if he was either sizing him up or getting ready to chop him to pieces. Norman did not look away.

"Tell me, Mr. Calicut, do you like selling insurance? Do you *really* like it, I mean?" Phelps' tone was emphatic and intimidating.

"Yes, sir, like I said, I enjoy my work."

"Do you like working here at the Freedom Life Insurance Company?"

"Yes, sir, I purely and surely do."

Phelps smiled broadly and leaned back in his chair. "That's good, Mr. Calicut, that's real good."

Suddenly, it seemed to Norman that the executive was either unaware or uninterested in why he was there. But he would be mistaken. With the considerable personal charm and the unrelenting undercurrent of the power he possessed, Phelps was using the subtleness that he preferred when handling problems, especially with *his* people. It was a long-practiced skill. Norman would surely recognize this, re-think his position, and politely excuse himself and cause no more trouble.

It would not quite work out this way, as one of them had underestimated the other.

"Mr. Phelps, I know you're mighty busy, but I have an important matter to discuss. It's urgent," he finally said.

"Of course, Mr. Calicut, what can I do for you?" Phelps leaned forward and crushed what was left of the cigarette in the ashtray.

"It's about a policy, sir. Actually, about a claim."

"What's the problem?"

"Well, the claim's been denied. I mean denied by our claims department. It's a claim that I think we're obliged to pay, sir."

"We always stand behind our policies and our customers. Have you run it by the underwriters?"

"Yes, sir."

"Well?"

"They say it's unclear. I believed they said *muddy*, or something like that anyway."

"What kind of claim is it? I mean what's the problem?"

"Of course it's a death. The death of the policy holder. But the folks down in claims say the policy don't cover it."

"And why not?"

"They say his death was an Act of War. But that's not true, at least the way I see it."

"What happened? I mean how did the client lose his life? I assume it's a *he*."

"Yes, sir. His name is, was, Ezra Burke. He was shot," Norman responded, with an edge of emotion and urgency.

"Wasn't he that textile worker killed over at Galway Mill? Involved with that union mess and those Northern agitators, as I recall." Phelps said.

"Yes, him, but I don't believe he was with the union, sir. He was only trying to go to work that day. That's what everybody says, and I believe it. I knew Mr. Burke. Paid his debit every week. Always on time. Never got behind. I declare, his wife is due this money, sir."

"What was he insured for?"

"Five hundred dollars. The usual payout for mill hill people."

"Hmm. Do you have a copy of the policy, Mr. Calicut?"

"Yes sir, right here, but it's all pretty standard." He opened the folder and, fumbling with the papers, drew out the policy and handed it to Phelps. Phelps rose and stood behind his desk, scanning the document.

After several moments, "Well, Mr. Calicut, I can certainly appreciate your standing behind your customers. Very admirable. But I'm afraid the boys down in claims are correct. An obvious Act of War, a condition that preempts payout of a claim."

"You mean we're not going to pay this claim?"

"No, Mr. Calicut. Can't do it. The company has no responsibility here. The policy is quite clear and precise, in my opinion. Not, as you say, *muddy*, at all."

"But Mr. Phelps, it wasn't an Act…"

"Look, Mr. Calicut, it was a most unfortunate incident. But there were soldiers involved. Mr. Burke quite clearly placed himself in what only can be described as a war zone. That's about it, I would say." His voice, soft and soothing, but resolute. It was clear the matter had been decided. Decided long before Norman had appeared in his office.

"But, sir—"

"Mr. Calicut," said Phelps as he looked at his watch, "It's well past the lunch hour and I have a two o'clock tee time at my club. So, if there's nothing else, Miss Carrington will show you out. Keep up the good work, Calicut. I think you'll go a long way with the Freedom Life Insurance Company."

***

    In fact, Norman Calicut would *not* go a long way with the Freedom Life Insurance Company. He had left his meeting with Phelps that day and resigned. He took a job with the Great Southern Extract & Elixir Company, selling what amounted to cough syrup, door-to-door. He had been able to obtain a position right off, for he was an experienced salesman with an education. In addition to being a high school graduate, he had successfully completed a correspondence course from the Holmes Business College of Akron, Ohio. And he had the certificate to prove it.

    But the day he left the Freedom Life Insurance Company, he drove to the mill village and pulled up at the curb in front of number Twenty, Fifth Street. He sat there for a moment before reaching down and drawing a pint of gin, wrapped tightly in a wrinkled, brown paper bag, from the floorboard beneath the seat. He straightened his tie, then suppressing a burp as he got out of the car, he walked to the porch and rapped sharply on the front door.

    "Afternoon, Mrs. Burke," he said to the attractive woman, whose smooth, brown skin shown even darker standing in the shadow of the doorway. He removed his hat.

    "Good afternoon, Mr. Calicut," she said softly but distinctly, with a brief, faint smile.

    "Well, not so good I'm afraid. I mean, I don't have good news for you." He hesitated. "They ain't going to pay your husband's—Ezra's—claim." He looked down at his scuffed shoes and fumbled with his hat.

    "I see," she said.

    "I tried, Mrs. Burke. I purely and surely did. I hope you believe that. I even went to the head man. He turned it down. I did all I could, but they just wouldn't listen. I hate it, Mrs. Burke, but I tried my best."

    She reached and touched his arm. Her touch was light to him. Soft as a morning breeze, he thought.

    "I'm sure you did, Mr. Calicut. It doesn't matter. Not really."

    "A bunch of cold-hearted bastards they are. Excuse my French, but it's true."

    "It's all right," she said.

    "Well, pardon me for saying it, but it ain't all right. You deserve that money. It's due you. That's all, it's your money."

    "No, Mr. Calicut, if I don't have it, then it isn't mine. But I never had it anyway, so it doesn't really matter, now does it?"

"It matters a heap to me. Ain't right!" he said, with a subdued, but sincere anger.

Then there was a silence between them. It seemed there was nothing else to say. Finally, he placed the hat back on his head and tipped the brim with his fingers.

"I'll be going now, Mrs. Burke. I guess all I can say is I'm sorry. Never been sorrier about anything in my life."

"All right," she said.

She continued to stand in the doorway, as he turned and walked across the porch. When he had stepped off the last step, he stopped and looked back up at her.

"I just want you to know that I can't make myself work for a company that would do somebody this way. I mean not pay a rightful claim. Like stealing, as I see it. I just couldn't do it. I quit the Freedom Life Insurance Company today. I just wanted you to know that. I couldn't stand myself if I didn't. I just wanted you to know that."

She looked at him for a brief moment, and then moved back into the house and quietly shut the door. For a moment, Norman Calicut sat in his car, gripping the steering wheel tightly with both hands, his forehead resting on the wheel. Then he reached over for the bagged bottle in the seat beside him. He uncapped it and sucked down what was left of the gin. He then started the engine and drove off slowly down the street.

EPILOGUE

I have been lightly dozing when I sense, more than hear, Captain Jorgensen reduce engine power. I wake, but do not open my eyes. Some light, pleasant thing that I must have been dreaming still tickles my brain but I cannot recall it precisely. I badly want to do so. Then I feel Ms. Bishop's touch, equally light and pleasant, on my shoulder. I open my eyes.

"Mr. Burke, Captain Jorgensen asked me to let you know we'll be landing in about fifteen minutes."

"All right. Thanks, Karen," I reply as I bring the leather seat upright.

"I laid your things out on the sofa in your cabin, Mr. Burke. Your overcoat and gloves. I think you'll need a scarf, too. It's very cold."

"Thanks," I say again, and turn to gaze out the oval window at the slowly-passing landscape far below.

The rolling hills I see below are thick with trees, all now leafless gray skeletons. Cars on the thin ribbons of glistening wet roads look like moving ants, small and inconsequential, from this altitude. The plane banks left somewhat sharply and in the distance I can see the city. It sits squarely and smugly, as always, on the plain just beyond the last of the mountains. New buildings, dull and dark and gray beneath the overcast sky—Downtown. Things must be going well here. Actually, pretty much a boom town is what they are telling me these days. Obscenely prosperous, despite bad times seemingly most everywhere else. Good for them, I say to myself. But I could not care less. You see, I don't really give a damn about Corinth,_____. We are descending rapidly when I hear and feel the dull but distinct thump of the landing gear being lowered.

The jet touches down somewhat heavily and I feel the reassuring firmness of the earth as the wheels click rhythmically over the expansion joints in the concrete runway. The clicking gradually slows and then stops. I don the overcoat, with Karen's competent hands needlessly smoothing the shoulders and lapels. I slip my hands into the black kid gloves and instinctively flex my hands. Perhaps they will stave off the cold that sometimes brings the aching to the joints of my fingers.

Captain Jorgensen self-consciously assists me down the extended steps. Just across the tarmac, a car is waiting with clouds of hot vapor pouring from its tailpipe into the frigid air. The driver, waiting in the warm snugness of the limousine, sees me deplane and quickly steps out to the front of the automobile. I think how foolish. Stay out of the wet cold I would say to him. I can open the door myself. Then I think perhaps it is me who is foolish, that I still do not take for granted the gratuitous things that people do for me because I am old and because I am wealthy. I doubt that they ever get the two confused, and I remind myself that I must guard against unwarranted cynicism as I age.

Tiny beads of moisture fall on the gleaming bill of the chauffeur's cap. He touches the edge of it with his long, slender, gloved fingers and nods as I approach. He is tall, thin and elegant, and appears to be an older man, though not nearly so old as me. He is black.

"Mr. Burke?" he asks with a clear deep mellow voice.

"Yes."

"Any bags, sir?"

"No, no bags. Just going to the cemetery." I reach to shake his hand, a gesture which seems to surprise and embarrass him, but one that I hope doesn't insult him.

"Sanders, sir."

"Well, I assume you have a first name, Mr. Sanders?" I ask good-naturedly.

"Name's Grover, sir, but I prefer Sanders."

"Of course, Sanders. Did anyone tell you where you are to drive me?"

"Yes, sir. The cemetery. Fairview. Fairview Gardens."

"Yes, the cemetery. I assume you know where it is located," I say, realizing immediately how obtuse this must sound to him.

"Yes, sir, I do."

"Well then, shall we stand chatting here in this miserable cold mist and catch our death, or get on with our chore?" Sanders moves adroitly to open the rear passenger door for me.

Arriving at the entrance of the cemetery, we pass through the open gate, above which is scrolled in black wrought iron, *Fairview Gardens*. Although I have been to the cemetery a few times over the years, it inexplicably occurs to me that I don't remember ever thinking much about its name. This time I muse. Fairview. A fair view of what? Death perhaps. Or maybe more than that. Like Moses, we'll give you a fair view of Canaan, but you just can't actually go there. I immediately recognize my cynicism for what it is and, once again, make a mental note to work on it.

Once inside the boundary of the expansive, gently undulating hills of the graveyard, we drive slowly, creeping along the narrow, wet lane that winds between row upon row of tombstones. Finally, I reach up and tap Sanders on the shoulder, and he steers the car over to the edge, onto the wet grass, and stops. Before I can grasp the handle, the door swings open.

"Leave the engine running and please wait *in* the car, if you will, Sanders." He knows it is more than a request and, considering the damp cold, I suspect he is grateful for it. I walk up the low rise alone.

In a small plot, outlined by a low border of granite stones, are two grave markers. One of them is little larger than the other, but the two tombstones are just as I remember them. The larger of them is more weathered, the stone darker and stained. I have not come here often, perhaps I should have, but I feel no guilt. They are not here. I have only now come to remember them, to remind myself what is real and what is not. What is permanent and what is transient. It has been a long and difficult road for me, but now I am content with the journey. The prospects, or I should say, the destination, is and always *was* irrefutable and unassailable.

On Papa's side of the larger tombstone are chiseled the words below his name, *Greater love hath no man than this, that a man lay down his life for his friends.* I wonder at this, as I have many times. I have no answer that soothes or feels exactly right to me. On Mama's side of the gravestone there are no words, other than her name, below which, is a crucifix chiseled in cold sharp relief, the dying Christ in his agony and passion.

Of the smaller of the two granite stones, I smile when I look at it and think of her. Below her name, chiseled in simple block letters, is only one word—*TEACHER*. Nothing to suggest all the fame and accolades, the years at Brown, the books she wrote. She was always, to herself, *just* a teacher. She saw no higher calling. She hasn't been gone long, and I miss my sister deeply.

As unlikely as it seems on this cold January day, I hear the distinct and unmistakable tweeting, more a screech, of a wren somewhere in the copse of trees nearby, and I turn to see if I can spot the bird. I cannot. But beyond, in the distance a few miles away near the bleak horizon, I can again see the gray outline of the city that I just flew over. The tops of its dull, unimaginative buildings seem ordinary and unprepossessing against the slate sky.

Standing lonely and almost surreal in the gray, cold mist, clustered some distance between where I am standing and the city beyond, are the rusting water towers and the lifeless smokestacks of the old cotton mills. They are like stiff, eerie man-made ghosts of a dead and archaic industry, I muse. But they are really nothing more than just sad, decaying monuments to a way of life, ancient and forgotten. They seem unable to accept the long-ago demise of their reason for existing, unwilling to accept what fate has dealt them. It puzzles me why they are still here—why progress hasn't swept them away.

The mills are all gone now and have been for many years. When the unions were crushed, the people returned to the drudgery of their virtual serfdom. It took time, and another World War, for the owners, whose holdings would later morph into faceless and austere corporations, to release their choking paternalistic grip. But the War brought an end to the Great Depression, prosperity followed, for *the Machine* had to be fed and it needed much cloth to quell such a voracious appetite.

The Company Stores closed; they could not compete when at last the workers had money to spend elsewhere—Downtown. It became unprofitable for the mills to provide and maintain the houses in the village, so they sold them off. The plants became efficient and became, essentially, printing presses for dollars. The owners became fat and complacent. But it did not last, nor could it have been sustained.

With exploding technology, the world shrank, became a smaller place. The machines, the looms, once new and efficient, became obsolete. The picker-stick is now only a museum relic. The workers' pay—labor costs—ate into profits. Places, distant and foreign, like Mexico, Sri Lanka, and China began to weave cloth from cotton. And to bleach it and to dye it and to cut it and sew it into garments. They were efficient and labor was plentiful and cheap. Cloth could no longer be viably made in the South or anywhere else in America. So the cotton mills, those gargantuan windowless ships of red brick, began to shut down. There was no longer a need for people, or villages, or Company Stores. The people, untrained and ill-educated, drifted away from their center, from the life they knew, that their fathers and grandfathers before them had known. They just seem to have melted away.

But not everyone suffered from this devolution of a single industry, of a way of life, into nothingness. The owner-families thrived. They had heard the gurgle of the death throes. Most just sold out to sterile, impersonal corporations and became richer and idler. And with means at their disposal, naturally preserved themselves. Why, some even came to deny any past association with cotton mills or with the now extinct *lint-head*. It had all been a mirage. They were not cotton mill people at all. They became developers of resorts, owners of dealerships that sold gaudy automobiles along gaudy strips of highway, or perhaps invested in a chain of movie houses someplace in the New South.

I realize it's just the ways things work out. But when I think back, which I seem to do more often these days, I think of the people, the way of life, and the myth of happiness and security that grew out of it. I think mostly, of course, of my father and mother, and of sweet Grace. As the mist turns into a light, cold rain on my face, I realize for the first time today that I won't likely be returning to this place. It does not make me sad or morose, as I would have supposed. I feel a completeness about it all. As if I have discovered it for the first time. Now I can let it go.

I turn back to the two tombstones and remove the glove from my right hand and lightly touch the wet, lifeless granite. It is cold. Strangely, I recall how I had always thought of the coldness of death, how people, loved ones are placed in the cold ground. That they are themselves cold. But I know now that none but the living feels the cold, the cold and pain of this world.

I breathe a short silent prayer, cross myself, and like all the others before me, walk away.

ACKNOWLEDGEMENTS

For many years I contemplated writing a certain kind of novel, and it finally sprang forth as *None but the Living.* The writing and publishing of this book would have been much more difficult, if not impossible, were it not for the involvement of some people who are very dear and important to me.

Thanks to my good friend Penny Beacham, teacher-extraordinaire, who was kind and brave enough to read the first, unedited draft. Her comments, suggestions, and encouragement will forever be appreciated by me.

Without the technical knowledge, savvy, and instincts of my daughter—and to an extent my alter-ego—Jennifer Smith Nicholson, this book would likely never have been published. Her critical eye, editorial expertise, and professionalism has given my work the polish that I could never have achieved on my own.

It has been said that no man is an island; I certainly am not. Nothing could ever replace the love, devotion, and unwavering support that Mary—my wife of many years, my companion, and my best friend—has shown me during this project.